KILL
THEM
ALL

Willow River Press is an imprint of Between the Lines Publishing. The Willow River Press name and logo are trademarks of Between the Lines Publishing.

Cover Design: Morgan Bliadd

Between the Lines Publishing
1769 Lexington Ave N, Ste 286
Roseville, MN 55113
btwnthelines.com

First Published: May 2025

ISBN: (Paperback) 978-1-965059-44-9

ISBN: (Ebook) 978-1-965059-45-6

Library of Congress Control Number: 2025934720

KILL

THEM

ALL

Mark Philbin

To my parents, Ken and Kay Philbin, who fostered a love of reading with a simple library card.

To my children, Stephanie and Andrew, who enjoyed countless nights of bedtime stories and always encouraged one more tale.

And, of course, to my wife Cathy. You have endured all things, inspired all things, and above all, believed all things were possible. Thank you for believing in me. This novel, and any that may follow, is ours to share.

Chapter One

The Bumper stared across the park from his bench. Normally, the emerging blossoms in Louisville, Kentucky, would raise the spirits of those who had endured another harsh northern winter. He felt none of that. Hired killers often spend the winters traveling for work.

He would occasionally look down, then up, appearing disinterested in his surroundings, but it was part of the charade, merely blending in until his mark showed up. After that, it was Game Time. Money Time.

Bumper Time.

Sunset in Kentucky in late April was around eight-fifteen p.m., so he had plenty of natural light at seven-thirty p.m. If his target was punctual, he should appear at seven-forty-five p.m., dog in tow, eyes glued to his smartphone.

Dogs could be a hazard, though. Unpredictable.

The Bumper had all but dropped his given name for the professional moniker he had established in Sofia, Bulgaria. An impoverished child turned self-professed thug, he spent his adolescence on the streets, where he found his violent skills and vicious temperament made him more money than working in restaurants, as his high school friends had. In the ensuing years, the young man gained a reputation that the internet naturally promoted and the dark web enhanced. He soon made all the right friends, did important people favors, and attracted wealthy clients. His ability to bump off targets with little evidence that a crime had been committed was nothing short of astonishing in a forensic world. His reputation grew as his targets became more prominent. The killer had a luxury afforded few paid assassins: The Bumper could pick his assignments. He answered to no one.

Which made his current predicament even more puzzling.

It was such a simple e-mail, really. The request arrived overnight in mid-November to his dark web account. It outlined the terms of the scheme, including the communication system, pay structure, and travel expense renumeration. Would he be willing to take on such a mission?

If so, reply within forty-eight hours.

Twelve kills in twelve months. An astounding one-hundred-fifty-thousand dollars a job. It was easily the most lucrative job offer he'd received, and he could multiply that by twelve! By Christmas of this year, he'd pocket one million-eight-hundred-thousand dollars. It was money only the starving child he had once been could scarcely dream of. Should he succeed and avoid detection (for both himself and The Client), there would be a seven-hundred-thousand-dollar bonus on the last day of the year.

Two-and-a-half-million dollars!

It wasn't just because of the money. It was the challenge, and The Client knew it.

The Bumper took the bait and replied within twenty-four hours.

He then spent the last week of November tracing the email in search of The Client. Was it a trap? After days of trolling code and outsourcing the search, he came up empty. URLs were dummies, rerouting was infinite, and replies came back scrambled.

Whoever had hired him was good. Very good.

But he should have known. Nothing is ever that easy. Not that he couldn't handle it; it just surprised him.

December saw a flurry of activity that began with the avoidance of all personal contacts, the creation of a discrete bank account, and the assurance the newly arrived encrypted cell phone was operational and hack-proof. Minimal packing was required as new clothes could be purchased throughout the year depending on the situation.

As outlined, he received his first target in another coded email package on January first. The Bumper flew to the United States to begin his deadly assignment by killing a young, single hipster lawyer in Missouri who had pissed off The Client. Few details other than a name, occupation, and address. The Bumper did a logistics search of both his neighborhood and his Kansas City office. He knew within days that neither was ideal.

Fate intervened. The Kansas City Chiefs had enjoyed a first-round bye in the National Football League AFC playoffs and therefore hosted the upset-minded Jacksonville Jaguars at GEHA field at Arrowhead Stadium on Saturday the twenty-first. Plenty of people, but few witnesses. An enormous crowd in search of transit after shivering in the cold for four hours, or drinking to avoid it, made for perfect by-standers.

The Bumper followed his target for five days to ensure he was easily recognizable from behind while walking. If he felt conspicuous, he could easily peel away until the next day.

After all, he had the entire month.

But Saturday, January twenty-first, was perfect. The Bumper felt little pressure as he walked himself through the day. He would enjoy his first American football game in person, then eliminate a man on the way out. He had to make sure the first kill was impressive for The Client. A botched January job would be both an end to his contract and a blot on his resume.

The secondary ticket market made getting a seat for the game possible, though expensive. He would pocket one-hundred-fifty-thousand dollars for his efforts, but spending fifteen-hundred dollars on a cold seat was a hefty expense.

An Uber driver picked up the mark at noon for the late afternoon kickoff. The target wore a black puffy winter coat and a signature red toque with the Chief's logo prominent on the front. He could so easily blend into the crowd if you took your eyes off him for even a second. The killer didn't worry at all. The digital GPS tracker he'd attached to the man's smartphone made trailing him child's play.

Within fifteen minutes of kickoff, the victim, enjoying the final three hours of his existence, arrived at his premium seat, easily affordable given his affluent lifestyle. The Bumper swiped, thumbed, and clicked a setting. Should the target move as much as five feet, the killer would get a notification. He settled into his general admission seat high above the field. He spent the game cheering when the crowd cheered, booing when the crowd booed, and listening for his phone.

At the beginning of the fourth quarter, The Bumper rose from his seat and walked up to the concourse level. From there, he could stroll the circumference of the stadium without notice. Concession stands and washrooms guaranteed ample foot traffic and cover.

He waited above the stairs where his target sat many rows below at field level. Gazing down the aisle, he saw the seats were at the mid-point of the field. The Bumper knew enough about sports to know fans coveted them, but only the chosen few could afford them.

He hoped that Kansas City would pull away from Jacksonville and empty the stadium early, but it was a tight game, and the mark showed no sign of leaving early. The Bumper watched the clock for the last five minutes of the game, which took almost a half hour.

Finally, as the seconds ticked down to a twenty-seven to twenty Kansas City victory, the crowd poured out of the stadium as one.

The Bumper stood against a back wall and watched his phone. His target was approaching, but slowly.

Impatience was not an option. That was how mistakes were made. Killers who became impatient didn't get a second chance.

Finally, the man appeared, alone, and joined the throng heading for the exit ramps and the parking lot where he would find his Uber waiting.

The Bumper had a couple of minutes at most.

He fell in behind Mr. January as they reached the ground level and passed through the stadium gates simultaneously, exiting into the parking lot. Thousands of joyous fans whooped and celebrated. Horns honked and headlights blinded pedestrians as the revelers darted across the exit roadways.

The target hiked along the sidewalk to the far staging area where Uber rides and cabs would hope for a big fare and a large tip. Along the side, Kansas City transit buses lined the sidewalk for those who wanted a cheaper ride and didn't mind the longer drive. They were party buses that night, with no one looking outside the windows.

The Bumper closed the gap and slapped the man's phone from his hand, hearing it crack on the sidewalk and disappear under a bus. Furious, the victim turned to confront his attacker. The Bumper was already a step ahead. He leaped with his arm folded and, with the force of his descending elbow, crushed the man's forehead, just enough to stun him unconscious as The Bumper slid him under the bus beside the fallen phone.

From slap to snap, it was over in seconds. No one was aware of what had happened at the end of the line, in the dark. The victim lay unconscious. Within seconds, the bus started up and moved forward, crushing him to death.

The job went perfectly. That wasn't the concern. The problem happened exactly five minutes later. That was the moment The Bumper felt his first regrets.

The appearance of tonight's target roused the killer from his memories. Mr. April was the oldest so far of the four. The man was also the strongest of the year's quartet. This job would call for more than a gentle nudge or a quick shove. He had to employ more than stealth.

The city park comprised interlocking paths and swimming pool-sized flower plots. It was fifty-five steps from the assassin's bench to the mouth of the victim's pathway. Having mapped it out earlier that afternoon, he watched as his target reached the all-important spot. The Bumper casually stood and began to walk.

As both approached the "Y" split on the path, The Bumper's greatest concern was realized. It was the dog. The animal reared and growled as the lawyer looked up from his phone in annoyance and dragged at the pet.

Animals always know.

The Bumper continued his casual walk along the 'Y' path, confident that the soon-to-be-victim would now follow, instead of lying in spasms in the bushes. He flicked the pocketed taser to 'standby'.

He quickly moved to Plan B as he took out the gum and waited at a trash can (his favorite surveillance spot) while the half-oblivious pair approached. The dog had settled somewhat but remained wary. That could still be a problem. The Bumper popped the gum into his mouth.

As the man drew closer, The Bumper turned on his charming smile.

"Alex? Is that you? Oh, my God. How are you?" and moved in for a shoulder embrace.

Alex Dunn accepted the confused greeting as the taser slammed fifty-thousand volts through him. He flopped to the ground, his eyes rolling and froth spewing from his mouth. The killer dropped and shoved the wad of gum down his throat as the now confused dog barked and whined in concern. Its yelps would attract attention in moments.

The Bumper knew that even with the cotton membrane he had attached to the taser, and the fact he hadn't gone directly on his skin, there would still be a scar. But it would only look like a burn mark.

What police would find, however, is a man who suffered from episodes of spasmodic dysphonia who had choked on a huge wad of gum while in a full attack walking his dog.

The Bumper made his escape down the path toward the side street that would lead to a main traffic road. But his mind remained troubled. It started in January and occurred in February and March as well. Would it happen tonight?

After inserting the wad into poor Alex's mouth and walking away, he began counting. When he reached three hundred seconds… five minutes… he felt better.

It would be short-lived. The telltale ding from his phone alerted him that his one-hundred-fifty-thousand dollars had been deposited into his account.

Four unrelated kills in four months in four cities. He'd been paid exactly five minutes after each kill.

The Bumper scoured the park entrance one last time before blending into the stream of pedestrians, making their way aimlessly through life.

After a short block and a quick corner, he found his car in the quiet strip mall. He looked around before unlocking the vehicle to ensure he hadn't been followed. Physically, at least. He knew he was being tailed, somehow.

He sat in the driver's seat and stewed. *'How did The Client know that he'd completed the job successfully on each occasion?'*

The Bumper had to acknowledge there was only one way.

The Client was watching.

Chapter Two

Robert Hannah was not a morning person. He'd never been a morning person. To him, the best part of the morning was midnight until about four a.m. That was always a great time. But these people who loved dawn and would go jogging…ugh. Not for him.

His ex-wife, Stacey, the adrenaline junkie, was like that. She was "seize the day" and all those goofy motivational phrases. When she left three years ago, he was free to live the life he wanted on his terms. At least that was what he convinced himself.

Robert cracked an eyelid as a pounding drummed against his consciousness. Was it a dream or last night's rum reminding him how much fun they had?

The thumping began again and sounded more insistent this time. He did his best to call out to ask the offending party to stop pounding, but it sounded more like a threat laced with enough expletives to get him tossed from a bar.

The pounding resumed with a voice adding, "Come on, Hannah. Get up. I can hear you dying in there."

Hannah rolled from his couch into a painfully seated position. He was naked and mildly hungover. A glance at his phone told him it was eleven-seventeen a.m.

"I don't have all day, bud," the voice shouted while the pounding resumed.

Hannah tried to organize his thoughts to determine whether the would-be intruder was "friend" (had virtually none of those) or "foe," perhaps a victim of last night's high-stakes poker game (he'd had several). Maybe the nudity could act as a deterrent. He stumbled to the condo door and feebly asked who it was.

"It's Tom Brady. Wanna play catch?"

Hannah groaned. If he had any friends left, it would be Curt Downey, but he didn't want Downey to see him right now. He didn't want *anyone* to see him right now. Not like this.

"Come on Pally, I've seen you naked before, and I've seen you look like shit before, so whichever it is, just open the door," Downey called from the hallway.

Hannah pulled the latch back and unlocked the door, swinging it open.

His friend stared wide-eyed. "Oh, it's both. Naked and shit. What happened to you this time?" He asked, brushing by Hannah on his way into the condo.

Robert Hannah's condo overlooked the Charles River in Boston, Massachusetts. While not the penthouse, the tenth-floor view was stunning and expensive. Most of the adornments had been left behind by his ex-wife, except the fully stocked bar. That was his.

"To what do I owe the horror of this visit?" Hannah asked. He watched his friend move about the condo, straightening things as he went, as if he owned the place.

"Jesus, did you sleep on the couch?" Downey asked.

"I woke up there a few moments ago, so based on that body of evidence, Mr. FBI Agent, I would say you are correct." Hannah answered.

Downey smirked and turned to his college roommate from so many years ago.

Hannah hated that look. That 'friend' look. That disappointed look. The look of pity.

"How are you, Robert?" It always started the same. Downey was like a one-man intervention.

"I'm naked and hungover at eleven-thirty on a Tuesday morning, Curt. How do you think I am?"

"It's Wednesday, Robert, and you look like shit."

Hannah leaned with his back to the door and, with no self-awareness of his current lack of clothing, swung it back open.

"Thank you, Curt, for that wonderful imitation of a cuckoo clock, alerting me to time and date, so if that is all you have today, would you not so kindly find your way back to the lobby and screw off?"

His friend tensed his lips to ward off the retort and purposely sat down. Hannah sighed. *"This was going to be a thing,"* he thought as he slammed the door.

"First," Downey said, "go put some clothes on. You're thirty-five, for God's sake."

"I'm thirty-four." Hannah fired back as he ambled to his bedroom. He grabbed a pair of cast-off sweatpants and a bundled t-shirt. He popped into the bathroom to answer nature's call, pronounced himself presentable, and wandered back, disinterested, into the living room.

A small box and card lay on the coffee table. '*What was this about?*' Hannah wondered.

"You are thirty-five, asshole. Happy birthday." Downey said.

Hannah's tough guy exterior dented a little. "That's today?"

"I'm pretty sure. I wasn't actually there when your mother pushed you out, but you claimed it was."

Hannah dropped defeated into a plush loveseat and rubbed his face.

"Not the way you thought you'd be celebrating your thirty-fifth?" Downey asked.

"I celebrate all the time! Look around. Every day is my birthday! No one to tell me what to do, no boss to let me know when to work. I live every man's dream life." Hannah answered.

"Uh huh," Downey said. "Still trolling Harvard for girls and poker games?"

"It's not trolling if they text you first. And it's very lucrative."

"The poker or the girls?"

Hannah shook his head. He would not get into it for the hundredth time with him.

Downey said, "I came to take you to lunch for your birthday and give you your present."

"Well, CD, I'm not hungry, so you can leave the box and card on the table and consider me grateful."

"Oh, the card and box are from Laurel. She thinks there's still hope for you. No, I have something far more valuable than a new silk tie."

Hannah paused. "Your wife bought me a silk tie? When would I ever wear a silk tie?"

Downey stood up. "Let's go to lunch. I will give you your present there."

"Is it a different tie?" Hannah asked.

"No," Downey answered, opening the door. "It's a puzzle."

FBI Agent Curtis Downey joined the agency out of Harvard, having completed his studies in mathematics and statistics. His interests in law-enforcement were limited but his expertise in analysis proved him valuable in a statistic driven world. He rarely saw danger if he could avoid it, and his unique abilities to weave bits of evidence into patterns of behavior were crucial in the growing field of algorithms. Agent Downey could sit in front of a computer screen all day but thrived in a team atmosphere where his strong presentation skills could command a boardroom.

He was going places.

Downey could have been an actuarial accountant, worked nine-to-five, made an easy six-figure salary, and lived the suburban life. But he also knew he could have ended up like his college roommate. Brilliant but unfocussed. A self-destructive genius.

Downey may be a rising star in the Federal Bureau of Investigation, but at Harvard fifteen years ago, he was just another classmate mesmerized by Hannah sparring with a professor over a theory of 'patternicity'.

"I understand, professor," Hannah would intone with mild condescension, "but there can be no 'clustering illusion' without 'confirmation bias'. They may indeed be two distinct features, but without pre-determined bias, there would be no 'clustering illusion'."

"Robert," the professor would patiently reply, knowing Hannah's first name in a hall of three hundred sophomores because of his frequent challenges, "the theory does not pre-suppose a bias, it merely allows for one. But a bias need not exist to uncover a clustering illusion."

"Of course it does!" Hannah would retort, the students weary from the constant interruptions. "If I see blue cars everywhere without being asked to do so, I have a bias toward blue cars."

The arguments always ended the same way. Hannah would be asked to remain after the lecture, where a more private dialogue would bring greater clarity to his concerns.

Downey graduated with honors, in awe of his roommate. Cracks in Hannah's personality, though, showed a defiance of authority and a rebellious streak toward the status quo, an unusual trait in mathematics majors where order was the name of the game.

Downey followed his love of math and duty to country, along with an adventurous streak to the FBI in Quantico. Hannah bounced from firm to firm, then job to job, until his marriage fell apart and his life spiraled. Downey caught wind of Hannah's high stakes poker lifestyle and knew that one day, he would forget when to fold them.

His friend and college roommate would either end up broke or dead.

They arrived at the deli around the corner from Hannah's condo and grabbed a small booth at the window. "You get an appetite yet, Pally?"

"Not much, but hey, it's my birthday."

The diner was crowded for a late morning, leaving only a couple of free tables from the dozen available. A view of the water was its charm. The prices on the menu guaranteed exclusivity.

Downey ordered a smoked chicken on rye and Hannah ordered a glass of water and an "I'll see in a bit." The server sauntered away.

"I'm sorry I haven't been around a lot lately, Robert." Downey said.

"Not a problem. I was busy training for the marathon, anyway. Then I slept in." Hannah said.

Agent Downey chuckled as he reached into the breast pocket of his overcoat. He pulled out a small booklet with a few sheets of loose paper.

"Pictures of the girls?" Hannah asked.

"The girls?" Downey parroted. "And their names are…"?

Hannah shook his head. Downey wondered how much damage the booze was doing.

"Emma and Bailey are good. They really are the cutest girls." Downey answered.

"They get that from their mother, I trust."

"Thank God," Downey quipped. "Last thing we need is a balding near adolescent in the house. It was our old dog that took after me."

The food arrived with Hannah's tall glass of ice water as Downey watched the silence unnerve his friend. Finally, Hannah asked, "So, the FBI agent said something about a puzzle?"

Downey wiped his mouth of the mayo and flipped open the booklet on the table.

"Before I say anything further, two important points." He stated.

"Agent Downey, may I interrupt to state that the first point requires extreme discretion by all involved? I am not to share the details of my birthday present, and you must not be identified as the source of this information."

Downey fought the urge to smirk. Apparently, the present was working. He was seeing glimpses of his old roommate.

"That is correct, Pally. The second is even more important. You must not work on the puzzle. Ever."

Downey watched the bewilderment wash over Hannah's face. As he sat stone-faced, the server materialized to ask how Downey was enjoying his sandwich, and if Hannah was ready to order yet.

"Pastrami on rye, please. Oh, with a candle in it, if that's OK? It's my birthday."

Chapter Three

"Never? What good is a puzzle if I can't ever try to solve it? What sort of masochist brings a puzzle you can't solve for a guy's birthday?" Hannah exclaimed.

"Because I can only show you part of the puzzle. I only want you to see if there is anything to solve. If there is no actual answer to the puzzle, then happy birthday. But if you arrive at a solution, tell me the answer, then leave it alone."

Hannah nodded. "So, you want me to write act one of a play without telling you how it ends?"

Downey shook his head. "Absolutely not. I want you to tell me if there is a play at all. I'll then determine how it ends."

Hannah flexed his hands as his face betrayed his wandering mind. Downey had seen it years ago in lecture halls, at poker tables, and occasionally late at night when he struggled to make use of his gifts.

Hannah said, "Remember the part in *The Firm* when Tom Cruise is making supper while the envelope with the law firm's offer is sitting on the kitchen table? His wife wants to open it, but he says not to because he knows what's inside?"

"Of course," Downey said.

"Is that my present today? A piece of a puzzle that you know I can solve, hoping I'll be drawn into the bigger picture?"

"No, Pally. I wish I had something that big for you. I am no Tom Cruise if you haven't noticed. So, I'll come clean. You guessed one part. I have a bit of a puzzle, but I don't have time to waste if it's nothing. But if it is something, I don't want to fluff it off. So, I thought, who better to take this on 'for free' than my college roommate genius? Do you still want it? Even if it is a waste of time and a bit of a pity present to keep you busy?"

"Wait," Hannah said. "You brought along some random FBI shit that may be nothing as a birthday present to keep me sober?"

"When you put it like that, I should feel bad, but I don't. Do you want it or not?" Downey asked.

Hannah smiled. "Hell, yeah."

Back at the condo, Hannah flipped through the half dozen photocopies of notes from Agent Downey. "Three people died over the past four months. Do you want to see if they are related?" He asked.

"Yeah. To go back to Harvard, my FBI confirmation bias is looking for a criminal pattern in the clustering illusion of these three deaths. But there is no evidence a crime was committed. Just three rich dudes who died."

Hannah laughed at the memory of the reference. "So, what's the puzzle?"

"Look at the deaths and see if there is a pattern. Is there any way they could be connected? I've googled their business associates, their common interests, and there is nothing."

"So, why are you investigating at all?" Hannah asked.

"Great question, Pally. We got a call from the Kansas City office about the guy in January who slipped under a bus after the Chief's playoff win. Crushed him. Me? I think…big deal? But they thought it looked too fishy, though witnesses were vague. Then we got a report from Lansing, Michigan, about a wealthy art collector who supposedly killed himself by taking a quick trip out of a twelfth-floor window."

"Supposedly?" Hannah asked.

"Yeah, apparently, his phone was chock full of appointments and exhibit appraisal meetings, so suicide was a shock to his associates. They urged an investigation, but it went nowhere. Disillusionment runs rampant in the Midwest. It happens."

"And the third guy?"

"This is where my stomach got the puzzle butterflies. A high-priced lawyer was found dead in a park while walking his dog in Louisville. When the EMTs arrived, they found a wad of gum lodged in his throat. There must have been two or three enormous pieces of bubble gum. Thing is, according to associates, the guy never chewed gum. Found it disgusting. I had them send the profile, and he suffered from a condition known as 'spasmodic dysphonia'."

"It makes your throat spasm and can affect your voice."

"Exactly. So, it was suspicious that a guy who hated chewing gum because of his condition would be found dead in a spasm position with a gag-inducing wad in his mouth."

"What have the police found?"

"Little to date. That only happened a couple of weeks ago. It crossed my desk last week."

Hannah sat back. Three men died in accidental or self-inducing manners within weeks of each other. Each in a different city. Total strangers to each other.

"I'll assume you've put this through the 'Improbability Principle'?" Hannah asked.

"Anecdotally, but outside of the strange details of their deaths, there is really no evidence of a crime. Each can be explained away as a tragic accident or suicide."

"Okay," Hannah said, "so let's do it now. How often do you get details of a strange death that appears to be accidental?"

Downey considered the question. "Often." He answered.

"How many of them are male?" Hannah asked.

"The vast majority of them. Most women die as obvious victims. Or by their own hand."

"Okay, how many are rich men?"

Downey paused. "That I would have to look up."

Hannah grew more interested in the details of the puzzle. "So, now the Improbability Principle shows itself. When you look up your 'rich men' statistics, see how many rich men die accidentally in clusters of three within four months. My guess is that rarely happens." Hannah said.

"Okay, smart guy," Downey countered, "but the Improbability Principle is supposed to thwart the belief that random things are just that. It confirms that most coincidences are actually more common than we believe."

"Precisely, Dr. Watson," Hannah said. "But, if someone, *or someones*, are involved in killing rich single men in monthly clusters that appear random but are in fact linked, then we don't have a puzzle at all. We have a *pattern*."

Downey blinked. "I didn't say they were single." He reached for the papers. "Are they single?"

Hannah laughed. "Of course they are. There isn't a single statement from a grieving spouse. One, two or all three may be divorced, but at the time they shook off their mortal coil, there was no one to mourn their passing."

Hannah collected the sheets, tapped them on the table to straighten them into a neat pile, and handed them back to his former college roommate.

"Find out how often four rich single men die accidentally in a four-month period, and you will have your solution. If the answer is 'never,' then you need to decide what to make of that. Either way, thank you for my birthday present and the puzzle."

Downey collected the sheet as he stood. "Four men? Do you think there is another?"

Hannah walked his friend to the condo door. "Yes, I do. And if there is, then that is the confirmation. Remember my Beatles party puzzle?"

Agent Downey laughed. "Oh, my God, you don't still use that on girls, do you?"

"Not as often now. Few know the Beatles by name. But if I asked, what four men are grouped when you hear the names, John, Paul…and of course, everyone says, 'The Beatles!'"

Downey finished the puzzle, "Until you say, 'Peter and Andrew'."

"If the girls quickly say 'Beatles', then I have a chance. If they say 'Apostles and Saints', then I leave them alone."

Agent Downey laughed. "You always got the girl, Pally. So, what am I looking for then?"

"You're looking for Ringo, CD. The death that confirms the other three. The fourth that completes the pattern. But at least you have a timeline."

"I do?" Downey asked.

"It would have happened in February. Look for a random accidental death of a single rich man in February. These sheets show one in January, March, and April. Find Mr. February, and you have your answer."

Hannah opened the door, but before Downey left, he turned and asked, "What did you mean when you said 'thanks for the birthday present and the puzzle'? The puzzle *was* your present."

Hannah softened his crusty gaze at his longtime friend. The only friend he had left. The only one who took the time. "No, Curt. You stopping by was my real present."

Chapter Four

The Client put the finishing touches on the May submission. The first four months of the year had helped to confirm the process. Dive deep into profiles, study album pics, engage if necessary to determine attitude.

After all, The Client knew they only needed one. If there was a choice, they simply kept the second as a consideration for later, provided they fit the criteria.

Mr. May had been on the radar since March. Wealthy, slick, and entitled. He was single by choice.

A player.

There were few pictures, but his persona oozed through the profile. Words such as "affluent", "cultured" and The Client's (least) favorite, "selective", as if interested individuals were nothing more than menu items.

They debated whether to add a concern to this package. The Client had high praise for the killer's work, but the terms insisted on discretion. They had left the manner of death in the hands of The Bumper, though there would be pertinent details from the soon-to-be victim's life that might enable him to tailor a specific action. But The Client had a growing concern the attacks were becoming too public, and therefore more likely to attract attention.

A click back brought up the news story of Alex Dunn, dubbed Mr. April. His manner of death in a park was public enough that a few enterprising witnesses had snapped some social media pics of the scene, and they had made their way on-line. The Client understood that perhaps an odd death would gain traction, but three of them had made the news in the first four months.

To The Client, that was the opposite of discreet.

It was vital to the plan that The Bumper carry out orders unimpeded to the very end. In fact, it was the purpose of the plan. If he should be caught, then the entire operation was a failure.

Twelve months, twelve victims.

The Client could jump to the very end, but the symmetry provided the beauty. No, The Bumper had to show more tact and less flair in his executions.

They added a note to that effect in the email and sent the submission through the routing channels. It would take almost eighteen hours for the file to reach his inbox only a few states away.

The Client might quietly admit that if the deaths were never connected, then the plan was proceeding as conceived. Still, arrogance was a luxury they could not afford.

Surely, no one would be gifted enough to follow all the breadcrumbs back to the source, but they hadn't expected the assassin to be so brazen.

"Perhaps I should have been clearer at the outset," thought The Client.

The calendar was ticking. Eight months to go. No one had yet made a single connection, and even if suspicions would be raised down the road, the separate law enforcement agencies would chase their tails. By the time anyone caught a whiff of the clues, it would be too late.

The game would be over before anyone knew one had started.

This made The Client smile.

They closed the laptop and turned to look out the window.

It was going to be another lovely day in the desert.

The Bumper woke to the familiar ping of his email notification. He gave himself a few precious seconds to clear his mind of sleep before opening it.

Much like his payment, The Client's profile submission always arrived within minutes of its allotted timeframe, the first day of the month at seven a.m. local time.

He got up from his motel bed and padded to the bathroom for nature's call. A quick shower, teeth brushing and a shave. Appearance was everything if you wanted to blend in.

At seven-thirty, The Bumper opened the submission and frowned at the accompanying note. It was the first time in which his methods were discussed, let alone criticized. He bristled at the word "discretion," as if his actions were impulsive.

The money was good, but this task was becoming bothersome. He considered a tart reply, but his better judgement chimed in. The Client was in charge.

"I won't let their apprehension cloud my process," he said aloud. What was that American saying? Ah, yes. "This says more about them than it does about me."

He let his anger dissipate before he clicked open the dossier. As he did, he felt another stab of irritation. It took too long from the email opening to the file opening. Surely The Client would receive timed notifications on both. They would know he spent some time reading the notes and gave it consideration. The consideration that made them regret hiring him.

The Bumper got up and walked around the room. He was losing his cool despite feeling justified by having his professionalism questioned. The Bulgarian assassin had to calm down, but it was a tough way to wake up. No one had a clue that he was a one-man execution team across the United States. No one could put it together by the time Christmas rolled around.

Eight more kills, then he could go home. He let that sink in.

He slumped behind the laptop. The Bumper studied the profile of another man who had encountered The Client. Big mistake.

The Bumper had long wondered how these individuals could have made such a horrible impression from so far away. In just four months, he had traveled to New York, then driven to Missouri. From there, he had weaved a web through the other states on the list. Clearly, The Client must be a jet-setter as well, because they were keeping tabs on him. Enough to know when the job was complete.

After reading enough about his May mission, he looked back at the location.

Where is Ohio?

Chapter Five

Hannah tried to silence his phone by blindly stabbing at the screen. It continued to ring unabated. Sliding it off the bed to the floor was unsuccessful as well.

Daylight seeped through the floor-to-ceiling drapes that shielded him from the view of the Charles River on sunny mornings. It was an expensive view to miss, but one he was determined to avoid. It would still be there in the afternoon.

The caller clearly had other ideas. Rather than leave a considerate voice message, they were committing a serious infraction. Rousing Hannah from slumber prior to the very moment he deemed the day to begin was a major faux pas.

Call once, an inconsideration. Repeated calls? A serious breach of etiquette that would cost them a Robert Hannah tongue lashing or something less emphatic. They might suffer the cold shoulder for a week.

Hannah slid his head down the side of the bed, spotted the form of his phone on the side throw rug, and retrieved the offending device. He made out the name of his ex-roommate and clicked the bottom green button. "You seemed to have forgotten a lot about me, compadre." he said.

"No, I was going to keep calling until I got a live human, even if they sound as dead as you do at eleven-fifteen," Downey replied.

Hannah cracked an eye fully open and searched his screen. Yup, eleven-seventeen a.m.

"What if I was busy with my latest conquest? Or out saving cats in trees?"

Downey laughed through the phone. "Dude, we are still hooked up on 'location finder.' I can practically see you in bed."

"Must be important if you called so early."

"Important phone calls come, Pally. Hell, telemarketers start before dawn. Calls around eleven-fifteen are what we refer to as 'wellness checks.' I'm making sure you're alive."

"I am good, CD. In fact, if you like, I'll download the SNUG app. Gives me a daily affirmation quote and everything." Hannah said.

"You do that, but in the meantime, I wanted to let you know I found some hits on your February victim. Wanted to run them by you to see which ones were more likely than the others. You awake enough yet?"

Hannah sat up, suddenly interested. While he hadn't forgotten his chat with Downey, he had expected nothing so soon. "Wow, I guess the FBI works faster than I thought."

"We have phones and the internet. It's amazing. You can do more than just play poker on it." Downey replied.

"Give me a second, Curt."

Hannah slipped on a pair of jogging pants and yesterday's t-shirt and slid past the living room into his open kitchen. He rinsed a dirty glass from the sink and grabbed some orange juice, and hit the speaker button on his phone.

"Okay, go ahead." Hannah said.

"Clean glass or dirty glass?" Downey asked.

"I'm hanging up now, Special Agent Downey."

"No, you're not. I found four suspicious deaths of interest. Not one of the four raised a red flag, but the victim in each case was noteworthy."

"The other three victims you told me about had similar circumstances." Hannah said.

"Exactly. I started with that process. Each of these guys was single and well off. I had a few others, but eliminated them because of circumstances. One had been missing after going hiking and was found days later, dead from a heart attack."

"In February? Who goes hiking in February?" Hannah asked.

"Rich guys in California. It's not cold everywhere, Pally."

"Right, so you narrowed it down to four."

"I did, so you have your choice of a slip and fall on concrete steps, a skiing accident, or one of two traffic fatalities." Downey said.

"The slip and fall would show a pattern after the January death in Kansas City. Is that too coincidental?"

"Yeah, maybe. I didn't like that as much."

"Tell me about the skiing accident," Hannah said, finishing the orange juice and refilling his glass.

"It was reported at a small resort as a tragic accident. Skier hit a tree and was killed. It happened off a groomed run, so they didn't know why the guy had gone off the trail. In fact, he may have laid there for as much as twenty or thirty minutes before anyone noticed him in the woods."

"Was he experienced?"

"I'll assume so, but I get why you're asking. Good skiers don't veer off into wooded areas." Downey said.

"No signs of a struggle? Any witnesses see a race or something?" Hannah asked.

"According to the report, no one saw anything. It was early afternoon, so a lot of skiers were in the chalet for lunch."

"Interesting. That has potential. Maybe he had taken an early lunch and someone had tampered with his skies. Stuck around to make sure it did the job." Hannah suggested.

"True. And if he was an experienced skier, he'd be on the tougher ski runs, so a snapped ski binding on a steep run would be fatal. I'll look into that."

"Where did that happen? Vermont?" Hannah asked.

"No. Indianapolis."

"What about the 'slip and fall'?

Hannah heard the shuffling of papers over the phone as Downey hemmed and hawed. "Uh, Madison, Wisconsin. The guy was found at the bottom of a set of stairs outside the main branch of the library. Slipped backward and banged his head. Died later in hospital."

"Rich guy who reads, huh? Leave it with me, CD. If I can come up with anything, I'll be in touch."

"Thanks, I appreciate it. Actually, I'd appreciate if you'd stay in touch even if you don't think of anything. In fact, if you make yourself presentable, Laurel and the girls would like to see you if you feel like popping over for dinner."

Hannah was touched by his generosity. "I'll think about it CD. Thanks for the offer."

Hannah took a long shower, trying to wash the sleep out of him. He mulled over the details of Downey's call, looking for the connection. He knew it was wrong to make the details fit any theory he could come up with. He had to let the facts lead him to the answer.

Hannah dressed in jeans and a thick hoodie, opting for a drive in his Audi rather than a walk around the corner. He wanted to think, not bump into people he may have out-hustled at a poker table. Hannah grabbed a coffee and muffin at a drive-thru and settled into the empty parking lot of a nearby baseball field. He strolled over to the metal bleachers and settled on a second-tier bench. The warmth of the sun and smell of the grass did wonders for his imagination. His mind automatically took him back half a lifetime ago when he patrolled the outfield, climbing the wall and throwing out runners. He had a cannon for an arm and an archer's aim.

He dismissively shook off the memories. So many missed opportunities, so many regrets.

Hannah finished the muffin, thinking about his buddy, Curt Downey. It had already occurred to him that Curt might play him, somehow. That Downey had already solved the case but was throwing his washed-up roommate a lifeline. The invitation to dinner seemed genuine, though. He should take him up on it. He wondered whether Laurel was truly enthusiastic about it.

Still, the details of the February deaths lingered. Hannah thought over the four of them. The two accidents seemed plausible, if not benign. Each of the other deaths, if they were part of a pattern, were so public and dramatic. Shoved under a bus, falling from a twelve-story window, choking on a wad of gum while walking your dog? Those were statement deaths. The type that would generate some buzz on-line.

"Humph," Hannah grunted. "Generate clicks?" He said aloud. His pulse snapped up a notch as he ran the two other February deaths through that lens. The "slip and fall" in Madison, Wisconsin, had potential because of the public setting, while the skiing accident in Indianapolis was the stronger contender for click generation on-line.

Hannah visualized the U.S. and drew a mental circle around the cities. Lansing was a state capital, as were both Indianapolis and Madison, so it couldn't be based on that criterion. Kansas City and Louisville were major cities, so the population made sense from a crime point of view. Lots of murders, not a lot to see.

So, would Madison or Indianapolis fit the bill? Both were large municipalities. A killer could easily blend in and get out with minimal attention.

Hannah sat up. "Wait a minute," he stammered out loud. "Kansas City was first, then this death, *then* Lansing and Louisville." He chastised himself for the blunder of organizing the clues in the order he'd been given, not the order of events.

Hannah opened a mapping app on his phone and moved to Kansas City. He shrunk the view to include Madison, Wisconsin. How long a drive would that be? A couple clicks later, it gave him the answer of seven-and-a-half hours.

Piece of cake. He cleared the search and tried Indianapolis. Seven hours, twenty minutes.

If these four men were murdered by a single perpetrator, then distance was a factor. Indianapolis, Indiana or Madison, Wisconsin, would be a day's drive from the Kansas City murder, giving the killer a month to scope out their next victim. Following this, the next victim had been killed in Lansing, Michigan. Again, not that far to drive.

Also, major cities had larger potential victim pools. Metropolitan areas were far more likely to have an abundance of affluent single men than smaller towns.

"Fish where the fish are," Hannah said aloud.

He gave the baseball field one more look, knowing he'd be back next week for another "session" and hopped down from the bleachers. He ambled back to the Audi, pocketing his phone when the answer struck him.

Hannah reopened his phone and punched in Downey's number. His impatience got the better of him as each automated phone prompt brought him no closer to his FBI ex-roommate. Finally, Downey picked up.

Before the agent could even say a word, Hannah yelled into the phone, "It's Indianapolis! And I think I know where he's going next!"

Chapter Six

Agent Downey worked out of the FBI Boston field office. His jurisdiction spread across much of New England, and he often worked with the other resident agencies in Massachusetts, Rhode Island, New Hampshire and Maine. Downey alerted his captain to his suspicions based on tips from local police agencies that had been floating around Quantico, the headquarters of the FBI Criminal Division.

"So, why you?" Captain Lockwood asked.

Agent Downey answered, "I got a hunch and a buddy from Harvard. I may have something."

Lockwood asked, "What do you need?"

"For now? Just a room and a few curious souls you can spare for a brainstorming session, sir. If it turns into something, I may need your support to work on the case."

"And this buddy?" Captain Lockwood asked.

"He's a little different, Captain. But he's the reason I think there is a case, so I can't ignore his hunch."

Downey prepared the briefing room for a small group of interested investigators and Hannah. Maybe Captain Lockwood would want to attend. He hoped not. Hannah could be off-putting.

"So, this buddy of yours is some math genius?" An agent asked, wandering into the boardroom. Agent Howard Bradley was a ladder-climbing pain in the ass. But Downey knew that if Hannah was right and if they had a cross-country serial killer operating well under the radar, Bradley would be the first guy to jump on the task force and the first to claim credit.

"Harvard math genius, but also a self-described puzzle guru. The guy is a pattern-finder."

"How does a Harvard math genius have the time to educate us lowly FBI agents?" Bradley asked, grabbing a coffee and donut.

"It's complicated, Howard," Downey said. "Play nice. He is a civilian helping us out with his unique skills and he may have something."

Agent Howard Bradley shrugged and wandered back out into the hallway, no doubt content to have fired his opening salvo of blame if this turned out to be nothing.

Downey's phone buzzed, and he texted back to bring Hannah upstairs. He stuck his head out of the boardroom and called to the six hand-picked agents for his team that their consultant had arrived. Three junior agents took their spots around the table, cautious of their locations. All three chose seats at the back, far from the whiteboard. Senior agents took the closer spots. Agent Downey would stand throughout the presentation.

Downey wasn't surprised that Agent Howard Bradley hadn't returned yet. He'd be fashionably two or three minutes late. He'd already gotten his coffee and donut, and was such a "busy guy."

Hannah strode into the boardroom with a confident ease, dressed in khakis and an off-blue flannel shirt. Downey was horrified that he'd put on the silk tie he gave him for his birthday. It looked hideous against the shirt, but at least he'd shaved and seemed purposeful.

Introductions were made as Hannah awkwardly looked at the remaining seats.

"Sit up here, Robert," Downey pointed. "Okay, as I mentioned in the memo briefing, this is Robert Hannah, my old college roommate. He has an advanced degree from Harvard in mathematics with a specialty in patternicity."

"When I'm not suffering from apophenia," Hannah interjected. He turned to look at the blank faces of the agents as Agent Bradley boldly strode in and plopped down at the front. "What did I miss?"

"You missed a fine introduction," Hannah said, turning to the tardy task force member. "Punctuality is not a thing in the FBI?"

"Robert," cautioned Downey, "you're a guest here. This is all pretty informal at this point."

"As to what you missed," Hannah continued as if his friend hadn't spoken, "that is the reason I am here. There is a series of murders taking place right under your nose that no one has detected until Agent Downey brought the circumstances to my attention. In the future, please take my time seriously and be prepared when the meeting is to begin." Hannah finished.

Downey's face rose to a level of pink knowing how Agent Bradley would spin the insult into a grievance with the higher-ups. This was not the way he wanted it to go.

"Let's just settle down here. Agent Bradley, thank you for giving us some of your busy time to help, and everyone, Robert, doesn't know the corporate culture or work habits of the FBI. But he has graciously offered to help us detect a pattern in these seemingly unrelated crimes."

"Oh, I understand the corporate culture, CD." Hannah said, flipping his birthday present. "I even wore a tie. But behavior analysis concludes that in every random grouping of people, there are statistical consistencies. For example, in a room here with nine people, there is always going to be the one person whose personality drives them to be late so that they might make an entrance. They know they will be coddled and explained away, so they don't believe it to be rude. In fact, it is a defense mechanism to hide their insecurities. That is apparently you, Agent Bradley. Of the other eight, one of you will always be the first in the room. You are highly motivated by the search and derive no pleasure from outside recognition. Two or three of you will slowly exit this task force when I am difficult to work with and the results are fruitless. In the end, there will be five of us when we apprehend our naughty friend."

"Well, thanks for wasting my time with an insulting circus sideshow, Agent Downey," Bradley sneered as he rose from the table. "I'm sure the captain will appreciate my update on your minor project." He stood straight as he buttoned his suit jacket before leaving the boardroom.

"Not nice to meet you," Hannah called after him.

Agent Downey grimaced as he closed his eyes in a failed attempt at stress relief. He knew bringing in Hannah was a crazy idea, but he'd hoped that his old roommate would have played nice long enough to prove his effectiveness before the eccentricities had the run of the boardroom.

"Robert, that was not smart."

"On the contrary, CD. It was necessary. I don't know that man from anyone else, but his presence was going to be a constant distraction and a colossal waste of time, and time is something we can't waste." Hannah stood up and moved over beside Agent Downey, who shuffled a little out of the way, unsure what was going to happen now.

"Agent Downey is probably my best friend. We were roommates at Harvard, and he brought this little situation to me last week. Puzzles and patterns, I know I'm good at. I play poker for a living, which requires not only strong math skills but also superior interpersonal skills. As they say, you don't have to know the cards your opponent is holding. Know your opponent." Hannah pointed to the door. "That guy is bad for this group. You don't have to agree with everything we talk about in here, but we trust that we all want the same thing. If I didn't believe in Agent Downey's leadership, I wouldn't be here. Agent Bradley is bad chemistry. You all have to toe the line in here, but I don't, and I don't want to work with him."

Hannah stopped and looked over at Downey, who shrugged in response.

"I call him CD because those are his initials and it rolls off the tongue well. He calls me 'Pally' because my last name is a palindrome. It is the same front as back. My first name is 'Robert', but I wanted to be Bob. Palindrome again. So, you can call me Robert, or Pally, or Hannah. I'm not a formal guy. I will always be on time and respect your time and talents. However, we should have no use for showboats and trouble-makers. Now, I may have gotten my friend here in trouble, but better that than get bogged down in his drama when we have so little time to catch the guy. Or girl."

Hannah turned and looked at the chart set up on the whiteboard. "It started in January of this year. I went back in an on-line search of December of last year and found no unusual deaths of affluent men. So, someone made this a New Year's resolution."

Two younger agents smiled, and Agent Downey felt a lightness in the room. Hannah seemed to have made a good call after all, even if there would be ramifications.

"Kansas City in January; Indianapolis in February, Lansing in March, and Louisville a couple of weeks ago in April. Four unrelated deaths of single affluent men, all made to look like accidents or suicides."

A woman near the back politely raised her hand and didn't speak until Downey pointed at her. "But we have been able to identify other instances where men who have died in the first four months of this year would have fit the pattern. Why aren't those deaths included?" She asked.

"Excellent," Hannah said, pumping the air. Downey was excited to see Hannah's reaction to questions. "Because they only fit part of the pattern. Not the entire pattern."

Downey turned to view the group. He saw six blank faces.

"What Robert is explaining is known as patternicity." Downey said. "If I gave each of you a solid shaped object of a different color and asked you to group them, how would you do it? Would you decide by the colors, or the shapes, or the size of the objects? They are the same objects, but how you organize them is different based on the criteria of the pattern."

An agent at the back spoke softly as he raised his hand. "Such as a 'see and say sequence?'"

"Not quite, but you're on the right path," Hannah said. "Five points for you. With those puzzles, you must determine the single hidden pattern that easily gives you the answer. The most famous one for children is the pattern of one, two, three, five, eight…what comes next?"

Downey watched five of the agents think over the numbers, while one stifled a yawn. Damnit, Hannah was right. We'll be down to five agents in the boardroom by this afternoon.

"Thirteen?" One agent called out. "Each number adds itself to the previous. Therefore, five plus eight is thirteen."

"And you get five points," Hannah said. "But what happens if I take those same numbers, but put them in a different order? Would the answer still be thirteen?"

Head-shaking and mumbles showed they didn't think so. Agent Downey knew they had to get to the crux of Hannah's insight or risk losing the momentum of the meeting.

"So, you see how recognizing the pattern is often key in solving crimes committed by habitual offenders, be it serial murderers or shoplifters." Downey said. "I know you know all that. But Robert has happened upon a unique pattern."

The room drew a collective breath of anticipation as seven sets of eyes rested on Agent Downey's friend.

Hannah turned back to the whiteboard and pointed again to the crimes.

"Kansas City, Indianapolis, Lansing and Louisville. Not Louisville, then Kansas City, then Indianapolis. No...Kansas City, Indianapolis, Lansing and Louisville."

The first young woman who had earlier raised her hand boldly spoke now without permission by asking, "Is this a geographical crime? Is the killer moving from east to west...or north to south?"

"No, it has nothing to do with the cities themselves." Hannah waited until he had the boardroom's full attention. He turned back to the whiteboard with a dry-eraser and slowly rubbed out most of the cities' names, leaving only their first initial.

Hannah stepped back to allow all to view the remaining letters, oddly spaced but obvious in their meaning.

The remaining letters spelled...K I L L.

Chapter Seven

The four men sat in the spacious windowed office, obviously paired for battle.

Agent Downey sat beside Hannah, while Agent Howard Bradley eased himself deferentially into a chair within reach of Captain Stuart Lockwood's desk.

Hannah did not know which way the wind was blowing on this, but he knew that regardless of his intentions, this meeting was inevitable. He just hoped it would not blow back on Downey.

"Agent Downey," the captain began, "I trust you informed your friend here that when one steps onto FBI property in service of this country, that they conduct themselves with the same sense of dedication that we ourselves have pledged to uphold?"

"Yes sir," Downey answered, but was silenced by a raised palm by the captain.

"I'm not finished." He turned his sharp gaze to Hannah, who found the exchange comical. It was as if they'd been summoned to the principal's office for laughing at a snitch.

"Now, Mr. Hannah," Captain Lockwood said, "I find it highly insulting to single out one of our agents in front of his peers for nothing other than a cheap prank to tilt the room in your favor. As a civilian, I expect you…no, I *demand* you demonstrate far more respect for this organization. Do I make myself clear?"

Everything Hannah had hated about Harvard, and accounting firms, and marriage came flooding back. The fake authority of the office when the mind was inferior. The stooping to bow before lesser intellects to get ahead. He knew by the temperature spreading upward from his neck that his thoughts would be betrayed.

Through clenched teeth, Hannah said, "Is this where I apologize to a disrespectful employee who so under-valued my contributions to this 'great organization' by not showing up on time for a meeting designed to save lives, or will you be calling my mother first?"

Stunned, Captain Lockwood pulled the glasses from his face and slammed them on his desk. His soothing voice had given way to a seasoned growl of rage. "Mr. Hannah, you have done yourself irreparable damage today. Your insolence and condescension are not welcome here. You have also represented Agent Downey poorly, making me question his judgement. You are to leave this building now and do not return."

Hannah sat stone-faced and waited. He tilted his head to Downey, who sat still with his crimson face facing the floor. '*Shit*,' he thought. '*I screwed Curt.*'

He sat and sized up Captain Lockwood in an instant, much like a poker player would. Lockwood was the loudmouth at the table who tried to bully the pot, except, in this case, he really had the authority to carry out his threats. Hannah ran through a dozen scenarios and landed on the one that might save his friend a severe reprimand.

"You're right, Captain. I over-emphasized my contributions today and overreacted to a hard-working agent who graciously stopped by to help with the investigation to which I was consulting." Hannah held up his hands defensively. "I'm not saying I like him, but that doesn't mean I can disrespect him. That is on me." He turned to indicate Curt. "As far as Agent Downey, he has a serious flaw in always putting the case before the organization. I suppose some might find it admirable that he cares so much about bringing justice, that he'd drag a troublemaker like me into a case, jeopardizing his own standing, in the heroic belief that it will get him closer to the solution. But that's my buddy. Captain FBI."

Agent Downey muttered, "Shut up, Pally."

Agent Howard Bradley said, "Apology…not accepted."

Hannah raised his eyebrows in surprise. "Oh, I wasn't apologizing to you. I was talking to the captain…"

Lockwood slammed his desk. "Oh, my God, enough! This is the Federal Bureau of Investigation, not middle school!"

"Exactly," Hannah agreed.

Agent Downey dropped his head as the crimson shade rose to his forehead.

"Look, Captain, I know have a love/hate relationship with authority. I love to hate it. But I have certain attributes of intellect that might be useful here. All I'm asking is that I work with Agent Downey and any other agents who might be assigned to this case. I promise I will play nicer from now on."

"What case?" Agent Bradley asked. "There is no case."

Hannah waited to see if Downey would come up for air. Like the champ he was, the question snapped him back. "Oh, we have a case." Downey said. "A case based on a pattern that only Mr. Hannah detected."

Captain Lockwood sat back in his chair, partly defeated, partly curious.

"So, Agent Downey, are you telling me we now have a case that only he can solve? I have to turn the boardroom and all our resources over to Mr. Hannah for his spiteful mental gymnastics?"

"No sir. I would like to remain in charge of a new task force to look into these killings."

"A task force?" The Captain said. "Who said anything about a task force?"

Hannah said, "Four murders in four months in four different cities across four different states. Even if one jurisdiction found one death suspicious, they wouldn't look beyond that case. That is the first over-riding safety feature. The killer is counting on incompetent communication, even if he were detected."

"Oh, come on. Not one of those three deaths was suspicious, let alone all three being murdered," Bradley said.

Agent Downey turned to his colleague. Hannah could feel the shift in his friend.

"Four murders. There are four. Hannah found the fourth and the link that ties them all together." Downey turned back to the captain. "Sir, today was a good example of what can happen when we drop our standards to make a civilian feel more comfortable. I exhibited poor leadership today. But his skills and our resources are what we need to nail this guy before he takes another life."

"What makes you think he'll strike again?"

"The pattern." Hannah interjected. "Four murders in four months. And the cities are part of the pattern. I believe he has a twelve-month killing spree in motion. Twelve perfect murders in twelve months. Then he's gone. We have to stop him now."

Captain Lockwood heaved a sigh and slowly rocked. He swung his glasses over to Agent Bradley. "Agent Downey, can you and Agent Bradley work together?"

"No sir, we cannot. His lack of professionalism today toward the entire team is not without precedent." Downey turned to Hannah, who stared dumbfounded. "We have no room on this task force for window dressers and naysayers. I need boots and minds. Agent Bradley and I have too much history now. Not to mention the fact that he ran to you as soon as he got his feelings hurt."

The Captain pursed his lips before glancing over at Bradley. "Yeah, that's what I thought. Leave it with me, boys. It sounds like the two of you need to go out for a beer like in the old days. Settle this somewhere else, other than my office. If I have to do it, one of you will be in Idaho. The other, somewhere smaller. Out you go. But work this out."

The three dismissed men all stood in unison. "You, stay," The Captain said without looking up. Hannah clapped his friend's shoulder to wish him luck and turned toward the door.

"I meant you, Mr. Hannah."

Hannah resettled himself in the same chair and waited for the door to close after Downey and Agent Bradley left the office. Once they were alone, he expected Captain Lockwood to lose his mind.

Instead, The Captain asked, "What do you think they are saying to each other right now, Hannah?"

Hannah pretended to mull it over. "I can't even imagine, Captain."

"Bullshit. Sure, you can. Agent Downey is as fine a young agent as there is in the building, and Agent Bradley is an ass-kissing ladder climber with brains, but too much ambition to risk using them. You should understand that if you're really that good."

"Risk aversion? Absolutely, sir. I play poker for a living. Some players would risk their pile to hit a huge hand, while others would fold any hand, regardless of having odds in their favor, if they fear loss. Is that Agent Bradley?"

"Yup. Don't get me wrong. I can work with the guy. I just don't know if I can promote him. We need leaders in the offices, not guys who never take their shot."

The conversation lapsed into momentary silence. Hannah guessed it was intentional, and not his place to break it.

After a few more seconds, Captain Lockwood said, "A Harvard educated mathematics puzzle solver who plays poker. Remind me not to sit at your table."

It was Hannah's turn to be surprised. "You play?"

"I dabble," Lockwood replied. "I lack finesse. Can you imagine?"

The two men chuckled, but Hannah knew the extended meeting wasn't for poker pointers.

"Sir," Hannah said, but was again shut down by the hand signal from the captain.

"Mr. Hannah, I have tremendous respect for your gifts. I came up through the ranks of the FBI when criminal profiling was the new science. Patterns, victimology, and tendencies were as important as fingerprints and photographs. What I don't have respect for is your attitude. Just like Agent Bradley, I can work with you without liking you. But, I can't fire Agent Bradley without cause. I can, however, can your ass with a text to the front gate. Do you understand?"

"I do, sir. It's just that, -"

"Uh, you had the right answer, then made the mistake of talking more. 'I do, sir' would have sufficed."

Hannah regarded the captain with growing disdain, but something kept the anger at bay. It was a strange feeling to fall back on his rebellious roots but have no heart in it.

The Captain must have sensed it as he asked, "Something you want to say, Hannah? It's just you and me here."

Hannah drew in a sharp breath and fought his growing agitation. He felt the same anger at being challenged he'd experienced his entire life, but either the setting or the authority figure didn't rouse the old animosity. He twitched with discomfort.

"Honestly, Hannah. You'll feel better. Let it out."

As his mind rose to form the condescending insults that protected his fragile ego, so did the realization dawn on Hannah that he was being studied. For the first time he could remember, he had been outplayed.

"I've been doing this a long time, Mr. Hannah. Are you getting it now?"

Hannah let out the breath with a strong exhale. He fidgeted with vulnerability. What was happening?

"Sir, it's just that I am always the smartest person in the room. I don't tolerate weaker theories or lesser arguments. When Bradley came in late, I had him sized up in a second. We can't get work done with assholes like that in the room."

"Okay, but what about right now? Why are you unsettled right now?"

Hannah struggled with his thoughts. His emotions were overriding his intellect, and he was off-kilter.

Captain Lockwood pressed forward on his desk and clasped his hands.

"Hannah, right now you are experiencing a type of emotional break. It's actually pretty normal. It is called stress. Your high intellect had always protected you from your emotions until I trapped you in this office and didn't let you take the big chair. You are reacting to not being in charge when you are in this room. I am. If you want to work here, respect that. Can you?"

Hannah gained enough insight to ask if it was a trick. "How did you know I would react that way?"

Captain Lockwood smiled. "I was a profiler for fifteen years, Hannah. You get to know a lot about people and their pressure points."

Hannah waited for his blood pressure to slow before asking, "So, am I banished?"

The question must have caught Lockwood off guard because he laughed. "Banished? Do you think I put you through this to kick you out? No, you have a job to do. And you will do it my way. Understand?"

Hannah nodded in agreement, stunned at the role reversal he'd been put through. "I understand, Captain. And thanks for the second chance. I don't get a lot of those."

"Most people don't, Hannah."

As Hannah got up to leave, he turned to Lockwood and said, "Downey would have asked if they were okay and wanted to get that beer. Bradley would have told him to fuck off."

Lockwood nodded and shot him the gun sign.

His instincts were still bang on.

Chapter Eight

Hannah sat outside the FBI boardroom at precisely nine am. Curt had answered the surprised text from the gatehouse at eight-thirty and brought him up.

"The meeting doesn't start until ten o'clock. Did you not get my text?" Agent Downey asked as they made their way upstairs.

"Yes, I did, CD. I just want to soak in the atmosphere and get a few questions answered before we start today."

"Which questions?" Curt asked.

"Like, how was your beer with Agent Dickhead yesterday?"

"Lonely. He told me to fuck off." Curt said.

Hannah smirked and veered off out of the elevator to head toward the boardroom. He sat himself in the visitor's chair by a watercooler and waited. He knew it wouldn't be long.

Hannah had spent last night filling out a ridiculous amount of paperwork the FBI demanded before one could be paid as a citizen consultant. Curt had warned him it wasn't a lot of money, and even then, he had ill-prepared him for the amount. Hannah had made more with a two-pair flop last week than he would see in a month here.

Hannah had given Downey the rest of the paperwork, which entitled the organization to do a deeper background check and provide credentials which would eliminate the daily trips to let him into the building.

Oh, and a parking pass. The all-American perk.

Hannah counted ceiling tiles and judged distances by the number of steps he would need to round corners or reach the elevator, just to pass the time. He checked his phone. It was nine-twenty-nine. His first answer of the morning would arrive within sixty seconds.

He was betting it would be the olive-skinned young woman who had initially raised her hand, the first to ask a question. An initial query in a room of peers was a vulnerable activity, yet she showed no hesitation. She was comfortable and confident. Hannah had to admit the quality was also attractive. She would move up.

He then ranked the rest by memory from not only their faces, but where they sat. Hannah understood the pecking order of the tightest of organizations, but internally despised the demeaning nature of seating arrangements. Perhaps that was only a deferential exercise when company was in the room, but still. He preferred the most attentive at the front, where engagement was cultivated and expected. Maybe today he would seat them himself.

"Would I be allowed to do that?" He wondered.

A swoosh of footfall on the carpet alerted him he was about to learn the first important detail of his new group. It stopped just behind him, as if the eager agent had expected to arrive undetected.

"Good morning, Jacco. Thanks for coming in so early." Hannah said without looking over his shoulder.

Agent Jacco Simms eased around to face Hannah with a sheepish grin on his face. "You knew I'd be first?" He asked.

"Actually, you were my second choice, but my first choice wore high heels, and they sound different on the carpet. Shall we go inside?"

Agent Simms held the boardroom door open for Hannah, and after following him in, moved to his seat at the back on the left-hand side. He removed his suit jacket, exposing a taut physique. The agent was of Asian-American descent, neatly groomed, and highly focused.

"Why do you sit there?" Hannah asked.

"It gives me a full view of the board. Also, with everyone looking forward, no one is looking at me."

"Ah, very good. I hadn't taken that into consideration. I assumed the entire arrangement was based on a pecking order of deference and seniority. But since you and Agent Rhonda Perez were sitting together yesterday, and I knew one of you would have been the first in when the meeting was called, I wondered why you were both at the back. Will she sit beside you again?"

"Yes, we graduated together and have been good friends. Just friends." Simms said, showing no surprise that Hannah had easily recalled their names.

Hannah chuckled. "Not my place. Thanks for that piece of info, though. Interpersonal dynamics are the most over-looked factors in team-building. Oh, everyone talks about it, but when the rubber hits the road, seniority and hurt feelings still carry too much weight."

Agent Simms sat and checked his phone while Hannah dropped his bag in the front corner of the room.

"Yesterday, before Agent Bradley came in," Agent Simms said, "you mentioned you suffer from apophenia. I looked that up."

Hannah said, "We all suffer from apophenia. As you now know, it's the condition by which we ascribe a pattern to random, unrelated events."

"Like when it always seems to rain on my days off." Agent Simms said.

"Exactly. It is a serious blind spot to avoid. It leads to confirmation bias where you look for the pattern you most want to see."

"I hope you don't mind, but I also looked you up, Mr. Hannah. It seems you have quite a reputation around the poker table. I would think it would be unfair for a man of your skills to be hustling college students." Simms laughed.

"To be fair, they are rich college students who suffer from delusions of grandeur. I am viewed as a bit of a challenge therefore, they seek me out, not the other way around."

Agent Simms put his phone down. "You play poker as self-defense?"

Hannah regarded the young man. He had a sharpness to his presence today that he lacked yesterday. Or perhaps he concealed it well.

Hannah answered, "Self-defense is a legal term. I play poker because I am invited. My reputation is my business card."

"Fair enough, sir," Simms said. "How do you avoid gambler's fallacy?"

"It's almost impossible to. Who has ever left a hot table or a fired-up slot machine? But that is why the house always wins. They don't have to cheat to gain an edge. They just have to understand human nature. Which is ninety-six percent of poker."

"What's the other four percent?" Simms asked.

"Pocket aces."

Agent Simms laughed and looked to the door as Agent Rhonda Perez floated in with a welcoming smile and a nod to Hannah followed by a puzzled look at Agent Simms.

"What's the joke, boys?" She asked.

"Poker, patterns and college students." Simms replied, standing to pull the rolling chair out beside him. Hannah noted the chivalrous act accepted graciously by the newest arrival. Simms and Perez would make a powerful pair of agents throughout their careers. Even if Simms was lying about the friendship status. Or gave up trying.

"Good morning, Agent Perez. Thank you for your rapt attention yesterday. Your grasp of the process of patternicity is an important tool we will need. I hope you will stay on the case." Hannah said.

"I serve at the pleasure of the organization. I would like to remain on this case, but that decision is not mine to make," Agent Perez replied.

"Fair enough. Just to be transparent, I have some latitude in the make-up of this small task force. Agent Downey will explain all of that when we begin this morning. Just a heads-up that you both are at the top of the list."

Agent Perez looked at her partner, who returned her puzzlement with a smirk. "He was early and busted me as Eager Agent Number One. He expected you, but was stuck with me," Agent Simms said.

"Oh, I see. Well, I take longer to get ready in the morning."

Hannah knew better than to respond to that.

At nine-fifty, Agent Downey walked into the boardroom without a hint of surprise in seeing Hannah with Agents Simms and Perez already seated and prepared to do battle against crime. He looked at Hannah. "So, was Perez the first in this morning?" He asked.

Agent Simms dropped a pen in mock disgust and threw up his hands. "Does no one think I am dedicated?"

They enjoyed the levity as Hannah said, "CD, monitor Simms and Perez. They'll be your boss before long."

Agent Downey shrugged with a grin and pulled sheafs of paper from a soft-sided briefcase that Hannah recognized from Harvard. "You still use that old bag?"

"What? This bag that you bought me for graduation? Yes, I do."

Agent Perez offered, "He calls it his lucky case. He only uses it when we're on the hunt."

Agent Downey announced, "We are expecting just two other members of the team this morning. Agents Bradley and Clarke have declined appointments, and Captain Lockwood has suggested we do not seek to replace them until we discover the extent of this case."

"Yes, sir," agents Perez and Simms replied in unison.

Hannah sidled up to his friend. "How should I address you in these meetings?" He whispered.

Downey smiled. Hannah understood his friend took it as the compliment it was. "I'd love 'Emperor', but I'll settle for Agent Downey. 'Curt' is too informal for serious meetings."

"Then, Agent Downey, it is. But can I call you Curt when I come over for dinner, or do I have to call you Dad?" Hannah asked.

Downey turned his back on the agents, looked at Hannah and whispered, "Name the night. If you actually show up, you can call me anything you want. After the girls go to bed."

Hannah stood frozen as he took in the inference. He knew he had been invited several times after Downey had gotten married and the girls were born, and he had maybe shown up once. There was always a stupid reason (mostly poker) why he begged off, but now he understood why the invitations dried up.

Apparently, Captain Lockwood wasn't the only one handing out second chances.

At ten o'clock, two other well-dressed agents entered the room with deferential greetings to Agent Downey and Hannah, along with perfunctory nods to Agents Simms and Perez. He filed them into the "Senior Agents" category. Hannah would have to use more discretion with them.

"Good morning, Agents Dennison and Farron. Thank you for agreeing to work on this case. I will do my best to not waste your time, and provide as much analysis as I can," Hannah said. He wanted the meeting to start off on a distinct note than the one just twenty-four hours before.

Agent Downey began the meeting with the requirements of the small task force as set out by Captain Lockwood, who would be kept apprised of the developments. "We are a fact-finding and process collecting team. Should we need to travel, we will receive further instructions and personnel with oversight from headquarters or Quantico. We are to collect data, analyze it, and make recommendations. As we then interview witnesses or potential suspects, again, Captain Lockwood may see fit to introduce other agents to aid in the workload or bring in some seasoned expert agents. But for now, we are the group. Is everyone comfortable with the instructions of the captain?"

Hannah tried to keep a straight face when Downey finished his opening remarks. Which of the agents would object to a direct order? He had to admit that his buddy was quite good at his job.

"As far as the role of Robert Hannah, as you all know, he is a good friend of mine, but in this investigation, he is a paid civilian consultant. His role is completely analytical and carries no authority over this investigation." Downey glanced down at Hannah, and added, "You can't tell people what to do."

The muted chuckles lightened the room a little as Hannah raised his hands in mock surrender. "I wouldn't dream of it."

Downey also chuckled as he passed out the clipped packets he had in his briefcase. "I would like everyone to take his analysis seriously and his recommendations graciously in the spirit in which it is intended. No, he doesn't understand our procedures, but I know Robert always concentrates on outcomes and the shortest route to arrive at them. Questions on Robert's role?"

"I don't have questions, Agent Downey," the large man to Hannah's left said, "but I would like to make a comment, if I may?"

Agent Downey nodded, prompting Agent Dennison to continue. "I found Mr. Hannah's behavior yesterday to be unprofessional and reckless. Frankly, I'm surprised he is still here. I respect the captain's decision to employ him, but I sincerely hope to not see that level of adolescent show-boating again."

Hannah turned a dark shade of pink as the embarrassment spread across his face. He looked up at Downey to see who should respond. Agent Downey took control.

"Thank you, Agent Dennison, for your candor, and you are absolutely correct. My colleague's behavior yesterday was not a reflection of the working conditions we aspire to create. His lack of decorum results from my negligence to inform him of our operating standards, and I take full responsibility for all embarrassment or insult generated from yesterday. We met with Captain Lockwood as a group and individually yesterday afternoon and have forged an agreement. Agent Dennison, thank you for sharing your views, and given the level of discomfort you experienced yesterday, I applaud you for continuing with this task force. I assure you I will not tolerate behavior such as that, and Mr. Hannah has sought to remedy that as well."

Hannah looked to his left at Agent Dennison, much as he would a poker opponent in the next chair. Agent Dennison avoided his eyes, but gave a frank head nod of acceptance to Agent Downey. Hannah understood. This was between the two agents.

Much like the meeting yesterday afternoon in Captain Lockwood's office, Hannah understood any unacceptable behavior reflected more on Downey than himself.

But Hannah couldn't leave it at that. He hoped he was doing the right thing.

"May I also make an apology, Agent Downey?"

His friend's eyes widened. Hannah took his shot.

He turned to Agent Dennison and said, "I'd like to apologize personally for my behavior yesterday. It was unprofessional to you all, whether or not you were the target. I will adhere to all procedures throughout this investigation, and I will work hard to repair and strengthen my working relationships with you all. I sincerely apologize to you, Agent Dennison, and thank you for your honesty to clear the room of the awkwardness."

The man frowned in concentration and slowly nodded his head in appreciation. Hannah felt his words had hit the mark. He turned to look up at Downey, whose face was awash in relief.

"Okay," Agent Downey continued, "in these packets are detailed notes of the four cases that we believe are linked by the city's name. The initials spell out the word 'KILL.' Kansas City, Indianapolis, Lansing, and Louisville. I am open to suggestions on the next steps, but I believe the most pressing issue is to prevent a fifth murder from occurring."

"Agent Downey," Agent Farron said, leaning forward to look at Hannah, "may I ask how you arrived at KILL in the first place? Perhaps in the process by which you discovered the pattern, we can better understand the next location."

Hannah had developed a quick appreciation for the people around the table. Clearly, he had underestimated what his friend did for a living, and the brain power behind the group. He really had been an asshole yesterday.

"It all started by factoring the possibility of three rich young men dying in questionable circumstances over a four-month period. It is possible, but highly unlikely. I asked Agent Downey if it was possible that a fourth had occurred, and given the parameters of months, seeing if there was February death? If not, then a random occurrence was a possibility. However, if there had been a February victim, then it moves from possibility to pattern. So, Agent Downey provided me with four deaths that fit the victimology of the pattern we were seeing. Rich young men dying in non-criminal ways. I still hadn't arrived at any certainty until I freed my mind of the pattern we started with and looked for any other. For example, one man in February had died after a slip and fall. That certainly bore the marks of the January death at the Kansas City Chiefs game. But March and April were vastly different. But it was only when I re-organized the cases into chronological order, not the order in when they were discovered, that I arrived at the importance of the locations. From there, once I had imported the city names into my puzzle generating mind, I landed on Indianapolis."

"And the word KILL?" Agent Farron said.

"Exactly. Again, what is the likelihood that four random deaths could be linked that would bear no similarities? None. If they are linked, then something must bind them together. Barring a different pattern, or patternicity, this seems to be the calling card."

Agent Downey let Hannah's explanation sink in before asking, "Are we good with this? Thank you, Agent Farron. So, next steps" …

Agent Perez raised her hand. Hannah wondered how long it would take her to shake that tendency, or perhaps it was in her DNA. He took the floor. "Yes, Agent Perez?"

The room shifted slightly as Perez appeared a little uncertain whether to ask her question. Hannah realized he had over-stepped too quickly.

"I'm sorry again, Agent Downey. To save time and momentum, I wanted to hear Agent Perez's question."

Downey, who had his back turned to the whiteboard, had missed the visual exchange. "No, of course. Now that we have gotten a lot off our chests this morning, I move we dispense with formalities. As long as we don't interrupt and conduct ourselves professionally, just jump in with questions, theories, or observations. Agent Perez?"

"Agent Downey, you opened by commenting that there might be several other avenues to open the investigation, though preventing another murder would certainly be the most helpful. To do that, we'd have to guess not only the next letter in the pattern, but the corresponding city. I wanted to know how possible we all thought that would be?"

Hannah immediately understood her query. She had another investigative start but didn't want to undermine Agent's Downey's authority or question his direction. Hannah liked her a lot already.

"That is a brilliant question," Hannah said. "How can we possibly guess the next step if we don't go back and fully investigate the first four murders, looking for the pattern within the pattern that not only links the four together, but will also point to the fifth, and probably the sixth murder, and beyond? Is that what you were asking?"

"I think so," Perez answered. "I realize time prevents us from doing a full scrub of the murders, but if we can grasp a hint of the puzzle, then if he slips through our hands in May, we'd only have one fresh case to investigate, not starting over with all five. But, if we learn enough from the first four killings, and we get lucky, maybe we will catch him before he kills this month."

Heads nodded around the table and Downey paused his writing to consider the question. Hannah, to bridge the gap, turned to Agent Dennison and asked, "Have you seen anything like this in your career? Have you been able to jump into a serial case in mid-method and conclude it successfully?"

"Well," Agent Dennison said, "I have experience in serial cases, but never where the time-line is so clearly marked. In every other case I've seen, we had no prior intelligence that shows when the next crime will be committed. In each case, we had conducted investigations believing that we would apprehend the offender before they could kill again."

Agent Farron added, "I think that is what Agent Perez is asking. Should we break into pairs? One pair does a deep investigative dive into the four cases to ensure their connection, interview family members, co-workers, good old-fashioned police work, looking for any consistency that determines the next city. The other pair works through the existing evidence trying to determine the larger pattern. For example, I think that there are not nearly as many cities to concentrate on as we fear. If the next letter fits a pattern, it will probably start with 'e', if the word is *killer*. Maybe it is 'a' if it is part of the phrase '*kill a*...what, *a man*?'"

"Kill a rich man?" offered Agent Simms, joining the conversation. Hannah was thrilled that all four were working together seamlessly. "Why *that* phrase?" He asked.

Agent Simms replied, "Because it has twelve letters, and the pattern also seems to show that by starting in January, there will be twelve victims."

Agent Downey had been writing points on the whiteboard. In large letters, he wrote KILL A RICH MAN. "That is great thinking, Agent Simms, and thank you, Agent Farron. What is the thought of breaking up the team into pods for the next two weeks with specific duties, but have daily access to fresh information and meet a couple of mornings a week just to stay in touch?"

"Sounds good to me, Agent Downey," said Dennison. "If the duties include more police work, I'd like to handle those. These puzzles give me headaches."

Agent Downey looked down at Hannah. "What do you think? Do we need six minds working on the next city in the same room, or is there an advantage to digging deeper into the past crimes?"

Hannah shrugged. "You tell me. The more information we have, the easier the pattern will emerge."

Agent Downey nodded before announcing. "All right, for the next two weeks, we will break into pairs. Agents Dennison and Farron, will you act as boots on the ground, working on the four murders as best you can, given the limited time available?"

Agents Dennison and Farron nodded enthusiastically. Two dogs with the same bone.

"Perez and Simms, you handle the data forensically. Work through the patterns. Were they raised as 'only children,' did they go to the same university? Patterns you can find on-line."

Agent Simms had already begun writing as Agent Perez sat straighter and matched the other's enthusiastic nods.

"Hannah and I will act as organizers of all new leads, patterns, and anomalies. No detail is too far out of bounds. We will keep everything in its place and feed each of you fresh information. A piece of evidence found by the investigators on Monday may make more sense with something the data team finds on Thursday. Communication is key here."

Hannah could feel the renewed energy in the room. He sat quietly, not wanting to derail the enthusiasm. It was like a game of poker to him. He knew he was sitting with a winning hand with this team. Don't over-play it.

Agent Simms looked up from his writing and asked Agent Dennison, "What specifically would you like us to provide for you right away?"

Agent Dennison looked over to Agent Downey before replying.

Again, Hannah marveled at the protocol hoops these agents jumped through to maintain respect and seniority. Even though Downey had clarified that they were all equal in the room, some habits die hard, if at all.

Downey said, "Please Agent Dennison, go ahead. Time is more important than protocol. My team, my rules."

"Okay," Dennison said. "Agent Farron and I will convene a very special meeting of our pair committee at twelve-hundred hours at the local diner of his choice. Following that, I will email our requirements."

A laugh lifted the room and prompted Downey to check the clock. They'd been at it for almost thirty minutes.

"Alright, in the remaining time before the subcommittee meetings break for 'strategy sessions,'" Agent Downey said, "It is May Ninth. If the killer follows the same pattern, he won't attempt the murder until the last week or ten days of the month. That gives us two weeks. How will we define success?"

Hannah turned to face the four stares around the table as they looked past him to study the details on the whiteboard. They believed the answer was up there. Hannah believed it lay within them. Some people play poker studying the cards. The best players studied the people.

Hannah broke the silence with an encouraging tone. "I know that when we reconvene in two weeks, we will have a better grasp of the four cases that have brought us together, and the information will give us a clearer direction that we can follow with confidence."

Hannah stood up and pointed to the list on the whiteboard, much like the Harvard professors he detested.

"A man has killed four people employing unique methods. He shoved a man under a bus. Publicly, yet without detection. He forced a man to ski into dense woods. Again, publicly. He either stood in a room and watched a man jump from his twelfth story window or hurled him out. But he was there. Finally, just a few weeks ago, he stood in a park in full view and shoved a wad of gum down a man's throat while his dog stood by. The killer is confident. He is chameleon-like. This guy can blend. He is experienced because nerves should have forced a mistake somewhere. Look for evidence that seems too obvious. Most killers try to hide their crimes or involvement. These crimes are so brazen as to be undetectable. If we can put together a profile based on those patterns, then it will have been two weeks well-spent."

Hannah sat back down as Agent Dennison spun in his chair to look at Agent Farron. "Experienced?" He asked.

Agent Farron answered, "Do you think he's done this before?"

Agent Dennison turned and looked directly at Hannah before looking up at Agent Downey.

"What if he was hired?"

Chapter Nine

By the end of the first week, Hannah felt they hadn't uncovered enough to determine with any accuracy the location of the May victim. He also knew that as the clock ticked, two things were happening. First, the task force was losing confidence in his ability to spot the diamonds among the coal, and second, the killer was getting closer to his intended May victim undetected.

Both gnawed at Hannah's self-confidence.

"Cheer up, Pally," Downey said. "We are doing better than you think. Just because we haven't hit the lottery doesn't mean that we aren't making progress."

Hannah looked over the latest information sheet shared to all on the task force. Agents Dennison and Farron had done a good job of law enforcement checks from investigating officers of each of the four victims. With not one case deemed a homicide, there was little evidence beyond their own observations to go on. Still, they had some good feedback once the police were given the suspicions of the FBI.

"The witness in Indianapolis is interesting," Hannah said. An officer investigating the death at the ski resort had notes from a witness that morning who identified the victim as someone who was weaving in and out of other skiers. "He got the impression the guy was a hot-dogger; a showboat. It's not enough to want to kill the guy, but it paints the picture of someone used to taking risks. Not a big surprise if he crashes into some woods on a steep ski run."

Agent Downey concurred. "Also, the canteen server who recognized him from his bright

ski pants as being rude and dismissive. Plays into that rich, entitled mentality that caught your eye. So no, we haven't hit the motherlode, but investigations are always built one brick at a time. You have correctly identified February's victim. That's something. I know the time frame is eating away at you, but we're doing good work."

Hannah got up from his chair in the boardroom where he and Downey spent their day. Fresh intel would find its way onto the whiteboard, often then photographed for charting, then replaced with new information.

He said, "Agents Simms and Perez are pretty smart and dedicated for recent recruits. Were you like that?"

Downey see-sawed his shoulders. "I don't know. Maybe? I'm rising quickly, but those two are extra special. It's good you see it. They feed off each other. They will make amazing partners when they reach full detective status."

Hannah paused. He hated feeling so vulnerable.

"Thanks again for trusting in me, CD. You've really put yourself out there for me, and considering I've taken so little interest in how successful you've been, it just shows how much I've lost touch."

Downey appeared surprised by the admission and stood up to move beside Hannah at the board.

"Everything written up here is because you've provided links and suspicions that were otherwise undetected. You've earned your spot here. Don't forget that. But if I have a skill that many people lack, it is that I can spot talent and I'm not intimidated by it. No way Agent Bradley back there would have ever had you inside on this. But I like talent, and I don't care if I get the credit or not. I want to nail the bad people more than I want credit for it."

"Well, again, I just want you to know I appreciate it."

"Want to show it? Come over for dinner tomorrow night. Unless you have a heavy poker game on the go."

"No," Hannah said. "My social calendar is wide open, Agent Downey."

Hannah watched as Downey sent a quick text, presumably to his wife, alerting her that there would be another spot at the dinner table tomorrow night.

"Now," Downey said, getting back to work, "what do you make of Perez's assertion on motive?"

"Uncertain. I don't know the order in which crimes are investigated. Is motive the most important indicator of suspects? Who had the greatest motive? Or is it opportunity? A mixture of both?" Hannah asked.

Downey answered. "It depends. There is no hard and fast rule. But I know what she is trying to do. She is trying to feed Dennison and Farron with angles of investigation. We can assume that the killer hates young, good looking rich guys, but there are lots of those. So, why kill one a month? Why not kill them all?"

"Or," Hannah added, "if the killer *was* hired, who is so angry that they pay someone to do it for them?"

"I have a problem with the observation, Pally. Most contract killers are hired by clients to kill specific people. I haven't worked in a case where someone hires a killer to bump off a stranger. If you hire a hitman, it's personal."

Hannah mulled that fact over. He hadn't considered that aspect of the killer's personality. His fingers flitted over the city names, as if hoping to elicit May's location.

"Hey, CD. Did you ever read Agatha Christie?"

"Not unless it was mandatory material from the Bureau. Why?"

"My grandparents had a huge cottage on a beautiful lake in Vermont. We'd go visit them in the summer. It was a great place to grow up. Swimming, hiking, climbing trees, meeting girls. But I loved their bookshelf. They must have had twenty or thirty paperbacks, with a bunch of Agatha Christie novels in there."

"How old were you? Were you a crime solving prodigy early on?" Downey teased.

"I just had a flashback to one of her books called *The ABC Murders*. In it, there were a series of deaths supposedly committed by a patsy whose initials made up A, B, and C. And all the victims' names were alliterations, starting with AA. Victim two's initials were BB. and so on."

"Heavy duty nineteen-sixties patternicity there, Pally. Did you figure out whodunit?"

"I don't recall. I just remember how clever it was that a pattern covered the singularity of the intended victim."

Downey asked, "So the killer created a patsy and started killing off victims to hide the one murder they had intended?"

"Exactly, and by the way, the book was published in the nineteen-thirties. I loved it. How patterns and alliterations were used not only to hook the detective into the chase, but blind him to the actual crime."

Agent Downey sat back and regarded his friend. "Is that how you'd do it? If you wanted to kill someone, would you make a game of it to make it harder to identify you?"

Hannah chuckled. "I don't have the temperament to kill someone, nor the nerve to cover it up. But listening to you talk about the motive, it made me think of the purpose of the pattern. In the book, the motive existed before the pattern. Maybe we need to look at that, much like we need to concentrate on the order of the killings."

"I like Agent Perez's thinking, though," Downey said. "There really are only so many motives that you can attribute to this victim base."

Hannah flipped through the latest combined report until he found her observations. "Envy of their unearned status, revenge for actual or perceived slights, retribution for career torpedoes, anger over stock market losses...the last one is interesting from a sociological perspective."

"Stalled social climbing?"

"We can ask Agent Perez, but I think it means another young, rich male denied entry into the exclusive club in which he believes he belongs. Therefore, he is 'clearing the field' of competition. There is a lot of pathology and entitlement there."

Agent Downey resumed his whiteboard scribbling. "January, a rich guy who has season tickets to the Chiefs is killed at a Chief's playoff game. That's a big F you. In February, a rich hotshot skier is killed while being a hotshot skier. F You, too."

Hannah wanted to warm up to the pattern, but didn't see the same enthusiasm for the kill in March. "Okay, but why throw an art collector out a window? Why not crush him with his collection?"

Downey lost steam as well and dropped his marker. "Frustrating."

Hannah reached over and patted his shoulder. "Not to worry, CD. Remember, we're making progress."

The door opened and Agent Simms handed over a two-page report to Downey.

"This is a statistical analysis of the next city on the list."

"A what?" Downey asked, staring at the sheets.

"I put together as many of the statistical factors of the four previous cities into an index, then correlated which cities share the most characteristics. Then, I singled out the ones whose first letters were most like to be used next if the pattern were indeed correct."

Agent Simms glanced at Hannah. "Which we believe it is."

Hannah was impressed with the clear-headed thinking and layout of the report. Statistics such as geographic location, population, median household income, propensity of affluence, support of the arts and culture, and high standard of living.

The ranking of those cities was then amended to shuffle them in a new order based on the initial letters.

"So, to cut to the chase, Agent Simms, am I reading this correctly? You think the top city on this list is the most likely spot for our May victim?" Agent Downey asked.

"Yes sir, I do. I've run this past Agent Perez based on her motive analysis, and she agrees that if we combine our reports, it helps to target the most likely area he will strike next, while Agents Dennison and Farron will find the evidence to help us identify the culprit while we descend on that city."

"How?" Hannah asked.

"We centered in on cities in the Midwest, and those with population bases over one-hundred-thousand people. Then, we factored in the rest of the criteria listed. Some of those cities have a higher rate of motive triggers, as identified by Agent Perez. With a tie-breaker on the list, we eye-balled some of the evidence Agents Dennison and Farron have accrued to see which cities would give the killer a greater chance of success should they continue with an audacious crime. For example, public transportation in January is used because of the weather, but may not be as big a factor in May, but a lake might be, which would have been ignored in January. Anyway, it is primarily hypothetical until a crime is actually committed or prevented to prove its validity."

Agent Simms stood ramrod straight while Downey flipped to page two for a second run-through. Hannah watched the ticks around Agent Simms's eyes dart as he fidgeted with his hands while waiting for Downey's assessment.

"Great work, Agent Simms. That is great thinking." Hannah said. "I think you will be proven correct on your list."

Simms broke contact with Agent Downey as if snapped from hypnosis. He looked at Hannah's untouched copy of the report. "But you haven't read it."

Hannah patted the top sheet. "I don't have to. Based on your criteria, I know the top city on your list. And I agree. It is the most likely."

Downey looked up at Hannah as he dropped the report on the table. "It is an interesting choice, though I don't see how you got there so fast, Pally. So, impress us with your deduction."

Hannah made a show of flipping the report to the second page without looking down. "Alert the authorities. We need to go to Erie, Pennsylvania."

Chapter Ten

Hannah arrived five minutes early for dinner at Curt and Laurel Downey's. He stopped by a boutique liquor outlet for a hostess gift for Laurel, along with a floral centerpiece.

Downey met him at the door with an enthusiastic handshake. "Great to have you over, Pally."

"Thanks again for the invitation," Hannah said as Downey's wife, Laurel, breezed past them. "Hello, Laurel. Thanks for the invitation."

"Our pleasure, Robert," she said on her way through the hallway.

Hannah slipped off his hikers as he remarked. "It appears the invitation may be one-sided?"

Downey answered, "What, Laurel? No, she's thrilled you're here. She is pre-occupied these days. It's all good. Come in."

Hannah handed the wine set he'd purchased to Curt, but held onto the flower arrangement, now believing he should make a heartfelt gesture to Laurel.

Squeals echoed up the stairs as two blonde girls bounced into the living room. They stopped as they spied the visitor.

"Girls, this is my friend Robert. Emma, you may remember him, but Bailey, you weren't born the last time he came over to see us."

"Hello," they said simultaneously, as only kids can. With that, they ran upstairs.

"They get big," Hannah observed.

Laurel passed down the hall into the kitchen without further acknowledging Robert.

"CD," he whispered, "I appreciate the gesture, but I don't want to be a problem."

"No man, I told you. It's good. Come on in and see her."

Downey led the way into the kitchen as Laurel was putting the touches on a salad. Hannah didn't need to check a thermometer. It was colder in there. He knew it would be. How could it not?

"Thank you, again, Laurel, for the invitation. I'm sorry I haven't been in touch. I brought along some wine and this gift for you." Hannah said.

"Thank you, Robert. That is very thoughtful of you. Make room for it on the table. Grab a beer, you two. Dinner will be ready in about ten minutes," she said.

She vigorously over tossed the salad before whipping around.

"Actually, Curt, do you mind getting the girls ready for dinner? Wash their hands and stuff, please."

"Sure," he said, heading for the stairs.

Hannah felt uneasy alone with Laurel in the kitchen, but she made it mercifully quick.

"I know Curt has made you his personal reclamation project. It is his greatest quality. He gives everyone a second chance, or a third chance, unlike me." She stopped stirring and turned to Hannah, a hand on her hip and eyes drilling into his. He unearthed a memory of seeing that pose for the first time.

"But his decisions have consequences now well beyond his job. He has two girls upstairs who need their father and his income. So, if your involvement with the FBI brings out your innate hatred of authority and blows back on Curt, your chances are over. It sickened me when he told me he got you involved. And, as you guessed, this little dinner party was his idea."

"Laurel," Hannah said. "You have every right to be concerned, and still mad at the way things have been, but I won't do anything to hurt Curt at work or at home, and I want you two and the girls to be so happy. I swear, I'm in this case to help where I can."

"Oh, you say that now, but which Robert Hannah will show up when the pressure is on? And I don't mean 'Poker Robert', I mean real-life Robert. Will you walk away from that commitment, too? Like me? Like Stacey? What do you think happens to Curt? His judgement questioned; his promotions stalled? This isn't a game, Robert." She fumed.

"Laurel, I know. I can't make up for what I did to you back at Harvard, and what happened with Stacey and me had nothing to do with anything but the two of us. Look, I will not stand here with flowers in my hand in your kitchen and say I'm a changed man, because I'm not."

"Are you still playing poker?" She asked.

"What? Of course I am, and that has nothing to do with this," Hannah answered.

"You are so thick, Robert. Your poker playing has everything to do with everything. When will you get that through your skull?"

"Not with this, Laurel." said Hannah. "I feel a strong connection with this case, and it's kicked something inside me. Curt's belief in me has a lot to do with it. But I understand your concerns, and hey, they are valid. But I won't do anything to bring more pain. I promise, okay?"

He walked over to her, probably too close. She raised her eyes to his. "Okay?" He asked again.

Her mouth froze in a straight line before calling out, "Supper!"

"And then your dad said that your mommy shouldn't be alone for Valentine's Day, so he called her up and invited her to go to a restaurant for dinner, and they have been together ever since," Hannah told the girls. He made a cross over his heart. "True story."

The girls giggled and looked at their mother, who managed a smile at the awkward memories shared like funny anecdotes. Hannah was doing a poor job of lightening the mood.

Downey had become quiet as the dinner progressed through the courses, and by dessert it was obvious to Hannah that what could have been a bit of a reconciliation among the three of them was just too broken to solve with wine, flowers and a lovely chicken casserole.

It was all on him.

"Laurel, are you still with the law firm?" He asked.

"I took a leave when Bailey was born, and I'm working part time with smaller cases for another year." She took a large gulp of wine.

"Well, that's good to hear. Emma, did you ever see your mother do her lawyer stuff? She is amazing! I know you think I'm just saying that to get a bigger dessert, but it's true." He looked up from the girls directly at Laurel. "She is the smartest person I know."

"Thank you, Robert, but flattery is not called for tonight."

Hannah looked over at Curt, who ate slowly without raising his eyes.

His eyes. Robert was an expert on eyes. 'Windows to the soul' but also windows to your triumphs and secret fears. Eyes gave away whether a player held a winning hand or a bluff job.

Curt's eyes gave away the game. Robert understood in an instant all he had missed this past week.

Motive. Curt's motive for calling him, inviting him to dinner, his defense of Laurel at the door. Curt wanted tonight to be a burying of the hatchet. Curt wanted them to move on.

Then the last detail clicked into place.

Laurel hadn't bought him the tie for his birthday. She wouldn't have cared.

Hannah realized Downey wanted them both in his life, but he couldn't, so he made a play. And it was ending in disaster. What's worse, if Hannah's involvement with the FBI was a failure, it would leave a stink on Curt he couldn't wash off, and Laurel was sick about it.

Curt hadn't consulted Laurel before doing any of this. It was all plain before Hannah's eyes and he'd missed it.

The first oath Hannah made was to Captain Lockwood that he would follow regulations. He made a second one that instant to straighten up his life for a friend willing to risk his family to give a chance to a guy who didn't deserve one, so he could bring peace to his wife, whom he loved above all else.

Dessert was served and enjoyed in relative silence. With empty plates and chocolate grins, the girls bounded upstairs to wash up and resume being kids.

Which left three adults with a shared history and a full bottle of wine.

"I'll go first," Hannah offered.

"No, I think I'd like to hear from Curt first." Laurel answered.

Curt bit a lip and shook his head. "I just don't know why everything between us can't get better."

"Oh, I don't know, Curt," Laurel said, going on the attack, "Maybe it's because you make power plays behind my back to force a reconciliation I don't want. You purposely didn't tell me because you knew what I would say and how I would feel and you did it anyway. How is *that* supposed to make me feel?"

"Because I want all three of us to be together again. I have my work and I have my family, then I have this big hole of nothingness where the three of us used to be. Even when we started going out after you two broke up, we got along. Look, I'm thirty-five and I want my friends back. Laurel, you are my wife that I love with all my heart. I do. But the three of us were something special. I always thought I'd be standing up at your wedding. Not Robert sitting at ours. So, yes. I won the lottery. I married you. But why can't there be room for all of us again?"

"What? Am I not enough for you, Curt?" She asked.

"Laurel, you're not listening to him." Hannah said.

"Oh, shut up Robert. You are the last person who should hand out communication advice," she answered, topping up her glass. "Why don't you go card-hustle coeds to feel like a man."

"Duly noted, counsel." Hannah said, knowing what a full glass meant to Laurel.

Downey said, "I know you were concerned when I hired Robert at the bureau, but I'd hoped that when you saw him again, you would see the changes I do. But I knew you wouldn't invite him, so I did. So how do you see that, and suddenly think you're not enough for me?"

"Because you're doing all this shit with my loser ex-boyfriend behind my back!"

"Laurel, you two haven't been together for over ten years! What's changed?" Curt asked.

"I haven't changed," Hannah deadpanned. "I'm the same."

"There! There you go," Laurel pointed as she lifted her wineglass for a gulp. "There's the real Robert Hannah. Mr. Jokester. Take nothing seriously. Take no responsibility for whatever pain and destruction you leave in your wake. You're a fucking hand grenade with a loose pin."

"Laurel," Downey began, but Hannah touched his arm.

"No, Curt. Let her finish. Get it all out, Laurel."

"What? Do you think I have some repressed issues about us I should spill in front of my husband? You are delusional, and I am so sick that you have come back into our lives. And you, Curt. What made you think that this will end any differently this time?"

Downey shook his head, apparently lost for words. He stared at the table like he was falling.

Hannah leaned back to give them space as he said, "Laurel, everything is different now, and what you are fearing will not happen."

"What I'm fearing?" She parroted between sips. "By all means, Professor Asshole, tell me what I'm fearing."

Hannah looked at the pain in his friend's wife's eyes. Eyes he had once stared at passionately, believing they would reflect in his forever. Now dulled by worry and sharpened by betrayal.

"You worry I will do to Curt what I did to you. That I will abandon him in his hour of need when he has so much more on the line than we did back then. Ultimately, you are furious that Curt has made it possible for me to hurt you again. Hurt your marriage." Hannah tilted his head toward the stairs. "Hurt your family."

A tear streaked down each of Laurel's cheeks as she grunted and finished her glass. Downey defiantly grabbed the bottle to prevent Laurel from a refill. She shook her head and stared at the ceiling, trying a laugh on for size to prevent more tears.

"You really wasted your major on mathematics, Dr. Hannah. You're quite a shrink."

"Poker pays better," he answered.

A silence settled over the table, borne of unresolved disappointments and resentments. Hannah shuffled in his seat, but Laurel raised her hand to prevent him from talking. She reached over and took her husband's hand.

"I love you, Curt, and I want Robert to hear this. If he hadn't been such a jackass, I never would have known that you are the man for me. I love our life, and those two beautiful girls. This is my life now. Free from all the shit he caused. But I've never thought of it from your perspective until now. If you want to work with him, if you believe he can help, that is your call. You don't need my blessing for it, and I shouldn't have reacted the way I did."

She turned and stared at Hannah. "But you. If you blow this, if you embarrass Curt, if you cause distress to this family, you will regret it for the rest of your life. Trust me."

Hannah stared back. "I do trust you. And I trust you, Curt. And I would do nothing to hurt those girls."

Laurel slowly nodded her head, her eyes locked on the wine bottle, still in her husband's clutches. He released his grip. "So, are we good now?" Curt asked, finally looking up. Laurel tilted the bottle over her glass while Hannah sat stoically, wondering if they could ever be like they were.

"It's a simple question," Curt said with an edge of authority. "I don't want any awkwardness in this home tonight, and I don't want any in the office on Monday. So, I will ask again."

Hannah saw curiosity cross Laurel's face as the two of them locked in on Curt.

"Are. We. Good. Here?"

Laurel went wide-eyed and gazed at Robert. He shrugged. "I'm good. But I'm not the one in the position to say."

Laurel sat back with a wine-induced smirk on her face, staring at her husband. "Did you just play us? Look at this, Hannah. The quiet man in the corner, all along taking notes. Agent Curt Downey. Just trying to get the band back together."

Downey's placid face gave nothing away. He'd be brutal to a suspect in interrogation.

"Yeah, I'm good," she said, looking up at Robert. "But my threats still stand. Hurt my husband, hurt my family? You'll regret it."

Robert bowed in acknowledgement. "Thank you for dinner and thank you for the chance to clear the air. It means a lot to me, Curt. And Laurel."

As they followed him to the front door, Robert turned and winked at Downey. "Oh, and Laurel, thank you for the tie on my birthday."

Puzzled, she asked, "What tie?"

Chapter Eleven

When Hannah arrived at the FBI boardroom on Monday, he wasn't shocked to find agents Simms and Perez already preparing presentations and comparing data. What he found pleasantly surprising was the early arrival of Agent Dennison. The three slid sheets back and forth as Hannah walked through the door, who mumbled a "hello" to avoid interruption.

"Agent Farron is grabbing coffee and pastries," Agent Dennison announced to Hannah without looking up. "Hope you like honey, sugar, and gooey things."

It was nine-forty-five am. Based on the amount of paper on the table, the relative ease of the trio and the fervent concentration, Hannah surmised they'd been there for at least thirty minutes.

The team had been communicating and wanted to get a jump at the ten o'clock meeting. Hannah was impressed.

Agent Downey walked into the room with an air of authority, greeting each agent by name, and finished up with Hannah as if he hadn't seen him since Friday. Any fear that working together would be awkward after Saturday night had dissipated. It was showtime.

"Thanks everyone for all your work over the weekend. Today is May fifteenth. Agent Simms has provided everyone with a preferred municipality list, ranking Erie, Pennsylvania as the most likely location."

"Other than the obvious midwestern location and population similarities, are we believing that the 'E' points to the word 'KILLER'?" Agent Dennison asked.

"That is my hypothesis," Agent Simms responded. "Clearly, I could be wrong, but in crunching pertinent details, Erie seems the most likely. But I believe the top five are interesting sites. Those cities are still too vast an area to patrol and prevent, but it gives us something."

As Agent Simms was summarizing his report, Agent Farron had arrived with two boxes of warm cinnamon pastries and a tray of coffees. He added without missing a beat. "I like Erie Pa. for another reason. The lake. Three of the four victims were outdoors doing activities that made them vulnerable. Football game, skiing, walking a dog. Now that it is warmer, beaches and boating become other dangerous activities where a young guy may have his guard down."

Hannah thumbed through the top five on Simms's report. The proximity to water seems to have been a consideration. Number two on the list was Cleveland, but the letter 'C' was problematic for him.

"What might the 'C' stand for?" Hannah asked.

Agent Perez answered, "It would have to start a different word, which may be 'CLUB'".

Agent Downey was writing points on the whiteboard. "Kill Club? Interesting."

Number three was Chicago, which made the most sense from a population and sheer numbers perspective. Hannah also saw the confirmation that "C" was Agent Simm's bias. Number four was Toledo, Ohio and number five was Detroit, Michigan.

Hannah was impressed with their thinking. He looked up at Downey, who was immersed in another report. Hannah asked, "If I may, Agents Dennison and Farron, do your findings on the past cases give you any ideas about these cities?"

Farron jumped in. "I love the water, and the more I looked into the first four victims, the more I am sure that their activities provided the opportunity for their demise."

"I agree," said Agent Dennison. "In fact, to be completely transparent, I'll trust Agents Perez and Simms, and Mr. Hannah on the geography. Puzzles aren't my thing. Now, you tell me where you think he'll be and I'll go all bloodhound on him. But if we could find areas where we think young single rich guys hang out in each of these cities, we may get some local help over the next week in spotting anything suspicious. I know it's a long shot, but even golf courses, marinas and concert venues. Places where young guys like to hang out with other rich guys."

"Great idea. Thoughts?" Downey asked.

So, it went for an hour. All the pastries eaten; all the coffee consumed.

Each agent was given a task of identifying areas of probability and contacting local forces in that city for help. Hannah knew it was a long shot, but also the only shot they had.

As they wrapped up, he said, "Thanks for all your work on this, but we won't really know until we either stop him or deduce where he struck again. But we have so much more than we did when we started two weeks ago, so thank you."

They all nodded in acknowledgement, packed up their papers and left the boardroom, leaving Hannah and Downey alone for the first time that morning.

"So," Hannah said. "Thanks again for Saturday. It was interesting."

Downey nodded, but his apprehension of taking it further showed.

Hannah threw his hands up. "Just wanted to say thanks. No need to rehash it."

Downey clapped Hannah on the shoulder. "We're good. Laurel actually thought we should do it again. Only properly, without a lot of anxious build up."

"Sounds good to me. I can buy steaks and take all the pressure off you guys. Name the time."

"How about in early June when we nail this guy?"

"I like the sound of that, Curt. But you know success this month is highly unlikely, right?"

Downey snapped up his case and gave Hannah's words consideration. "I know, because if we are wrong, another young man dies. But the actual crime would be to not learn from it. You never know. We might get lucky. Stay sharp. We won't meet again until we have to, so let me know if anything occurs to you in the meantime."

"I will Agent Downey," Hannah said. "Good luck.

Hannah drove home as his mind buzzed with the many tidbits the team had amassed. It was like having seven hundred pieces of a one-thousand-piece jigsaw puzzle. It wasn't enough to spread them out on the table. You had to fit them together. And maybe when the picture emerged, they would know where to find the other three hundred pieces and end it.

He was struck by Agent Dennison's observation about lifestyle spots. If that was the case, how would the killer know so much about the habits and lifestyle? It seemed easy enough. Any rich guy would want NFL playoff tickets, and a guy with a dog would take it for a walk.

But Agent Dennison was right. Not a single killing had been committed at a workplace. Even the jumper in Lansing flew from a penthouse window, not an office building.

His mind wandered to Agent Perez, as it sometimes did. She was dazzling, with her olive skin and shiny hair. But he was drawn to her quick thinking as much as anything. She had introduced the possibility that the word 'Club' might be next.

Clubs were something that rich guys joined. Society clubs, country clubs. Men only clubs. Very exclusive.

He pulled over and texted Downey a quick request.

'Find out if the four victims were all members of a club or fraternity.'

Hannah wondered if the killer was a victim of bullying years ago and exacting revenge now.

Agents Simms and Perez were working on connecting the cities, and Agents Dennison and Farron were working to find a connection among the victims.

Hannah knew it would be up to him to find the connection between them all.

Chapter Twelve

The Bumper did not know Ohio could be this hot in May.

It took minimal research to understand the importance of the Memorial Day long weekend. Americans commemorated the fallen heroes of the U.S. military every May. It was also the kickoff to summer. Barbecues would be flaming, golf courses would be stuffed with tee-times, and everyone would be out celebrating the hot weather of the weekend.

It made The Bumper's job that much easier.

The dossier on today's victim was light on details. It was clear how the deed could be accomplished, and given the undeserved reprimand he'd suffered weeks ago, he followed the perceived suggestion to the letter.

As The Bumper often wondered, *if The Client was within sight of the kill and had such deadly insight, why hire him?*

The reasons ranged from obvious to intriguing. Intriguing because it could be a dress-rehearsal for a much larger plan with bigger fish. After this one-year audition, would he become the house assassin for a wealthy oligarch or despised business executive?

Obvious because he knew it was more likely that The Client wanted the job done with an easy fall guy who would be betrayed on New Year's Eve. He suspected that this was the most likely, but the latter possibility kept his head in the game.

For the former, though, he began working on a year-end exit strategy. Once the December dossier arrived, he would know how to execute the last kill and exit stage right with his life, reputation, and anonymity intact. If The Client was indeed honorable, the money would arrive as promised.

If betrayal was the real end-game, The Client would be left holding Santa's sack. The Bumper would be in the wind plotting his revenge.

He had scoped out the location for the murder weapon and found the spot just down the street from the target's two floor condo overlooking the Maumee River, which flowed into Lake Erie.

The sprawling neighborhood was easily one of the more affluent in the northern Ohio city where crime was a constant threat. Immaculate sidewalks crossed groomed lawns. McMansions abutted McMansions, and smaller condos filled in gaps where pie-shaped properties made monstrosities impossible. The victim's condo had to have cost a small fortune when he bought it. The place looked more like a stand-alone small home, but the grounds and up-keep were too consistent with the neighbors not to be a coordinated condominium complex.

On Saturday morning of the long weekend, The Bumper went down to the park and was pleased to find the murder weapons in abundance. Had he been unable to find any, he had a back-up plan somewhere else, but didn't want to risk missing Mr. May.

He secured the weapons in a small plastic container that wouldn't arouse suspicion if anyone saw him near the condo. He placed it in his car within sight of the unsuspecting victim and walked around the wealthy enclave like any other neighbor enjoying the day.

Just after nine a.m., the mark followed his usual routine of going outside to start up his luxury Jaguar, after dropping his gym bag into the trunk. He settled into the driver's seat to engage the air conditioning before going back into the condo.

The Bumper had studied this routine for the past four days. He would be inside anywhere from two to four minutes. The killer retrieved the container from his car and counted in his head as he slunk to the Jaguar, shielded by the over-hanging shrubs in the short driveway.

He slipped on his work gloves and quietly opened the rear passenger door of the luxury sedan, struck by the fresh smell of the upholstery. Of course, it was new.

Only the best for Mr. May.

The Bumper undid the top cover of the container, careful not to arouse the concern of the residents. He considered simply releasing them, but if the driver noticed their presence too soon, he might abandon the car altogether. Best to let the bumps of the road stir them from their sleep. The Bumper then closed the door as his counting reached ninety seconds. He slid behind the shrub nearest the passenger front door to give him a secluded view of the victim.

Within a minute, the target whistled out the door, unaware that his life would soon slip away in whatever agony awaited him. He popped open the driver's door and buckled himself in for the final ride of his life. Mr. May backed out of his driveway and slipped down the street, unaware of his deadly passengers.

The Bumper jogged to his car and took up the slow chase. He already knew the destination, so following the route was not a concern. Being there at the end was a different matter. He had to retrieve the plastic container.

As The Bumper turned from the neighborhood, he saw the Jaguar had pulled over to the side of the road at an odd angle, as if narrowly missing a collision. But the killer knew otherwise.

He parked in a small alley laneway and walked over to the car.

The driver was gasping and clawing at the window, apparently relieved to see help arrive. Two of the five bees were still crawling on the man's face as the stings had found their target. The other three were flying around, waiting for a place to land.

Mr. May stared wide-eyed, pleading for help while The Bumper waited. A car drove by slowly before speeding up and passing the scene.

No one ever wants to get involved. Even if he did circle back to be a good Samaritan on a gorgeous Saturday morning rather than enjoy whatever his pleasant day entailed, he would find The Bumper gone and a dead man in a car. It would now be that guy's problem.

The man's eyes were sliding north as his mouth contorted. One of the first bees, already faced with its mortality, flitted onto his tongue and fell into his throat. The expensive glass of the Jaguar buffeted the sound of the gagging, but the victim's lurching showed that the bee hadn't gone down without a fight.

Most victims of anaphylactic shock succumb within half an hour, but those with serious allergies who become envenomated by a bee sting have even less time. Five bee stings? Say goodbye in minutes.

The man's tongue swelled as his breathing stalled, and as the fifth bee made a landing on the back of his neck, Mr. May could not make even the feeblest of swatting attempts. The other winged assassins slammed against the window, unaware of the role they played in their own demise.

Such is the circle of life.

Slouching forward, the victim became motionless. The Bumper hustled around to the passenger rear door and opened it to retrieve the plastic container. The bees were already in their final death throes, silent witnesses to The Bumper's latest perfect crime.

He removed his work gloves, strolled to his SUV and drove away from the scene with his eyes alternating from the windshield to the rearview mirror.

There was no one behind him and no one to connect him to the scene. Even if the passing witness of a few minutes ago raised a concern, all he could describe was a curious walker who might have happened upon a dead body before running away.

It's not like it was a murder or anything!

The Bumper pulled into a nearby school parking lot to wait. It didn't take long.

Within seconds of pulling over, his phone dinged the notification, and he was one-hundred-fifty-thousand dollars richer.

With a focused fury, he slammed his open palm on the steering wheel. He yanked open his car door and stood spinning his head, looking for the spy. There was no one.

He dropped back into his SUV and seethed, snorting his anger.

The Bumper slammed the steering again for good measure, growling in Bulgarian. "Predatel…predatel"!

Traitor…traitor!

He shoved his door open and spat on the ground, calming his anger. It would do no good for The Client to know his current state of frenzy.

Five perfect, undetected kills down. Seven more to go.

And he was seven-hundred-fifty-thousand dollars to the good. He calmed himself and vowed that he would not let this bother him. If this truly was an opportunity to prove himself to what they called in Bulgaria a *bogatiyat chovek* (a great, wealthy man) in America, then so be it. Let the rich man watch. He would control his temper and ease his passions.

He would be professional. For the next seven months, at least. Then?

Time would tell.

The well-dressed stranger strolled from the condo just down the street from the doomed Mitchell Graham. If one didn't know better, which The Bumper clearly did not, one would be convinced that the older gentleman lived here. In reality, he had secured the residence for the month of May through a property sharing website.

He pulled out of the driveway in his non-descript tan sedan and drove along the same route he'd seen Graham take just minutes before.

As he passed the parked Jaguar, he regarded the man staring inside the automobile with a casual glance, if only to gauge his stress level. It certainly appeared as if everything had been executed to plan. This Witness, a key component of the scheme, tapped the brakes to appear concerned, as a bleeding-heart neighbor might, but then zoomed off.

He rounded the first corner and parked in a small strip mall, knowing he'd have about three minutes before his most important task of the month. He wandered into a variety store and grabbed some chewing gum and a soda, all the while watching the road for The Bumper's SUV.

The man got back into his car and sent the message to The Client that all was well. The Witness waited to ensure delivery and verification. He felt, as always, that his timing would be impeccable.

The phone buzzed as the assassin coasted past the store. Sixty seconds to the auto-deposit into The Bumper's on-line account. He started up his car and pulled into the light traffic, well behind the SUV.

The Witness watched The Bumper pull into a neighboring school parking lot, and as he counted out the sixty seconds to elapse, he whispered aloud "Boom," as he drove past the school.

In his rear-view mirror, The Witness watched The Bumper leap from his SUV and scan the area, looking for his tail. He didn't understand the man's frustration. Surely, he should know there would need to be a verification of services rendered.

He understood the importance of discretion. What was wrong with the assassin?

The Witness, fully packed for his next assignment, got onto I-Eighty and drove east. It would take a few days to arrive at his next destination, but he would have almost a week's head start to cement himself with his role. For this, he would slightly dye his hair, shave his mustache, and wear glasses. No ball cap or t-shirts. Always button up short sleeve shirts.

He would be in place when The Bumper arrived, ready to report on the progress of the operation.

So far, so good. Five months in and five kills. Just seven months to go.

The Witness resisted the urge to input the destination into the GPS system.

You just never know what these computers could keep.

Chapter Thirteen

The Boston task force met on Wednesday, May Thirty-first. Agent Simms was first in the room again, arriving at eight-fifty am. Everyone was there for the ten o'clock meeting by nine-forty-five. Hannah was impressed with their commitment.

Agents Farron and Dennison had been scouring the internet and calling police sources in Erie, Cleveland and Chicago looking for telltale signs of a strange death. Nothing was cropping up, but then they knew that one life, precious in God's eyes, would be a needle in a haystack to investigators. How do you find a death not investigated?

Agents Simms and Perez cross-referenced keywords such as 'drowning,' 'falling,' 'accident' or 'crashing.' Several hits provided few leads as the Memorial Day long weekend produced a handful of such cases, but none involving affluent single men. They broadened their search yesterday to include all the United States and struck out again. There were tragedies reported, but none fit the profile of their pattern.

"Maybe he is going to strike today. It's still May," offered Agent Perez.

"Or maybe he already has, but it hasn't been reported or discovered yet," said Agent Farron.

Downey filled the whiteboard with sparse details and what few leads materialized, looking for any clues. "Robert? Do you see anything?"

"No, not yet. I agree that it simply hasn't been reported yet because what you guys have found in a few short days this week is remarkable."

"But not remarkable enough," added Agent Dennison. "I hope we are wrong and that he has already gone to ground, because I'd hate to think we couldn't prevent another murder, then follow that up by not seeing it!"

"Not seeing what?" Captain Lockwood asked, entering the boardroom. The agents scrambled to their feet in respect. Lockwood waved them back into their chairs.

Agent Downey filled him in. "We were just in the first stages of looking into any cases that fit the existing profile before perhaps expanding our view."

"Nothing in Erie?" Lockwood asked.

"Nothing so far, sir," Agent Farron said. "There were the expected accidental deaths accounted for over every long weekend, but none involved the victimology we are investigating. None in Cleveland or Chicago. But they are large cities with active police forces, so I feel confident, sir, that if our killer did strike, we should have a knowledge of it within hours. "

Hannah watched the captain move his gaze around the room. The man could simultaneously intimidate and encourage his troops. The two locked eyes before Lockwood grinned and asked, "And what do you make of it, Mr. Hannah?"

"I agree with Agent Farron, sir. Even if we take a few more days, it will be a tragedy to learn of another victim, but it will both reveal and confirm the pattern. That brings its own clues and strategies to draw us closer."

"And your thoughts on expanding the view?"

Hannah paused. "Expanding the view, sir?"

"Yes. Agent Downey said that if a victim couldn't be determined by existing parameters, then perhaps the group would expand its views. Wasn't that your term, Agent Downey?"

Downey seemed wrong-footed. "I meant we wouldn't simply give up without exhausting all possibilities. Sir."

"No, I understand that, Agent Downey. But what I am asking Mr. Hannah is whether he agrees we need to expand the view or whether we need to narrow and focus our view."

Captain Lockwood gave a fatherly smile to the group. "Food for thought, everyone. Let's find that connection, otherwise this investigation will be dead in the water. If he's out there, let's get him. But if you can't prove he's there, then we are done here. Agent Farron said you should know by Friday. I will alert Washington of your deadline. They want to know."

Captain Lockwood walked out of the boardroom to a deafening hush. Only the squeak of Simms's chair broke the silence.

Agent Downey said, "He's right. If we can't prove that a May victim exists, then everything we've been working on is a mirage, anyway. We're chasing a ghost. We need to get big fast."

Hannah sat still, staring at a spot on the table. "We have to go smaller, not bigger."

"How do we go smaller to be more effective?" Agent Dennison asked.

"I've been thinking of all the big public deaths he's pulled off so far this year." Hannah said. "They were extravagant and bold. So, we've blown this guy up to be some invisible assassin. But let's think about the victims. Sure, they are rich, but they are ordinary people who would be treated in ordinary ways. So, we have to think small, not extravagant."

"Where would we start?" Agent Downey asked.

"I would start with hospitals. Has a body entered a morgue with an unusual death that didn't require a police presence, or was so standard that it escaped detection?"

Agent Farron flipped his laptop and started typing. "I'll get a database of hospitals in Erie and Cleveland and consult them. I should have an answer within an hour. A lot of them are linked through health units and share their data."

Hannah said, "If you can get answers within an hour, contact the hospitals in the top ten on the list. Go after as many as you can."

"What can we do?" Agent Perez asked.

"Think like a victim, not the perpetrator. That's what thinking small means. Narrow the search. Where would a victim of an accidental death be?

"Hospitals, morgues," said Agent Simms, "or missing persons?"

"Excellent," Hannah said. "Check missing persons from the top ten cities on our list on-line to see if any fit our profile."

Agent Downey scribbled notes across the whiteboard as the room buzzed with new determination. Hannah checked the clock. If they could find anything by the end of business today, they'd be on their way.

But if they were no closer when the clock hit five p.m., the search would be over.

Agent Farron cradled his laptop in his arm as he pushed open the boardroom door with his shoulder. "Got it," he yelled.

Hannah instinctively looked at the clock. It was almost three o'clock.

Agent Downey uncapped a fresh marker as the rest of the team, alerted from their desks, scrambled around the table. "Where?" Downey asked.

"Toledo. Number four on our list. Saturday morning," Farron said, nodding acknowledgment to Simms and Perez.

Hannah locked on the 'T' He knew the next letter. They all would.

"A guy was found dead in his car. Get this…a Jaguar!"

"Why weren't police reporting the accident?" Downey asked.

"Because it wasn't an accident. What they had was someone who stopped because the Jag was parked at a weird angle. When they got to the window, they sure wish they hadn't. The driver was slumped, dead, with scabs on his face and swelling on his neck. At the hospital, they found he had died of multiple bee stings. Maybe four or five of the little buggers. Turns out, the guy has that allergy to bees. He died of one of those attacks."

"Anaphylactic," Hannah said.

"That one," Farron agreed. "So, there is no case. Can't charge dead bees with murder. But, a Jaguar? Bee stings in public? It must be it, right?"

Hannah looked around, waiting for the agents to make the call. Instead, they all stared at him.

"It's him, all right. This is a classic case of, pardon the pun, overkill."

Hannah stood up. "Has anyone in this room ever driven and found a bee in their car? It happens. Have you ever had five bees in your car simultaneously?"

Eyes darted around the table as it sunk in. "The clue isn't simply the victim, but the mathematical probability of five bees being in a car with its windows rolled up, driven by a man whose death would be certain if even one or two of them stung him."

"How can you guess the window was rolled up?" Dennison asked.

"If it wasn't, then the witness wouldn't have had to walk close enough to see inside. The tint of the window made identification impossible from afar," Hannah answered.

Agent Simms reiterated the execution. "Five bees in a car. Eerily brilliant."

"But sloppy as well, Agent Simms, because we have found the victim within hours."

Agent Perez tapped the keyboard of her tablet asking, "What was his name?"

"Uh, I have it here. Hang on," said Agent Farron. "Mitchell Graham. Age, thirty-two."

As she typed, Agent Downey asked, "What are you looking for?"

She hit enter with a flourish and stood straight. "Our killer somehow knew that putting five bees in Mr. Graham's car would kill him. He also knew that our April victim had a condition that enabled him to choke to death easier than the average person. The killer knew the January guy had season tickets to the Kansas City Chiefs. How would anyone get that kind of personal information?"

Hannah grimaced in thought as the others gave silent shrugs. Agent Perez looked down at her screen, gave another tap, then turned her laptop around.

A man's picture was in a side column with script running the length in various fonts with paragraphs highlighted in bullet form patterns. It was simply a screen capture of a page, so accessing the full scope of the search wasn't possible without a password. But Hannah knew what she had found.

Agent Perez truly was a genius.

"What is that?" Agent Farron asked.

Agent Perez looked up at Hannah, testing him. He smiled and clapped his hands, silently congratulating her brilliance.

"It's a dating site profile."

Chapter Fourteen

Agent Perez continued her deep dive into the dating website. The screen grab was from a site called 'Hearts Elite.'

The logo elongated the first initials, making the word HE the prominent feature.

"It is an exclusive, affluent dating site, and the only one I can see where the men are free to join, and women pay to be on it. Virtually every other site is the other way around."

Agent Simms pointed to the copied profile. "On his hobbies, we can only see a snippet, but he lists hiking outdoors but must avoid open meadows with bees. It was right on his profile."

"That was the thread that I snagged with my search. A cache photo of his dating profile," said Agent Perez.

"Why would it be public if it's a pay-to-play site?" Asked Agent Downey.

Hannah answered. "Like everything else, I bet the site allows you minimal access to see the goods before paying to sign up. I bet a small portion of hobbies and pictures would be available for free, but not contact information."

"Can we check the other victim's names?" Asked Agent Simms.

"It wouldn't hurt to try, but in this case, his profile doesn't actually say Mitchell Graham. The browser must have caught an email address when I searched."

"So, this guy is on a dating site looking for women to date? He's rich? Why does he need to advertise?" Agent Dennison asked.

Agent Perez answered, "It's not advertising. Dating sites claim to match people based on the algorithms of their profiles. You put in your likes, dislikes, and preferences, and the algorithm will search out other profiles that fit that pattern. With this 'Hearts Elite' site, men who are affluent enough to be accepted on the site fill out their preferences and women who pay to have access to these guys fill out their preferences, and the algorithm does the rest."

Hannah was thumbing his phone, downloading the 'Hearts Elite' app. "How long would the verification period last?"

"What? Are you signing up?" Asked Agent Downey.

"We have to get on there to see if all five of our victims are members of 'Hearts Elite.' If they are, we've found the hunting ground."

Hannah took the victim's files and browsed the 'Hearts Elite' website back at his condo. He had hoped that by simply typing in a name, a profile would magically appear. He was surprised that this app was not like other social media sites. There appeared to be a great deal of protection from personal information that couldn't be gleaned by simply surfing, though Agent Perez had been lucky enough to find Mitchell Graham. Hannah was given a certain amount of freedom within the site as a prospective client, in much the same way a potential paying customer would be given a taste of the banquet before swiping the credit card.

Importing names and locations did little to narrow the field. To test his theory, he typed all he knew about Mitchell Graham, including the bee allergy concern. The search revealed a match with dozens of men. Even including Toledo as his hometown excluded only five. The search parameters were broad, which wouldn't help his investigation. But again, this was a dating site for affluent people, not a crime database. Without an actual name, it might prove impossible.

Hannah inputted Alex Dunn, the April victim, and got nowhere. He included *dog owner*, *Louisville*, and *lawyer*. Hundreds of profiles remained. Hearts Elite was clearly in the match-making business; there were no parameters to love among the wealthy.

He closed the app and turned off his bedside lamp. It was strange to call it a night before ten-thirty p.m.

But he had a day job now. The university student poker crowd, having thinned after that spring's graduation, was all gone. He fell asleep thinking of what his 'Hearts Elite' profile would divulge. A little of this, a little of that, but certainly one thing had to be there.

Some passion of his that would be certain to pique a killer's curiosity.

Some flaw that would point to his death.

Friday morning, June second, Hannah woke to his cell phone ring. He snapped awake, though he was sure there wasn't a meeting scheduled. He bugged his eyes to force himself awake, relieved it was eight-fifteen am. "Hey, buddy," he said to Downey.

"Sorry to call so early on your day off, but I wanted to give you an update to see if you wanted to be part of today's investigation. It isn't really a part of your skill set, but if you are available, it might be helpful."

"Sounds good, CD." Hannah agreed, rubbing his hair to wake his head. *How do early bird risers do it?* He wondered. "What time and what's going on?"

"There's a lot going on," Downey informed him. "Washington is going to get involved in the case, so I'll be introduced to a Quantico counterpart, but that's nothing you have to worry about. If this case gets blown wide-open, it would probably be kicked upstairs to major crimes, but that would be a good thing. The more resources, the better."

"But we'd lose the case? All this work just to hand it over?"

"Not necessarily, Pally. Besides, it's not a contest. There's a lot of coordination and cooperation that would still need to be done, so we wouldn't be on the outside. But I want to tell you about the warrants we're drawing up."

Hannah flung his feet to the floor. "You have a suspect?"

"No, we're not getting the full cooperation of 'Hearts Elite' to access their membership information. We're going through the legal channels, and it looks like we'll have the warrant by noon today. I have a standing 'face chat' appointment with the COO of the company that owns the dating app this afternoon, provided the document is all-encompassing."

"Ok, but what do you need me to do?"

"I'd like you on the chat. You have a way of reading people. You can watch her body language and listen to her replies. Look for tells, evasions or out-right lies."

"The COO of 'Hearts Elite' is a woman?" Hannah asked. "That surprises me a little. I assumed it was another privileged, entitled, trust fund guy creating a safe space for pompous asses."

"Well, maybe her business partner is a younger brother. Can you be here for one-o'clock?"

Hannah arrived at the boardroom at twelve-forty-five. Curt, Agent Perez, and Agent Simms were already there and seated near the front.

"The full squad is not on the call?" Hannah asked.

"No," Downey replied. "Dennison and Farron are in Toledo, getting statements from neighbors and checking the hospital. Cops have been informed of our suspicions and taking meetings."

Agent Perez handed Hannah a report file on the 'Hearts Elite' dating service as they knew it.

She caught him up to speed on its contents. "'Hearts Elite' has been on-line since twenty-eighteen. According to its charter, it seeks to provide cover and control for affluent men who don't want the hassle of fending off 'gold-diggers' that they encounter on more mainstream dating sites. The site is owned by a California shell company that operates various web properties, all legal. Here is what's good for us. The most active mainstream dating site boasts a monthly average user base of seventy-five million active users. 'Hearts Elite' only has seven thousand, and that includes users around the world."

Hannah thought that still sounded like a big number, but in comparison, he understood her point. "Does this site use comparative algorithm technology that could help us locate our victims and see who contacted them?"

"Perhaps, in theory, but we won't know until we ask."

"Why, in theory?" Hannah asked her.

"We assume that not all profiles are one hundred percent accurate, especially if we believe the killer is hunting here. He may have several accounts, for example, or may purchase one masquerading as a woman. We may find the profile of a 'match' that led to communication, but it could lead to a dummy profile deleted after the killing."

Agent Simms added, "Or we may find that Mitchell Graham was the only member among the victims, rendering our request useless."

Hannah nodded. "So, they could cooperate with us and not put us any closer."

Agent Downey added, "True, but we find even one or two other of the victims had profiles, and if they cooperate, we will need their input on how to snare the killer this month before he strikes. Because we don't need access to all profiles yet, we can concentrate on identifying victims and setting a trace. That's what we want to know. Would they cooperate in moving forward?"

Hannah had already done the math in his head. If membership was dispersed among the population, though concentrated somewhat in larger urban areas, there should be roughly fifteen hundred single, affluent men in a city of one-hundred-twenty-five-thousand people. Of those, Hannah estimated that two-thirds of young adults would be on a dating site, or roughly a thousand potential profiles across all platforms. Knowing the user base ratio he'd just formulated, he guessed how many male subscribers to 'Hearts Elite' he was looking for in June.

Hannah flipped open the folder and found the name of Elaine Stafford, COO of 'Hearts Elite'. There were enough letters after her name to justify her position. She had been with the company from the outset and was installed as COO in twenty-twenty-one.

As with so many things that involved patterns and coincidences, Hannah wondered if that was pertinent information, or was he was indulging his apophenia? Was he just trying to find patterns in random events to justify his chair on the task force?

He might have to add "Imposter's Syndrome" to his long list of shortcomings.

The centre console tablet buzzed as the whiteboard flashed an incoming meeting. Agent Downey tapped the screen and looked up at a wall camera just above the board. He was now displayed in the small box in the bottom corner. In the mainframe was a well-dressed, poised woman of forty-years-old. She made an immediate impression of confidence. Her camera awareness was perfect. She was neither too close nor too far, and though her camera was also off center, she maintained total eye-contact with the room, ignoring her screen.

"Agent Downey?" She cooed. "I am Elaine Stafford, Chief Operating Officer, responsible for the interests of 'Hearts Elite.' I have been briefed by my attorneys that your warrants are in order, though, in the interest of full disclosure, this is just too vast a fishing expedition. I will cooperate to the best of my ability, but I caution you to not view any concerns I raise as being evasive. I simply loathe having to disclose privileged client information on a wide scale for what may very well turn out to be nothing."

Hannah had to give her credit. Elaine Stafford was ready for this meeting and took control early. Maybe they should send her the morgue picture of Mitchell Graham after the bees had done their worst and have her compare it to his profile pic.

"We understand your position, Ms. Stafford, and you have the FBI's appreciation for your cooperation." Agent Downey volleyed back.

Hannah sat back to watch the verbal tennis match unfurl.

"Without getting into too much detail, Ms. Stafford, we suspect that five of your clients have been murdered in the past five months. What we are asking for is a report confirming that the five men we sent you were active clients on your website. We know one of them was and suspect they all were. Once that is confirmed, we would like access to their profiles to see what information they disclosed that would have made their lifestyle attractive to the killer. Then, we'd like a history search to see who contacted each. There should be very few who would have been in contact with all five. That last information should lead us to a killer."

"Agent Downey," Elaine Stafford answered, "and I assume you are a lead agent and that you speak for the rest in the room, you still have not risen to the level of confirmation in my eyes. We host a highly specialized clientele. They are a very select group. 'Hearts Elite' flourishes because we do not disclose any data from our gentlemen. As you know, the selling of data is the goldmine of the internet. Our currency is confidentiality for the men, and the metadata of the paying consumers, and even I would balk at betraying our female clients."

"Ms. Stafford, I understand your concerns, but five clients have died."

"And Agent Downey," Stafford interrupted, "you cannot verify that they were clients, nor do I have to cooperate in confirming their status. My lawyers may be satisfied with this charade, but I am not. Prove to me that these unfortunate victims died because they are clients of 'Hearts Elite' and I will cooperate in bringing them justice. But I will not risk sullying the name of our site and the men who trust us all for the sake of a theory. Do you have any other questions today, Agent Downey?"

Downey paused just long enough to convince COO Stafford that she had made her point, and was prepared to end the video call. Hannah cleared his throat.

"I have a question."

"Yes," Stafford said. "Which one of you said that?"

Hannah raised his hand and leaned around Downey into camera view. "My name is Robert Hannah, Ms. Stafford, and I have just one question."

"Go ahead, Agent Hannah. This has gone on long enough."

Hannah looked over at Downey. *"Do I have to correct her"*? He mouthed. Downey rolled his eyes.

"Ms. Stafford, Mr. Hannah is not an agent. He is a consulting specialist in this case but has the authority to be present today."

"Ask your question, please." Stafford said, clearly impatient.

"Do you like puzzles?" Hannah asked.

Elaine Stafford leaned nearer the camera as if she could not believe what she heard.

"I'm sorry, what? Do I like puzzles?"

"Yes, little mind games. Puzzles. Do you read mystery novels, or catch up on true crime podcasts or streaming documentaries? Do you have an inquisitive mind?"

"Mr. Hannah, I do not know what you are trying to elicit with this detour from the case at hand…."

It was Hannah's turn to interrupt her and gain an edge in the meeting.

"Not at all, Ms. Stafford, because this case, at its core, is a puzzle. It was conceived as a puzzle, it has been executed as a puzzle, and it will take a puzzle master to solve it. If you do not have an inquisitive mind capable of imaginative thought and curiosity, then the fault is all ours for contacting you. Who might fit that description in your management hierarchy?"

There was a long pause before Stafford spoke. "What does 'being a puzzle master' have to do with your case?" She asked.

"Because I am going to enter into a trustworthy relationship with you. I am going to give you the pieces of our puzzle. You simply fit them together one by one. You don't have to reveal what it looks like when it is done. But what it will do is confirm what we have said all along. You will have the confirmation that you seek. There will be no divulging of any information about your clients. You can merely investigate and confirm for yourself."

Elaine Stafford moved back from the camera, stretching her lips in thought.

In Hannah's poker terms, it was 'a tell.' Elaine Stafford was a visual thinker. She had a more active exterior than she exhibited at the beginning of the meeting when she controlled the flow.

"Just so I understand, Mr. Hannah, you will provide me with the details of your queries, and I am to confirm them for my peace of mind? That is very magnanimous of you."

Hannah instinctively recognized 'tell number two.' The exaggerated bluff. She was interested but couldn't admit it. He would call her on it.

"No, Ms. Stafford, it is not at all, and you know it. It's a business arrangement. You get everything you need to protect your precious website from a predator, and in return, I want one little number. From there, we'll move forward with our arrangement. Do we have a deal?"

There was a hint of concern in her eyes, but curiosity was winning out.

"Do you agree with Mr. Hannah, Agent Downey? Would this give you all you need if I am free to investigate through my channels without divulging privileged information?" Stafford asked.

"Yes, ma'am. But understand that time is our enemy. We believe that our next victim has already been chosen and will be in the crosshairs before the end of the month."

Elaine Stafford raised her chin in a defiant pose and struck the bargain. "Send me the information on your five victims. I can do a quick search with my IT team and get enough confirmation of your suspicions within thirty minutes. If there is no merit to your concerns, will you trust me and allow 'Hearts Elite' to continue without interference?"

"Of course, Ms. Stafford," Hannah said, "but I know you will be overwhelmingly convinced. In which case, we have to trust that you will live up to your end of the deal. But once you realize the liability of doing nothing, you will truly see what a bargain you are receiving."

Stafford paused. Hannah watched her with card shark eyes as she weighed her options. To Hannah, it was a straightforward decision, unless there was more at stake than he realized. Was there something else going on at 'Hearts Elite' that she did not want exposed?

"If I am satisfied beyond a doubt that this investigation has merit and that my cooperation will shield my company, then yes, you will get what you ask. What is it you want, Mr. Hannah?"

Hannah made his request.

"That's it?" She asked.

"That will be more than enough. I have worked out what the number will be, so I'll know if you exhausted your search, or are wasting our time. Once we have established that trust, you will help us locate our killer. I guarantee it."

Elaine Stafford looked at the bottom of her screen. "It is almost ten-twenty in California. Give me two hours from the moment you scan and send the information, and I will respond with the number you need. Is that a satisfactory time frame, Agent Downey?"

"Yes, Ms. Stafford, it is. And thank you."

With that, she ended the call, darkening the whiteboard.

Hannah ran his hands through his hair to relieve the tension as Agent Perez ran the profile sheets through the scanner to send to Stafford. Downey slapped Hannah's shoulder.

"Good work. Strange request, though."

"Not really. It's the next piece of the puzzle."

They scrambled back into the boardroom just before four o'clock, Boston time. A little over two hours had gone by since Stafford would have received the five victims' names, locations, hobbies, and profiles.

Also, the dates of death. Hannah hoped that a lack of user traffic after those dates would also go a long way in convincing Stafford of their hunches.

Within seconds of sitting, Stafford's face appeared on the screen with a much different countenance. Gone was the defiant gate-keeper scowl with the glazed eyes and placid glare. Here was a woman fresh from the hunt with answers.

"I regret to inform you all of my search within the profiles of the five gentlemen you sent along." Her timing was impeccable. "I regret it because you are right. All the information you expected to find were in those profiles, and yes, they have been dormant beyond the dates specified. Thank you for the opportunity to maintain their confidentiality even beyond death, so I am, therefore, willing to fulfill my end of the bargain, though I do not know how it will help." Stafford said.

Hannah leaned forward and wrote a number on a scratch pad within reach and held it up to the room, out of sight of Stafford.

She looked at him across the miles and said, "We have twenty-seven subscribers in Hartford, Connecticut."

Hannah turned the note for her to see the number 26 scrawled across the page.

"Close enough," he said.

Chapter Fifteen

The Bumper arrived in Hartford on Saturday June third. He located his first motel on the southern outskirts off Interstate Ninety-One. It wasn't as hot now, and The Bumper was relieved to be out of Ohio. He checked in under his new assumed name for the next six nights until moving closer to his intended victim.

June meant he was almost halfway through his mission.

After sorting out some clothes, he opened his laptop and reread the dossier, which included the strange, encouraging attachment. The Bulgarian thought his English was good, but he worried about the context. Was he being challenged or…. comforted? Was that even the right word?

"Don't worry yourself with the speed of payment. It is apparent you are concerned with the oversight, but it is all part of the plan to ensure its success. You remain the most important player in the game. Concentrate on your role and trust the plan. Good luck."

The Client saw all. But The Client also knew that The Bumper now knew.

That bothered him as he drove out of Ohio, through Pennsylvania and across New York State. But the letter he had opened seemed to want to calm his troubled mind. Keep him in the game.

But these drives! Bulgaria from tip to tip was only about two hundred and fifty miles. The drive from Toledo to Hartford took all day and about six hundred and fifty miles. His latest SUV was comfortable, but he wasn't used to such long trips as Americans must be.

He read the note again. He concentrated on the first words.

Don't. Worry.

They seemed…what? He knew the word he was looking for in Bulgarian.

Not Predizvikatelen

"Ah," he said aloud. "Not confrontational." He expected a firm hand was guiding his actions, but this letter was more…*uspokoyavashto*…reassuring.

But he would take its advice and stick to the plan. Expect to be paid but keep his eyes out for The Client.

The Bumper opened a new window on his device and ran a general search of Hartford for the target locations. He found Americans had so many of them, but wondered why they were all so out of shape?

"Too many hamburger joints as well," he said, chuckling to himself.

He embedded the victim's address into his map and panned out, looking for a good first intersection point. From there, he could scope out his routine until the opportunity presented itself for the execution.

And the opportunity always presented itself.

The Bumper showered off the weariness of the road, dried himself with a flimsy towel, dressed in fresh casual clothes, and set out in search of American hamburgers.

As The Bumper drove out of the parking lot, The Witness, two rooms away, noted the assassin's latest vehicle and watched him drive off.

June was underway.

Chapter Sixteen

"Good morning, Agent Downey. I'm Agent Michael Watson."

Hannah sat at the boardroom table as Downey was introduced to his counterpart at Quantico, the main office of the FBI. Unsure of whether he should he even be in the room during this meeting, Hannah was assured it would be beneficial for the three of them to make that early connection.

The zoom call started precisely at ten a.m. Hannah was amazed at the continued precision of the FBI.

"Thank you, Agent Watson, for your attention on this case." Downey said.

"My pleasure. I am intrigued by the novelty. It seems outlandish that this could be true." Agent Watson replied.

"Let me introduce my colleague. This is Robert Hannah. He has a degree in mathematics from Harvard, and was my roommate. Pretty well, the smartest guy I know."

Agent Watson cracked a smile. "That is a good guy to know. Hello Mr. Hannah, pleased to meet you."

"Thank you, Agent Watson, but please call me Robert."

"I have nicknamed him 'Pally' over the years because his name is a palindrome, his favorite numerical sequence." Downey explained.

"So, you are good at picking up on puzzles and patterns, Robert? Good to know."

"As I stated in my latest report, it was Robert who happened upon the connection among the killings. You have read enough to know where we are now, Agent Watson?" Downey asked.

"I have, and I am impressed with the work of your team. I suggested to my boss here that I would like to act more like a liaison between Quantico and Boston until we can confirm the actual killings are that of a serial predator. As strange as it sounds, we would need empirical courtroom proof before we'd announce it. But the circumstantial evidence is more than compelling enough to continue an investigation. Tell me, Robert, how did you land on Hartford for June?" Watson asked.

"As you know, Agent Watson, the city names are spelling out a warning, or the motive. We had KILL after the first four and believed Erie Pa would give us the first five letters of KILLER. But with Toledo, we now believe the first seven letters with spell KILL THE. So, given population abundance, as shown by the initial chosen cities, Hartford is the largest city in the east that begins with the letter 'H'," Hannah said.

"And this dating site seems to be the hunting ground? That is amazing work in such a short period, Agent Downey. Is there anything we can do at headquarters to guarantee greater cooperation from them?"

"No, thank you, Agent Watson. Unfortunately, we would almost need to see a June victim as a client to prove it to them, something we are trying desperately to prevent. If either scenario occurs, a death or a prevention, and we're working hard towards the latter, that should give us all the leverage we need with 'Hearts Elite' to encourage full cooperation without warrants."

Agent Watson nodded before asking, "Robert, what do you think this individual is looking for this month?"

"Great question, Agent Watson. I just wish I had an answer. If we are going with the theory that their wealth and lifestyle provide the opportunities to kill them, then we must think in terms of what activities are most likely to attract the killer. I was wondering last week whether, in fact, the killer chooses the most vulnerable of them, or simply one that angers them the most."

"Right," Agent Watson replied. "If a profile stated that he liked to bungee jump without a helmet…" He let the implication float.

"Exactly. He'd be an easy target. Or maybe he looks for the most arrogant profile and wings it from there."

"We asked for access to all twenty-seven profiles in Hartford, and were denied. I understand their concern, particularly if we were wrong like we were in Erie, but Agents Dennison and Farron will spend a few days in Hartford with the police to work on a surveillance system. Anything to alert officers of a unique threat."

"Why aren't they there now?" Agent Watson asked.

Hannah answered. "The killings have all taken place at the end of the month. A scoping period precedes it. We know that when the killer strikes, it won't be before the twenty-second or twenty-third of June."

"It's going to be nearly impossible to monitor the activities of two dozen young rich guys."

"Agreed, Agent Watson, which is the same concern 'Hearts Elite' voiced. I did, however, have a thought about how we might narrow the field." Hannah said.

Downey turned to his buddy with a puzzled look. "When were you going to share this?" He asked, as Agent Watson chuckled on the screen.

"I just thought of it. We could ask Elaine Stafford, the COO of 'Hearts Elite,' whether there was a common thread that runs through many of the profiles. Are they all golfers? Do they all own a boat? Do they all hike? See which are the most common and narrow the field of concern."

"Do you think she'll cooperate?" Watson asked.

"I don't see why not. As long as she can dispense the information, she feels in control. It's worth a shot." Hannah replied.

"Hannah can be pretty persuasive. She was impressed with his number trick on Friday. I think she'll take his call." Agent Downey said.

"I will leave the communication up to you, Agent Downey. Please contact me with any information you deem worthy. Should we be contacted by any individual who seems related to the case, I will reach out. You have my cell number, and I wish you all the best. Nice meeting you, Robert. Keep that brain spinning."

"Thank you, Agent Watson, and I'll stay in touch," Agent Downey said as the screen went blank.

Hannah followed up by e-mail with Elaine Stafford on his request. He left the timing open-ended, but the urgency was there. He just didn't want her to shut down the lines of cooperation if he got too pushy. Way too early in the game to go "all-in."

Agent Perez moved into the boardroom with her laptop and set up shop in her familiar back corner. "Everything okay?" Hannah asked her.

"Oh yeah, just gets noisy when the adrenaline is running in the pit. Need some quiet," She said.

"Hmm," he murmured. "In poker, that is why some players wear glasses. Yes, it disguises the eyes, but it also dulls the peripheral vision. If you take in too much sensory input, it clouds your vision. Noise never bothers me, but too much movement is a major distraction."

"You're always looking for 'tells,' right?"

"Sure, but too much movement is the same as no movement. If a player has been disciplined and plays the same when they have a winning hand and when they're bluffing, then you can't tell. But if suddenly they scratch their hairline, cough, and look around, then you know they are disguising their real tell when the pressure is on."

Perez typed, scrolled, and printed. Hannah sat and fiddled with his phone, looking for clues about Hartford while he waited for Elaine Stafford's response.

"What do you think he is doing right now?" Perez asked.

"Who? The killer?" He asked.

"Yeah." She looked at the clock. "He is only a few hours away. He doesn't know we are onto him. I wonder what he is doing."

"Watching. Planning."

She pushed her chair back a bit and sat straighter. "But how does he know what to plan? I understand the metadata from the profile gives him an edge into their vulnerabilities, but how do you tap into that? Use that info to kill someone?"

"Unfortunately, Agent Perez, there are lots of ways. The easiest way is to bond with someone over a shared experience. How many times have you seen strangers hug each other at concerts? That isn't even planned. It just happens organically. My fear, of course, is that he doesn't even plan at all. If that is his process, then I don't think we'll ever catch him."

"But he had to have collected the bees. He had to have scoped out the park where he killed the guy with the gum."

"True, but none of those things alerts authorities to anything criminal. He doesn't break into their homes, doesn't steal a car, and probably does nothing that would get the police involved. He never runs a yellow light, never breaks the speed limit."

"Now that, Robert, sounds like profiling," she said with a chuckle.

Hannah found he was genuinely enjoying her company, and while he knew that asking her out wasn't breaking any protocol, it would jeopardize the coherence of the group, which seemed more important to him.

This new world within the FBI was doing strange things to him, he thought.

Instead, Hannah said, "Let's build a profile on the guy right now." He stood up and grabbed one of Downey's markers and made a large rectangle on the whiteboard. "Tell me about him."

"Like, what I think?" Perez asked. "I don't have nearly enough profiling experience to tackle that."

"Neither do I," he answered, "and yet, here I am."

Perez paused and stared at the board. "He is their age."

"Good," Hannah said, noting the observation on the board. "Why do you say that?"

"Because he has blended in. If he was significantly older, he would have stuck out, especially at a ski slope."

"Great. What else?"

"The killer is also single. He understands the dating sites and how to use the profiles," she said. "He must have a profile somewhere, or *had* a profile somewhere, but I don't believe he has an actual account on 'Hearts Elite.'"

"For someone with little confidence in profiling, you have wonderful insights," Hannah said, jotting her points in the rectangle. "So, we have a man in his mid-thirties, single, with a history within dating sites. Tell me about his personality based on his approach."

"He is highly organized, especially for a serial killer," Perez surmised.

"But is he a serial killer?" Hannah asked.

"Of course. Five kills in five months in five different cities? What would you call that?"

"I don't know nearly as much as you do, but the lack of recognition factor bothers me. Don't most serial killers make a bigger splash? Play 'catch me if you can' with the police? Send letters to newspaper? This guy is killing and we can barely prove that they are truly murders!" Hannah finished.

"Okay, but he is highly organized. With that comes patience, execution, and escape. With each of the first five deaths, he has avoided leaving clues at any stage of the crime. Nothing before, nothing during, and nothing after." Agent Perez said.

"So, he's professional?" Hannah asked.

"Professional?"

"Yeah, do you think he's done this sort of thing before?" He asked.

Perez chewed her lip as she pondered the question. "Yeah, I certainly think he's killed before, but as to the notion that he makes a habit of killing in secret, that would be hard to find out."

"That's my point about labeling him a serial killer. I agree he has done this before. To have killed no one in your life, then suddenly be so adept at avoiding detection, is virtually impossible. You know how many things can go wrong," he said.

Hannah turned back to the whiteboard. "Do you mind if I add a couple of other characteristics? Tell me if you disagree."

"Ok," she said, standing up and moving beside him.

Hannah felt the unease move down his fingers as he wrote. Was this turning into something?

When he finished, he capped his marker. Perez looked over at his comments.

"I agree. He is professional and intelligent. But explain why you think he is handsome and small in stature?"

Hannah looked into her eyes. He could see the curiosity and interest behind the stare. This was a dangerous moment if he took it any further.

"Because he has gotten close to his targets. If he was the least bit intimidating physically, perhaps the dog walker would have avoided him, and the art dealer in Lansing wouldn't have let him into his twelfth storey condo. Why do I believe he is handsome? He is very confident in public, something unattractive people often are not. He doesn't believe his appearance will scare away the victim. That is something worth considering."

Agent Perez gave him a pleasant smile and walked back to her seat. He watched her sit down.

"I researched you, you know," she said. "You have a bit of a reputation at Harvard, outside of the lecture halls."

Hannah stood still, wondering where this was leading. Perez hadn't yielded a single personal comment or asked a personal question before this moment.

"I'll admit a man of your intellect and drive is very appealing, but I'm a career agent so I am very grateful to work with you, and am relieved you haven't made things awkward by asking me out," she said while resuming her scrolling. "Besides, I think you know my heart belongs to Jacco whenever he gets his handsome head out of his ass."

Hannah laughed as his disappointment dissipated like fog in the face of her honesty. He truly had met no one like her. Agent Simms would soon find he was a very lucky man.

Hannah thought he may just have to tell him.

Agent Perez looked up with her winning smile and said, "Don't bother telling him. He won't believe you, and things will get all awkward."

Smiling himself, Hannah returned to the rectangle on the whiteboard and captured the image of the impromptu profiling session. He would save this for Curt as more information became available.

He stared at the 'professional' characteristic.

Could he be a contract killer?

"One last thing, Agent Perez," Hannah said formally, to clear any lingering impressions of their relationship being anything but professional. "Why now? Why has he started this killing spree now?"

She widened her eyes in thought as she looked at the board and across at Hannah.

"I don't know," she said. "But that's a brilliant question."

Chapter Seventeen

The Bumper walked past the target's high-rise apartment complex, concentrating on the flow of pedestrians, the roar of the traffic and the distance to the gym.

There were four workout studios within an eight-block radius of Mr. June's apartment, and the assassin would start with the assumption he walked to his preferred choice.

He had been alerted in the dossier that every one of the target's pictures on-line involved lifting, pumping, or posing. The method of disposing of this guy was obvious.

His physique, though, made it worrisome.

It was a warm mid-June Saturday morning, and The Bumper enjoyed the exercise. Anything to free him from his hotel room. He longed for his studio in Bulgaria with its balcony and city sounds so different from the cacophony of America.

After over an hour of walking, he found what he was looking for. Having struck out at the four workout studios, which looked nothing like the gym in which the victim's pictures were taken, he spotted a personal trainer's studio across from his last stop. Of course. It would be 'personal training.' Expensive.

The color of the walls and the setup of the equipment matched the photo background perfectly.

Intersection point number one.

The Bumper surveyed the scene. The front door access made privacy impossible, while the street cameras at a nearby bank branch could track his movements should anyone become suspicious. He walked to the side alley and pulled on a couple of doors. All locked.

The assassin put on his best tourist face, and with a ball cap and light sunglasses to mask his appearance, he entered the trainer's gym. There were three guys in various workout routines. Two were hard at it with free weights while the third was fast-pedalling a stationary bike.

No televisions. No talking. The Bumper tried to think of the American expression. *'Right,'* he said to himself. *'Hard core.'*

A hard-bodied man of about forty-years-old appeared from a side office. "Can I help you? You looking for a place to train?"

"Yes, thank you," The Bumper said, playing the timid tourist while laying on his accent. "I'm only in town for about a month and I don't want to go to one of those places," he said, motioning to the gym across the street. "Is there a month rate I could buy to work out here with you?"

The trainer gave him a quick look. The Bumper understood the assessment and unzipped his jacket to display his hard, flat torso and six-pack abs. His arms were quite defined within the jacket.

Apparently satisfied, the man negotiated a fee. "I don't operate like that, but I can see you know your way around. How about one-hundred dollars for the month, cash, and you can use it as much as you like? You won't find it as busy in June and July, anyway."

"That is very…uh…generous of you. Is that the word? Generous?" The Bumper asked.

The trainer scowled, seemingly uncomfortable with 'this foreigner.' "Yeah, I'm generous," the trainer said.

The Bumper made a mental note to come back for this asshole.

"I thank you. I will bring money tomorrow morning," he said, walking out the door.

The assassin jogged across the street against the lights and used the ATM at the bank on the corner, extracting five hundred dollars. He'd need one hundred for his registration fee that would never see a tax form or balance sheet, and four hundred dollars for workout clothes.

On the way back to his hotel, he stopped at a fitness outlet and bought a couple of Under Armour muscle shirts and shorts, a bag of socks and a pair of high-end sports shoes.

He had to look the part when he went back to Lonzo's Training Gym in the morning. Perhaps he would meet Mr. June tomorrow. Or the day after that.

He knew it wouldn't be long.

Chapter Eighteen

"Mr. Hannah, as much as I want to cooperate with your investigation, I cannot simply allow you to run roughshod through our client profiles."

Elaine Stafford glared through the screen into the boardroom at the FBI office in Boston.

Hannah looked at Agent Downey before returning to the screen. "You know we're all on the same team here. We want to save your clients from what we believe is a serial predator." Hannah reiterated.

"And I am both grateful and sympathetic to your cause, but there is that nasty little thing about privacy protection. And I won't surrender it." She said.

Agent Downey entered the fray. "We're not asking for a blanket assault on your client list, Ms. Stafford. You have twenty-seven profiles in Hartford. We believe that one of those is being targeted as we speak."

"And again, Agent Downey, until you show an actual threat, I am not obligated to provide you with information. Because, to be frank, gentlemen, I know where this is going. Should there be an attack on one of our clients this month, you will be back next month. Am I correct?"

"Yes!" Hannah said. "Of course. But are you willing to sacrifice one life for some meaningless protection clause? Don't you think if your clients knew the risks out there, they'd be furious you did nothing to protect them?"

Stafford seemed to wrestle with the concept when Downey asked, "How about this? Is there a way to track who has been searching their profiles? Is there a way to find a common account?"

"Theoretically, but only if they make contact. We employ what we call 'Triple A' scanning surveillance. The triple A's stand for 'Abnormal Algorithm Analysis.' This detects catfish attempts, or ACT. Our 'Anti-Catfish Technology.' This is an important part of our site. These rich bachelors do not want to get catfished." She said.

"And by catfished, you mean…?" Downey asked.

"Oh, if a person is 'catfished,' it means someone pretending to be someone else who is trying to lure them into a relationship to drain them of their cash. The surest sign of a 'catfisher' is the reluctance to meet in person. I can say I'm a beautiful thirty-year-old law school graduate looking for a man on our site, who then becomes interested in her. She says that she is interested, too, but can't afford to go out because she is strapped with too much law school debt. That sort of thing. Then, after a few weeks of stringing him along, he agrees to give her twenty-five-thousand dollars to pay off some debts, and she accepts the money, but never shows for the date. Well, it turns out 'she' was a fifty-year-old sophisticated hacker with a drug problem. Catfishing."

"What technology do you have that fights that?" Hannah asked. "Rich guys, dropping cash on beautiful women, has been going on as long as money has been around."

"True," Elaine Stafford said, cracking her first smile of the meeting. "But in our case, we employ a 'time detection code' that is self-administered. We encourage our clients to enable the feature, and after accepting contact, the clock starts. If after fourteen days regular contact has continued, the client will get a pop-up asking questions about the customer. It gets them thinking clearly about their match. The ultimate question is whether a rendezvous has been suggested but rejected. That sends the clear warning to our client, and they are to report the customer to the embedded link in the pop-up. That link comes directly to my office."

"An impressive feature." Hannah said. "How many reports have you received?"

"This year, or throughout the life of the site?" Stafford asked.

"Actually, both, if you could look that up," Downey said.

"I don't have to look it up at all," Stafford said with obvious pride. "We've had only one, and that was within the first three months of operation. After that, word got out that we were the safe space for introductions and our clients have been protected from fraud. And it doesn't cost them a penny."

"As far as you know," Hannah replied.

"I'm sorry?" She asked.

"As far as you know, no one has been defrauded. As you said, it is a self- reporting technology. Perhaps a client ignored the warning, lost a bundle and chose not to report it to you. I bet that happens all the time,"

"Not on my site," Stafford said, hooding her eyes. Hannah knew he'd struck a professional nerve.

Risking antagonizing her further, he said, "Oh, come on. Sexual assault statistics are clear that a small percentage are even reported. Once embarrassment and humiliation are factored in, the reporting process becomes less appealing. Now, bilking money from the wealthy is not nearly as dehumanizing as sexual assault, but the blow to their ego guarantees that you'd never know."

"Mr. Hannah," Stafford answered, "we take our responsibility seriously in protecting our clients."

"I know you do, as proven by the lengths you will go to, even though their very lives are at stake. But you are relying on their candor and honesty. I've not seen a lot of that among the wealthy. They rarely have use for honesty, and even less so for transparency."

Stafford bit her lip and sat back from the camera. Hannah knew she'd been stung by his assessment but found her loyalty to the clients admirable.

"Still," he said, "no one deserves to be killed, so if there is any edge we can get that points us in a direction, even if it's paring down the potential victim list this month, we have to ask."

Hannah watched the internal struggle spread across her face. Finally, she asked, "What 'edge' would you be looking for?"

Hannah watched Agent Downey pull a sheet from his binder. Apparently, he was ready if she offered the help. "The most notable areas are public hobbies and obvious points of intersection. For example, golf is a popular activity for this group. It would be natural to play and get paired up with a stranger on a golf course and think nothing of it. So, any of the profiles that mention 'golf.' Same with leagues; softball or tennis. Clubs or public gymnasiums. Places where it is natural that you would be vulnerable to strangers."

Stafford nodded as she scribbled off-screen. "When would you need this information?"

Downey looked at Hannah. "As soon as you can."

Hannah nodded. "We are assuming June twenty-fifth will be the day, for no other reason than it seems to work out for the killer. It has not yet gone to the last day, and the twenty-second of the month was the earliest. But we'd need time to get this information to local police to keep an eye out at these areas, so the sooner the better. Even if you trimmed the list of twenty-seven down to the more obvious dozen, it would be an enormous help."

Elaine Stafford sighed in resignation. "I'll see what I can do, but no promises. And Mr. Hannah, I can assure you, not one of our clients has ever lost a penny in a scam from this site."

"Oh, Ms. Stafford, I can assure you they have. The early catfish attempt you employed to test the technology has given you a false sense of security. It's a different world than even four years ago." Hannah said.

Stafford's wide-eyed double blink gave her away. "What?" She muttered.

"Hey, it's your website," Hannah said. "You set up your own catfish test to make sure the client self-reports it, and then you have them put together a testimonial talking about the safety. It's no different from handing out samples. It's not illegal, though perhaps unethical. But again, we're talking about the wealthy here. Ethics is less important than honesty and transparency."

A crack showed in Stafford's armor. "You seem to know a fair a bit about the affluent, Mr. Hannah."

"I went to Harvard. I know."

Somewhat deflated, Elaine Stafford promised to stay in touch and hung up on the call.

Agent Downey shook his head. "You just keep amazing me. How'd you figure out that the catfishing email came from her?"

"I'm just skeptical of all the hocus-pocus, mumbo-jumbo algorithm stuff. It's a questionnaire to see if you're being scammed. Since it goes directly to her office, of course she would want to try it out. It's hardly a stretch to see rich guys ignoring that. The part that disappoints me is the time frame."

"How's that?" Downey asked.

"If the killer chooses a kill a month, then he can't be taking more than a few hours to peruse profiles looking for his victim. I doubt he makes contact, or if he does, there is no way it continues for at least two weeks. The killer isn't looking for money or a relationship. He's looking for access."

"You think their algorithm is bullshit?"

"I don't think it's helpful. If the killer is just treating the profiles like a real estate guide, then how would we know who has been chosen? And if it is as easy as that, then the killer could create a new profile every month to search, then delete and start over next month to cover his tracks."

Downey rubbed his face. "You're depressing me right now."

"Well, cheer up. It's the fourteenth. We have about ten days to shrink the victim pool and maybe we'll get lucky. I'll tell you this. The killer doesn't know what we know. That's powerful."

They packed up the boardroom, and Downey walked Hannah to the front door. "I'll call when I hear from Stafford. If you think of anything, shoot me a text. Otherwise, I'll see you when I see you, Pally."

Hannah walked to the Audi, thinking about his wealth and privilege. '*Am I like them*?' He wondered. Then decided that if he was, it really was time for a change.

Chapter Nineteen

The Bumper got in a few workouts before encountering Mr. June.

The assassin had been going to Lonzo's Gym for four straight days before the hulking figure in the back made his acquaintance. He made it appear random and inconsequential, and the mark paid little attention after the casual greeting.

The Bulgarian got to work on his program, going only seventy percent so he could monitor the powerful figure he'd have to subdue and kill in the next week. The guy was a beast.

After his workout, The Bumper made a stop in the back corner of the studio, then thanked the owner and commented on his target.

"Did you get that guy into the shape he's in?" He asked with an exaggerated accent.

"Who, JoJo? Oh, my God, I swear he was born that way. He is committed to his training." The owner replied.

"Does he compete or something?"

"He has done a few competitions, but it's really just about his physique. The guy digs himself."

"Digs?" The killer asked, pretending to be confused.

131

"Oh," the owner laughed. "What I mean is, he likes himself. A lot. When he isn't here, he works out at his apartment. He has a home gym as well."

"Well, he is very strong," The Bumper replied, laying on the 'dumb tourist act.' "Maybe I have seen him?"

The owner reached behind the counter and pulled out a pamphlet. Two of the same photos The Bumper had been sent were on the front of the gym leaflet. "He is on our pamphlet, so you may have seen a flyer in the neighborhood."

"Oh yes, maybe." The Bumper reached out. "Thank you again for letting me come in. I don't know when I will be back because I am almost done with my work. So, thank you for your help with my workouts."

"You're welcome," he replied. "I didn't know if you were serious when you came in here, so stop by the next time you're in Hartford. Seeing as you only popped in a few times, you can work out for free next time."

"Thank you," the assassin said with a small courteous bow, "but I doubt I will be in Hartford again."

The Bumper lingered within sight of the target's luxury high rise. He ran through his process a few times in his head to perfect the approach. He gripped the water bottle he'd pilfered from the target, waiting for him.

The hulking figure followed along the same path a half-hour later. The Bulgarian waited until he was almost to the front lobby door when he jogged up, calling him.

"Hello, sorry, hello?"

The man, irritated, turned and stared at The Bumper. "Me?"

The Bulgarian turned on his full accent. "Yes, you were at Lonzo's. We met today, though now that I am changed you probably don't recognize me. But, I am sorry, I think I took your drink bottle by mistake, so I have been following you, but you are in very good shape." The killer laughed with self-deprecation.

Relief spread over the man's face. The lost bottle was clearly on his mind as he steamed home. "Oh, great, thanks. I wondered where it was. I've had stuff stolen from there before, and I thought it had happened again."

"Who would steal something from someone as huge as you?" The killer joked.

The man laughed in reply. "You never know. But thank you. What were doing at Lonzo's? I haven't seen you there before. You new around here?"

"Yes, I am doing contract work, so he gave me a monthly…how you say…rate? But I didn't like the studio. Old equipment and not very serious about training." The Bumper stumbled.

"Lonzo's is okay, but you're in great shape, so I can see what you mean. I bought my set of free weights, so I only go in for a change of scenery."

"Well, good for you. I don't want to bother you, just to return your bottle." The Bumper turned to leave.

"Hey, thanks for bringing the bottle back. If you're looking for a place to work out, I offer some workouts in my home studio. I'll give you a cheap rate for your honesty."

"That is kind, but I am not in your…. what is word…"

"League?" The hulk replied.

'Yes, league,' the killer thought. He said, "I would be embarrassed to work out with you."

"Hey, not at all. Here…here's my cell. Shoot me a text if you change your mind. I'm free in the early mornings and on Thursday evenings. And thanks again." The man turned and walked through the lobby, unaware of how he'd set his own trap.

The Bumper folded the sheet with the number and slipped it into his pocket.

He would buy the burner phone tonight and text him tomorrow for a session on Thursday night. He had a few days to work out the method, but a general plan was taking shape.

For the first time this year, he had a small tinge of…something.

This guy didn't seem so bad.

What had he done?

Chapter Twenty

Hannah woke to the sound of his cellphone ping. He reached over to his night table and took a peek.

It was a text from Downey. 'Can I call?'

Hannah groaned. He thumbed back, "Hang on. Fifteen minutes."

He raised an eyelid at the clock. Eight-fourteen a.m. It was still too early. Hannah had been back at the poker table the night before and didn't hit the sack until almost three o'clock in the morning.

He slowly woke up in the shower, feeling guilty about last night. It was a strange new feeling. His time was his own, and Downey had not told him to stop playing, yet somehow, he felt like he had relapsed. The game itself lacked its usual spark, anyway, but Hannah chalked that up to a lack of practice. But this morning, he thought it might be something else.

He felt…bored. Now, in the shower at nine o'clock in the morning, he was curious and excited to hear what Downey wanted to talk about.

He threw on some shorts and a Red Sox t-shirt, grabbed a clean glass and filled it with orange juice as he texted the "all clear."

His cell buzzed seconds later.

"Sorry to text you so early on your day off," Curt said, "but I need your eyes on a list from 'Hearts Elite.'"

"Want me to come in?"

"No," Downey said, "I can forward the email. Stafford pared down the profiles in three categories, which is smart. They are ranked in order of most to least accessible by profile activity and public interaction."

Hannah checked his phone to confirm the date. "Today is Tuesday, June Twentieth. You think we have enough time to make a call?"

"Hope so. I'll send the list. Can you look it over and give me your thoughts in a reply email this morning?"

"Sure thing. Talk soon." Hannah hung up and drained the glass.

He walked over to his dining room table and flipped over his laptop. While it fired up, his mind drifted to Laurel, his old girlfriend, now Curt's wife. He made a mental note to ask Curt how she was doing with all this. Then he thought better of it.

He searched his contacts and hit her number before he could change his mind. He expected to get voicemail anyway, because she was busy, but more likely because she would check the display. A nine-a.m. call from Hannah was not something Laurel would be interested in.

"Well, isn't this an unusual surprise?" She said after a single ring. "Is everything okay?"

"Yeah, I just got a call from Curt, and we're getting closer to this guy. I was thinking about what we talked about and wondered how you were feeling about it. I mean, it really isn't any of my business but, you know." Hannah paused. "This all sounded so much better in my head sixty seconds ago."

Laurel made a pensive "humph." "No, I think it sounds just right. You're trying new things, Robert. Caring about how people feel is a bold step for you."

Hannah felt a stab of irritation at the jab, though he knew it was deserved. Laurel always knew where to pierce the shell.

"I also wanted to tell you something, and I don't know why. But since you always knew me better, maybe you can explain it to me."

The phone went quiet. "Can I guess?" Laurel teased.

"Well, okay, but it was a serious observation." Hannah answered.

"I bet it is. So, tell me, is she still there?"

Hannah paused. "Oh, no. It doesn't involve a woman. I was going to tell you I went and played poker last night and I feel like shit about it this morning."

"Same thing," Laurel said. "Poker is your sex. The girls have always been the trophy for winning. I should know. I sat on your mantel a long time before I understood."

Hannah sat and placed his phone on the table. He hit the speaker feature as Laurel seemed to wait. "Did I strike a nerve?" She asked.

"Always have, always will," Hannah said, staring out the window. "I'm sorry I bothered you, Laurel. I just wanted to tell you."

"You aren't bothering me, Robert," she interrupted. "I'm very glad you called. Curt has told me about the case and how much you've helped. But now I know what it means to you, and that is a wonderful thing."

"What does it mean to me?" He asked.

"Yeah," Laurel said. "If poker has always been your sex, and now you feel boredom, or even shame, it means it has been replaced. In fact, it feels like you 'cheated on it' last night."

"What? This case is my 'new' poker?"

"I was going to say it's your new thrill. This case has clearly awakened something in you. It is filling some space that poker can't. Go with that. It will bring out the better 'you.'"

Hannah pondered her insights. She had a way of 'knowing' that used to irritate the shit out of him. Now it gave him pause. "Thanks, Laurel. Good talking to you. I expected voicemail when you saw who it was."

"Robert Hannah," she said formally. "You still, to this very day, do not truly know me. And it's too bad. Because I think I have a pretty good handle on you. And from now on, I'll always pick up."

"Okay, thanks again," Hannah said, clicking off. He continued his gaze out the window, something he did every morning when he and his wife would have breakfast, and he couldn't stand to look at her with the pit in his stomach. He would stare out the window until Stacey couldn't take it. She knew. It was slipping away.

Hannah owed her a phone call, too.

He slid back around to his laptop and opened his email. At the top was Downey's forwarded list from Elaine Stafford at 'Hearts Elite.'

There were thirteen profiles, each listed under one of three headings.

The first seemed to be the most likely victims given, which Stafford listed as 'highly approachable activities' stipulated in their profiles. There were four who fit under that heading. The second grouping of basic approachability and intersection had five guys who fit, and the third group had another four.

She also made a bottom list that, to save time and resources, she deemed to be unlikely targets.

There were no names, but Hannah was sure Elaine Stafford knew which profile fit in each category.

The first grouping all had outdoor activities. Golf, softball, camping/hiking, and boating were big with this quartet. The second was less accessible, which listed restaurants or the theatre. One profile was heavy into travel. These guys could be on the killer's radar, but it would take more work. The third group comprised guys whose livelihoods matched their lifestyle. One guy was a pro hockey player, while another owned a series of local workout facilities.

Hannah printed out the list and went to work on it.

The hired assassin had two days to prepare for Thursday night. JoJo had readily accepted The Bumper's offer of a shared training session at his condo studio. He was expected at seven o'clock for a one-hour workout to be finished at eight.

The Bumper expected to be finished and washed up by seven-thirty.

He made a trip to a local Walmart where he purchased a new ball cap, sunglasses, workout gloves, and a hoodie. To complete the camouflage for the security cameras, he bought a package of men's t-shirts and baggy sweatpants. Then he moved over to the grocery section and bought a couple cans of Red Bull and Gatorade, along with a water bottle that closely matched Mr. June's.

He felt confident that he could be in and out of the condo (and out of the city) well before anyone would know that JoJo had suffered a terrible accident. Given his single lifestyle, it might take a few days for the smell to alert neighbors.

The only concern was gaining the man's trust. Everything was easier if you appealed to his sense of dominance. Then the assassin would use it against him in an instant.

He laid everything out on the hotel bed, checking the inventory. Anything he had missed he could buy tomorrow, but it all looked to be in order.

The Bumper tried not to think about where The Client was right now. Was he in the hotel? Across the street? Was he situated somewhere near the victim, knowing that the killer would have to go to him, anyway? He tried not to let it consume his thoughts, but the puzzle ate at him.

But after Thursday, he would be halfway through the year. Six months. Six victims.

A wave of satisfaction passed over him as the accomplishment filled his mind. He was nine-hundred-thousand-dollars richer with another near million to go. Then, the bonus money.

A smile crept across The Bumper's face when he thought of the hapless law enforcement officers in America who were completely unaware that a silent killer was operating undetected in their midst.

He was so good at his job.

Chapter Twenty-One

Hannah called Downey after lunch.

"I've done a preliminary ranking based on Stafford's list and shuffled a few profiles. I wonder if we can send those to her and get some names. Maybe if we only suggested five or six, she'd be more cooperative."

"We can only ask. Scan your work to me and I'll send it back to her. Hopefully, we'll get it back by Friday." Downey said.

Hannah sent the list, the only sizeable switch being the move of the workout gym owner from the bottom list to the top.

It was just a feeling.

Thursday evening, The Bumper checked out of his hotel after wiping down all surfaces and checking for all his toiletries and clothes. He didn't want to be known as the contract killer who got caught leaving boxer briefs under the bed.

He parked his car in a long laneway that led to a downtown park. There were no cameras and a good flow of pedestrians. He had scouted the area and found that most people who walked downtown used it as a shortcut. City planners would be proud.

He hoisted the full gym bag over his shoulder after ensuring he had a towel, his workout gloves, shoes, a bottle, and drinks. He could be stopped along the way by police who had stumbled on his plan, but they would find no weapons. None. The Bumper didn't need any. He was that good.

He strolled along without a care in the world in his baggy new workout sweats, disguising his trim, muscular legs. The killer wore an equally baggy three-quarter zip-up pullover hoodie jacket with six -t-shirts taped around his midsection. He looked about thirty pounds heavier than he was.

If what he had heard was true, the camera adds even more weight.

'Good luck, security cameras, on nailing him by the description on the screen.'

As he approached the front of the building, he pulled his ball cap tighter to his forehead and casually pulled his sunglasses off the bill of his cap. Sliding them on, it guaranteed that no one could recognize the stranger, should anything require investigation.

He strolled past the elevator and turned down the right hallway.

As he approached condo one-oh-four, he slipped his sunglasses and ball cap into the front zipper pouch of his bag, grateful for the lack of cameras once he turned the corner away from the elevator. The Bumper pulled the taped pouch of t-shirts from his abdomen and slid the bundle into the side stairwell at the end of the corridor for safekeeping. Satisfied that he looked like the harmless tourist that JoJo was expecting, he knocked on the door while steeling his nerves.

A heavy foot padding preceded the fast door opening, and the man named JoJo extended his hand to greet his new friend.

"Hey, thanks for signing up. I'm happy to meet a new workout buddy. This is great."

"It is likewise," The Bumper said in his broken accent, playing the part to keep his target's defenses down. It was unnecessary, but the assassin didn't want to vary the approach he had planned last night.

The condo had an impressive view of the back garden, and with the sun setting in the west, the killer took in the opulent condo. "Wow, you have a beautiful apartment. You are very lucky."

"Not so much lucky as having the money to pay for it. But it's a magnificent spot. And my neighbors don't complain about the noise so much. Sometimes the music gets pumping when I get pumping, but they are pretty cool. What kind of music do you like?"

'*Something very loud,*' the killer thought, but replied, "Whatever you like is good. I am not a music...huh...buff?" He pulled out his shoes from the knapsack and peeled off his overhead jacket. He looked the part of a ripped lifter looking for a spotter.

"You look good man," JoJo commented. "I have a few cardio reps I like to use before we get into weights and stuff. You good with that?"

The Bumper spied what he had hoped to find. His luck was unstoppable.

Nodding to the stacks of blocks, he said, "As long as we can do some box jumps, I'm good. I need to work on my lower body strength and flexibility."

"Oh, for sure, we can do that, of course," JoJo said.

The Bumper went into the small kitchen and pulled out his water bottle, running the tap while he filled it with a pre-workout concoction. He filled it three-quarters full and gave it a quick shake before coming back into the expansive living area, filled with exercise equipment organized into workout stations.

"It looks like you live in a gym," the killer joked to cover his growing adrenaline rush. He knew he had one shot to do this right. The victim would not give him a second chance if he didn't finish him quickly.

"Workout palace out here, love palace in there," JoJo said, pointing to a sliding door shielding his bedroom. "The ladies love the playroom."

The Bumper laughed accordingly and started his routine stretches, awaiting instructions from the giant who had minutes left to live.

JoJo slid an app on his phone and pounding beats exploded from hidden speakers in the walls and ceiling. He started hopping in place as he stretched his neck and shoulders.

"Let's do two minutes of stretches, then we'll move through the stations, starting with the box jumps," JoJo shouted.

"Yes, thank you," the killer yelled above the music. "How high can you go?"

"On the boxes?" The victim asked. "I've never really tried. You?"

"I can go four feet, but not every time," he said, moving closer. He took a fake sip from his bottle. The power of observation was a curious thing. JoJo turned and took a pull from his matching bottle before resuming his stretch.

After a couple of minutes of stretching, The Bumper made his way over to the boxes and piled them to three feet. He then cleared an area behind for leaping without interference. The killer rolled away a large weight bar with a set of dumbbells already prepared for lifting. It wouldn't do to have that lying around in their way.

"You first?" The Bumper asked. JoJo did a deep knee bend, then sprung to the top and hopped back down. After a session of three jumps, he moved aside. The Bumper also did three, though with a slower pace to preserve some energy. In his mind, time slowed down. His window of opportunity was opening.

He turned to JoJo and, because of the volume of the music, mimed another box going on top to get it to three-and-a-half-feet. JoJo gave a thumbs up, clearly enjoying the challenge.

The hulk dipped again and exploded, landing the first jump. He did a second successfully but wavered on the third. The giant of a man stumbled against the wall of his condo, and The Killer reached out an arm in support. "You did real good," he yelled in his ear. Turning back to the launch area, he leaped to the top of the box with ease on the first two jumps but also stumbled on his third. JoJo gave him an encouraging fist bump.

"You can go to another box?" JoJo asked.

The combination of the music and the thrill of the kill had filled The Bumper's body with superhuman strength. "I can try." JoJo grabbed the last of the boxes and secured them to the four-foot mark. When he moved back, The Bumper stepped into the launch spot. He closed his eyes and knew what success meant. An instant challenge. If he failed, his plan was useless.

The Bulgarian dipped deep and exploded with both arms flying up over his head. He hit the top lip of the highest box with the tips of his shoes and lightly propelled himself for a landing. The killer hopped down, giving his soon-to-be victim a smile of achievement. He bowed and waved his arm as a maître'd might do in a fine restaurant. "It is your turn."

JoJo curled his arms and clenched his fists as he squatted to his ankles. He exploded from the crouch and reached the top box with a glance of his shoes, but stumbled to the right, a few inches short of making the leap. His face clenched in anger at falling short.

"So close," The Bumper said. "Do one more try. Your disappointment is all the fuel you need." He turned to the weights he had rolled away earlier. "Then you can show me what you are very good at."

The victim nodded his head in total concentration as he crouched down in slow anticipation of his explosive lift-off.

The Bumper took full advantage of those precious seconds to roll the bar back into position, just to the right of the box, but out of the victim's sight.

Time stood still in the assassin's mind. He instinctively knew that everything had to happen simultaneously. He had played the scene over in his mind dozens of times today and was ready for the moment.

The Bumper counted to three in his head, and with deadly precision, moved to the launch square as the giant hit the top box, unable to land the jump owing to the spent energy of his first failed attempt. The killer expected that. He moved to the front corner, seemingly to help catch JoJo when he stumbled, but instead, grabbed the man around his solid torso and spun him to the floor in a crunching, wrestling drop.

The man's head struck the bulging dumbbell plates. His immense weight, coupled with the speed and force of The Bumper's takedown, was all that was needed to crush his skull.

Arcing to his right, the killer rolled from the drop, careful to keep his feet off the floor. He lay panting on his stomach, arching his back to keep his feet in the air. The Bumper watched his victim for signs of life. There weren't any. The skull had been crushed, with blood sprayed along the wall and pooling on the floor. He rolled himself to his back and slowly untied his shoes, slipping them off before rising to survey the scene as a witness would.

JoJo tried to jump a top box setup and had stumbled and fallen on a poorly positioned nearby weight bar. The Bumper stared at the blood spatter and wondered if it was consistent with a single-person accident, or whether it would show someone else had been there.

After using a cloth around his index finger to shut off the music, he padded to the bathroom, careful not to leave fingerprints or blood droppings. A second blood trail would be no good at hiding his presence.

He had more blood on him than he expected, but it *had been* a powerful tackle. Most of it was sprayed, though a streak ran down the side of his head where he had driven the man by his shoulder. As tempted as he was to wash it, he had seen enough documentaries to know that you could never, ever really clean up all the blood in a sink or drain.

The Bumper stripped out of his workout clothes and wiped himself down with his shirt and shorts. He had worn them under his baggy clothes, expecting their use after the man's death. The Bumper caught a look at himself in a side mirror and spun around to ensure there were no blatant spatters he had missed.

He pulled up his baggy sweatpants over his boxer briefs and then wrestled the jacket hoodie over his bare chest. The Bumper grabbed JoJo's bottle and replaced it with his own, filled with an elevated level of workout protein. He donned the ball cap and positioned the sunglasses on the perch, ready to drop them into place if needed. He stepped over to the crushed victim one last time and noticed the angle of his head, now slumped down on the slippery barbell. What the crushing blow hadn't done, the broken neck would have taken care of.

With a coroner's certainty, the killer pronounced him dead.

The Bumper stood at the man's door with his hand on the doorknob, now wearing rubber surgical gloves. This was the moment. If a neighbor stood at the door about to complain about the noise, the killer would have to eliminate the threat in moments. He was ready for that. If there were two people? He'd have to improvise.

The Bumper turned the silent door handle and risked a peek through the doorjamb. Never out the door where a visitor would look, always at the hinges.

The hallway was empty.

The assassin took off like a shot to the stairwell and retrieved the bundle of t-shirts. He stuffed them into his workout bag and walked back down the quiet hallway until he reached the lobby.

Again, gut-check time. A part of him knew it would be empty, a part of him knew there could be a weary owner home from work who would pay him no mind as he waited for the elevator, and a part feared there would be a dozen cops. Time to find out.

As he stepped around the corner with his head down, a woman passed him beside the elevator. No casual greeting. No scream about dripping blood.

He walked through the automatic sliding lobby doors into the cooling breeze of a June Thursday night in Hartford, Connecticut. He continued his walk until he reached the first street corner, certain he was blending into pedestrian traffic.

As he waited for the light to turn, he stood up straighter and slowly spun around, making his presence conspicuous.

'*I am here, and I did it,*' the killer seemed to say.

Within seconds, his phone pinged. The deposit had been made.

The killer smiled as he stared straight ahead, no longer concerned he was being watched. It now gave him a renewed sense of purpose.

He was part of a team.

Chapter Twenty-Two

Agent Downey and Hannah sat subdued in the FBI boardroom. It was Monday morning, hours after notification that a conspicuous death had occurred in Hartford, Connecticut. Agent Dennison had made the dawn call to Agent Downey.

"I moved that guy to the top tier. There was something about owning a gym that made him vulnerable to me. I wish I had pressed sooner." Hannah said.

Agent Dennison, on the speakerphone from Hartford, said, "I'm not sure it would have made a difference. No offense to your talents, Mr. Hannah, but this really has the feel of a tragic accident."

"Do the Hartford police still have the site closed off?" Agent Downey asked.

"Yeah, we've asked for a deeper check of the condo. It's a pretty gory scene. It looks like the victim fell hard while doing box jumps, missed the landing, and fell back on a barbell, crushing his skull. A lot of blood."

Hannah pulled his face as he crossed his eyes. He shook his head at Downey. He was not interested in going there.

"Can you photo the place and send them back?"

"Will do. Anything else?" Dennison asked.

Hannah said, "I know I'm asking a lot, Agent Dennison, but is it possible for you to work the scene as if it was a murder site? By that, can you look specifically for evidence that someone else was there?"

"Well, we did that initially, primarily because of this case, but everything seems to show that a gigantic workout fanatic got juiced up on some workout drink and took a tragic header. But Farron and I will walk the scene again later this morning."

"Hey, can you ask the coroner to check to see if there was anything else in his system that might have contributed to him being amped up? If he is otherwise clean, then our guy may well have gotten away with another one." Hannah asked.

"I hope you're wrong, Hannah," Agent Dennison said, before hanging up. "I hope this guy is not a client of that website and just had a terrible fall. Because this is a shitty way to die."

Agent Downey had sent the notice to 'Hearts Elite' within minutes of the early morning notification, requesting confirmation that the profile of the gym owner was thirty-three-year-old Joe Johansen of Hartford, Connecticut.

"There must have been easier guys to kill than this Johansen. Dennison said he was massive." Downey said.

"Gravity would have been the only way. Our killer has been successful because he can blend in. He appears non-threatening; friendly even. But, in this case, he must be fit enough that Johansen would allow him in his condo for a workout."

"Could it have been a woman?" Downey asked. "She gets invited over and he puts on a show, then 'bang,' she gives him a shove?"

"No, it's our guy," Hannah pronounced.

Downey sat back. "How do you know?"

Hannah replied. "The workout drink. In fact, it's overkill. It's like the five bees last month. Get Dennison to check this guy's garbage and pantry shelves. I bet you don't find any of this stuff in his pantry. It isn't his."

"So why would the killer make the workout smoothie? To make us think he got juiced up and passed out while jumping?" Downey asked.

"Maybe," Hannah replied. "Probably. He had to give us a path to convince the cops there was nothing to see. If we hadn't been looking in Hartford, this would have been filed as a tragic accident."

Downey texted the request to Agent Dennison and turned back to his laptop. He refreshed his email constantly as Hannah watched the frustration take over. Checking the clock, Downey grabbed his phone and called Elaine Stafford.

The call went to voicemail, but within seconds of his leaving a message, Downey's email pinged.

He said to Hannah, "Are you free for a few minutes?"

Elaine Stafford sat rod stiff on the screen as Agent Downey filled her in on what they had.

"Based on the evidence, he'd been dead twenty-four hours before discovery. He died of a massive fall against a set of weights, crushing his head. We would like you to fully cooperate in telling us whether he was one of the thirteen profiles you grouped together last week."

"Agent Downey, I can tell you he was not." Stafford said.

Hannah moved from his seat. "He's not? He isn't the gym owner I moved from the bottom tier to the top?"

"No Mr. Hannah, he is not. In fact, a search of our Hartford database does not show the man's name at all. His death is no doubt tragic, but he is not connected to 'Hearts Elite.'" She said.

"Could he have been a client but deleted his account in the last month?" Hannah asked.

"No, his name would have remained in our internal records in case he reactivated his account in the future. His preferences would be on file," she said. "Once a client, always a client."

"Damn," Hannah said.

"Now, if there is nothing further gentlemen…" Elaine Stafford said.

"Thank you for your cooperation, Ms. Stafford. If needed, we will be in touch."

"Good luck, Agent Downey. I trust this concludes our participation in this case," Elaine Stafford said, hanging up on the video call.

Hannah blew out a breath, leaning back in his chair. "There's something wrong here. Something we're missing."

"It happens all the time, Pally. Agent Dennison and Farron were going to stay in Hartford for a couple of days. They'll work with the local police and will let us know if there is a connection we missed. It isn't always obvious right away."

Agent Farron's call caught Downey off-guard. He expected a text first.

"Sorry, but I just finished a strange interview. Our guy was a client of a personal trainer by the name of…Lonzo Garcia. We found a stack of brochures for the gym in the victim's closet. Our victim was the model on the brochures."

"Okay," Downey said.

"Yeah, so Lonzo was pretty broken up when he heard about his buddy's death. We didn't get into any of the details, other than his routines. Get this: he never used pre-workout drinks. Never touched the stuff. Only water, or the occasional power drink."

"On its own, it proves nothing." Downey said.

"But get this. Lonzo claims that some ruddy guy had been in the gym for a couple of weeks who was a tourist or something. Wanted just a monthly membership to workout. Lonzo said he was pretty fit and knew his way around the weights, so he charged him a hundred bucks to come and go. The guy paid in cash. This same dude was seen striking up a conversation with JoJo just a week ago, but that he claimed to be leaving town a couple of days later."

Agent Downey grabbed his personal cell and shot Hannah a text. "Go on," he said to Farron.

"I'm going to save the best for last, but Lonzo just wondered if this guy might have had anything to do with the accident." Agent Farron said.

"I don't suppose he has security footage of the guy?" Agent Downey asked as his phone pinged a return text from Hannah.

"No, just dummy cameras for insurance."

Agent Downey asked, "So what's the gold nugget you're saving for last?"

Agent Farron stretched the silence before replying, "Lonzo Garcia is a member of 'Hearts Elite.'

"This Lonzo is the gym owner? Are you sure?" Hannah asked. He raced back to the office after getting Downey's text.

"No, I'm not sure. He is *a* gym owner, but the coincidence is too strong to ignore. Could our killer have gotten the wrong guy?" Downey pondered, staring at the large phone in the centre of the table.

Agents Perez and Simms sat quietly, hunched over their laptops. "Lonzo Garcia seems squeaky clean," Agent Perez said. "Nothing online about him, and he doesn't show up in our database."

Hannah looked at Agent Simms. "What do you think, Jacco?"

"This is our case. We just don't see it yet. There are too many coincidences to not be right. It happened in Hartford, at the end of a month, and the case surrounds a personal trainer. All the pieces are there."

"Like another puzzle," Hannah said.

The centre console phone buzzed and Elaine Stafford appeared on the screen, sporting reading glasses. "Agent Downey," she said without offering a greeting, "this is becoming tiresome."

"Our victim in Hartford may have been a case of mistaken identity. The gym owner where he worked out is a member of 'Hearts Elite.' His name is Lonzo Garcia. I can get a warrant, but let's skip the formalities. Is his profile the gym owner from last week's list?" Downey asked.

Stafford looked off the screen as her lips pursed in concern. "It is, Agent Downey. How did you arrive at that? Did you ask him?"

"Of course we did. Mr. Garcia gave our investigators the information when he was being notified about the victim."

The room drowned in silence as Hannah thought through the details of the murder. "How did this guy who had met Lonzo Garcia mistake him for the JoJo guy?" He asked aloud.

"I'm sorry?" Elaine Stafford asked.

"I'm thinking out loud," Hannah said. "If he is hunting his prey from the profiles on your website, how did he mistake the victim with Lonzo Garcia?"

"He would have a group of photos to choose from," Agent Perez replied, clearly warming to his train of thought. "He hadn't made a mistake yet, so why this time?"

"Do they resemble each other?" Stafford asked.

"Not all gym rats look alike," Hannah replied. "Apparently, the victim was massive. In fact, he posed for the brochures for Lonzo's gym."

"There is little resemblance," Agent Simms said, "Lonzo is about ten years older and a good four or five inches shorter. He's stocky. The victim is a hulk."

"So, how did the killer get them confused? He selected his victim. So, what happened? Did he change his mind? Was JoJo suddenly a greater challenge?"

"I may answer that question, Mr. Hannah." said Elaine Stafford. "Mr. Lonzo's account shows an upgraded profile. There are only a few ways you can achieve an upgrade since payment is not required of our gentlemen. One is to engage with on-line support concerning site enhancements. Take part in monthly surveys, that sort of thing."

"He wouldn't have time for that," Agent Perez said. Hannah could read the disdain for the website's COO in Perez's tone. He'd make sure Downey was aware of it. He didn't blame her, but they needed Stafford right now.

"What else?" Hannah asked.

"The more likely path would have been client referrals. He has enough 'clout,' we call it, to have suggested three men to join. Now, they don't have to join for Lonzo to achieve the upgrade, simply stop by with an email address to receive a digital invitation video. Once the video has been viewed, it sends a code to Lonzo's account, and he receives his 'clout.'"

"I don't want to know what he cashes that in on," Agent Perez stated, clearly voicing her disgust. Hannah saw Downey shoot her a firm but sympathetic look.

"Actually, it doesn't allow him any more perks than any other member, but what it does is boost his profile in the algorithm. His profile would rise higher in searches than it would have without the 'clout.' Plus, he has the designation on his profile page, which would appear to be a status symbol for those scrolling through."

"And you're sure that our victim isn't one of the referrals? The guy posed for his brochures and was an active member of his gym. He'd be a perfect candidate for a referral." Agent Downey asked.

"We don't track video views, only positive engagements, so he may have been sent the video, and may have watched it, but we have no accounts in the name of Joe Johansen, in Hartford, or anywhere else." Elaine Stafford replied.

Hannah snapped to attention. He turned a puzzle piece around and suddenly it fit. "Sorry, what did you say? Joe. Johansen?" He enunciated.

"Yes, we do not have an account under that name," she insisted.

"Try *JoJo Hansen*."

Hannah watched her type below the screen, and after a pause, her face crinkled.

"I thought the name was Johansen."

"It is, but the guy went by the name contraction of JoJo. When you say it out loud, it sounds the same…*Joe Johansen*…but the play on words would look different on-line." Hannah said.

Elaine Stafford looked on the screen, removed her glasses and leaned forward on her elbows.

"We have an account for a JoJo Hansen in Connecticut."

Chapter Twenty-Three

The Client typed up the dossier for July, impressed with the Killer's progress. He was becoming more imaginative in his methods and cooperative with the process.

They had chosen well.

The Client sent the missive and sat back in their chair, admiring the scene outside. They were sure twelve months would be ample time to complete the project, but now there were doubts.

The plan could always be shortened if the situation grew worse, but it was too annoying to ponder. To change the game in mid-stream was infuriating, but too much was now out of their control.

The Client closed their eyes as the soft sounds of the yard floated around the little corner of the world. So invisible, so inconspicuous, so forgotten.

So non-threatening.

A wistful smile perched on their lips before sleep snatched them away.

Chapter Twenty-Four

"How did we miss him?" Hannah yelled, pounding the table.

Elaine Stafford jumped at the outburst and answered. "I will check his profile in greater detail, but whatever he listed didn't make him an attractive choice for the victim. Also, he didn't include Hartford specifically in his bio. The man had a few activities and only three pictures. I'll check his response rate, but it doesn't appear he is a...was a...very active client."

"We are going to need full access to your entire website profile pages, Ms. Stafford." Agent Downey announced. "The FBI will notify you and will expect your full cooperation."

"I understand, Agent Downey, and I will prepare for that. I am truly sorry for all that is happening. Is there anything I can do right now?" She asked.

"No," Downey answered. "Your future cooperation will be more than enough throughout the investigation."

"Hang on," Hannah interrupted. "What about a notice put up on the website alerting clients to a threat? Wouldn't that be a responsible thing to do now that we are convinced?"

Elaine Stafford blanched at the suggestion. Hannah knew it would be bad for business. "Lives are at stake here."

Agent Perez was blunter. "Why don't you shut the website down?"

"I will cooperate with the FBI throughout the investigation, but I will not willingly shut down operations without a warrant." Stafford said. "Even then, it would tip off the killer who could easily move onto another site."

"Ms. Stafford, you will hear from my federal counterparts today. They will provide you with the next steps." Agent Downey said, ending the call. He left the boardroom, Hannah guessed, to notify Agent Michael Watson at Quantico.

Hannah mulled over the puzzle. Six perfect murders of young affluent men linked to a rich dating site. A killer so adept as to leave no trace of his crime. Six city police forces that couldn't find a connection.

"Can we get a sketch of the ruddy guy that Lonzo described? He has to be the killer," Hannah suggested.

"On it," Agent Simms said, following Downey out of the boardroom, leaving Hannah and Agent Perez alone at the table.

Hannah took a shot at lowering the temperature. "I get it. You believe the guys who sign up for the website are treating women like used cars and expect them to pay for the privilege. They are rich and entitled. But they don't deserve to die."

"I didn't say that, did I?" Agent Perez fired back. "There is an inherent risk in aligning yourself with a shitty group of guys who look down on the rest of us. No, they don't deserve to be killed, but don't be surprised in this day and age that people hate them."

Hannah gazed at her. "Is there a part of you that is cheering for this guy?"

She groaned and lowered her head. "No, but I'm having a tougher time feeling badly for the victims. Go ask traffic cops how they feel when they arrive at an accident where the driver was doing one-hundred miles an hour and slams against a tree. Sad? Yeah, but whose fault is that?"

"Not the same analogy, Rhonda. The guys didn't sign up thinking there was a risk."

"No, they signed up to be the predators. *'Look at me, I'm rich, and I demand you pay money to have access to my inner life, and if I find you worthy, perhaps I'll give you a chance to spend time with me.'*"

"What's happened?" Hannah asked her. "You didn't feel this way a couple of weeks ago."

She shook her head. "The more time I spend researching victimology, the more disparity I see. Women are victimized and trafficked in percentages far higher than men, and especially rich men. Yet, here we are. There is a reason 'Occupy Wall Street' and 'Eat the Rich' have trended. My guess is that if the story were ever broken, the killer would attain anti-hero status. There will be social media accounts for him and trending cycles."

Hannah was gaining a greater insight into the pressure of the agents. He could dispassionately toss in his cards in a poker game, but Downey and his cohorts had to carry the hands they were dealt.

"Can we explore that? Do you think the killer is motivated by hatred of the social class?"

"Yes, I think so. Anyone could surf any other dating site, but he goes to the most exclusive."

"A modern-day Robin Hood?" Hannah asked.

Perez had clearly had enough. She bundled up her laptop. "Yeah, something like that," she said as she, too, left the boardroom.

Hannah went back to noodling the puzzles. Hartford had been the correct guess for the 'H', but they had already tried to fit an 'E' city into the equation and were wrong. Would 'Erie' Pennsylvania be right this time?

A connection formed in his imagination. Is the phrase being spelled out *Kill the Elite*? It had twelve letters and mirrored the website's name. He grabbed a scratch pad and scrawled other possibilities, aiming for twelve letter phrases.

Kill the Elite was the leading contender in his mind. He wrote other choices, but none had twelve letters. Unless…

He sat back. What if the second word wasn't *'the'*? What if it was *them*? Or *their*?

Kill Them Dead had twelve letters, but didn't have the same urgency that *Kill the Elite* had.

Twelve months. Twelve murders. Twelve Letters. Hannah's logical puzzle brain was sure of it.

"Let's get the 'E' city right and not have to worry about the rest," he said aloud in the empty boardroom.

Chapter Twenty-Five

Justin Harrow locked his Mercedes GLC Coupe with a press of the fob and walked over to the paved dock path. He bypassed the marina store and canteen, preferring to avoid the weekend fishermen and out-of-state family boaters.

Harrow flipped through his phone as he made his way along the marina pathway before turning right, heading to his dock slip. The boater stopped and looked back to see if he was being followed, an annoying feeling of paranoia that had gripped him over the past week.

The radio shock jock stepped aboard his Regal LS36 Luxury Crossover and tossed his day bag onto the nearest bench. He was looking forward to spending the weekend with a woman who would faun over his good looks, charm, and, of course, his yacht.

He grabbed at his phone and flipped open the 'Hearts Elite' app for the umpteenth time this morning. There it was.

The warning.

"Because of unprecedented circumstances, we are suspending operation of 'Hearts Elite' in your area. We apologize for any inconvenience this may cause,

and will correct the situation in haste. Please be aware that we take the safety of our clients seriously and will work to eliminate all threats against customers."

Harrow should have known that it wouldn't work out. He'd never had much luck with traditional dating sites but had run through all suggestions by his handful of close friends. Every single one of them had been more interested in his celebrity, his money, and Instagram 'likes' than in forging a relationship. Not that Justin was paving a road to the altar himself; he just wanted a woman who wanted him, not just his money.

So, on the advice of a real estate buddy, he'd stumbled onto 'Hearts Elite'. The male dominated logo and color scheme certainly looked different from every other hook-up site on the web. The intro video was male dominated in its imagery and language. As a radio guy, Harrow was drawn to the smart marketing package.

It was worth a try. Within two weeks, he had had two connections, but both had figured out who he was despite the vague profile. The dates ended with the regular sexual escapades, but no call backs. Sure, the women were hot, but he could get those anywhere. He was looking for something…different. Exotic, maybe.

'Danica' had dropped into his message box, showing interest, but asking for details. It was strange, at first. Justin intentionally kept things private to avoid 'cat fishers' or loyal listeners. He playfully sent back a *'what you see is what you get'* reply and got an even more playful response.

'Promise?'

What followed was a two-week avalanche of introductions and messages. She divulged her disdain for conventional dating sites as she was affluent herself and wasn't put-off by the vibe of 'Hearts Elite'. It allowed her to be choosy as well, or as she put it, she could *fish where the fish are.*

After the first week, she admitted she lived in the Midwest and wasn't close to Erie, Pennsylvania. He replied with disappointment. Then, she asked the big question. Was he looking for local hook-ups, or a serious chance with a successful woman who also wanted a relationship? Because if not, she would not fly across half the country to just be another notch on the bedpost.

Harrow fell hard. He replied that that is exactly what he was looking for and spilled more details about his popular radio show. He sent a picture of his Mercedes and his luxury yacht, which he had named 'Justin Time,' as well as a few shirtless pics.

She sent along a couple of headshots and the view from her penthouse condo.

The radio jock could see himself waking up there one morning.

He had invited her here for the weekend, where Harrow would treat her to a wonderful dinner and a day on the yacht.

Then, the website blocked. Harrow hadn't received a reply from Danica, and he couldn't let her know about the 'Hearts Elite' warning. Would she get the same message if she tried to access his profile? He didn't want her to think she had been ghosted without so much as a first meeting.

Harrow tossed his phone up onto the dash above the controls. He removed his workout shirt and slipped out of his jogging pants and stood in his bathing trunks. The yacht captain walked back to the bow area and looked back along the pier. He kept hoping he would see a woman standing there, puzzled, looking for him.

The dock was empty.

The Bumper stared at his reservation sheet and the berth slip of his rental boat. It didn't look exactly like what he had ordered, but what did these days? He made sure it was gassed up and let the teenager run through the safety features and rental regulations in his annoying, droning voice. The assassin knew the kid really hated his job.

After getting the 'all-clear,' the Bulgarian slipped out of the marina into the mouth of Lake Erie. He'd seen enough of the area to know that if he turned to the starboard side and travelled far enough, he'd get to Buffalo, New York and soon after, Niagara Falls. As much fun as that would be to dispatch of a lonely soul over the Falls, he'd stick to his plan. The killer turned port side and went left along the shoreline for about fifteen minutes. He slowed his engine in a small bay and dropped anchor.

The Bumper pulled his hat lower on his forehead and flipped his phone to check the coordinates. He was only a ten-minute cruise from the target's marina who had planned a lovely voyage for the day with a woman who, apparently, wouldn't show up.

The Client was a very cunning individual who fed him the information he needed. Once the assassin had been given the name of his boat last week, The Bumper attached a digital beacon to the bow. With the app, he would know not only when Mr. July was on the water, but exactly where he was.

This may prove to be the easiest job yet. He was outdoors on a beautiful lake, not in a condo trying to wrestle with a beast in Hartford.

The six-time killer popped a Red Bull and sat back. He didn't care how long it took.

Life was good.

Justin Harrow cranked the engine on his small yacht and eased out of his slip. The morning was not only the smoothest time of day on the lake; it was also the quietest. On July weekends, it could be standing room only at the pier by the early afternoon. He hated the crowds on land and despised them on water.

He popped the engine as he felt the swell of the lake take his bow and turned starboard out to the middle of Lake Erie. At its widest point from the marina, the lake was about twenty-five miles to Long Point, Ontario, Canada. The shipping lane to the Welland Canal was in the direct middle of the lake. Harrow didn't have his passport with him, so he would stay in American waters.

The lake was serene, and he felt the pang of anger that his rendezvous with Danica had been spoiled by that stupid app. Harrow gunned the engine as he pictured her sitting behind him in a bikini, sipping a margarita, before taking her top off…

He thought of his motto. 'My yacht, my rules.'

The radio jock pulled back on the throttle and allowed the cruiser to drift. There was little chop, and marine traffic was light. There were a couple of lake freighters on the western horizon, probably six or seven miles away.

He threw on the radio and cranked the music. Harrow had to overcome his frustration, so he grabbed a waterski vest and dove into the water. The cool of the water energized him, and as he surfaced, he decided he'd hit another hook-up site tonight and play the field again.

He'd go fishing where his fish were.

The Bumper tracked "Justin Time" out of his marina into the middle of Lake Erie. He waited for the inevitable drift spot, and when the beacon stilled, the killer started up his boat. The app informed him he was four-point-three miles from his target.

He gunned his pathetic rental boat, thinking it sounded more like a go-kart, and less like what he was used to back in Bulgaria. As he drew to within a couple of miles, he was pleased that his target preferred to be alone on the lake.

So did he.

Harrow climbed out of the lake onto his dive platform, drying himself off. He caught sight of a small boat approaching him from the east. It was an enormous lake, so he found it odd that it was coming straight toward him.

He moved to the captain's chair and started up the engine, turning to check the other's closing distance. The boat had moved farther to the port side a few hundred feet before reaching him.

Harrow walked to his dive platform as the boat flew past with a wave. He waved back and shook his head.

The other boat cut its engine seconds later. Harrow watched the inexperienced mariner in what was clearly an old rental boat. *What the hell was doing way out here*?

Mr. July putted over to the other boater and called out to him. "You're way too far out with such a small boat!"

The stocky man in the vessel gave him a wave, seemingly not comprehending what was being said. "Thank you!" He yelled back.

"No, I'm saying your boat" ...Harrow stopped. It didn't matter. The guy didn't get it.

He pulled up alongside the guy and asked if he was okay.

"Oh, I am having great day," he replied in broken English. "It is beautiful lake. You have beautiful boat!"

"Thank you, yeah," Harrow replied. "It's just that this boat shouldn't be more than a couple of miles from shore. Are you sure you have enough gas to get back? Do you have a radio?"

"Oh yes, radio," the man replied, looking for the instrument. He pulled one from his knapsack in the back. "I am good. I am sorry if I am too close to you. I wanted to see how far until Canada, but it looks too far for me."

"Yeah, it's about another twenty miles. Not a good idea for you."

The man laughed, as if Justin had made a joke. *'What a character,'* Harrow thought.

"Thank you for asking. You have a fun day," the man said.

Harrow turned back to his captain's chair and throttle when he heard the unmistakable sound of a boat engine misfiring. He turned back to the rental. The man was trying to restart his boat, but it wouldn't catch.

"Shit," Harrow said. It could be anything from spark plugs to low fuel. And this clown was out in the middle of Lake Erie.

'Thank God I'm nearby,' he thought.

The Bumper over-primed the pump for the boat, ensuring it would flood if he tried to start it right away. He smiled back at his victim, who appeared concerned about the predicament.

"Give it a few minutes," the man yelled back. "Sometimes it floods after a long whip over the lake. I'll stay here to make sure it fires up."

"Okay," The Bumper replied with a smile. He 'tried' a second, then a third time, to no avail. He stood back, frustrated.

"I be okay," he called to the yachtsman, "but thank you for concern."

"No, you don't leave a boat in distress on the water. Hang on."

The man zipped up his ski vest and dove into the water. He sliced through the twenty feet of chop to the assassin's boat. The Bumper moved aside his knapsack to give him access to the rubber club and weight pouch.

As the man reached his boat, the killer offered his hand to pull him aboard.

Harrow was angry at this idiot who was ruining what was already a frustrating day. He stroked through the water and arrived at the boat. The man gave him a welcoming hand out of the water.

"Look, if you can't start this old rental back up, I'll just tie your boat to mine and tow you back to shore. You really shouldn't be out this far."

The man turned towards the front as he said, "Oh, that won't be necessary, Justin," and whipped back with a fist.

Harrow reacted far too late, glimpsing a black club whipping towards his temple.

His head exploded in pain as he rocked to keep his balance before crashing to the deck. He felt the man grab his legs at his ankles and unzip his flotation vest. Justin struggled to sit up when the club pummelled his other temple.

He felt his ankles pulled together as he slipped from consciousness.

His final thought on earth before he hit the water was, "*How did this guy know my name?*"

The killer watched as his victim's body descended into Lake Erie, ankles tied with a nylon fishing rope, weighted with a small anchor. It was more than enough to sink him to the bottom, and heavy enough to ensure his death, even should he regain consciousness.

The Bulgarian started up his boat and putted over to 'Justin Time.' He tied his boat to the yacht and climbed aboard, looking for the man's phone. The Bumper found it above the controls and prayed it hadn't locked. He quickly swiped and found luck continued to be with him. He closed the app that provided the music. The lake went quiet.

The killer thumbed through messages and photos to make sure he hadn't contacted land or taken his photo as he approached.

There was nothing. Which means he had sent no one a photo of the day.

The Bumper took a deep breath and watched the lake for the victim. He had not resurfaced. It had been at least five minutes since he had been in the water.

Five minutes. The Bumper's phone was in his knapsack. He thought it impossible but wondered if it had dinged while aboard the victim's boat.

That would be impressive.

He chucked the victim's phone over the side and heard it drop into the water, where it would float along until it emerged somewhere after Niagara Falls.

The killer considered returning the loose ski-vest, but thought better of it. Why not add to the

mystery? A missing vest would hint at a tragic swimming accident.

Before leaving the yacht, the killer reached under the back ledge and retrieved the directional beacon he'd attached. He hopped down to his rental and stared at the floor. Was there any blood? He had found none on his hands as he hoisted the lifeless body overboard, but one couldn't be too careful. It looked clean. The killer untied the craft and pulled away from the bobbing vessel. He gave the lake a three-hundred-sixty-degree look. There was no one within miles.

The Bumper hit the throttle and bounced toward shore with no connection to the abandoned yacht floating in the middle of the Great Lake. After a mile, he tossed the vest overboard.

He slowed before entering the marina and checked his cell.

His phone hadn't dinged. No payment yet.

The killer steamed ahead and docked the rental smoothly into the slip. He pulled his knapsack from the back as he climbed ashore.

As he straightened himself up, he heard the buzz of his phone. He smiled, guessing that he had little cell coverage on the water, but plenty back on land.

When The Bumper reached the end of the dock, he stopped and gave a little bow, then walked to his rental car, already packed for his August destination.

Chapter Twenty-Six

Hannah struggled to get out of bed, ignoring the series of texts he'd received from Downey, vowing to hand in his resignation from the task force.

Who was he trying to kid? He was a mid-thirties, washed up, poker playing adolescent pretending to be an adult while people were being killed.

Three men had died since he had stumbled onto the code, and he wasn't prepared for the crushing guilt that followed.

Hannah slid from the covers and stumbled to his bar. The pounding resumed in his head as he tried to focus on the labels.

His bottle of choice was empty on the kitchen table. In a rage, Hannah dropped to the couch, cursing himself. He hated Downey for getting him involved.

Hannah was sure he was replaying the first encounter with the case in his mind when the door pounded.

"Come on, man. Let's not do this again." Downey called from the hallway.

"Go away, Curt. I mean it." Hannah yelled.

"Nope. I know you're hungover. Just tell me you're dressed."

"I'm serious, Curt. Get lost. I'm done." Hannah groaned.

The room went quiet until a light swoosh came from beneath the door. He could hear Curt's footfalls moving away.

Even hungover, Hannah's curiosity got the better of him. He stepped to the door, where he found a small envelope.

"I hope it is explosives," he said aloud.

He opened it and found details of July's missing person in Erie, Pennsylvania. Was this supposed to make him feel better?

Curt had written beneath the report, *"You found the pattern, you picked Hartford and you were right about Erie. We need to catch this piece of shit, and we can't do it without you."*

Hannah dropped the note on his table and stumbled into the shower. He stood motionless, letting the water try to wash his sins, but he still couldn't shake the guilt.

He was Robert Hannah. The Smartest Guy in The Room.

He'd lost his friends, he'd lost his jobs, and lost his wife. Now, his arrogance was costing lives. Why would the FBI want him around?

He threw on some sweatpants and a t-shirt and lumbered around the corner for coffee.

Hannah would take the rest of the morning to compose a friendly letter to Curt and resign.

Agent Simms finished importing pictures, evidence, and witness statements into the file marked "Justin Harrow," a popular radio host in Erie, Pennsylvania. His boat had been found adrift five miles out from shore on Saturday, July twenty-second. The coast Guard found a missing ski vest this morning near the shore a mile down the lake.

His body had not been located.

While local authorities were leaving it open as a missing person's case, Simms and the task force knew otherwise.

Harrow had been a client of 'Heart's Elite' and had a few profile pictures taken aboard his yacht on the website. There were no such things as coincidences anymore.

He closed up the file and looked around for his partner, Agent Perez. She had moved to the boardroom to give him some quiet while doing some investigations of her own. Agent Downey had appointed her as the assistant to Agent Michael Watson of Quantico. It was a nice feather in her cap. Simms should be jealous, but Perez deserved the recognition.

He stuck his head in to check on her. "Need a break?" Simms asked.

"Always," she said with a smile.

'One day,' Simms thought as he eyed his partner, *'I'll get the guts to tell her how I feel.'*

Instead, he said, "I'm all done inputting the evidence, such as it is."

"Great, thanks. But you don't have to report to me, Jacco. It's all just a formality if Downey isn't around. It should be you, anyway."

"We both know that isn't true, Rhonda, but thanks for saying that. What are you working on? Can I ask?"

"A few things. First, warning the guys was useless, because even if they took it seriously, the clients would be wary of a *woman*, not a man. I'm looking for legal precedents to go after the site itself and broadcast our suspicions."

"Good luck with that. Even this Justin guy is only a missing person to them. And we gave the cops a warning." Simms said.

"Also, do you know how much a Regal LS36 Luxury Crossover costs?" Perez said. "I just found a used one on-line for three-hundred-thirty-five-thousand dollars! We are in the wrong line of work."

Jacco laughed. "Who would dive out of one of those? It's worth more than my condo!"

Agent Perez leaned back to stretch and asked, "Do you think Hannah will be back? He was pretty upset after Hartford and Downey said he wasn't answering his door this morning."

"I hope so," Jacco said. "He's a good thinker, even if he doesn't understand law enforcement. What about you? He clearly likes you."

"He clearly likes me?" Perez repeated. "What does that mean, Jacco?"

He put up his hands in defeat. "I'm just stating my observations. He talks to you more than anyone, respects your opinions, and I think he would ask you out if you weren't working together."

"Well, he did almost ask me out," she replied, "so we're clear on where I stand on that. And, to answer your other question, he talks to me more because I interact more. I told you, Jacco, you are smarter than everyone else I know, but just being first in the room doesn't help you if you are the quietest in the room."

Jacco nodded. "So, he asked you out."

Agent Perez sighed and stood from her chair. She stepped over to Simms and leaned into his face, leaving a couple of inches.

"Take your shot," she whispered, closing her eyes.

Jacco froze, wondering if anyone could see in, or if it was a trap.

"Hurry," she said, "I need to pee."

Jacco laughed, leaned in, and locked on.

Agent Downey wrapped his day by filing the reports from Agents Dennison and Farron from Erie, PA, engaging in another stern email exchange with Elaine Stafford at 'Hearts Elite,' and sitting through a bizarre meeting with Agents Perez and Simms.

'What was going on with those two?' He wondered.

"Until I can convince Hannah to come back to the table, the puzzles fall to you two," Downey said. "We have KILL THE…but what comes next? Get to work on your algorithm so I can squeeze Stafford at 'Hearts Elite.' I need another city."

"Will do, Agent Downey," Agent Simms said, with a huge grin on his face.

Perez and Simms snuggled under the covers at her condo. It was early evening, and both agreed that dinner could wait. If at all.

Simms had made the gentlemanly suggestion that he would not spend the night. She agreed to keep that door open. It was quite a first kiss.

He lay on his side, looking at her. She smiled self-consciously, asking, "What are you thinking about?"

"What every guy thinks about when they are in bed after making love to a beautiful woman? How lucky he is, and when can we do it again?"

She moved in closer and rested her head on his shoulder. She felt the same way, but words always failed her. This was Jacco. If it didn't work out, she would lose more than a lover. She would lose her best friend.

Why did she always start with self-sabotage?

"You okay?" He asked.

"Mm-hmm," she replied, worried he'd read her mind. "I'm just trying to soak this all in. You and me after all this time."

He sat up and looked at her. "Things will not change with us. I mean, well, this changed. You are still my best friend and partner. I don't want you to think that this changes my feelings for you. It elevates them. Please don't be afraid of this."

Perez bit her lip, exposing her doubt. Jacco, of course, caught it. "Aw, Rhonda, no. I will never hurt you. I practically love you."

She stifled a swallow and croaked, "Practically?"

He grinned. "No, I completely love you but wanted to leave wiggle room if you found that too creepy."

Tears filled her eyes as she reached up to him with a laugh.

"Then love me again, Jacco."

Chapter Twenty-Seven

Hannah slunk into the boardroom at nine-forty-five, averting Agents Perez and Simms's eyes. He needn't have bothered. They hadn't looked up.

He slid open his laptop and listened to their quiet chatter. *'Good for them,'* Hannah thought. *'It's about time.'*

Agent Downey walked into the room with a flourish and stopped when he spotted Hannah. Downey dropped his files on the table before giving him a small nod, which Hannah hoped meant as a 'welcome back.' Downey looked up and said, "Agent Watson will join us by video this morning. We'll be getting more resources from Quantico."

"Good to hear," Agent Perez said. "We still need an August city. Jacco and I were just narrowing down the list."

"What do you have?" Hannah asked.

Agent Simms replied, "We're leaning toward a city that starts with 'M'. If the phrase is KILL THE MEN, or KILL THEM DEAD, we get an 'M' either way. It's a crap shoot, but we believe 'M' is our best bet."

"Minneapolis?" Agent Downey offered. "Montpelier?"

The agents nodded as the center phone buzzed and Agent Watson appeared on the screen, haggard and worried.

"Good morning, everyone. Thank you for your attention today. The FBI will ramp up our involvement in your investigation. While it appears we don't have an actual single murder, the circumstances of the events, combined with the insight from Mr. Hannah, make for a compelling case."

"What do you need from us, Agent Watson?" Downey asked, with no hint of disappointment in the investigation being pulled out from under him. Hannah was continually impressed by his friend's composure.

"Business as usual, Agent Downey. We will add six investigative agents to assist Agents Dennison and Farron, and the work of two criminal profilers who will take your information and give you a better grasp of who might be responsible."

"Thank you, Agent Watson. Is the help available right now?" Downey asked.

"Yes. What do you need?"

"We were just discussing viable locations for Mr. August. As you know, Robert has been correct in the last two cities, but we could not prevent either crime or pinpoint the correct victim even with cooperation from 'Hearts Elite'. I'm hoping that once we determine our next city, that the investigators could fan out and begin greater reconnaissance to see if we can spot our perp before the end of the month."

"Of course. I'll let them know they could be on the road as early as tomorrow morning. The profilers are already working on a psychological make-up of the killer, including tendencies and approaches. He is visually non-threatening, yet lethal."

Hannah added, "And very disciplined and patient."

Agent Watson nodded. "I'll send those thoughts to the profilers."

"There's something that's been bothering me about his on-line search methods," Hannah said. "I couldn't put my finger on it until last night. I was actually drafting a resignation letter from this task force…"

Agents Simms and Perez physically reacted to his admission.

"…but I changed my mind, only because when I was writing it, I finished it with the date, July thirtieth. On the line above, I had written the last victim's name, Justin Harrow. A new connection jumped out, so I went back to the other victims to confirm it."

He turned to look at Agents Simms and Perez. "Do you see it, Simms? I didn't until last night. Something has been bothering me until I remembered what you said in June. Why would a killer who had access to the profiles of the clients in Hartford not choose the over forty-year-old Lonzo, *who he actually just met*, and instead stick with the jacked-up JoJo Hansen? In fact, why, of all profiles, would he have chosen the most difficult victim to kill?"

Hannah watched confusion and embarrassment creep into Agent Simms's expression until a spark lit his eyes. Recognition erased the doubt.

Jacco clicked open a folder on his laptop, taking seconds to scan the list for confirmation. He looked up at Hannah before turning to Agent Downey and Agent Watson.

"The victim's first name initials all coincide with the months of their deaths."

"Jacob, Frank, Michael, Alex, Mitchell, JoJo and Justin." Agent Simms pronounced as Agent Watson left the call, with the information for the profilers.

Hannah said, "After I realized there was a pattern within the pattern, I deleted the resignation letter, but I still feel so slow in picking up the puzzles. So much of this has been right in front of me. It's a classic blunder. Solve a pattern and fall into the trap of self-congratulation, which prevents you from seeing the more important one embedded inside."

"*The ABC Murders*," Agent Downey said.

"The Agatha Christie novel?" Agent Perez asked.

"Pally told me about it when we started this back in April. I read it a couple of weeks ago. Genius." Downey said.

"That's the one where the victims all had double letters and the killer's initials were A, B, C?" She asked.

"Yeah, except, being Agatha Christie, the whole pattern was a ruse to hide the actual killer and the real pattern, which was, of course, no pattern at all." Hannah said. He turned to Agent Simms. "Sorry, Jacco. Spoiler alert."

"I've read it," he said without looking up from his laptop. "And Hannah, you don't get to carry the blame on your own. I've got a chart here with the letters corresponding with the months staring me right in the face. This one is on me as well."

Agent Downey said, "Now that we know that the August victim begins with an 'A,' we can go back to 'Hearts Elite' and subpoena the profiles of all guys with that initial in cities that start with 'M'."

"Or, all clients whose name starts with 'A' in the Eastern USA and see what cities pop up. 'M' is only the choice as the most likely, not the guaranteed location." Hannah said, looking over at Agent Perez.

She was staring off at the corner of the room, lost in some detail. Hannah had seen that look across the poker tables when a player had gained an insight. "What is it?" He asked.

Downey and Simms followed Hannah's eyes and looked at Perez, who shook herself from her thoughts.

"No pattern at all. You said the pattern was that there was no pattern at all. Agatha Christie created a pattern so that an obvious crime could be masked in the camouflage."

"Right," Hannah said, "but here, we do have a pattern. In fact, we have two of them."

Perez sat straighter. "Why? Why do we have a pattern at all, and why do we have *two* patterns? We haven't stopped to ask ourselves...*why*?"

The room remained silent as Agent Perez continued. "If the killer simply wanted to kill a rich guy every month, he could just move from city to city in a smaller pattern than this geographical criss-crossing. The methods for these killings are the least efficient model imaginable. Then, consider the killing of JoJo Hansen when the likelier victim, Lonzo Garcia, who was also a client, drops into his lap. Why? If he is using this dating site as a hunting ground, why not take out Lonzo and move on?"

"Because by moving from city to city in a wider pattern, the killer is counting on law enforcement not finding any connections. That is why he has to move." Hannah reminded her. "And Lonzo's first initial is wrong."

"Okay, but why take the chance that a Robert Hannah, or a Jacco Simms, will figure out the pattern? My question is, just like Agatha Christie, *why do a pattern at all*?" Perez asked.

Blank faces stared back at her. "Look," she said, "this killer is so adept that he doesn't leave a single clue behind. The killings don't even register as murder. So why create a pattern that could trip yourself up? I think there is only one answer."

Hannah tried to keep up, but even he was unsure what she would say.

"What if the killer doesn't know?"

Chapter Twenty-Eight

"He's a contract killer?" Hannah asked.

"We've asked ourselves this before, and that's what I think," Agent Perez said. "If he was controlling his own hunt, there is no way he would have killed Hansen after meeting him and Lonzo. He'd have made the switch. I think he's not the one pulling the strings. He is doing a client's bidding."

"Okay, let's back this up," said Agent Downey, moving to the whiteboard. "You think our guy has been hired to carry out these killings, and is...what? Given his victims a month in advance?"

"Yeah, but I don't think that's important. I think what is important is that there is a client who has established a pattern that is unknown to our killer."

Agent Downey wrote the word 'Client,' on the whiteboard, and said, "This is an intriguing theory. It also answers the question of why the killings are being carried out the way they are."

"Undetectable?" Agent Simms asked.

"Exactly. The Client has a desire to kill these rich young guys, but lacks the experience, or nerve, or both, and hires a killer capable of dispatching of the victims without bringing attention to the crimes *or the Client*." Downey said.

"Oh," Agent Perez realized. "It also answers why he didn't go after Lonzo. He did not know that 'Hearts Elite' is the hunting ground, or that it plays any factor in the selection of victims. The killer probably doesn't even know that Hearts Elite exists."

Hannah sat back. "Whew, that is quite the insight. Our killer does not know who he is killing or why? He just does as he's told?"

"It's the very definition of a contract killer," Agent Simms said.

Agent Downey wrote these points on the board. "So, let's work with this for a while. What does it mean to us? How can we use this to our advantage?"

Hannah started pulling the pieces of the puzzle apart, looking for the thread that linked them together. The puzzles were vocabulary-based, with initials being the pattern. First initials of victims tied to their month of demise. Their city corresponded to a phrase not yet spelled out.

Agent Perez said, "We need a deep interview with Lonzo Garcia in Hartford. He is the only witness who can identify the guy. That is number one. We need everything he has on him. Did he sign anything, so we can analyze handwriting? What name did he give so we can cross-reference hotels and AIR BNBs?"

"We need a sketch artist," Agent Simms offered. "If it's true that the killer does not know what he is weaving, then he won't expect anyone to expect his moves. If we can get a good sketch, and find him before he strikes again, he will not know we are even there."

"Good, good," said Agent Downey, jotting and talking. "Robert, what are you thinking?"

"We also need to find where the killer got his boat in Erie. He either rented one or stole one. Either way, there has to be a record or a police report."

Agent Simms said, "The victim was moored at a luxury marina, but Erie has a few smaller ones dotted along the lake. I bet he attached a tracking device to the victim's yacht, so he didn't have to follow him around the docks."

"I'll confirm with Dennison and Farron to check all the boat rentals. They came up empty at Justin Harrow's marina."

Hannah added, "And find one without security cameras who will take cash. See if whoever worked that shift can identify the guy."

"Will do," Downey said as he fired off a text. "Anything else?"

"It's not my place to make this suggestion, but I believe Agent Perez would do well working with the Quantico profilers as our eyes and ears." Hannah said.

Agent Downey looked down at the table. "You okay with that, Perez?"

Agent Perez perked up at the compliment. "I'd love to work with them."

Downey said, "Done. I'll pass that on to Agent Watson." He looked over at Hannah. "Good call. Do you have any other amazing suggestions?"

Hannah looked at Agents Perez and Simms, not wanting to interrupt if they had something. "There is another important angle I believe we should investigate," he said.

"What's that"? Downey asked.

"The Client. We need to use 'Heart's Elite' to sniff him out."

The 'Hearts Elite' COO stared defiantly through the screen. "Absolutely not." Stafford said.

"Ms. Stafford," Agent Downey said, "we will bear the full resources of the FBI on this case, but to save time, I would much rather do this cooperatively."

"If I put a warning label across the top of my website that even hints that clients are being selectively targeted, I can close up shop for good," she said. "Again, I am committed to cooperating with the FBI, not only for the sake of my website, but for basic human decency, but a warning banner is like yelling 'danger' in a movie theater. I'll have clients running for the delete button."

"What was the feedback or fallout from the northern Pennsylvania blackout?" Hannah asked.

"Well, traffic was eliminated, of course," she replied, "but I have received no sign of any long-term grievances. But you're asking for an entire eastern United States warning? The impact that would have in New York and Boston alone would be catastrophic to my brand."

Hannah was both sympathetic to her concerns, and Downey's. "Elaine, I have an idea that may work for both of us."

Downey flipped Hannah an eyebrow while Stafford said, "I'm all ears, Mr. Hannah."

"What if the banner doesn't look like a warning? What if it looks playful, yet protective of its client base? If the language fits your 'brand,' as you call it, it could help us both." Hannah said.

"I don't see how, Robert. Can you think, off the top of your head, what it might sound like?" She asked.

"What if it said something like, 'Thinking of doing something naughty around here? Now, now. Play nice.'"

Agent Downey said, "That sounds more like we're tipping off 'The Client' that we know someone is trolling the site for victims, rather than protecting customers."

"Who's 'The Client'?" Stafford asked.

Downey grimaced as he uttered, "Sorry, I shouldn't have said that. It's part of our new theory."

Hearts Elite COO Elaine Stafford said, "Oh, you think the killer isn't the same person accessing our customer profile base?"

"We don't know for sure, but it's a new avenue of investigation."

She paused and looked away from the screen. "It makes a bit more sense, I think. I have been giving this a lot of thought, gentlemen, even if you find me obstructive. I couldn't equate the subtleness needed to engage men at this level on-line, then act so brutally in the field. It is two distinct skill sets."

"Subtle? So, you think it could be a woman?" Hannah asked.

"Of course, it could be a woman. On-line, it can be anyone. With artificial intelligence, anyone could craft a greeting to make them sound as gentle as a kitten, be it a man or woman. What I meant by subtle is that the aim of your 'client' is to engage and select, which is far different from the killer's need to hunt and eliminate. I believe you are right. It could be two different people."

"Elaine, the FBI is putting a couple of profilers on the case. We could use your input on personality traits of men and women who sign up and use your site to help shape the individual we are looking for, either the killer or 'The Client.'" Hannah said. "But we also have another special reason to be in touch. We have cracked another puzzle. The initial of the victim matches the month of their death. So now that we know that, any man with 'A' as their initial is vulnerable in August, and we have a handful of prospective cities. If we send those along, could you pare down a potential victim list and send it to us? Not just the profiles, but the actual names with addresses? The clock is ticking."

Stafford chewed her lip before nodding. "I am trusting your discretion as you are requesting my cooperation. Send the list to my direct email and I will do my best within the next forty-eight hours. How large are the cities?"

"Combined? Around two million people," Hannah said.

"Well, then get me that list, and I will see what I can do. The initial 'A' will help to narrow the list."

"Thanks, Elaine. Talk soon." Agent Downey said, ending the video call. "I'll get Simms on the details. What cities are you thinking?"

"I'm leaning toward the letters 'E' and 'M'. Minneapolis, Memphis and Milwaukee all have sizeable populations, and after Erie, the smaller cities of Evansville, Indiana or Elizabeth, New Jersey might be in play."

"Get your thoughts to Simms before you go today. We need that list to Stafford by day's end," Downey said, capping his smart marker. "You really think we can tip The Client that we are on to them?"

Hannah answered, "It seems like using a tank to go after a butterfly, but anything that looks suspicious to them might make them careless, or, if we are lucky, make them bolder."

"Why would that be lucky?" Downey asked.

"We have to look at it from The Client's perspective now. He or she is a character in this whole drama we didn't know existed. They are invisible, but brilliant. They have put together a puzzle within a puzzle, and if we are right, hired a killer incapable of detecting it, or at least unable to change it." Hannah sat forward, staring at Downey. "They are now on month eight. It is going perfectly. The killer has been totally effective. But a playful new banner appears on the 'Hearts Elite' website. The Client wonders if they have been detected after all. How would they react? I'm hoping they react the way any puzzle player would."

"Change their pattern, making it easier to catch them?" Downey offered.

"No, they would, in fact, make it more puzzling. They would contact 'Hearts Elite'. Maybe they email asking about the banner, but doing it in such a way as to make it sound like a puzzle, or even better, to claim credit for the necessity of the warning itself."

"The taunting email. Classic." Downey said.

"It would provide confirmation that we are right, and will leave a digital trail back to The Client. There had to have been some communication."

Downey twirled the marker in his hand as he tapped the table. "That could work. Can you think of other warning ideas they could post on the site? I know I'm asking a lot, but, as you said, time is ticking."

"I'll go sit with Simms and Perez and brainstorm a bit."

"Yeah, well, don't sit too close. I think something is going on there. Someone is going to have to have the uncomfortable chat with them soon." Downey said.

"Why, Agent Downey, I did not know you were against young love," Hannah mocked.

Downey smirked. "Partners who have personal feelings make unstable decisions in the field. Not good. I get that it's an HR nightmare, but it's best that the higher-ups know. It's why we don't have spouses as partners. Just bad logistics."

"So will they have the choice of what kind of 'partners' they want to be?"

"It depends what they think is happening. But I just want them to understand what they are getting into."

"Yeah," Robert said. "Love can be a bitch."

Downey shook his head. "Not what I was thinking."

Chapter Twenty-Nine

The Bulgarian assassin enjoyed his breakfast at Millie's Outdoor Café in the city's downtown core. Of all his stops across the eastern USA, this was his favorite so far. He enjoyed the scenery, as well as the proximity to power. It was so intoxicating to know how close he was to the hub of the free world.

Five victims remain. Only five more deaths. Then he'd be home two-and-a-half million dollars richer. He had already decided he would take the next year off, lying low. As much as The Client craved anonymity, The Bumper wanted to ensure there was a push in his reputation. He didn't think there was an 'Advisor Website' for hired killers (Leave five stars!) but he wanted a testimonial that carried currency within his world. He would have to think about that as November and December rolled around.

The Bumper finished up what the diner called The Devil's Mess (with avocado toast) and left a healthy tip. He slipped his sunglasses back on and strolled to his rented luxury ride. The killer slid behind the wheel of the stone silver Lexus RX and checked his mirrors.

Of course, no one paid him any attention. This man, who has killed dozens in his official capacity in the underworld, as well as seven this year, looked the part of the white-collar, upper class power broker.

He pulled out into traffic and set off north toward Westhampton.

It was time to meet Andrew.

Chapter Thirty

Agent Downey rushed into the boardroom with Agents Simms and Perez streaming in his wake. He hit the speakerphone before sitting down.

"Go ahead Agent Dennison."

"Everyone there?" He asked.

"I'll catch Hannah up later. Where's Farron?"

"He's inside getting the photo." Dennison said.

"We have a photo? Of what?" Asked Agent Simms.

"More like of whom." Dennison answered. "We found a low rent marina down the shoreline that rents boats by the day. Some college kid works the Saturday midday run. Usually pretty quiet. Serious fishermen have their own boats, and even renters are usually on the water before eight o'clock. This guy starts at nine o'clock."

"Tell me he worked Saturday, July twenty-second," Agent Perez said.

Dennison answered. "He did, and as a precaution at the marina, when the customer fills out the rental slip, the cashier snaps a picture with a small, attached camera off to the side, out of sight from the main window. The place can't afford

a security camera set-up or offsite digital storage, so they came up with the next best thing. When they are printing the receipt, they just hit the photo button on the laptop. If the boat comes back on time and is in the same condition, they just delete the photo. If there is damage or any question, they have a credit card and a picture."

"Oh. My. God." Downey said. "This place still has the jpeg image on the computer? Was there damage to the boat?"

"I don't think so, no. They only have the photo because it was so dead that day, and all the boats were back, that the kid had permission to close-up shop early. In his hurry to get to wherever the party was, he forgot to delete the pictures!"

"You've been over the boats? Have local police run them?" Downey asked.

"We have, and they have. They all look pretty clean, and in fact, they have all been rented out a few times, but there was no evidence of blood, or dents from a struggle. They just look like old rental boats."

"Great work, Hal. Is Agent Farron sending us a digital copy?" Downey asked.

The boardroom tinkled with the sound of a store door opening somewhere in Erie, Pennsylvania and he could hear Agent Farron in the background. "They are just matching the photos with the timestamps. We are going to send three pictures." Dennison said.

"Have Farron send it to my personal email account. I'll distribute from there," Downey said as he flipped his laptop opened and turned on the whiteboard. His laptop filled the screen on the wall.

While they waited for the pictures, Agent Downey worked his cellphone, texting Watson at Quantico that they may have the first concrete lead in the case, copying Hannah on the thread. He dropped his phone on the table and stared at his account.

The first ping arrived seconds later. Downey stabbed the email and clicked on the jpeg file.

The photo was of a scruffy, mid-sixties man wearing an old ball cap and sporting an annoyed expression. It was a profile of the guy staring above the laptop, as if the attendant was ruining his day.

"No," said Agent Perez. "Not him."

"What's the timestamp on the photo?" Agent Simms asked.

The bottom right corner bore the imprint. Agent Downey read off, "Nine-eighteen a.m."

"Okay, he may not be our guy, but he may have encountered the killer on the dock, or remembers something about him." Simms said.

"I'll get you the details of all three guys who rented boats that morning." Agent Dennison said. "According to the credit card, this guy is Oscar Bellamy."

A second ping followed as Downey clicked. A second photo filled the screen.

It showed a chisel faced man with a tight jaw-line in over-sized sunglasses, clean ball cap pulled tightly over his brow, and a dickey just below his chin. He was looking away to the water, as if avoiding any further conversation.

"Nationality?" Agent Perez asked, standing up. "He looks Eastern European. Croatian? Turkish?"

"Is this our guy?" Agent Simms asked. "Time Stamp?"

Downey said, "Nine-forty-three a.m."

"This is the guy. I can feel it," Agent Perez said. "Look how he is avoiding the attendant. He just doesn't want to give him a full-on look. He's probably darting his attention as he is standing there. What is the name on the credit card?"

Agent Dennison exhaled into his phone. "He paid cash, including a security deposit that wasn't returned."

"This guy!" Perez yelled. "Print this guy's picture."

A third ping echoed as Downey hit 'print,' linked to a copier elsewhere in the office. He clicked open the third picture of a strong looking young man in a muscle shirt, sporting a shoulder tattoo and military buzz cut. He was service or wanted to be. Without waiting for the question, Agent Downey said, "Ten-oh-four a.m."

Agent Simms asked, "So no one else rented a boat that morning?"

Agent Dennison, still on the line, answered, "We only asked for men of a certain age who rented alone. There was a grandfather who took his grandson out for a fishing trip. We ignored him. And also, anyone who fit the description of a man capable of doing what our killer has been doing who was on the water by ten-thirty. The Coast Guard found Justin Harrow's boat drifting around one p.m. The next guy who might have fit the bill didn't rent until early afternoon. It's these three guys, or our killer got his boat somewhere else."

Agent Downey also printed the third picture. "Did this third guy rent with a credit card?" He asked.

Agent Dennison replied. "He did."

"Great work, Agent Dennison, and congratulate Farron for me. You guys did great. Pay a visit to the two guys who paid with the credit cards. If they are in fact still in Erie, PA, we can cross them off our list. If they are nowhere to be found, we keep them on file as suspects. Get all you can in Erie, then head back. I'll get these pictures to Quantico."

"It's got to be number two," Agent Perez said as Downey hung up the speakerphone.

"I agree, but we can't be too sure of ourselves. I'll send all three to Agent Watson and let him make the call."

"Did you notice that number two was the shortest of the three guys?" Agent Simms said. "If we assume they all stood in about the same spot, he looked like he was about an inch or two shorter than the first guy and about four inches short of the last renter."

"What do you make of that?" Downey asked.

"Eastern Europeans make great weightlifters and bodybuilders. They are not tall, but they are strong. A sturdy, compact suspect who clocks in under five foot nine or five foot ten wouldn't be overly intimidating to the eye. That last guy must have been six-foot-two. He would have scared the dog-walker in Louisville and might have made the art dealer in Lansing think twice about letting him into his condo. The first guy is, of course, way too old."

"And the second guy paid cash to avoid a paper trail." Perez said.

Agent Downey forwarded the photos to Agent Watson at Quantico with their thoughts on suspect number two, and Agent Dennison's upcoming interviews with two of the suspects.

"Okay, we've got our first solid lead. We can put a body in a boat at the same time Justin Harrow would have left his marina. Let's let Quantico handle the next steps with the photos. We need to find one of those three guys in a city we believe is our August destination."

"Is Hannah up to speed?" Agent Simms asked.

"I've texted him the details. Do you need his input?"

Agent Simms darted his gaze to Agent Perez. "What?" Agent Downey asked.

Perez answered. "We wanted his thoughts on a new theory we've been working on. It's pretty far-fetched, but when we thought of it, we didn't have what we have right now."

"So, is it still valid, or did you just want to run it by him?" Agent Downey asked.

"It concerns The Client, the one pulling the strings. What are the odds that the list has already been made? Especially since we know August is in motion already and only four months remain. We were thinking there might be a way of manipulating The Client into making a mistake."

"What kind of mistake?" Agent Downey asked.

Agent Simms leaned forward. "We know so much more than the killer thinks we know. We now also believe that there is a client who is acting as puppet master. Neither of these two individuals knows we are on to them." He looked at Agent Perez. "We believe it is time to make that work to our advantage with so little time left."

"How?"

Agent Perez looked over at Agent Downey. "We think it's time we open a 'Hearts Elite' account."

Chapter Thirty-One

The Bumper strolled the leafy neighborhood until he identified five different escape routes from Andrew Sisteck's spacious home. More to the point, from his property. Thankfully, the killer wouldn't actually be in the house.

That would be poor planning and terrible execution.

He would have to be on site, but would need a quick, unobserved escape. One leap and two turns should do the trick.

The Bumper listened for dogs and cancelled those backyards from his mental checklist. As he walked, he could hear the splashing of the swimming pools. Again, a terrible choice.

After six days in different workout gear, and at different times of day, he jogged, walked, and bladed around the blocks of Westhampton, selecting his five routes. Two were out the front of the house, turning in different directions, and three were from the back of the house. The killer would employ his new toy to help him rank the five selected pathways in order of preference.

The Bumper returned to his luxury Lexus and popped the back hatch. He gave his vicinity a quick eye and found no one watching him in the parking lot behind the local church.

Small parishes couldn't afford security cameras, and even if they could, what was there worth stealing?

The killer eased the drone high into the air and settled onto the back open hatch of his SUV. He watched the laptop as the image of his Lexus grew smaller. When the elevation reached three hundred feet, he moved the device over the neighborhood until he spotted Andrew Sisteck's two-storey ranch with its wrap-around driveway and ivy trestles. The Bumper had shaken his head when he'd laid eyes on the victim's house. *'Why not just leave a ladder out'*? He wondered.

He rotated the view from the drone to follow his first possible getaway out the front yard and turning east. There were five houses to the corner, and depending upon where he parked, he could be at the Lexus within forty-five seconds. But he would be in plain sight to any of those five neighbors who might be at their windows. The killer pivoted the drone back to its original spot and turned it the other way to see what a western escaped looked like. It was worse.

He would have to park on the same street and run past at least a dozen homes, though he might be remembered as someone fleeing the scene for safety, rather than avoiding detection. But it wasn't worth the risk.

The Bumper positioned the drone back over Sisteck's home and panned around his back neighbors. To the east was a large fence with a rock garden that would make hopping it a perilous leap with an uncertain landing.

Suddenly, the confidence he had with five routes had shrunk to two. He pivoted the drone to the west and calculated the fence jump as do-able and liked the hedges that separated the side neighbors as a bonus.

All eyes would be on Sisteck's house, and perhaps a shadow hugging the shrubs would go undetected. The problem was the driveway. It was also circular and made the escape from the backyard to the parallel street dangerous. He dropped the drone to one hundred feet and tilted it to get a look at the back of the house. Oh, no. He would have to run right beside a sliding glass door that led to the backyard, and what appeared to be a large dining-room window beside it. If those neighbors were home, or, heaven forbid, entertaining that night, he would hop into a yard of witnesses with no easy sprint to safety.

That left the main backyard neighbor.

It fortunately had what he guessed was some kind of elm tree that would make the fence hop easier, but then it was an open sprint to a driveway that ran as an extension to the concrete back patio. The tree had a large tire hanging from it, which remained motionless in the late afternoon sun. He could see no vehicle, so determining who might be home at what time would require a bit more surveillance.

He chose that route as the most likely and decided upon a sixty-second duration from one ignition to the next.

He flew the drone back to the Lexus and hopped out of the back hatch to the parking lot. Had anyone seen the spectacle and wandered back for a look, he was ready. Drones were cool. He'd be magnanimous and let any kids take a look. They made horrible witnesses anyway and never took down licence plate numbers.

No one cared.

"I think it's a great idea," Hannah said. "But September would be too soon. Maybe we put together three accounts, one that would coincide with October, November, and December. Since we know the criteria of the initials, all we'd have to do is choose a city we believe would match the phrase."

Agent Downey stared at his friend. "You know I can't let you put an address down, then have you live there, waiting."

"Why not?" Hannah asked.

"Why not? Because the FBI is not in the habit of using civilians for bait, even if we believe, in this case, you are expendable."

Hannah twirled the spaghetti on his fork and shovelled it against his spoon. "Come on, Curt. We both know we'd have the lovebirds watching over me."

Downey took a bite of his garlic bread, and stringing the cheese out, laughed as it hit his chin. "I talked to Simms today about it. They are going to make the call to HR. I guess it's real."

"What do you think about three different accounts? Maybe an Oliver, a Nathan and a Derek? I'll help put together the profiles that we think would trigger The Client to want to choose either of them. Hopefully, it would be 'Oliver' so we can get the guy."

"The profilers at Quantico have pored over the metadata of the seven victims. Perez could get you access to their profiles to meld them together. See what links them, or what they might have in common. The lack of strong friendships keeps showing up. It's easy to get these guys alone and vulnerable." Downey said.

"It's the language I'm interested in. Again, in poker terms, I don't care what pocket cards they were holding when they signed up. I'm interested in the vibes they were sending out."

Downey drained his wineglass and pushed it aside. "Do you agree it was boat renter number two?"

"Absolutely. Perez is right. He seems jumpy even in a still photo, and the cash is a red flag. Do you have any misgivings?" Hannah asked.

"Nope, I feel the same. Just don't want to color your view with my thoughts, that's all."

Hannah spooned another helping into his mouth. "The killer does his research," he said in between bites. "If he was just picking up his boat rental around ten o'clock, he knew when Harrow would have been on the lake and what his boat looked like."

"I like Simms's insight. We're pretty sure the killer placed a tracker somewhere on Harrow's boat. It's the only way he could have found him out there that morning." Downey said, pulling out his credit card and placing it on the table in view of the passing server.

"You don't have to do that." Hannah said.

"Actually, I do," Downey answered. "If we're talking business, it goes on the expense account. Thanks again for your help. I also didn't thank you for not resigning."

"God, I felt so stupid. Still do. It feels so simple, but that makes it hard to catch him. There is no way Stafford can trace a common account back to The Client?" Hannah asked.

"She claims she can't even if she wanted to. Messages disappear after twenty-four hours if there is no ongoing conversation. My guess is that The Client is too tech savvy to leave a digital fingerprint. Many accounts and off-site proxies would come up as dead ends," Downey answered.

"What about the surveillance photo? Quantico running with it?"

"Agent Watson is sending it around. Our hope is someone knows the guy and can give us a hand. Even just to get a name."

The server came by and printed out the check. Downey swiped his card and stood to leave. "Thanks Pally. I'll be in touch if anything materializes. You do the same if you think of anything."

Hannah paused before saying, "I will, and thanks again."

He watched his FBI contact and best friend walk out of the restaurant. Hannah should have told him about his new 'Hearts Elite' account he opened that morning.

The three of them, actually.

Chapter Thirty-Two

The killer stopped at four area thrift shops before he found the perfect black windbreaker, gloves and sweatpants. He would have to make do with the shoes he'd purchased in Hartford.

The Bumper set out on his final reconnaissance mission before tomorrow night's performance. He parked near the church, a block closer to Sisteck's house than yesterday. The assassin jogged down the street and turned one street farther before checking the timer on his watch. As he passed the home directly behind the victim's, the stopwatch clicked to sixty-two seconds.

Precision was everything. He would have to park fifty feet closer. The killer didn't want to run faster. That would look suspicious. And he didn't want to park on the same street. That would look obvious.

He continued his jog, wondering what it would be like to live in this neighborhood. Washington D.C. was far enough away as to not impact the city, but it was close enough for those who craved power. Maybe when this was all over, he would come back here to live. It was clearly the most beautiful of all the cities he'd visited so far.

The Bumper grinned as he thought of what would happen to the housing market in the Westhampton neighborhood after tomorrow night. He knew one building lot that was about to become available.

The Client felt the first twinge of anxiety.

'It couldn't be.'

A search of keywords, owing to the change in the men's initials and city names, always produced a fresh crop of bachelors. Favorite words included 'cultured, prestigious' and the nauseating 'entitled,' as if any man believed that their social standing entitled them to anything.

Having prepared the September dossier, The Client's attention turned to October, the beginning of the home stretch. For the first time since the project began, there was an account that listed all three words. It was as if the profile was tailor made. Even the name set the pulse racing.

One click sent their heart sinking. The account had been created that morning.

"It just can't be," The Client whispered aloud, this time with a soft wheeze that was invading their speech.

Fingers tapped the photos of the young man in his early to mid-thirties. "Harvard graduate," they spat out loud, as if clearing their throat of the irritation. One click closed the on-line album and returned the page to the profile status. It was just too perfect.

"I am a cultured man searching for an intelligent woman who is fond of puzzles, as am I. You must have prestigious credentials to back up your impressive resume. As a self-made success, I am entitled to the finest life can offer. When I find you, I will know. You won't get away from me."

The Client's heart raced and understood the implied threat.

"…who is fond of puzzles, as am I."

Had this man figured it out and was setting a trap?

When I find you, I will know. You won't get away from me.

The Client was the hunter, not the prey. Anxiety morphed into indignation. How dare he try to match wits? With one last look at the full profile, the instigator thought, *'Too bad Oliver Goodman. You live in the wrong city.'*

Chapter Thirty-Three

Andrew Sisteck turned into his circular driveway at precisely six-oh-three p.m. He was looking forward to tonight, not simply because it was Friday, but because he'd cleared his social calendar to enjoy a weekend alone. His fiscal business-year ended in August, and he was in the mood to celebrate.

He climbed out of the BMW and stood admiring the front gardens he'd had tended. The air was scented with barbecues riding a warm breeze. He would open an older bottle of wine from his collection and savor it on the back patio at dusk.

Sisteck keyed in his passcode on the front door and walked into the air-conditioned foyer. He had too much house by far, but a man of his stature had a certain reputation to uphold.

Mr. August brushed off a flake of dirt from his fingers as he shed his tan shirt and cream suit and walked into his shower, letting the spray and steam ease away the tensions associated with being a millionaire businessman at thirty-six. He dried himself off and donned a black bathrobe, and padded down to the kitchen. It was still too early to chill the wine, but it wouldn't hurt to have a look. He stepped downstairs into the wine cellar and tapped the sensor, which triggered an overhead glow. The room was always chilled to sixty-four degrees. He ran his fingers over the corks of his collection until he brushed a Chateau Latour Grand Vin Pauillac two-thousand-six. That would do nicely.

He set the bottle aside on the serving table and retreated to his bedroom to dress in an evening outfit befitting his mood. Sisteck grabbed shorts with a cotton shirt that felt right as he ran his fingers through his thick wavy hair. He stood back from the mirror to appreciate the look.

Sisteck went downstairs and prepared a chicken stir-fry dinner with groceries purchased by the housekeeper that morning. He looked about the kitchen and living room, searching for flaws in her work, but was pleased to find none.

As the dinner seared, he stood at the patio door watching the child behind his property swaying on the old tire swing. Andrew marvelled at how good it must feel to be so young, so carefree, with so much life ahead of you.

'*Just like me,*' Andrew thought.

Earlier that day, The Bumper dusted the keypad for prints and slipped the tape over the residue. He ignored the slight apprehension he felt, knowing no one would question him. He was driving a rich car and looked like he must be a buddy of Andrew's.

There were no fingerprints on numbers one through five. He hit pay dirt on six. When he found none on seven or eight, he groaned at the adolescent nature of his victim. The killer knew the code had to be six digits, so with his gloved fingers, he pressed six-nine-six-nine-six-nine, the door silently unlocking.

The Bulgarian moved downstairs to the storage room that ran along the far side wall of the house, beneath the ivy trestle. He hoisted himself to the ledge and unlatched the window. He knew that when he locked the house, it would arm all the circuits. The window just had to be unlocked. He wouldn't need to open it from outside until later tonight.

He made a couple of trips from his SUV and unloaded his shipment into the empty cavernous room, careful to position it below the window.

The killer pried open the first box and spread the powder around the top layer. Once it caught, the show would begin.

He wished he could stick around to see it.

Sisteck enjoyed his last dinner at the dining room table that over-looked his patio. It was a warm August evening just a week ahead of Labor Day. That was a busy time for him, though not nearly as busy as the Fourth of July. Thankfully, the demand stayed crazy this summer. The pandemic had slowed his inventory, but it was all coming back now.

At eight o'clock, while there was still a hint of daylight in the western sky, Andrew Sisteck, owner of "Sis Boom BAW Fireworks," loped down to his wine cellar to retrieve his celebratory bottle for his best sales year ever.

He turned back to the stairs when he heard what sounded like a metallic latch shut. Sisteck opened the games room door beside the wine cellar and saw nothing amiss. He again turned when he heard a strange hissing behind him from the basement storage room.

The Fireworks King couldn't imagine what could make a noise in there.

After all, it was an empty room.

The Bumper waited for the signal. When he heard Mr. August moving downstairs, he dropped the five lit sparklers onto the box of fireworks in the storage room. The gunpowder he'd strewn across the top would blow the room in seconds, the three cases of fireworks would disguise the true nature of the blast, and the low-grade dynamite should take care of it all.

The killer didn't wait to make sure the flares hit their target. The Bumper crouched and dropped the flaming sparklers into the basement storage room through the side window he'd unlocked earlier that day and raced up the side of the property and was over the fence in seconds. He slipped along the hedge line and stood behind the large elm tree as the first blast blew out the basement windows. At that, the killer sprinted past the back neighbor's house, sure that all attention was drawn from the road. As The Bumper peeled past the front of the house, he jogged to the right, ignoring the urge to remove his earbuds. He was just another jogger out for an evening run.

As the killer passed the adjoining driveway, the next blast blew out the remaining windows of Sisteck's house. A patriotic red, white, and blue hue emanated from the growing inferno.

The Bulgarian got to fifty seconds in his head as he rounded the corner just steps from the Lexus. The last explosion shook the night, surely engulfing the house, killing all inside.

Such a tragedy.

The Bumper settled into his seat and started up the engine. It would do no good to linger in the neighborhood, and no one could blame anyone trying to get away from what could have been a gas-main explosion.

The killer pulled away from the curb and drove straight down Patterson to I-Ninety-Five.

On his way, he passed several fire trucks and first responders, no doubt racing to the ferocious house explosion of Andrew Sisteck, the Fireworks King of Richmond, Virginia.

As he eased north onto I-Ninety-Five, his phone pinged.

Another satisfied customer.

Just four months to go.

Chapter Thirty-Four

"We got the first initial right," Hannah said, disappointment overshadowing the meagre accomplishment.

"Andrew Sisteck." Agent Perez recited. "His charred remains were found in the burnt-out hull of the basement in the hallway. Crime scene investigators seem to think he might have sparked the accidental explosion. According to his staff, he was in a good mood, going home to celebrate his best sales year yet." She dropped the report on the table. "Apparently, it must have included sparklers and maybe a box of fireworks he wanted to bring upstairs."

"Richmond, Virginia. It wasn't even on our radar," replied a despondent Agent Simms.

Agent Downey stared through the wood of the table as he said, "I don't know what it's going to take. We've been so close." He slammed his palm on the table in a rare show of anger. "We must shut down 'Hearts Elite' to send the message that we're onto the killer. Maybe they will make a mistake."

Hannah waited a few seconds out of respect for his friend's outburst before replying, "I believe that would be our mistake."

"No, Pally, we don't use innocent lives as bait. We need to shut this down before it goes any further. We'll go public and warn people about what is happening."

"And say what? That these eight random monthly deaths result from a genius serial killer? The FBI is under intense scrutiny right now. You need proof we don't have."

Agent Downey looked around the room, seemingly for support, before dropping his eyes. "We can't let this go on any longer."

Agent Simms sat up straight. "I believe that our next victim, which will begin with an 'S', will live in a city that begins with 'I'. The phrase has to be *KILL THE RICH*."

Hannah shook his head. "That only has eleven letters. We need to get more creative."

Agent Perez addressed Agent Downey. "What does Quantico have to say?"

"It's all hands-on deck now. But we are to stay in touch and update our investigation. The profilers have put together a psychological make-up of both The Client and the killer. By the way, Agent Perez, they speak highly of you. Great work. It will arrive today. Study it and we will meet up again tomorrow." Downey said.

Hannah raised his hand. "Can I get something off my chest?"

The center phone console interrupted all conversation as the display screen identified Agent Watson. Downey hit the connect button as everyone turned to the video monitor.

"Good morning, Curt, good morning, all. We may have our first real break in this case, much as it pains me we didn't have this sooner, but through cooperative channels within law enforcement, we may have a positive ID on the suspect from the boat renter photo from Erie, Pennsylvania."

"Is he a local?" Agent Perez asked.

"From Erie? No," Agent Watson replied. "He's not even American."

"Did the ID come from Homeland Security?" Agent Downey asked.

"No. He's never been here before, which might explain why he was recruited. We would have no record of him. The help came from Interpol." Agent Watson said.

"Interpol?" Hannah said. "So, he's a known criminal?"

"You could say that, Mr. Hannah. They believe he is Zach Betes, a Bulgarian contract killer from Sofia. His specialty is getting in, getting the job done, and getting out before anyone notices a crime had been committed. He is practically undetectable."

"Sounds like our guy. Any aliases we should search?" Agent Downey asked.

"None that would show up through a standard search. We have requested his folder from Interpol and an agent who has intel on the guy. He'll be here in a few days."

"That's great news. What do you need from us here?"

"Keep digging. You were the first to put this together. Keep following the trail. Find the next city. Let's save the next guy," Agent Watson said.

Hannah lifted the boat rental surveillance photo from the case folder and looked at the man who has eluded them since the day Curt Downey knocked on his condo door and changed his life. "Zach Betes. Where are you right now?" Hannah asked.

"Good question, Mr. Hannah." Agent Watson said. "And by the way, he might not use any aliases, but he has a nickname. He calls himself 'The Bumper.'"

As Agents Perez and Simms headed back to their desks, Downey turned to his friend and asked, "You had something you wanted to get off your chest?"

Hannah pursed his lips and exhaled. '*Maybe this wasn't such a good time,*' he thought.

Downey stared. "Tell me. What is it?"

"Okay. I set up a 'Hearts Elite' account."

"What? When?"

"It was a few days ago, before Richmond. I can cancel it if I jumped the gun before the profilers' information got here." Hannah said.

He watched Downey run through the myriads of problems and solutions in seconds. "What was the hook?" Downey asked.

"I used the name Oliver Goodman."

Downey blinked. "Good. Man. Okay, not subtle, but go on."

"I couldn't wait for Perez to feed me the details, so I looked through the profiles of the seven victims and found recurring phrases or words. I used those as well." Hannah said. "Plus, I mentioned the puzzles."

"How?"

"Just that I was into puzzles and I need a woman who was as well. Also, I referred to finding them," Hannah said.

"What city did you choose?" Downey asked.

"It was before we found out about Richmond. I expected Milwaukee or Minneapolis. I guessed it would be the letter 'N', and that the phrase might be 'Kill the Money.'"

Downey reacted. "Kill The Money?"

"I know, it doesn't work now, but with so many potential victims, I needed to channel the killer's vision and The Client's psyche. Kill The Rich wouldn't work, but Kill the Money might. It has twelve letters."

"So where was the 'N'?"

"Apparently, Oliver Goodman hails from New York."

"Any bites yet?" Downey asked.

"Nada. Nothing. But that doesn't mean The Client hasn't seen it. But that Richmond helps to spell KILL THE 'R', means that September must be a vowel before we even get to Oliver's month. I believe Agent Perez is right when she believes the next city will begin with 'I'". Hannah said. "There are few cities in the Midwest that start with 'I', especially since Indianapolis has already been chosen."

"Okay, I'll get Simms and Perez on that list. But I think you were premature to set up an account without our input. You probably blew your cover if The Client searches for keywords."

"You don't think that maybe it might spook him?" Hannah asked.

"The Client?" Downey asked. "Maybe, but you can't just copy and paste the same profile into multiple names from multiple cities. The keyword search would give you away. If there were suddenly ten profiles with the same information, The Client would know their cover was blown, and that someone was onto him. And what would make it even worse is that The Client would know we were fishing. The multiple accounts mean we don't have a clue who they are, where they are, and who they are choosing. It does more damage than good. And if we're right and September has already been chosen, then there are only three more names to go. I doubt The Client would choose one from a fresh account. Too risky."

Hannah nodded. "Very true, CD. Hadn't thought of that. I doubt any damage was done because we now know The Client won't go looking anywhere near New York in October. The city initial doesn't work."

"Hey, it was a bold try. Tell you what, though, Pally. Leave the account active just in case. You never know who might meet. You're a catch, you know."

"Exactly what I was afraid you'd say."

The Bumper made his second pit stop of the day toward his September destination. He knew little about America, but he was guessing he wasn't going anywhere as pretty as Richmond. The internet search revealed that one thousand miles lay between Richmond, Virginia and his next stop on the journey. He could handle all sixteen hours in a single day, but that was how mistakes were made.

After finishing in the bathroom, he strolled across the parking lot to the new rental, only to be interrupted by a ping on his phone. He had shut off the notifications to all his apps on the burner phone, and the only person who might contact him was The Client, who hadn't done so between dossiers and pay days.

The killer looked around the lot to see if he was being followed. Perhaps The Client was even closer than he thought. He pulled the phone from his pocket while scanning cars for abrupt head movements.

The Bumper had a text from an unknown number. He thought it must be spam when he read the only word.

Detected

He clicked on the text, which revealed a link beneath the cryptic message. Again, he scanned the parking lot before pressing it.

His stomach dropped as he stared at an old picture of himself that he knew was on file with Interpol. He had been thrilled to be so important. Now, it was a major millstone around his neck.

The brief report simply warned that The Bumper was rumored to be in the United States and was dangerous.

He hustled to his car and fired up the engine.

The killer took three deep breaths and thought about the situation. The Client was watching his back. He had found the report and had sent it as a warning. 'No more big shows' was what he'd meant.

But who had found out where he was? Again, his ingrained suspicion expected a double-cross from The Client to avoid paying out the bonus money. Had The Client begun setting the trap by leaking his location to the authorities? But then why send him a warning text? Just to make him paranoid?

He calmed himself as his mind dismissed that theory. "No," he thought, "I must have been photographed or identified." He thought back to Richmond and the backyards. There was no one with a camera, no one with a computer, no one with…

A computer. The killer closed his eyes and tried to remember where he'd been at a laptop. Then he remembered.

Erie, Pennsylvania. When he rented the boat.

The cap and neck scarf were to make it harder to remember facial features because the kid's mind would jump to the hat and scarf. But a picture could be analyzed for hours, and then, compared to existing photos with other agencies using facial recognition, like Interpol.

"*Mamka Mu*" the killer swore under his breath. He'd been linked to the boater's death.

He scanned the lot one last time before pulling out of the spot and roaring down the ramp onto Interstate-Seventy-Six, heading west.

The Bumper needed time to think. Perhaps it was time to contact The Client.

Chapter Thirty-Five

After the lunch tray was removed, The Client opened the laptop and signed into 'Hearts Elite.' They scrolled through the recent searches and found his name.

Oliver Goodman.

The name, Oliver, was troublesome because of the 'O.' Too much of a coincidence that a man with that initial should open an account this close to October. It was possible, but the name seemed so…fake.

The trembling fingers hovered over the keys, as indecisive as the mind. If it was someone to be feared, they should know. It may very well change the strategy for the last months. If it was just a coincidence, then no harm was done. To Oliver, anyway.

A right-click of the keypad allowed a copy of the account's link, which then opened a second window to search for the origin. The Client coded an outdated but accessible password and slipped beyond a firewall into the global department's database. From there, they entered the name of Oliver Goodman and uploaded the photo. They checked the wall clock, accounted for the time difference, and waited.

With any luck…

The status bar flew across the screen as it neared the end of its search.

Zero contacts located.

A smile spread across the computer genius' face, feeling delighted to have been so adept at sniffing out the ruse. The Client had intentionally kept the parameters tight to ensure as exact a match as possible. The fact the IRS had no record of such a man in New York confirmed their suspicions.

Oliver Goodman did not exist. At least, not as Oliver Goodman.

The Client typed a complex code to access the TOR browser and entered the dark web, being no stranger to the workings of the internet. Their fingers, so jittery when dormant, now danced across the keys with purpose. The picture of the pursuer was uploaded, and The Client set off on another search to locate the credit card used to open the account.

When The Client had devised the scheme so many months ago, they had already stumbled upon the abomination known as 'Hearts Elite.'

The All-Rich-Male-Entitled-Club.

It made their blood boil. The Client took less than a couple of days of light hacking to mirror the infrastructure of the site and access the personal information of the members. It was then so easy to hunt for victims without ever appearing on the site. If someone had discovered the trail, they'd be looking out front. No one would look back here.

The credit card from the anonymous Oliver Goodman was a standard Visa card, which was another red flag. So many of the profilers had black cards. Such status.

The Client copy and pasted the information and dropped it into another search engine. With both databases on the hunt, the searcher lay back and rested their eyes.

Memories flooded back from when The Client was a pioneer of the tech industry so many years ago. Their father had been an engineer by day and a tinkerer by night. Radios, televisions, and the earliest computers fascinated him, as well as his ever-attentive child. It didn't take long for the budding genius to become interested in the information side of computing, and learned the language of coding.

From there, it was the wild west of the industry. A new frontier had opened before their very eyes. The Client had been there at the forefront, working for Apple in the early days, before being shoved out in their search for younger men, eager to prove themselves. They moved on to code for many of the start-ups that made their twenty-something CEO's billionaires while they were being ignored, passed over, or downsized.

Younger men with no vision were trained by The Client, then became the bosses. Co-workers received patents. Friends became strangers. Everyone became enemies.

Within a decade of the computer boom, this bright, dedicated visionary was a footnote in the forgotten tsunami of nameless faces who had shaped the new computerized world.

No fame. No glory. No wealth.

Not so much as a thank you.

The Client had sat in the room when the concept of 'transferring digital music' had been introduced and discussed. They had taken part in the coding to develop what became 'jpeg imagery.'

It was child's play to refine search engines, pattern algorithms and they distinctly remember the day someone uttered the phrase 'browser.'

It sounded all so quaint now, but years ago, it had been revolutionary.

Until it was all taken away.

Academia replaced passion in the technology sector. Degrees from prestigious schools outranked imagination, experience, and loyalty.

Nineteen-hour days were a badge of honor and weekends were for slackers. Like the machines they were creating, the human overlords ate them up and spit them out. No room for emotion; there was too much money at stake.

Start-up tech companies dotted the landscape, and the larger beasts swallowed the smaller ones in billion-dollar lunch deals. A handshake, a faxed copy, and BAM! You were now a zillionaire, just eighteen months out of college.

Not The Client. The always single, hard-working computer expert deemed well past their 'sell-by' date, and everyone else in the same boat, was sent out to pasture.

Even now, the fire roared in their stomach as the world watched the growth of the entitled young men who suffered nothing on their easy climb through the ranks. The Client detested the trust-fund babies, the tech barons, and the banking elite who received bailouts when their unsavory schemes cost hard-working, honest people their homes and their nest eggs.

The Client shook as if in response to an unheard voice. It was never good to dwell on too much now. Water under the bridge and all.

The telltale "ping" brought The Client back to present concerns, alerting them the search of the credit card information from the Hearts Elite account in the name of Oliver Goodman had found a match.

It listed an address in Boston, Massachusetts, but not in the name of an "Oliver Goodman."

The murderous Client, whispered, "Hello, Robert Hannah. It sure will be nice to meet you."

Chapter Thirty-Six

Steven Karron pedalled hard up Coral Ridge Avenue, which bordered the University of Iowa in Oakdale, a suburb of Iowa City. He loved the fall more than any other time of the year. The University of Iowa Hawkeyes football team dominated the sports pages, and cycling season slowly wound down from a busy summer race schedule.

He had travelled a lot this past summer to make up for lost time. As a fit, thirty-seven-year-old former college athlete, he knew that time was fleeting. It wouldn't be long before the pounds wouldn't just 'fall off' in the spring. He had to watch his weight and the calories.

Karron zipped around onto Oakdale Boulevard and coasted into the University of Iowa Driving Safety Institute parking lot. He hopped off his TCR bike and rolled it into the back storage room before unclipping his helmet and removing his backpack.

The bike came first, then everything else.

The Driving Safety Institute was an innovative facility that studied factors that contributed to driver safety, or the lack thereof. A growing interest in automated cars had made centers such as this critical in their modelling of self-driving automobile integration with all vehicles. Their simulation lab was popular with youth, and their outreach efforts through SAFER-SIMS made for an in-demand program.

Karron walked to his office and dropped his backpack on the side sofa. As a research scientist and Director of Drugged Driving Research, road safety was his life. He was obsessed with traffic patterns, innovative highway design and all discussions that lessened the reliance on automobiles in the private sector. Sure, he owned a nice Mercedes AMG CLA35 4MATIC Coupe, but he loved his racing bike.

A junior researcher popped his head in. "Good weekend, Steven?"

"Yes, sir. Living the bachelor's life. You?"

"Yeah, not bad. Did you bike in this morning?"

"I did, but probably not much more. I'm not competing again until the spring and there's too much farm equipment on the back roads for my liking." Steven said.

"Yup, safety first," the staffer said, slapping the door jamb. "Talk fantasy football later?"

"Sounds good. Save me a spot at the table."

The Bumper fidgeted in his motel room, occasionally checking the parking lot through the closed drapes. It was an odd feeling being pursued. He was no stranger to the scrutiny of law enforcements. No thug ever was. But he was a stranger in America, where technology was everywhere.

One laptop in Erie, Pennsylvania might have given him away.

He'd been in Iowa City for three weeks studying his prey, a bike racing enthusiast, but had a hard time concentrating on the task at hand. It was difficult to be creative when survival seemed more important.

Now, he feared failure. He was running out of time, though the means were obvious.

If the victim continued his routine, opportunities abounded.

But it was Monday, September twenty-fifth.

Steven Karron should be dead by now.

The older gentleman who walked the campus of the University of Iowa was a stranger to the grounds. He did, however, have the knack of blending. His non-descript features and calm demeanour made him practically invisible in a distracted world. While everyone stared at their devices on buses, in parks and across tables in coffee shops, he watched. He could follow a mark for blocks without detection. It was his evasive experience; the rest being the oblivious nature of today's society.

Cyber crimes and theft identity stole the headlines from the more mundane mugging and purse snatching.

Oh, for the good old days.

The Witness reported back to The Client on The Bumper's mental state, which seemed to lack confidence. He'd been holed up in his motel more this month since the report of his presence in the USA. It was natural, of course, but little cause for alarm.

He was in Iowa City, for God's sake.

The Client replied with gratitude on his surveillance and expressed patience in the interim. It would be handled.

He walked past the University of Iowa Driving Safety Institute, stealing a glance at the grey building.

It was Monday, September twenty-fifth. Shouldn't Steven Karron be dead by now?

Chapter Thirty-Seven

Hannah left the FBI offices in the late afternoon on Monday, September twenty-fifth. There had been no news of any unusual deaths, particularly of affluent men, in the four cities they were monitoring. While they believed his first initial would be 'S,' the range of names was too vast.

Agents Dennison and Farron had scoped Annapolis, Maryland, for a week, earning the cooperation of the locals. They moved on to Ithaca, New York and spent time with detectives, building the profile of what might lurk in their city.

They came back to Boston on Friday, waiting to see if this was the month they got him. Hannah spent the weekend surfing news sites in the other two likely centers. Independence, Missouri and Iowa City, Iowa. With Kansas City, Missouri already having been chosen, Hannah was slowly convinced that Iowa City made the most likely target.

He was sure it had to be an 'I'. but if the phrase was *KILL THE RICH*, why were there only eleven letters?

The agents spent Monday morning coordinating leads and working on a possible October victim. Agent Downey had 'Hearts Elite'

COO Elaine Stafford on speed dial. She agreed to provide the profile names and addresses for all members with the first letter 'O' in cities that started with 'C', which was troublesome. Cleveland, Cincinnati, and Chicago combined for a population of three million, four-hundred thousand people. The geography alone would make it almost impossible. It had been a long and fruitless day.

As Hannah walked into his condo, he received an unusual ping on his cell phone. Shedding his jacket, he cracked a beer and flopped on the couch.

Hannah had received a contact on his 'Hearts Elite' account. He stared at the start page and looked for the icon, signalling the message. He flipped through his preferences and noted that all notifications, and their sounds and icons, were active, yet he couldn't find the message.

Hannah thumbed through the screen until he found a 'chat' feature he'd overlooked. He expected that the notification would be more like an email or a formal text.

As he slid the feature open, his eye locked on the message.

"Hello Mr. Puzzler," was all it said.

His hands shook as he took a screen shot and texted it to Downey. It took less than two minutes for his answer.

"Don't reply to it."

Seconds later, Hannah's cell rang.

"Did you get my text?" Downey asked before Hannah even checked the screen.

"I did, and I have done nothing. Is it The Client?" Hannah asked in return.

"We can't take the chance if it is. It could be an opening volley from a random interest, but this seems too pointed toward the puzzle aspect to be a coincidence." Downey replied. "When was it sent?"

Hannah held his thumb on the message and the imprint *'eight minutes ago'* appeared. "Less than ten minutes ago." Hannah said.

"Are you back at your condo? I'm still at the office. Can you meet us somewhere within twenty minutes?"

"Sure, who's 'us?'"

"Simms and Perez will be with me. They will want in on this."

Drinks arrived at the back table of the Silver Badge Pub while all four stared at Hannah's cellphone, strategically positioned in the middle of the table, untouched as if radioactive. "I have to reply soon. If it is The Client, we don't want him to be completely sure that I'm *not* Oliver Goodman. Why would I wait to say hello?" Hannah asked.

"Well, we didn't come out here to just stare at it," Agent Downey agreed. He looked at Simms and Perez. "Flirty? Serious? Non-committal? What do you two think?"

Agent Simms offered, "Casually, but follow-through on the puzzle. I'd say that you play along with their lead, but remember, you are kind of a jerk." Agent Perez nodded along as she sipped her margarita.

"Okay," Hannah said as he scooped his phone up and thumbed a reply. He made a few corrections before flipping it around for their approval.

"Hello Miss Puzzle Piece. What do you need solved today?"

All three stared and slowly nodded. "I like it," Downey said. "Send it."

Hannah slid his thumb over the text and placed his phone back in the middle of the table, as if someone else could now have a turn. He sat back and took a pull off the beer bottle.

"Sympathetic tone," Agent Perez said. "By calling her just a 'puzzle piece,' you are minimizing her. That you believe you can be her solution makes you arrogant. An excellent start. The Client will be fooled into believing that you are who you say you are. Unless it really is an attractive gold digger, then you can forget it."

"Believe me," Hannah said, "I'm good either way."

The ping surprised them. Hannah gingerly pulled the phone back and slid the screen open.

"Just one question, Oliver. Are you really a Good Man?"

Hannah blurted, "Am I busted, or is she flirting?"

Agent Downey pulled the phone from Hannah's hand. "The capital letters on G and M seem like he's mocking the name. I think you're busted. Perez?"

She shrugged. "It sounds like something I would ask. Could be legit."

Agent Simms gave her a look.

"What do I reply? I can't stop now." Hannah said.

They lapsed into silence when Agent Simms offered, "Answer a question with a question. Here." He picked up Hannah's cell, flew through a text, and held it out for them to read.

"Are you looking for a Good Man?"

"Excellent. Send it," Downey said, while Perez gave a throaty chuckle.

Hannah was amazed they weren't even hiding it anymore. "Something you want to share with the class, Perez?" he asked.

"Oh no," she answered in a singsong. "I don't share."

The cellphone pinged its reply. Hannah asked, "Who's up? Who gets this one?"

Agent Downey grabbed the cell and thumbed open the message. He held the phone still and slowly raised his eyes. "I think we've got ourselves a live one," he said, slowly rotating the phone.

Hannah was sitting too far back in his chair to get a clear look at the reply, but the reactions of Simms and Perez told him it wasn't good.

He sat forward and took the phone from Downey. The strained look on his friend's face should have prepared him for the shock of the reply.

"I'm not looking for anyone, Robert. But I know you are."

"I should have replied," Hannah insisted the next morning around the boardroom table.

"No way," Downey said. "The Client took one look at your fake account and dug enough to find your true identity. And he isn't even hiding it. This guy is confident, resourceful, and clearly ruthless. You don't answer that."

Captain Lockwood turned in his chair to look at Hannah. "You seem to have made quite an impression."

"Not a good one, sir."

"I don't know, Hannah. I'm not one to run from a fight, and this character clearly wants to size you up. If he wasn't worried about your abilities, he wouldn't have reached out. He'd have ignored you. No, I'm with Robert. I'd keep the lines of communication open. Monitored, but open."

"How would you have us reply, sir?" Agent Simms asked.

"Well, let's hear from Agent Watson from Quantico before we craft our next romantic arrow, but if you are just asking me? I know I only have so much time before the end of the year, so I'd drop the bullshit. He knows your name, ask him his. Be bold. Make him uneasy. This guy isn't going anywhere. He'll play along." Lockwood said.

On cue, the console phone buzzed as Agent Watson appeared on the screen.

Without preamble, he said, "We've got our people on the search, but it appears to be a dead-end female account and a proxy server. It just keeps looping us back to the beginning. It certainly helps that the dating website is cooperative, but this guy is a pro."

"Agent Watson, we were just discussing next moves. Whether we should continue to engage, or cut," Captain Lockwood said.

"Captain, I'm uncomfortable putting Mr. Hannah in harm's way, but it was his original profile that piqued The Client's interest. I doubt, though, that any reply would even be received. The account is now dormant, and corrupted," Watson replied.

The room fell silent until Agent Simms said, "It's in our best interest to maintain contact. Time is running out. Today is September twenty-sixth, so the killer may strike today. If we are right, we only have a few months left. There is an easy way to keep him intrigued, even if we can't find him."

"How is that?" Asked Agent Downey.

Hannah answered for Simms. "Constantly update my profile. Suspend all pretense of romance or attracting a woman. Go 'all in' on luring The Client. It will be irresistible to him. Even if he doesn't reply right away, he will continually come back if he knows there are new messages. He'll eventually get in touch again through a new account."

"What will you say, specifically, Mr. Hannah?" Agent Watson asked through the screen.

"I can do it right now. Give me a second to plan it, then let's discuss whether I send it."

Hannah's thumbs flew over the keyboard. He paused before finishing the text, hoping to strike the right tone.

"Okay, this is what I wrote. '*Here's the location that hits the mark. What kind of bird cannot see in the dark?*'"

Agent Watson frowned and said, "I don't understand. I thought we were going to dispel with all pretense and go after this guy. Why talk in riddles?"

Captain Lockwood answered, "Because it was the puzzle aspect that drew him to Robert. We are speaking The Client's language."

"Thank you, Captain," Hannah said. "I am baiting him to reply to my challenge. I believe I know where The Bumper is right now and where he will strike."

"Where birds can't see in the dark?" Watson asked.

"Yes, the answer is a Hawk Eye. I believe The Bumper has to be in Iowa City. The University of Iowa Hawkeyes is in the city's heart. If I'm wrong, he will taunt me with my mistake, but we need to try something. I'm convinced it is Iowa City."

"Quantico okay with that, Agent Watson?" Captain Lockwood asked, "because I like it. I think you should update the profile with that and see what happens. We might still catch this guy before he kills again."

Agent Watson silently chewed his cheek for a three count. "Do it."

Hannah swiped his profile update tab and checked to make sure it was active. His heart raced as he looked at the riddle on the screen.

His mind cast back to Laurel's warning that night at the Downey house, one he couldn't have imagined would come to pass. "If you put my family in danger…" He looked over at Downey, who sat passively, waiting for a reply that was not expected.

"We'll have to assume," Hannah said, "that if The Client can find out so much about me through a dummy account, he can find my connection to Agent Downey and everyone in this room." He stared at Downey. "And our families. We need to be very diligent from here on in."

Hannah watched the comprehension spread across his friend's face. He meant what he had said back in May in Curt and Laurel's kitchen, and he meant it now. Hannah would be the one waving the red cape in front of the bull.

He owed that to Curt, and he especially owed that to Laurel and the girls.

Hannah continued. "It's one thing to embark on a secretive murder spree with a plan no can detect and hope to pull off all twelve killings attracting no attention. It's another to be this close and suddenly be challenged. We don't know whether the plan will continue unabated, or whether my interference needs to be dealt with. But I feel safe with you in my corner. And I know I want to nail this arrogant son-of-a-bitch."

"Mr. Hannah, while I commend your courage and dedication to justice, we have people who have been trained for situations like this," Agent Watson reminded him through the video screen.

Hannah answered, "But he doesn't *respect* you. You are too closely associated with the men he hunts. Also, he has had ample time to taunt you with emails or blog posts. Even old-school 'Jack the Ripper' style letters to newspapers. Nothing. If he wanted the FBI involved embarrassing them, he'd have started that back in January. No, he'll take up the challenge now, but it's with me, not the police."

Hannah wasn't surprised it was Agent Perez who asked the insightful question. "So, why you then? If he has learned all he needs to know, he saw you went to Harvard, you live in a nice condo, drive an expensive car, and already worked yourself through a first marriage. You have more in common with the victims than anyone else in this room."

Hannah gave her a proud grin. "Great question. It's because my affluence led to my downfall. I'm tarnished goods. I'm no threat. Look at me. I'm yesterday's garbage. I am the poster child of what The Client has been creating. A world where the young elite are toppled by their own greed and arrogance."

"Yeah, but you are more than that," Agent Simms replied. "This guy shouldn't underestimate your abilities."

Hannah said, "Oh, but I am sure he found out I play poker. So, this guy knows all he needs to know. I am exactly what Agent Downey saw that morning back in late April when he brought me the first puzzle. A hungover, poker-playing hustler who cared about nothing beyond my self-interest. That is what The Client is counting on. It's my chance now to prove him wrong."

"We don't put civilians in harm's way," Agent Watson recited. "But I'm glad you're in the room."

The sound of Hannah's phone was so unexpected that everyone froze. He slid it over and opened the 'Heart's Elite' app.

There was a notification. Hannah swallowed and caught Downey's eye, who nodded. He pushed the notification and opened the chat box below. Hannah quietly read the contents, scanning the words as he went along.

"The Client?" Captain Lockwood asked.

Robert nodded as he slid it across to Agent Downey, who read the message aloud.

"*Bravo. But now a riddle for you! What do delayed trains, slow ambulances, and curfew breakers all have in common?*"

Agent Watson pursed his lips while Agent Simms began scribbling. Captain Lockwood asked, "Can you read it again, slower?"

Downey said, "*What do delayed trains...slow ambulances, and curfew breakers...all have in common?*"

Hannah arrived at the sickening answer as Agent Perez broke the silence in a choked whisper.

"They are all too late."

It was Agent Dennison who called Curt Downey just before ten p.m. It was almost nine o'clock in Iowa.

The bloody, broken body of a biker had been found on the outskirts of Iowa City, seemingly the victim of an unfortunate accident. There was no sign of foul play, no skid marks to indicate the man had swerved to avoid an accident, and nothing to show anything other than an unfortunate spill that had caused catastrophic damage to his head and neck, despite wearing a helmet.

Broken necks were something you just couldn't prevent and rarely survive.

His body had been discovered by a late evening jogger. The victim had flown so far, he may not have been found until morning. A dented bike lay almost twenty feet from the corpse. The Good Samaritan told authorities that he had known enough CPR to check for a pulse, but the flashlight on his phone illuminated the full damage. "There was so much blood," he told them.

Steven Karron, ironically a driver safety researcher, was thirty-seven.

Chapter Thirty-Eight

"Steven Karron was alive when he sent that message, the son-of-a-bitch." Hannah shouted. "It wasn't too late!"

"Yes, it was," Agent Perez fired back. "There was no way for us to mobilize the manpower to scour the city, and it would have been impossible to have alerted any of the potential victims. It was, literally, too late."

"It's not on you, Pally," Agent Downey said, trying to soften the blow. "This is what it feels like when the bad guys win another round. But you just have to keep your head in the game. We're on to October. A victim's name that starts with 'O', and the city that starts with 'C'? Are we going with RICH for the last word?"

"Yeah, but that only allows us eleven letters. That throws the symmetry off." Hannah said.

He caught Agent Simms's eye, who nodded when Hannah had said the word "symmetry." "What?" He asked.

Agent Simms sat straighter. "I have a thought on that angle. I believe the full phrase is KILL THE RICH, and that the spree should run eleven months. What I think will happen is that the killer will be double-crossed and eliminated in December."

Hannah chewed that over for a few seconds. "So, the killer believes it was twelve months, was probably *told* it would be twelve months, but doesn't realize that he is the last victim?"

"Precisely. I've been mulling that over for a few weeks," Simms continued. "This Betes guy must be getting paid after each murder to keep him engaged. But when I saw how The Client so easily hacked into your life from a simple dating profile, I realized it would be nothing to kill The Bumper and take the money back from his bank account."

"Who does The Client hire to kill The Bumper?" Hannah asked.

"Probably The Client himself. And it will look like an accident." Simms replied.

Hannah nodded. "Eleven months. So smart. It's the famous Four Goats Prank. University seniors released three goats into a faculty building before graduation, and numbered them one, two, and four. The professors were so pre-occupied spending the entire day looking for the phantom goat number three that they never stopped to think about the full nature of the prank."

Agent Downey said, "Plus, the killer will be on the homestretch and eager to finish the job, that he might very well miss the signs. He could get sloppy."

"But that means there are only two more victims to go, and all we have is a grainy laptop photo and a brilliant Client capable of hacking on a whim." Agent Perez said. She turned to Hannah. "Can you get a profile change to help us narrow down our October search?"

"That's the plan," Agent Downey said. "We'll need some ideas right now. October first is Sunday."

"It can't be confrontational, and it shouldn't be congratulatory either." Agent Simms suggested. "But it better be engaging. Raise the stakes."

They batted around a few ideas, including riddles and rhyming couplets. Hannah thought of what Simms had suggested. Raise the stakes.

"I think it's time to see how adept at puzzles this guy really is. I'm going to send him a cryptic crossword message. Let's see how he handles it."

Hannah grabbed a pen and a tablet of paper and started scribbling phrases and lines until he was satisfied.

"What we need is a tip-off to the location or the victim. It would be best if he gives it away without knowing. So, I'll send him this clue."

Hannah tilted up the writing pad for everyone to see what he'd scribbled down.

One could leave this city after such style (seven)

"Pally, what the hell does that mean?" Agent Downey asked. "Are you making shit up?"

"No, the answer is solved by following the words. The number in the bracket tells you how many letters are in the answer. 'One could leave' means what?" Hannah asked.

"Depart?" Agent Perez tried.

Hannah shook his head. "No, simpler."

"Go?" Simms asked.

"Yes!" Hannah exclaimed. "The second part, 'after such style.' What is another word for style? Again, we're looking for a clue about the killings, notably the city."

Agent Simms brightened up. "Oh, 'chic' is the word for style. So, the answer 'One could leave' is GO...and it follows *after such style,* which is CHIC. The middle *this city* is the crux. It's seven letters, so the answer is CHICAGO."

"Exactly," Hannah said. "Since The Client was forthright in admitting Iowa City, even though it is torture to know we were so close, perhaps his ego will give him away here and he will tip his hand."

"What if he doesn't solve it?" Agent Downey asked.

"Then we'll try something else later." Hannah said. "But can I post this?"

Agent Downey looked around the room. He shrugged. "Worth a try."

The Bumper battled the morning traffic. He had no one to blame but himself, having waited so long to kill Mr. September. He should have taken care of him sooner. The all-night drive was punishment enough for his lack of speed. This traffic jam just made everything worse.

With nothing but time, the killer stitched and separated the threads of his ever-growing concerns. His picture was being made available to law-enforcement departments across the country, yet he could get in and out of Iowa City without detainment. Was The Client intentionally choosing these cities to avoid larger police forces?

'No,' he thought. '*Kansas City and Indianapolis were large urban centers, and look where I am this morning!*'

And then there was the witness.

Yes, The Witness. The invisible tail reporting his successes back to The Client. He was sure now that they were two separate people. Following killers while remaining invisible was an art form, needing strong nerves and chameleon-like instincts. Not once in the nine months he'd been in the United States could The Bumper swear he'd spotted the third member of the team. What he couldn't decide was whether this witness was a friend or foe? Was he simply along for the ride as verification, or was he an expensive one-man mop up crew in the event something backfired? Could the killer count on The Witness for help, or was he the ultimate safety net protecting The Client?

The Client clearly was the brains behind the operation. With top-level computer skills, it seemed ridiculous that he would get his hands dirty in the field. This, more than any other revelation, convinced The Bumper that they were a trio on a collision course towards New Year's Day. The killer nodded to himself in the car's rear-view mirror.

"They don't know that I know what they are up to," he said.

The Bumper silently congratulated himself on his brains. They couldn't put one over on him.

Before traffic thinned, he stole a peek at the dossier on the passenger seat to check the address. His exit was coming up. He caught sight of the name Owen Ratchford.

"Mr. October is Owen Ratchford." He sang to himself. "Owen is October. That's funny," he said, wondering if the first initial was just a coincidence.

Chapter Thirty-Nine

The Client woke early again. The pain wasn't debilitating yet, but it was severe enough to interfere with so many basic human functions, such as sleep. They spied the digital clock on the nightstand. The sun wouldn't be up for another hour, but the investigators would already be chasing their tails on the east coast.

The Client sat up, remembering it was October first.

Three more deaths to go, then there will be peace.

The instigator of The Game closed their eyes and tried to drift off before the demons stoked the fires of rage. The long, unabated hatred of those who denied them all that they had so diligently worked for only to end up like this.

A shadow crept across the bedroom floor. Sleep would have to wait. The sun was calling, and there was so much to do.

Chapter Forty

The Bumper stared at the passing throng below his hotel window. The Witness could be any of the thousands who filtered past and he wouldn't be aware of it. But he knew he was out there.

He was now sure of it.

Owen was October. He cursed himself for missing the obvious factor in his recruitment. He was poor at English.

The Bumper had believed his hype and was pleased The Client had selected only the best assassin for such a tough assignment. It never occurred to him to look beyond the dossiers and find a pattern. He went back over his past victims, and by May, it was painfully obvious he was being played. They all had names that started with the months they were killed.

What made it worse, is that The Client intentionally hired someone who could not put that together. The pattern.

The Bumper knew enough that patterns can be detected. Patterns can be expected. Patterns can get you captured if you aren't careful.

Patterns can get you killed.

The photo from Erie, Pennsylvania. Of course, someone had already detected the link between the victims and the names. But how? They had known enough to look for a man named Justin in July!

As he stared longer out the window at the sheer mass of humanity, he realized the folly of his logic. There must be thousands of men named Justin in America. There were probably fifty of them right now on the street.

His stomach turned to acid as he conceived another possibility. Was there another pattern? He thought back to January. No, Kansas City and January have different first letters. Maybe he was getting paranoid. Indianapolis, then that city in Michigan. His mind had trouble keeping the order straight, so he returned to the dossiers. When was Richmond? Was that last month? No, that was the month before.

He pulled out a sheet of hotel paper with the free pen and wrote out the cities with the first names of the victims to confirm his suspicions about the names. Yes, the first names and the months had the same first letters. That was clever, but again for him, very dangerous. The Client had sent him out, convincing him it was all random. No, it had been set up from the beginning. The killer should have asked more details about the twelve victims, but he was clearly so transfixed by the money and what Americans would call the "audacity" of the undertaking, that he charged ahead without thinking about any potential traps until it was too late.

His eye found Erie on the list, the city where he'd been spotted. How could anyone have known to search there?

It was followed by Richmond. He read the cities back. Hartford, Toledo, Louisville, Lansing, Indianapolis, Kansas City. He read them forward, looking for the pattern. It wasn't until he arrived at Erie again that something registered.

The hired assassin knew enough English that the word "the" was very common. Toledo, Hartford, and Erie, when read down the page, spelled out the word 'the'. Was *that* a, what do you call it? A coincidence? He knew it wasn't when he read down the first four cities and spelled out KILL.

The Bulgarian sat back, both enraged and terrified. He filled out the last two cities and mouthed the phrase KILL THE RI. What was the rest? He again hated that his lack of English was a factor in his being hired.

The Bumper rushed to the window and worked October's city into the phrase. It could fit, he guessed, but wasn't fluent enough to know what letters might follow to complete the twelve-letter phrase.

Then, like a flash, he saw him. The Witness. Both on the street and in his mind.

He wasn't simply there to ensure the job was done. His mission was to ensure The Bumper never figured out the pattern. Never questioned his orders.

"His job is to make sure the stupid Bulgarian did what he was paid to do, and never stopped to think about why," he said aloud.

He stared at the older gentleman who stood on the sidewalk, allowing the crowd to pass him by. Not close enough to the shelter to be waiting for the bus, but not so far away that he appeared threatening. Just an older guy with nothing to do but stand and stare up at a hotel.

The Bumper closed his eyes, spinning the card rack of memories, looking for his face. Where had he seen him? He must have, or it would not have registered so clearly just now.

Toledo. Yes! He'd been driving the car that passed him while he waited for poor Mitchell to succumb to the bee stings. What about before that? Oh. Lansing. The man he'd mistaken as the condo doorman simply because he'd held the door open for him on his way out. All it had taken for the disguise was a nice jacket and matching cap. The Bumper missed it.

And, of course. Iowa City. Just a few nights ago. The convenient night jogger who 'discovered' Steven Karron's body, giving details that allowed The Bumper to slip away, free of suspicion.

What a fool he'd been. The third member of the trio had been with him all along.

He opened his eyes, ready to confront the shadow.

The man was gone.

Chapter Forty-One

The Client finished breakfast, such as it was. A bit of fruit with some toast would hold them over until lunch. Appetite was the least of their concerns.

The computer genius slid the tray over the bed and opened the laptop. Within seconds, they were free again, pulling the entire world into their room. The Client opened one of the many 'Hearts Elite' backdoor holes and found the updated profile of Robert Hannah in Boston.

Oh my. He was persistent.

They clicked it open, stunned at what they saw. It was a cryptic crossword clue.

A broad grin broke over The Client's face, the first in years. "*I haven't done one of these in forever,*" they thought. It took less than a minute to solve the phrase, but they still gave this Robert fellow begrudging credit. It was a bold attempt.

Had he earned a reply? Stringing along Robert Hannah wasn't part of the plan, and The Client was so close to the end that any deviation could have *unforeseen* consequences.

Those were the worst kind.

They wavered between not wanting to appear rude (which was ridiculous) and not wanting to waste time on such a meaningless distraction. No matter what this Hannah had found, he was in no position to be of any threat to the project. They had planned for so long and come so far.

What could the harm be? "This man was making the effort, so I could as well. But what does one say to someone who believes they are so clever?" The Client asked aloud.

They thought of another cryptic crossword device and thought it fitting. *"Not too hard, and not too revealing."*

They puzzled the language as they crafted the phrase, settling on *"Life is disappointing when you're grown (five)"*

'Disappointing' the keyword pointing to 'grown.'

An anagram of *wrong*.

The Client hit "post" and saw it settle beneath Robert Hannah's fishing expedition along the shores of Lake Michigan in Chicago.

Correct letter. Incorrect lake.

"Shit," Hannah said. "Not Chicago."

"He could be lying." Downey challenged.

"I doubt it. I wouldn't have gotten a response if I was right. He takes pleasure in my being wrong. But at least he answered. Are you sure there is no way to trace these?"

"Not only can we not trace these," Downey said, "but Stafford doesn't understand how they get there. They have no account affiliation or code stamp…or something like that."

Hannah got up and paced the boardroom, looking at the clock. It was almost lunchtime. "This asshole's also ruining my appetite."

"I'm sure he's not doing it on purpose, Pally. Just a fringe benefit."

Hannah went back over the profilers' findings, along with the analysis of Agents Perez and Simms. The Client is highly organized, extremely intelligent, and very motivated. Everything about him screams high achieving. "Why is he so angry?" Hannah asked rhetorically. "Other than he sleeps late."

Downey looked up. "You think he's a night owl?"

"No, I sent the clue over three hours ago, and he finally got around…"

He paused. He looked at the clock and back at the profile page.

"What?" Downey asked.

Hannah waved him off as he flipped through his earlier notes. "Of course. OF COURSE!"

Downey spread his hands. "What? What is it?"

Hannah slapped his hands on the boardroom table in disgust. "How many times am I going to miss clues right in front of my face?"

"Specifically, which clues, Pally, because I'm clearly missing them too."

"The time, for one. We got the first contact from The Client at the end of business day, then worked into the evening at the pub. Then today, we don't hear from him until lunchtime! Why do I keep missing the obvious?"

Agent Downey leaned over and grabbed his wrist. "Tell me…now…what you found."

Hannah puffed his cheeks. "The Client lives on the West Coast. He doesn't have a sleeping problem. He's three time zones away across the entire country."

Downey leaned back, tapping the table. Hannah kept going.

"In fact, that is why all the murders happen east of the Mississippi when possible. It stays far away from him. Kansas City is the only glaring exception, but it was the first. At that point, there was no pattern. No reason to look for him."

"And The Client is a computer whiz. Silicon Valley, California." Downey said.

Hannah shook his head. "It's the *ABC Murders* all over again. Hide the obvious in an obscure pattern so you miss the actual trail. "

Downey got up and moved to the whiteboard. "So, how many patterns do we have? Initials match the months, and the cities spell a phrase. The Client is nowhere near the crimes. What else?"

Hannah bit his lip. He stared at the cities and names. "I don't know."

"Could there be another?"

"Sure, there could be," Hannah said, "but there has to be a limit on how complicated you want to make it. I mean, the killer still has to execute the plan."

Downey tapped Bêtes' picture. "Bulgarian killer, not American. Bulgarian. Hired on the dark web. Why?"

"His methods. He's known for clean murders and quick getaways." Hannah said.

The boardroom glass door swung open. Agent Perez stuck her head in. "I heard shouting. Anything new?"

"Get Simms and come in. The Client is West Coast. Probably Silicon Valley."

Perez disappeared around the corner while Hannah asked, "Do you think the killer's limited literacy in English is a factor?"

Downey answered, "I think his lack of experience with America, geography, and the English language all combine to make his selection optimal. Do you know how many qualified assassins there are in America who could have done these killings? More than a few. Yet, our guy goes off grid to find the best killer with the least amount of American experience."

"So how come he hasn't slipped up yet? How come we haven't caught him?"

Agent Simms walked in as Hannah was finishing his question. "Perez mentioned the West Coast?"

Downey and Hannah filled him in on their theories, while Perez returned with her laptop and folders. "This is making more and more sense. The distance, the expertise, the puzzles. All designed to distract us from the real underlying theme of the murders," she said.

"Which is?" Downey asked.

"Revenge. In fact, I've been spending a lot of time with the profilers and their work, and I think we've missed a crucial element. It would be an anomaly, but that's what makes it significant to me," Perez said.

Hannah looked at her. She was laser focussed. "What have they found?"

"The victimology pattern is indisputable. All young, single, rich men. All chosen from an elite dating site where they are the coveted choice. It smacks of elitism. It plays right into the ongoing climate of 'Eat the Rich' and 'Occupy Wall Street'. They are disposed of in ways indicative of their lifestyle. The profilers centered in on that. Signals given on their profile page or photos tip off The Client as to their prized identity. They feel completely untouchable. The Client uses that as the opportunity to get the killer close."

"Excellent, but that's nothing we haven't already guessed. What else?" Hannah asked.

"The choice of assassin. A Bulgarian with no ties to the States. Why? An assassin with no ties to the victims. Why? Word puzzles with a pattern spelled out to no one. Why?"

Agent Perez held the attention of the room. Hannah hoped she had an answer.

"Why go to all that trouble, taking no opportunity to take credit? We believe there can only be one reason."

Hannah looked at Downey, who seemed equally transfixed.

Perez said, "The profilers work with the belief that killers are not born, they are created. Something flipped a switch in The Client. Something so profound that they would create a scheme so elaborate. The profilers wonder if The Client experienced the death of a loved one at the hands of a rich professional. Someone they now blame for their death."

After a heartbeat of silence, Hannah asked, "How did you figure that?"

Agent Perez continued, "Because now everything is about distance. A far-off assassin. If you are right about The Client living on the west coast, then the murders are committed clear across the country. They are spaced a month apart. Distance, distance, distance. The Client never has to meet the victim and look them in the eye. Never have to push them out of a window or shove them off a boat. The Client has never met the assassin, so there's no possible identification. They must just email or post a link about the next victim. Weeks later, thousands of miles away, a man is dead. Then, when December is over and the pattern is complete, nothing can be tied back to them. Their hands are clean."

"So why the puzzles if not to taunt investigators?" Agent Downey asked.

"The puzzles of the initials and the cities are just fun clues for amusement. The Client is brilliant and would never dream of engaging in a scheme so outlandish in a mundane fashion. It wouldn't be enough to just kill. It has to have some flair. That is who they are."

Hannah understood. "So, just like the victims whose profiles give away a means of killing them, so these clues, or 'profile', of The Client are giving away who he is?"

Agent Perez held up a finger. "I'll return to that important point, but that is how the profilers see it. One very intelligent person with nothing to lose and a grudge to fulfill. But that isn't even the biggest part."

Robert turned. "It isn't?"

"Not by a longshot." Perez said. "There is the anomaly. The exception that proves the rule. Why The Client could work unimpeded without detection."

Perez paused for obvious effect. Hannah held his breath.

"The Client is a woman."

Chapter Forty-Two

Owen Latchford spotted the man again.

No one would have accused Latchford of being the paranoid type, but he was skeptical by nature. Any new acquaintance was only after his money.

This man, though, had yet to approach Latchford. But this is the third or fourth time he'd seen this guy around the branch. The guy was always alone, always appearing aloof, but his darting eyes always seemed to find Latchford's. It was weird.

Latchford didn't recognize him as a client, but he could be an on-line investor, trying to summon the nerve to complain about the dip in the stock market.

'If you can't take the drop, don't get on the ride,' he often advised.

Still, he could simply confront the man and ask what he wanted. But there was something off-putting about him. A man to be left alone.

Latchford locked his filing cabinet and spun the blinds in his corner office, leaving just a few minutes before the investment offices closed. He stepped into the carpeted hallway and glanced toward the front door.

The man was gone.

Owen Latchford, the most successful of the investors in the branch, and a rising star in the Cleveland business community, walked down the back stairway to the staff parking lot, and pushing the crash door open, strolled the few steps to his new black Cadillac V-Series Blackwing.

When you were the king of the money hill, they gave you the best parking spot. Might as well have the right car.

The investment banker fired up the engine and inhaled the fresh smell, as intoxicating as a narcotic. Money was Latchford's drug of choice.

He backed out of his spot and wheeled to the edge of the sidewalk before turning right and gunning into traffic.

As he did, his eyes darted to the rearview mirror. As he had flown out of the lot, he could have sworn he was being watched.

The strange man in the branch was sitting across the street on the bus stop bench.

He was staring at the car.

Hannah sat at his kitchen table, trying to make the puzzle fit.

A woman? Could a woman be behind this? It was certainly possible, of course.

He thought of Elaine Stafford, COO of a successful, multi-million-dollar on-line venture. The internet was second nature to her. She understood technology and had the means to data-mine the membership list. But could she sit stone-faced over the remote calls and give nothing away?

Hannah wondered what it must be like providing the services to these pampered playboys looking for lovely playthings. Would she grow disillusioned? Could she grow to despise them so much that eliminating them became an obsession?

Hannah looked at the small writing pad. He had written three questions.

Who else had the means to search the database undetected?

Who else could control the flow of information regarding the clients to Curt and the task force?

And the most important question.

Who else knew the FBI was onto the scheme and recognized my fake account?

It was that last point that burrowed the suspicion deep into Hannah's psyche. Within hours of him setting up his account, it had been sniffed out. *How?*

Elaine Stafford had the means and the opportunity, but did she have a motive? Surely killing off members was a sure-fire way to torpedo the website's success. But if Perez and the profilers were correct, there was no other woman involved in the investigation who had anywhere near the information Stafford did. She knew the cities being targeted and the importance of the men's names.

He continued his search of Stafford on-line and found the normal business contact websites and the occasional speaking engagement. She had never been the subject of an unsavory article, or the defendant in any litigation.

'*She has cooperated to an extent, but we aren't really any closer.*' Hannah thought. '*Is she truly helping?*'

He checked the time and thought that eight-thirty was too late for a texting session with Downey. He fiddled with his phone as a strange *déjà vu* came over him. It was as if he'd once before been sitting at the table, holding his phone, unsure whether he should text.

Of course, he'd done it before. Many times. It was to his ex-wife, Stacey.

His mirror opposite. Where he was cerebral, she was spontaneous. When he was cautious, she was adventurous. Stacey was unbridled, but he was staid. Only now had Hannah understood how much he gave up when he let Stacey walk out the door.

So many times, he'd thought he should reach out to her, but resisted. Anger? Pride? Hannah did not know if she had the same cell number. They had had no meaningful communication in over two years. But the pull felt so strong tonight, and he was now powerless to fight it.

He thumbed her name out of the contacts list and typed, "Hey." He let it sit there like a talisman, hoping that some magical phrase would follow, but all he had were those three letters.

'Hey,'

Was that all he had? Had he always been so detached that simple communication was foreign to him?

Hannah looked back down at the screen and let honesty be the best policy.

"Hey, I was thinking of you today and wanted to see how you are."

He hit the send button before he could change his mind. Hannah dropped the phone, suddenly fearing a reply, and grabbed a beer from the refrigerator. He stood by the window waiting for the ping. After a minute, he rushed to grab the cell to make sure his volume was up when a ping sang in the palm of his hand.

He read the quick reply from his ex-wife. *"Funny, because I think of you every day."*

It stunned him. His quivering lip gave way to a silent tear that fell onto the phone's screen. *She still thinks of me?*

He bit his lip to forestall the tide threatening to pull him out to uncharted territory when Stacey sent another text.

"Still not good at replying, huh?"

Hannah's thumb hit the letters before he realized what he tapped.

'I'm here. I just don't know what to say.' He hit send. Then he added, *'Except I'm sorry.'*

Hannah felt good sending it, but also knew she was owed a better apology than a quick text in the late evening. So much wasted time. He watched the conversation bubbles pulsate along his screen as she tapped out her reply. Then they stopped before starting again.

He thought maybe she was having a hard time as well when his phone pinged.

"The apology was a pleasant touch, but nothing was as kind as 'I'm here.' That was good to read."

Hannah started a longer text, but knew it was time to act like an adult. *"Are you free for dinner sometime soon? I'd like to talk to you, if you are available."* He took a swig of beer as his phone rang. He hit the button and pushed the speakerphone key.

Stacey chuckled through a throaty sob. "Is my ex-husband asking me out?"

Chapter Forty-Three

The Bumper walked from his hotel, head spinning to glimpse The Witness. It was Saturday, October twenty-ninth. His shadow must know that it would go down tonight. Not only was the killer running out of days, but there were only so many opportunities.

He walked to the party supply store to pick up the prized piece of his Halloween costume. His choice was a formal selection, given the occasion. The killer paid for the small box with a pre-paid debit card and strolled back to the swanky hotel room, always aware of his surroundings. The Bumper preferred small highway motels off the beaten path, but proximity mattered this week.

The annual Halloween Gala to benefit the Cleveland Historical Benevolent Society was a formal costume affair that, tonight alone, would raise over two million dollars. It was held in a restored ballroom, befitting not only the soiree, but the organization itself. There would be over five hundred of Cleveland's richest benefactors.

Including Owen Latchford.

The killer had already purchased the black suit along with the silver bow tie. All he needed was the proper mask. He removed it gracefully from the packaging and placed it over his face, walking to the full-length mirror to stare at his reflection. It was perfect.

The Bumper left the mask on while he donned the formal jacket for full effect. It thrilled him to look so good. He was pleased The Client had made him aware of the circumstances of the Gala and pointed him toward the appropriate mask suggestion.

The Bulgarian wondered whether Owen Latchford would also be masked. No worry, he would have access to the seating chart.

Owen Latchford arrived at the Starlight Ballroom minutes after six o'clock. The champagne hour would run until seven o'clock, when guests would be seated according to an arrangement chart. The investment banker was making his way closer and closer to the front of the room each year, and tonight expected to be seated at a front row VIP table.

His induction to this group of Cleveland's elites was courtesy of a client who had made introductions years ago. Since then, Latchford had made financial commitments in the hundreds of thousands of dollars, as well as generous bids at the Gala auction. His enthusiasm for the organization was attracting attention, and soon, the old money followed. Latchford estimated that for every five thousand dollars he had donated to the Cleveland Historical Benevolent Society, he gained fifty thousand dollars in management fees from new clients. It was just good business.

He completed the look of his costume as he strode, alone, into the ballroom. Several heads turned, no doubt wondering who this confident man might be. Latchford smiled beneath the mask, knowing the mystery only added to his allure.

He stretched his arm to snatch a glass of champagne from a server's tray as he gracefully spun into a bow towards a group of women dressed in royal ball gowns. Their appreciative laughs and murmurs gave him a thrill. He sipped the champagne and let the bubbles dance over his tongue as he surveyed the room. Perhaps one hundred people had arrived for the opening at six o'clock, so Latchford had time to find his seat on the chart.

As he made his way to the arrangement board, he was disconcerted to find another man studying the table chart in the same costume. Latchford knew it was popular enough that he would not be the only one of his kind, but it stunned him that this gentleman looked so good. It was as if this man were the original, and Owen Latchford was the imitation.

Sensing Owen's presence, the other turned and reacted to finding his reflection standing beside him. "Don't we look like a pair?" The man asked Latchford in a veiled accent. Latchford wondered if it was a part of his mystique or his natural voice.

"Perhaps there will be mystery afoot this evening." Latchford replied, in character, with no hint of the annoyance he felt. After all, the man could be very wealthy, and in need of financial advice. Latchford decided he would do well to keep his eye on him throughout the night.

The other Phantom of The Opera turned and said to Owen Latchford. "Oh, there will be. I am sure of it."

For the next hour, Latchford mingled and schmoozed with the upper crust of society, introduced by colleagues and clients alike to their friends and associates. His choice of costume made him a dashing figure, and he was pleased to be seated at Table Number Eight beside an appellate court judge and his wife.

And their very attractive, very single daughter.

Latchford paid special attention to the judge and his wife, who were long-term patrons of the Historical Society. It was becoming obvious that the woman was eyeing Owen's interest in their daughter.

The parallels of their interest in a historical society and ensuring the underpinnings of the shared traditions through generations, were not lost on him.

Their wealth would eventually pass to their daughter. History dictated the future.

Latchford gracefully turned his attention to the young woman, who seemed bored with the stuffy ceremony. He was certain that she would much rather be anywhere else for a Halloween party than being put on display by Mom and Dad.

Latchford looked around the table of ten, seated as four couples, along with the daughter and himself. It was certainly possible that, as a single, he would be seated at a table where there were also an odd number of patrons, but he wondered if this arrangement wasn't pre-meditated by the judge's wife.

He got a smile out of the young woman that was magically transferred to her mother's beaming face. It had become so obvious. He knew there was a way to use this to his advantage tonight.

Within minutes of dessert being served, the Master of Ceremonies began a live auction of noteworthy, donated items. The first handful were experiences offered by patrons. One could bid on a week-long lakeside house retreat complete with boat usage, chef, and maid service. Others were similar packages, but in farther destinations on tropical islands in the winter. Of course, there was no actual cost involved. The wealthy donors generously surrendered their property for a week to benefit their favorite cause. In reality, they'd simply go to another of their homes for seven days.

As the bidding began on a weeklong stay at a Bahamas mansion outside Freeport, Latchford turned to the young woman. "Have you been to the Bahamas? Snorkeling is so fabulous there."

"No, I haven't been to the Bahamas. We have a condo suite in Turks and Caicos." She said.

Message delivered. *'The Bahamas is beneath me.'*

Latchford's interest grew.

"Perhaps you should try it. A different slice of paradise," he said, raising his paddle as the bidding reached nine-thousand dollars.

The young woman's eyes widened at the ease of Latchford's bid and the underlying invitation. Her mother squirmed in approval. The judge was oblivious.

He was quickly outbid as it raced beyond ten-thousand dollars. Latchford tapped his paddle in disinterest, content with taking part as the young woman tilted her head.

"Should I bid again?" Latchford asked.

The woman teasingly shrugged. "It's your money."

Latchford's shoulders returned the gesture. "Yes, that is true. And I could easily find similar accommodations for half the current bid. But why would I pay all this money to go alone?"

The judge's daughter laughed and turned away. Her mother looked like she wanted to scream.

With a casual flick of his wrist, Owen Latchford raised the bid to fifteen-thousand dollars, and a murmur of approval accompanied light applause at the gesture. The young woman smiled back, but wouldn't meet his eyes. "I sincerely hope you aren't doing this for me," she said.

"For you?" Latchford chuckled, feigning insult. "I hardly know you. No, I could always find someone to join me if my interest in helping the historical society entitles me to a week in the Bahamas at the Senator's winter home."

The judge's ears perked up and his eyes fell to the auction program. Latchford had already read it front to back and knew who had donated what.

"Are you acquainted with Senator Perkins?" The judge asked Latchford.

"I've met him professionally a handful of times," Latchford answered, as the auctioneer kept his eye on him, expecting a return volley should another paddle be raised. "The Senator trusts me to oversee his foundation. His financial holdings are managed within my portfolio. I like to support my many clients who share my spirit of philanthropy."

The judge nodded his approval, while his wife was hyperventilating.

"Going once...going twice..." the auctioneer called. Latchford casually watched the man as if he had no interest in the outcome. "Sold!" the Master of Ceremonies yelled, "to the handsome man in the Phantom's mask for fifteen-thousand dollars."

Owen acknowledged the compliment and the ensuing applause by standing, and with a slight bow, he theatrically waved his paddle like a sword. An approving roar from the patrons filled the ballroom as the young woman beside him rewarded his generosity with a sparkling smile. The judge called over a nearby server and ordered another bottle of champagne.

The judge's wife was on the verge of passing out.

Table Number Eight toasted the winning bid as the auction continued. Paddles flew around the ballroom while the dollars rolled in, spurred on by Owen Latchford's example. As the gavel struck to sell the last item, over two-hundred thousand dollars had been raised in the hour-long event. An art auction was announced in the side foyer for six historical pieces. The investment banker had little interest in that portion of the evening, and remained with the judge's daughter, who also did not leave the table. Within the hour, a dance band was scheduled to play until midnight, and Owen, who normally left by ten o'clock, suddenly was interested in staying late.

"You are under no obligation to join me in the Bahamas," Latchford stated, "but I do believe a dance wouldn't be out of the question."

She sipped her glass of champagne before responding, "I'll check my dance card, but I'm sure I can make room for you. Excuse me while I go freshen up."

As Latchford followed her hip sway to the back of the ballroom, his eye caught the stare of the man from earlier that evening. The other Phantom. There were at least a dozen others in the identical costume, but this was clearly the same man. He was locked onto Owen's face and did not look away or avoid embarrassment at being caught. Latchford raised his glass in a mock toast spanning dozens of near empty tables.

The man did likewise.

An uneasiness seeped into Latchford's confident demeanour. He waved the obsequious server over, ordered another bottle of champagne, and asked for two fresh champagne flutes. When the bottle arrived, he stood straight and slow marched to the man who remained seated, making no attempt at escape. Owen wondered if the meeting was intentional. It certainly seemed inevitable.

"Do I know you?" Owen asked, lightly, opting for curiosity over confrontation.

The man, still masked, tilted his head up, motioning for Owen to join him at the table. Latchford displayed the bottle and glasses and sat with a seat between them. He poured each a full flute and settled back in the chair.

"Congratulations on your trip," the man uttered. Owen was caught unaware. Not only had this man been interested in the coincidence of their costume, but he'd been watching him.

"Who are you?" Latchford asked, dropping all pretense. "Have you been spying on me?" He suddenly thought of the man at the branch. Could it be?

"Hardly," the man said with a gruff, cultured laugh, draining the champagne glass. "I'm an affluent man in a sea of competition. You're the real deal." The man reached for the champagne bottle and refilled his glass. "To you!" He toasted as Latchford drank his in acknowledgement.

"Can I ask you something?" The man suddenly leaned forward, as if a conspiracy was about to be hatched. "When you look around the room, what do you see?"

Latchford refilled his flute, gave a second silent toast and sipped another generous portion. "I see my future. The money in this room needs someone to look after it. To protect it. To grow it. That's where I come in. I would never have to steal money. They give it to me, and I'm paid handsomely for the privilege."

"To money!" The man re-toasted with a slur encroaching upon his guttural accent. He wavered slightly as the glass reached his lips and he downed the golden liquid as Owen chased his flute to the bottom.

The man stood with a slight shuffle. "I thank you for the bottle, my Phantom friend, but our time has drawn to a close. I must go, and your young lady awaits."

Latchford turned to see the judge's daughter had returned and was scanning the room.

"Mustn't keep your future waiting." The man turned and shuffled away.

Owen Latchford left the empty champagne bottle and stood to walk back to his table and the enchanting young woman who had released her tight hair design, letting it cascade over her shoulders. Her lips pouted with a fresh red application until she caught Latchford's approach. Her eyes widened as her mouth tensed in a line.

Owen wondered what had caused the concern as his legs fell out from under him. He grabbed at the collar of his tuxedo as the air escaped him. His heart raced as he struggled to stay alive, his lungs incapable of drawing breath. She dropped to him as he rolled onto his back, seeking help. Worried faces huddled over him as he sought the second Phantom. *What had he done to me?*

A fountain of bile escaped Mr. October's mouth as the champagne made its unwelcome return, and the choking began, only to cease as his eyes flew wide open and his heart stopped. The young woman screamed and backed away as security and medical attendees swarmed into action, but it was too late.

Owen Latchford, seeing his future in the room, had missed all the signs.

He was thirty-six.

The Bumper removed the bottle of champagne and the two flutes from the table as the man fell to his knees, all attention turned in that direction. He played his role of an attentive waiter to perfection. The Bumper calmly walked back into the kitchen and removed the medieval jester's mask all male serving staff had been ordered to wear throughout the evening, pleased that his imitation had been noticed by no one. He snatched a plastic bag, placed the bottle and flutes inside, and twirled the bag shut in his hand as he strolled out the back door into the chilly late October night. Disposing of the bottle and glasses would be easy on his way out-of-town tonight. Ensuring he was not noticed or followed was his chief priority for the time being.

The killer of Owen Latchford kept his head down until he turned the corner to his hotel, stealing a glance behind. There was no reaction to his head movement and few pedestrians in the vicinity. He continued into the hotel lobby and waited for the elevator when the thought hit him.

The walk from his hotel to the ballroom was seventeen minutes. Given the time it took him to retrieve the bottle and flutes, bag them and depart from the backdoor, it might have added another three minutes.

Owen Latchford had died a horrible public death of his own doing, twenty minutes ago.

The Bumper had yet to be paid.

Chapter Forty-Four

"Fentanyl?" Hannah asked. "It was an overdose?"

Agent Dennison relayed the information from the Cleveland police concerning the strange death at the Gala over speaker phone. "Well, it was more of a poisoning, but yes. Fentanyl. The scourge of the drug community. They found some cocaine in the glove box of his car, so they were working the toxin check at the lab with the autopsy. It doesn't look like murder."

Hannah wasn't so sure. "A rich young guy with the initial 'O' dies in Cleveland under tragic, but understandable, circumstances. He, also, just happens to have been a member of 'Hearts Elite'. Guys, this is exactly the murder we need to investigate."

Dennison said, "Yeah, I see your point, but the Cleveland Police don't understand our angle. They've got their hands full and don't have the resources to dig deep when the cause of death is apparent to them. Plus, they have a few other cases from the weekend to investigate."

"Okay Agent Dennison, thank you for everything. Work as much as you can and stay in touch," Agent Downey said, hanging up. "This case is impossible."

Agent Simms looked up from his laptop. "Latchford was no saint, but he was quite the philanthropist. He is often photographed at galas and charitable benefits where his wealthy clients turn up. Lots of pictures on-line."

Hannah asked, "So where are we, Agent Perez? The profilers think a woman is behind this, and that, what? She's a puzzle genius? How does any of this help us track her and stop the killing?"

"The profilers believe it's a woman because of the victimology. How many men kill women out of frustration? It would be the same situation, given the obvious list of victims in this case."

"The profilers believe it's a woman because the victims are men? Is that what you're saying?" Hannah asked.

"Strongly possible, but not a certainty. They believe it *could* be a woman. But as for the rest of your question, we have only weeks to stop November and prevent December." Perez answered.

Agent Downey asked Hannah, "Like putting bees in the car, do you think The Bumper put poison cocaine in Latchford's glove box and waited for him to snort? Seems passive for him."

"I agree," Hannah said. "The bees would attack within minutes, so just swapping out cocaine packets and waiting for the inevitable death snort isn't in his method. He had to know that before the Gala, the guy would fill his nose."

The center console buzzed, and Agent Downey hit the green button. "Yeah," was all he said.

"It's Dennison. We may have something."

Hours later, on Monday, October Thirty-First, Agent Dennison reported back to the boardroom in Boston.

"The body was found in an alleyway behind the hotel that sits beside the ballroom where the Gala was. It was a middle age guy in a tuxedo, dead from what now appears to be a fentanyl overdose."

"Two guys are dead following an overdose at a rich gala? The charity can't be happy with that publicity." Agent Perez said.

"And get this," Agent Dennison added. "The guy in the alley still had his costume mask on him when he dropped in the alley. It was a 'Phantom of the Opera' mask."

Hannah waited for the connection. "What does that have to do with Latchford?"

Dennison answered. "Sorry, I guess I didn't tell you before because it wasn't important. Latchford was also dressed as The Phantom of the Opera."

Hannah spun to Agent Simms, who began typing on his laptop. "The Killer had to have struck at the Gala. He didn't know which of the 'Phantoms' was Owen Latchford, so he…what? Dropped fentanyl in the food?"

"Drinks," Dennison stated. "Witnesses said that before Latchford died, he was seen sitting with another guy who was dressed alike. They were sharing a bottle of champagne."

"But how does this Bumper guy get a hold of a bottle of champagne to spike without having it go somewhere else?" Agent Perez asked.

"Because he's dressed as a server," Hannah said. "I bet he hovered around Latchford's table all night waiting for a chance to slip him something. He must have ordered the bottle, then rather than just sit and drink it, he took it with him to introduce himself to the other Phantom."

"Oh My God," Simms said. "The absolute worst example of 'wrong place, wrong time'."

Agent Dennison said, "They are having a hard time identifying the guy because he didn't have a wallet. It's possible it was taken after his death, but they are working on prints to see if he's in the system."

"But he's definitely not Bulgarian?" Agent Downey asked.

"No, he is not, and he is too old to be our guy. I'll text you the crime scene photo now for records. In the meantime, Agent Farron has been knocking down hotels within the easy distance of the club, looking for any clues where the killer has been hiding out. So far, just one lead from an upscale place downtown that had an Eastern European gentleman stay for two weeks, but disappeared overnight, as his room was vacant this morning. He hadn't officially checked out. We're running the ID and name, but it takes time."

"It would have been a fake name anyway," Agent Downey said, as his cell phone pinged with the picture's arrival. He thumb-swiped the screen and enlarged it.

It was an alley-scene with the body positioned on its back, staring at the heavens. The contorted mouth was the only clue as to the horrendous pain that preceded certain death.

The man was in his mid-sixties with a light scruff of beard, an otherwise clean complexion, and wavy hair. He looked to have been healthy, and not a habitual drug user.

As Hannah took the phone for a look, he thought of the victim as being a man in the wrong place, at the wrong time, in the wrong costume. Until he put it together.

He asked, "Where have we seen this guy before?"

"What?" Simms said.

Hannah ran through the case in his mind.

He pointed to the whiteboard. "Show the pictures from Erie, Pennsylvania."

Agent Downey asked, "What pictures?"

Hannah answered, "From the boat renters. Show me picture number one."

Agent Simms found the thumbnail pic and posted it to the whiteboard. It was of the older man who seemed annoyed waiting for his boat rental.

Hannah said, "The man dead in the alley after meeting Owen Latchford in Cleveland had rented a boat thirty minutes before The Bumper in Erie, Pennsylvania. How's that for a coincidence?"

"Wait, that's this guy?" Perez asked, getting her first look at the text.

"We dismissed him because he didn't fit the profile of the killer. But he was in Erie when Justin Harrow was murdered, and he was there last night when Owen Latchford was killed."

Agent Downey said, "He's been there all along! Maybe it was his job to monitor the killer to make sure it went as planned."

Hannah, who sat puzzling over the development, calmly added. "He may be the missing piece we've been struggling to find. We've been hunting *two* suspects, The Bumper and The Client. There have always been three."

Agent Simms spoke up. "If Perez and the profilers are right, and The Client is on the West Coast, then it makes sense to have boots on the ground in the Midwest. This guy was an accomplice."

Hannah looked over at Downey. "Or maybe he was the guy to kill the Bulgarian in December. If so, did the killer catch on? Now what?"

"Now what?" Downey repeated. "We get to work. We need to find out who this guy was."

Chapter Forty-Five

"According to fingerprints, his name was Mel Fitzpatrick. He was a retired software engineer, turned security professional." Agent Downey said. "There seems to be more money in protecting the technology than creating it."

"Any idea when he made the job switch?" Hannah asked. "It may be why he exacted revenge on the rich guys. If he felt hustled out of his job, he could have learned the means of revenge."

"It doesn't say. But what is known is that he fell off the radar about eighteen months ago. He was a regular free-lancer for top firms in Silicon Valley but hadn't been heard from since. Agent Farron made some calls last night and found many people who knew him, but didn't know where he was now. And it isn't our job to satisfy their curiosity." Agent Downey said.

"That would fit." Hannah said. "He concocted his revenge scheme and disappeared to work out the kinks. He'd know how to go deep on-line, maybe contact an overseas killer, and being a software engineer, could easily send him details of the victims without leaving a trail. It would be child's play. Then he followed The Bumper around to make sure the job was done. Maybe he is The Client."

The room was silent as they pondered Hannah's theory.

Downey asked, "But what about the west coast?"

"He'd have enough time to travel back and forth," Hannah replied.

Agent Perez said, "It certainly looks like he could be The Client, but without locking in on the profiler's description, he doesn't really fit it. He's clearly involved, but I guess we won't know until late November."

Hannah didn't want his theory flushed just because it didn't fit the FBI's vision. "The profilers only work with theory and abstracts. We have a computer programmer dead at the scene of the last murder, and proof he was present at one other. The only thing that makes sense is that he is The Client."

Simms asked, "So, if Fitzpatrick is The Client, is the case solved?"

"Not entirely," Hannah said. "It is likely that November's victim has been earmarked, and the package may have been auto-sent. The killer could scope out a victim unaware that The Client is dead. We still need to find The Bumper before he kills again."

Forty-eight hours.

It had been forty-eight hours since he killed Owen Latchford, and no money had made its way into his bank account. The Bumper wrestled with the skeptical side of his brain that convinced him it was part of The Client's exit strategy. Withhold payment for October, so he would be preoccupied in November. Then, Bam! Take out The Bumper and retrieve the money. He seethed with hatred for The Client but had no proof. His professional side preached restraint. There were many reasons there had been a glitch.

The Bumper was curious about the body that had been found in the alleyway beside the Stardust Ballroom. He knew it would have been the guy sharing the bottle with Latchford. That much was obvious and unavoidable. The identically dressed man would have been an unintended casualty that added to the mystery.

He read an on-line story about the victim this morning, but it wasn't until late that identification had been released. The Bumper searched the name on-line.

He physically reacted to the photo. The man found dead in the alley was the same man The Bumper had called The Witness. He was standing below The Bumper's hotel room in Cleveland just days ago.

The killer paced his new room as his current situation became apparent.

He hadn't been paid because The Witness was dead. Who would be alive to let The Client know the killer had succeeded?

A chill ran through The Bumper's veins. Surely The Client would know that The Witness's death was a total accident? The man was wearing a mask and talking to the victim. How was he supposed to know who the man was?

A thought streaked through his mind.

The Witness had to know who Latchford was. Why would he put himself in harm's way, knowing what was going to happen to him?

And why would he dress in an identical costume? Then the answer floated in.

"Latchford's death has been reported on the internet," the Bulgarian said aloud. "The Client would know he was dead, so I should be paid."

He dropped into the seat behind his laptop, opening the final dossiers he had received last week with both November's and December's victims. It all made sense.

"I was not paid because there was no Witness. Only Client. And The Client, he is dead."

He read over the two victim profiles, then closed his laptop. Those two would be spared. He would get a good night's sleep, then drive to New York and fly home. It had been a lucrative trip to America, even if it was cut short. He wondered how he could parlay his feat into a selling point. Add to the legend.

He fell asleep late, and awoke refreshed at seven am, November third.

He thumbed through his phone, checked his messages, and found an entry that arrived at exactly midnight.

A wire transfer notice that one-hundred-fifty-thousand dollars had been deposited into his bank account.

He clicked on the message's origin and found it to be identical to the others. The only glaring difference is that it had been scheduled to arrive at midnight days after the killing, not delivered manually five minutes after the deed was done.

Had The Client always scheduled the deposits and manually overrode them when he had confirmation of the kills?

The dead man in the alley had all the means to arrange payment any way he wanted.

But the most important thing for The Bumper, he decided, was to finish the race. He rose with certainty that he would be paid for each of the remaining kills by schedule, and if he wanted to be one of the greatest assassins of all time, then he would act professionally and finish the list, even though The Client was gone.

After showering, dressing and ordering a room service breakfast, The Bumper began a deeper read into the life of Nathan O'Neill, an orthodontist from Harrisburg, Pennsylvania.

Chapter Forty-Six

It had taken only an email to convince Elaine Stafford of 'Hearts Elite' to provide the names and contacts for all men whose first initials were 'N' who lived in cities that began with 'H' to the FBI.

The final pattern had revealed itself. The phrase would no doubt conclude in November as *KILL THE RICH*. With Owen Latchford's death, along with that of the supposed client, The Bumper was on a collision course with authorities hunting him without his knowing. The full resources of the FBI were working on contacting forces from Hoboken, New Jersey to Hanover, Indiana and every 'H' in between. Hannah was convinced there would be an attempt over the Thanksgiving weekend when police forces would be short-staffed and a victim's guard would be down.

How might it happen? Because he had not yet predicted the means of murder, Hannah couldn't guess the victim. He'd been trying to hone an intuition, but nothing had sunk in.

He sat with stacks of printed profiles and separated them into piles. In his mind, he called them 'likely' and 'unlikely.' Again, the criteria would make sense only to him.

Hannah started with the cities. Which city would be the most likely? Then he reversed course. No, which city would be the most unlikely. He put those into one pile. There were only three, anyway. He continued to do that until he had roughly equal piles. That made sense to him. By a rough count, he had an equal number of profiles in each stack, the most likely being from one of four cities.

The heated discussion yesterday had been the elimination of Hartford. Hannah argued the killer had yet to repeat a city when given the chance with Lansing and Louisville, as well as Indianapolis and Iowa City, and didn't expect him to start now. Perez wasn't convinced, calling it a stroke of genius to choose a city he had already researched and been more familiar with as the weather turned colder.

Hannah sat in his condo, staring at an atlas map of the eastern seaboard of the United States. The page was covered with lines between victim cities, highlighted routes, and likely locations circled in orange. It was a mess from a visual point of view, but important to Hannah. The map was the full visualization of the hunt that had consumed him since late April.

What held his gaze tonight were the open spaces. It reminded him of the board game "Battleship." The best place to hide your ships was to put them into clusters. The mind wanted to imagine them spread out over the entire board given equal distance between each ship. It was symmetrically pleasing, but a poor strategy. Hannah stared at the congested clusters and wondered why, other than the initials, they were lumped together, and why some areas were left alone.

New York had been completely ignored. It would have been the easiest city to hide a murder because of the sheer volume of people. In fact, if the initials weren't important, the killer could have stayed in New York for the entire year and reeled off twelve perfect murders with less fanfare than driving around from state to state.

What was the purpose of the puzzles? Why the initials?

Hannah pushed the map aside and retrieved the file on Mel Fitzpatrick, The Client. He had been a divorced loner who had thrown himself into his work with several of the leading firms in Silicon Valley before either being replaced or burning out. Suddenly, he reappeared as a security specialist. He had few friends outside of work, and had shown little personality that made him memorable. His frustrated work experience, coupled with his loner persona, made him the perfect Client. But Agent Perez's analysis with the profilers nagged at him.

As did the money. Mel Fitzpatrick, at the time of his death, had about three-thousand dollars in the bank, and a small monthly pension on top of any freelance security work he had done before disappearing. How could he have hired an elite killer to take part in such an elaborate scheme, and continue to kill every month, with no money?

Mel Fitzpatrick also wasn't a woman. He didn't appear to be known as a puzzle solver, or even a gifted programmer. He was a grunt employee. A worker bee.

Yet, there he was, in the middle of at least two kills. Probably more. Maybe all of them.

Mel Fitzpatrick worked in Silicon Valley. The Client lived on the West Coast. Could he have been travelling every month from his home to the kill sites to oversee his assassin? With what money?

A simulated wind chime broke Hannah's concentration as his cell registered a text.

He was pleased to hear that tone after such a long time, and the thought of another text from his ex-wife, Stacey, was a welcome distraction. He snatched his phone from the table.

"Thanx again for dinner and chat. And thank you for the text this morn. I meant what I said, but you did surprise me. Good night."

A warm glow replaced the pit in his stomach that accompanied thoughts of Stacey and their life together, which he now realized he had destroyed. A marriage counselor would have been proud of his honest assessment of the night before over dinner, taking responsibility for his actions, and lack thereof. Stacey had been wary of his intentions and remained unusually guarded. She had been blunt when asking whether the dinner was to seek her forgiveness, or whether it gave him the outlet to forgive himself. It had been a tough question then, and a tough one to answer even twenty-four hours later. He had sent her a good morning text, with a "nice to see you" gif, and let her be. No invitations to another dinner, or follow-up questions. He owed her the right to answer if she wanted.

And she had. Hannah was relieved to see it, but knew better than to imagine it meant more than what she said. But it was enough.

He returned to Mel Fitzpatrick's profile but had lost his train of thought. His eye fell on the word 'divorce', and after the reply from Stacey, his mind made a mental leap.

The Client might be a woman. Could The Client be Mel Fitpatrick's ex-wife? Would she have become enraged at the treatment of her husband and divorced him because of his weakness in the face of the entitled?

Mel Fitzpatrick was a worker bee. Not the Queen Bee.

If Mel was in the field following the killer, who would be the best choice to remain home and organize the scheme? The Ex-Mrs. Fitzpatrick.

Hannah sent a quick text to Agent Perez to make finding Fitzpatrick's ex-wife a priority. He left out his concerns, preferring to keep those close to his chest for now.

He wanted also to text Stacey back, but thought better of it. "Give her space. Give her time." He said aloud.

His phone pinged Agent Perez's reply that they were working on locating Fitzpatrick's ex-wife and next of kin.

Robert replied with a thumbs up emoji, wondering whether the woman was already aware.

Chapter Forty-Seven

Dr. Nathan O'Neill of Harrisburg, Pennsylvania, was growing a thriving orthodontic practice. He had been fortunate to graduate at a time where several prominent practitioners were getting long in the tooth and looking to retire. O'Neill bought one of them and gambled that the conglomerates that would scoop up the rest would operate 'hands off' impersonal practices.

He had chosen wisely. O'Neill Orthodontics, with its now recognizable double 'O' logo, was a fixture in the medical community, local media and on-line.

At thirty-eight years old, O'Neill had dedicated the first ten years of his practice to solidifying his future. As the orthodontist closed in on forty, he decided it was time to play.

O'Neill went out and bought a cottage, complete with fishing boat and jet skis. He had dabbled in dating but wanted more than what Harrisburg's single life offered.

The orthodontist wanted someone more successful, more worldly. Not some local hand-me-down, or a divorcee he'd gone to high school with.

Dr. Nathan O'Neill signed up for 'Hearts Elite' and was stunned at the range of women who were available. Recognizing the competition, he creeped other men's profiles to see how he could up his game and began choosing his words more carefully on his status updates and posting more adventurous pictures. O'Neill found that recreating his image was just as much work as finding the perfect mate. He received messages and travelled to meet these fascinating women in New York and Philadelphia. Dr. O'Neill felt there was chemistry, but each relationship fizzled out when Harrisburg was mentioned.

No one was interested in settling down with an orthodontist in southern Pennsylvania.

He had his wavy hair styled differently and colored his natural brown a tad lighter. He photoshopped his pics to take off a few pounds and cleaned up the backgrounds of boring shots.

But the biggest change was using more confident language in his welcome profile. He was initially almost apologetic for being a thirty-eight-year-old successful bachelor. That had to change. He had to appear choosy, as if he had been saving himself for the perfect woman. Nathan wanted to make the women who clicked on his profile feel as if they were the special one. They were lucky to have found him. O'Neill used words like "successful," "driven" and "adventurous," though those words would never have escaped his lips.

Deep down, he was just Dr. Nathan O'Neill of Harrisburg, Pennsylvania. But this was the on-line culture, and competition was fierce. He would have to puff himself up more than he had been to gain any kind of attention.

You never know who was out there reading this stuff.

The Bumper grew impatient. He knew it might happen as the calendar year ended, but with The Client dead, and no one supervising his methods, he just wanted to get the jobs done and go back to his native Bulgaria. He was tired of the travelling and hotels.

The killer recognized why a man named Nathan would be killed in November in a city called Harrisburg. He thought it funny that everything was easier when you knew the pattern.

But it was the end of the phrase that concerned him. *KILL THE RICH* had only eleven letters, and there was a twelfth dossier. Was it a dummy? Was it a trap?

Was he the last victim?

The sooner he killed Dr. Nathan O'Neill, the better he'd feel moving on to December.

The Bumper had located and followed the good doctor for over a week, and it made him uneasy. The killer was a professional and good at his job, but the orthodontist had registered no clue he was under surveillance. Dr. O'Neill didn't appear to be anything but polite when holding doors or entitled when speaking to patients or staff.

He was nothing like the others. He seemed friendly, courteous, and kind. Not entitled, arrogant, and self-centered.

How had he ended up on The Client's list?

Chapter Forty-Eight

"Her name is Sonya, and she divorced Mel Fitzpatrick in twenty-twelve." Agent Simms read off his laptop. "She still lives in California and is remarried."

"Has Cleveland police notified her of Mel's death?" Agent Downey asked.

"I don't know. Agent Dennison hasn't checked in yet. Want me to reach out to her?"

"I think we should." Hannah said. "In fact, I'd like to talk with her if I could. I think she may know more than she realizes."

Agent Downey laughed. "Six months in an FBI boardroom, and you're a seasoned interrogator now?"

"Well, I wouldn't call it an interrogation." Hannah answered. "I thought she might be The Client pulling Fitzpatrick's strings, but I don't think so now."

"You think she may know who is, though?" Downey asked.

"Yeah, I do." Hannah said. "Fitzpatrick didn't have the background or the resources to pull off a year-long caper this involved. But he could have been someone's eyes and ears."

Agent Simms jumped in. "His background seems ripe for revenge on the rich. There must be so many others that think like him. So many techies who worked themselves to death only to watch others enjoy the riches. He could have been part of a group of disgruntled castoffs. Maybe one of them took things into his own hands?"

Agent Downey followed up. "And he asked ol' Fitzy, now a security expert, to help on the road? Divorced and broke, he'd be the perfect soldier. Cover the expenses for him, and he will pay Mel when the work is done? That would explain the depleted bank account."

Hannah turned to Downey. "Or he had the killer take out Fitzpatrick when he was no longer necessary and wouldn't have to pay him at all."

Agent Simms looked up. "That's cold."

Agent Rhonda Perez burst into the boardroom with her laptop balanced on her palm. "We may have a slight break. An agent at Quantico sent along an email. He got a tip from a cop buddy who read the bulletin about the killer. The cop's kids get their teeth straightened by a Dr. Nathan O'Neill who lives in Harrisburg, Pennsylvania. Check out the initials. The 'N' matches and the 'H' matches. While he was at his daughter's appointment yesterday, the cop noticed that the guy had dyed his hair. The orthodontist joked that it's helping him with his dating."

Hannah flipped through his pages. "Harrisburg is one city that seems likely." Seconds later, he stabbed the paper with his index finger. "Nathan O'Neill! He's a member of 'Hearts Elite.'"

"Perez, forward me the email. I'll craft a reply to get the cop to monitor the dentist." Agent Downey said.

Agent Simms resumed his searches and found a current photo of Nathan O'Neill. "What is he? Forty? Seems older than the usual ones found on the list."

"It will be the profile." Hannah said. "Whatever he wrote meant more to The Client than just the age and pictures. Besides, forty is the new twenty-eight."

"If you say so," Simms replied.

"Nice work, Perez," Downey said. "We're going to investigate Mel Fitzpatrick's ex-wife. When we get her on the screen, do you want in on the talk? You've learned from the profilers a few things that may tip you off on her demeanour or evasiveness."

"Absolutely. If The Client is a woman, it will have to be someone who was close to Mel. He was someone she could trust. Who closer to start with than his ex-wife?"

Agent Simms added, "It also explains why Mel's bank account was light. All the money for their year-long killing spree would be held by her. He wasn't worried about not being paid. They were using their money."

Thanksgiving was over two weeks away and The Bumper was sure the victim was hapless enough that waiting for the right moment was unnecessary. He had killed no one this early in the month yet, but not only were rules made to be broken, who was around to criticize him?

The killer was crouched in Nathan O'Neill's cottage kitchen, re-clamping the gas line behind the stove. It probably wouldn't be lethal, but The Bumper had made a few adjustments. For example, he had stripped the heading to ensure the leak would be continuous. The cottage would fill with carbon monoxide slowly throughout the week. The killer had learned Dr Nathan O'Neill had planned to close his cottage this weekend, instead of Thanksgiving. After three days of the leak, the undetectable gas would smother anyone who arrived on Friday within a short period.

The Bumper would stay on a nearby lake and monitor the situation with the occasional drive-by until he was sure the deed was done. Then, he'd move in, unclasp the hose to look intentional, and leave the note. It seems orthodontists have high suicide rates.

Chapter Forty-Nine

On the afternoon of Friday, November tenth, the task force was huddled around the boardroom table, watching a nervous woman of uncertain age on the whiteboard screen.

Sonya Fleming, once Sonya Fitzpatrick, had been devastated to hear of her ex-husband's death. The San Jose police officers who had handled the notification found her reaction credible and had provided information following a background check. She had never had so much as a speeding ticket, had never been involved in a police investigation, neither as a suspect, witness, or victim, and lived in a comfortable neighborhood of stable, middle-class families.

Hannah and Agent Perez exchanged a look. Sonya Fleming was the opposite of what the FBI profilers were looking for in The Client.

After introductions and words of condolence, Agent Downey asked, "How did you and Mel meet?"

Sonya Fleming took her time answering, fidgeting with her hands as she said, "It was in the late seventies, I guess, when the computer boom was starting here in California. I got a job with a small company with big dreams, but it was tough for a woman to make a go of it. This guy took me under his wing, and that was Mel. He was sweet and kind, and all that. We got married a few years later."

"How long did you work in the industry, then?" Hannah asked.

"Oh, I got out as soon as we got married. Mel was working eighteen-hour days, going on cocaine binges with the other coders. I stayed home and tried to raise our kids. It was a wild time, but it wasn't for everybody, that's for sure." Sonya said.

"Tough on a marriage?" Downey asked.

"Tough on everyone, unless you owned the company. Everyone wanted to get ahead, be the next genius. We started hearing about Apple, Steve Wozniak and Steve Jobs, Bill Gates' name was bounced around. The money started flowing and everyone got weird."

Agent Perez asked, "Did you and Mel get some of that money?"

Sonya Fleming's nervous gaze cracked and broke into a laugh. "Hell, no. That was big shit money. We were the lowly expendables. Mel was smart and driven, but there was always someone smarter and more driven. The fact he had a family held him back. There was a time in America where the family was a good thing for a man to have. In Silicon Valley, it was a crippling distraction."

"So, you were married...what, thirty years?" Hannah asked.

Sonya bit her lip in thought. "About that. The last few years probably didn't count anyway because of the separation. We were done by the time the kids left. It just took a while for the paperwork."

"All because of Mel's job?"

"Yeah, but he had changed, too. The kind young man I fell in love with had grown into a bitter old man by the time he hit forty. He came home furious every day at what was going on at work, and at how he was being ignored or shoved out. The 'work culture' this, the 'work culture' that. He had high hopes for himself, for both of us, but in the end, he just felt he was a failure. I couldn't pull him out of it. So, I stopped trying. Mel stopped trying. One day, we both just stopped."

"Mrs. Fleming," Perez asked, "Is that a common story in Silicon Valley? Frustrated, overworked employees who felt unappreciated?"

Sonya shifted in her seat and leaned in toward her computer camera. "Miss, not only is it common, it is inevitable. It's like everything else in California. The Klondike gold rush of the mid-eighteen-hundreds that opened the state. Some got rich, but most died trying. Look at Hollywood, darling. Everyone moves there expecting to become the next movie star, only to be used up by predators and spit out when they don't need you anymore. Silicon Valley is no different. Everyone who moved in during the heydays of the late seventies, early eighties wanted to get rich and famous, but only a few did. The rest got old and bitter. Different industry. Same story."

"Except, there is a difference, Sonya," Hannah said. "Silicon Valley isn't just the luck of finding gold in a stream, or bumping into the right agent in Hollywood. There are patents and inventions and skills in demand. People should have been promoted on merit and been compensated for their worth for the good of the industry, right?"

"Oh, please," Sonya spat. "You sound like a man, all right. Do you know how many women worked their ass off, only to get ignored when the buyouts and mergers picked the best and brightest? Pretty well all of them. Some things never change, and that was one of them. If you were a woman, or, like Mel, if you were kind and non-confrontational, you got left behind. To the victors go the spoils? Well, the victors were assholes."

A silence followed her outburst, but it convinced Hannah that Perez and the profilers had a point about The Client. It may not be a woman, but it would have been someone Sonya had just described. Someone who had had enough of the hierarchy but now had the time and means to exact revenge on the elites of Silicon Valley. The Client was using the internet's largest meeting place, a dating website, to select faceless victims.

Just as The Client had been perceived.

Nameless. Faceless.

"Mrs. Fleming, I'm sorry if I came across as insensitive. That was not my intention. I guess I am very naïve as to what goes on there," Hannah said. "But can you think of particular people who you might have just described? Were there people you know whose lives were ruined, or careers destroyed who might have been angry enough to do something violent?"

"Violent? You think Mel was mixed up in something?"

Agent Downey answered. "We think there was a reason he was in Cleveland, doing some security work for a client, and his death was an accident."

"Oh," Sonya answered. "Collateral damage. Got it. Sounds like something Mel would get caught up in. I'm telling you, this place changes people."

"Was Mel the type of guy to get caught up in someone else's scheme?" Hannah asked.

Sonya paused. "Maybe. Mel was more like a sidekick. He was no push-over, but he wouldn't be the type to start trouble. But he would have your back if you needed him."

"Was there, maybe, a group he hung out with? Other castoffs you might say that he would have stayed in touch with?" Agent Perez asked.

"I'm sure there were a few. They looked out for each other and traded war stories. I don't remember all of them, but he had a few buddies who came to the house a lot in the last few years when the pressure got too much. Marriages that broke up before ours sometimes meant that a buddy slept on our couch. Crazy times."

"Do you think you could write a few names that come to mind?" Agent Downey asked. "If someone was involved in what happened to Mel, even if it was an accident, we'd like to talk to them. It would be a great help."

"Okay, I can do that. I've been away from that world a long time, but there may be a photo album around here somewhere. Send me an email and I'll reply with a few names. That's all I can do." Sonya said, shrugging.

"One last thing, Sonya. Did Mel like puzzles?" Hannah asked.

"You mean jigsaw puzzles?"

"Any kind," Hannah replied. "Crosswords, jumble words, word searches."

"No, he was too analytical for that. No puzzles or mysteries. What you see is what you got with Mel."

"We appreciate your time, Mrs. Fleming, and again, we are sorry about your ex-husband. We'll do what we can to bring his killer to justice. If you can assist us by completing that list of names, it would be a great help." Agent Downey said, signing off.

Agent Simms immediately typed out the email to Sonya Fleming and sent it.

"Thoughts?" Downey asked.

"The Client is someone from Mel Fitzpatrick's past, a castoff like himself." Perez said.

"If it was a woman, I don't think Sonya knows her. When she talked about women being ignored, she would have mentioned an example if she knew one." Hannah added.

"We'll see when the list comes in." Agent Downey replied. "Anything more on our November victim's list, other than the orthodontist in Harrisburg?"

"Dennison and Farron are running rabid between Pennsylvania and Hanover, Indiana. The police forces have a picture of The Bumper and all eyes are out."

"That's all we can hope for." Downey said. "Have a good weekend, everyone."

Simms and Perez slipped out of the boardroom in anticipation of two days off. Downey closed up his case and asked Hannah, "What have you got going on this weekend? Want to come over for supper tomorrow night?"

Hannah replied, "Thanks, CD, but I'll take a rain check." Hannah paused, unsure if he should continue. "I had dinner with Stacey last week."

Downey stopped, then sat back down. "Wow, is this a good thing?"

"Yeah, I think so. It's not the path to reconciliation. I just felt that I had to smooth things over. I've got a lot to make up for."

"That's great, man. Good for you." Downey replied, then added. "By the way, Laurel's good. You don't need to take her out."

Hannah laughed as he said, "Damnit. She was next on the list."

At that moment, four hundred miles southwest of Boston, Dr. Nathan O'Neill shoved the last of the weekend bags into his Outlander and set off for his cottage. The weather had stayed sunny, but a biting wind tugged at the last stubborn leaves, threatening to ruin the bonfire he'd planned for the other cottagers.

It was a peaceful drive along the Susquehanna River on Highway Twenty-Two, north into the country until he reached his cottage road just past Millerstown. There were plenty of spots to stop along the way for gas and snacks.

O'Neill wasn't paying close attention to his speed when he spied the flashing lights in his rearview mirror. He glanced down and was relieved to see he was barely over the posted limit, but still felt the anxiety of the police presence. He pulled over and watched the officer slowly walk forward on the driver's side.

"Afternoon, Dr. O'Neill," the officer greeted him, removing his sunglasses.

The orthodontist recognized him as the father of a couple of his patients. "Oh, hi officer. I'm sorry I don't remember your first name, but I know your daughters are patients. Was I speeding?" He stammered.

The man shook his head. "Not at all, Doctor. Could you step out of the vehicle, please? I just want to have a little chat."

Chapter Fifty

Hannah spent Veteran's Day, November eleventh, huddled in his condo. He kept his phone charged and his calendar empty, just in case Stacey texted. He had to be honest with himself that he was indeed willing to try for a reconciliation but clearly understood her reluctance. Once bitten, and all that.

He wrote out his theories on the case, then jumbled the pages, looking for other connections that weren't as obvious.

The elephant in the room refused to be ignored, so Hannah dropped his pen, rubbed his eyes, and turned his attention to the glaring inconsistency.

The phrase.

KILL THE RICH only had eleven letters.

Hannah jokingly supposed that punctuation could end the phrase, but what city would that point to? No, it had been intentional. There was a reason only eleven men would be targeted. It was the prank of the three goats. By painting the number four, the searchers assumed that a loose goat remained wandering.

Could The Client have killed the eleven whenever he wanted, but knew that if he started in January, it would create a distracting pattern?

Hannah cursed himself. He was doing it again.

Pareidolia. Clustering illusions. Taking random points and forcing them into a pattern so it would make sense.

He thought, again, of the classic Agatha Christie gem, *The ABC Murders* he'd read at his grandparent's cottage. Was the twelfth murder the one true target, or was it the Bulgarian?

Puzzles, twists, reveals. Patterns within patterns. So much planning.

He gave that some thought. How long would it have taken to put it together? Mel Fitzpatrick had fallen off everyone's radar about eighteen months ago. Had he been recruited then? Told to lie low because of a big year-long job coming up?

Then, there are the cities and profiles. If The Client had already chosen the phrase, then selecting cities could be done in minutes. That would not have been hard. But finding the victims to match the monthly initials might have required some luck. Or was that part of the challenge?

Hannah returned to the profile pages, wondering if The Client would contact each of the victims when it hit him.

Contact The Client.

Hannah's Hearts Elite page was still active. If Fitzpatrick was The Client, then any contact would be fruitless. If not, then it would be possible that he would get a reply.

Hannah stared at the Charles River and tried to concoct a riddle so enthralling that The Client, if he were indeed alive, would want to answer. Would *have* to answer.

He stepped back to the table, sat down, and wrote out a message.

"What is wished of an enemy but found in a friend?"

Hannah thought it was okay for a first draft, but realized that time was in short supply. Besides, if The Client was dead, it would go unread anyway.

He hit the green 'post' button and watched the riddle settle in the member profile box.

It was just after three p.m. in Boston, so it was lunchtime in California. The Client had replied quickly before.

If he was alive, perhaps it wouldn't take long,

The Bumper left his small roadside motel room and drove past Nathan O'Neill's cottage for the third time today. *Where was he?* It was just after four o'clock and he hadn't shown up for the weekend. Perhaps he'd encountered car trouble, or was called back for an emergency, but it was so frustrating. The killer wanted to be finished with Pennsylvania, actually done with the entire contract, and be home, alive and safe.

None of that could happen until the orthodontist was dead.

The Bumper considered breaking into the cottage and repairing the gas line, but that could be catastrophic. And what would happen if O'Neill showed up while he was in there?

No, it was best to leave it alone. He would just have to find another way.

But he sure wished it had ended on the lake. He couldn't stand the thought of even one more night in a road-side motel.

Dr. O'Neill looked at his phone. It was only four o'clock. Was he expected to stay in all weekend? The shocking revelation on the side of the road was too much for him to handle, so he took the officer's advice and headed back home. Stay indoors and play it safe. Just twenty-four hours later, he was bored with the strategy.

Why would a killer be targeting orthodontists? The cop was short on details, just that they'd gotten a tip. Being alone in the remote cottage wasn't the safest place right now. Stay home.

O'Neill peeked through his curtains and spied the cop car sitting on watch at the corner. It must have been a convincing tip. He had never been threatened in his life, let alone become the target of a random killer.

O'Neill plopped down on his sofa, and for the third time today, fired up another true crime documentary on his television.

It had to be someone else, some other orthodontist.

Who would want to kill *him*?

Chapter Fifty-One

Monday morning brought a flurry of activity. Hannah was in the FBI offices by eight-forty-five, passing Downey in the parking lot. "You not sleep well, Pally?" Downey asked as they marched in together.

"I have news," Hannah answered.

Agent Simms and Perez were already seated in the boardroom, organizing their weekend discoveries. Downey jumped in to say good morning and ask them to be ready early. Apparently, they all had a lot.

At nine-thirty, the meeting convened with Agent Downey giving an update from Harrisburg, Pennsylvania.

"The orthodontist Nathan O'Neill was stopped on his way to his cottage Friday afternoon by the officer who emailed the tip, and convinced him to go home and hide out. He made up some bullshit tip about someone targeting orthodontists, and the guy bought it. On Saturday afternoon, the state police were called to the area near that same lake by a neighbor who found a squirrel dead on O'Neill's window ledge. Neighbor stuck his head at the side door to call for the guy when he felt light-headed. Long story short, authorities found the place full of carbon monoxide. No idea how long the stove leak had been active, but enough to soak the crevices and kill the animal. State Trooper described it as a 'total tamper job'. O'Neill was notified of the incident and lost his mind." Downey finished.

"Mr. November," Agent Perez said.

"Yup, sure looks that way," Hannah agreed. "But since the killer failed, he will be twice as careful and more violent over the next two weeks."

Agent Simms asked, "You don't think he'll wonder if the cops are on to him?"

Agent Downey replied, "That's a good possibility, Jacco, but it was the squirrel who gave the gas away, and if the killer was watching the cottage for signs of O'Neill, he wouldn't know why he hadn't shown. It still looked like a leak to the police, and the killer isn't aware that we know otherwise."

Agent Simms nodded. "Do you want me to start a search of possible Harrisburg Hotels where the killer may stay? There would likely only be so many, and we have a picture."

"Work on the list, and we'll tackle that problem this afternoon. First, let's go over your reply from Sonya Flemming, Jacco."

Simms clicked open a second folder and printed off copies of Sonya's reply email. She had typed out four names of past associates who had remained in touch with Mel that she could remember. Whether they were dead or alive, active or burnt out was unknown to her.

"The list contains the names of three men and one woman who were long-time friends of Mel Fitzpatrick," Simms said theatrically. "I have already done a quick dive into all four, who are still alive, by the way, and none seem to be gainfully employed."

Agent Downey flashed the four names on the whiteboard:

Gerald Smith, Diane Jenkins, Paulo Rodriguez, Lonnie Banks.

"Everyone will get a copy of the email to have these names on hand. Agent Simms will be a busy boy this week tracking these individuals down, as well as tracking down the hotel where The Bumper may be holed up. If anyone wants to help, feel free," Downey said.

Perez waved her hand with a grimace.

"Thank you, Rhonda. What do you have today?"

"Considering what happened in Harrisburg this weekend, I got a late-night note from one profiler yesterday. He said that the killer may be spiralling. That he struck so early in the month may be a sign that he's rushing to finish the job."

"I agree," Hannah added. "In fact, slicing a gas line is not his usual method. The Bumper is a hands-on killer. He is not the type to set a trap and wait."

"How does that help us?" Downey asked.

"Well, it means he may make a mistake." Perez answered. "Overplay his hand. Take risks. We know where he is, we know what he looks like, and we know his intended victim. He may come out of his burrow and expose himself. We need to be there when he does."

"Agent Watson at Quantico has a surveillance team in place in Harrisburg. There's no way the guy gets close to O'Neill." Downey said.

Agent Simms asked, "What happens if the killer gets the vibe that we are on to him and we overplay *our* hand? What if he just disappears?

"At this point," Downey said, "anything that saves Nathan O'Neill is worth it, even if we lose The Bumper for the time being."

Hannah said, "He won't give up."

Agent Perez looked up. "How can you be so sure?"

Hannah pulled the cellphone from his jacket pocket. "Because The Client is still alive."

The three agents wheeled on Hannah like he had dynamite. "What?"

"In all the confusion after Mel Fitzpatrick's death, I forgot my account was still active in 'Heart's Elite.' So, I uploaded a riddle to my status to see if I could get a hit, and I did late last night."

"What does it say?" Downey asked.

"I sent out this riddle. *'What is wished of an enemy but found in a friend?'*" Hannah watched Agent Simms, expecting the agent who had shown a growing mastery of the puzzles, to guess correctly.

He turned to Hannah. "An end?

"Exactly. You want the end of your enemy, but the actual word is found as the last three letters in 'friend'. I wanted to make The Client aware the end is near and we know it."

"And you got a reply to that?" Downey asked, trying to read over Hannah's shoulder.

"I did." He turned his phone to the group. In the chat square beneath the original riddle were three words.

When I say.

Chapter Fifty-Two

For the first time, The Client felt they'd made a mistake. They should not have been baited into responding to that juvenile riddle. This Robert Hannah clearly knew more than he should. It had taken two days before The Client had learned of Mel's death, and the grief cut deep. They should have ignored the status. 'Hearts Elite' was no longer part of the plan.

'Why did I go back again?' The Client wondered, despite knowing the reason.

That damned city. Chicago. The first riddle. Hannah had guessed the initial.

The Client had even made the connection without realizing it. This Hannah guy had asked about Chicago when the action was in Cleveland. Had he solved the riddle of the cities? He clearly had figured out the initials of the victims.

It was too late to pull out of Harrisburg, even if The Bumper could be reached. He would have to be careful. *'If they apprehend the killer, it shouldn't expose me,'* The Client thought, *'but this isn't over until the very end.'*

With the click of a trembling finger, The Client opened the December dossier and read it one more time. So much time had been spent ensuring its exact instructions, including the method of death. All The Bumper had to do was complete the November task, then head to the finish line with a twist no one would see coming.

Not that anyone could follow the trail.

Although, this Hannah fellow seemed persistent.

Chapter Fifty-Three

The FBI had set up rotating pairs around the clock following Dr. O'Neill. He had been begged to close his office and hunker down for the rest of the month, but O'Neill felt that if the FBI couldn't protect him, what was the use in hiding? Besides, he couldn't bear to make his patients suffer.

Each morning, O'Neill checked in with the night crew that he was awake, and would wait until given the 'all clear' to move about his house to get ready for work. He would be driven to and from the office in a state car with a team remaining outside. The receptionist desk was staffed by two assistants, both of whom were told to report any suspicious cancellations or strange new patient requests. The orthodontist carried an alarm fob in his smock that, when pushed, would alert the cavalry.

Nothing unusual happened.

Days turned into weeks and Thanksgiving was upon them. The Feds had expected at least one cursory attempt from the killer to test the strength of O'Neill's protection. A strange email to see if it would be intercepted, or a late-night phone call. Pay a kid to deliver a pizza box to find out if agents would jump out of the bushes.

Something. Anything.

This was the worst time to let their guard down. But at least O'Neill had made no plans for the holiday, so maintaining surveillance was far more manageable.

Each team had a full file with the Interpol photo of Zach Betes, aka The Bumper, as well as mock sketches of what he'd look like in various disguises, such as a mustache, a shaved head, or glasses, along with toupees and wigs. All persons approaching O'Neill's home would be detained.

Let the fine folks of Harrisburg, Pennsylvania scream about their civil liberties.

They had to keep Nathan O'Neill alive.

The Bumper spent the days leading up to Thanksgiving in a rage-fueled fog when he learned the orthodontist was now being guarded. The gas line plot had been foiled. How had it happened? The sheer number of officers who had descended on the victim's cottage eliminated the possibility of a quick kill. Nathan O'Neill had been identified as a high-risk target.

As the killer had feared over the passing weeks, he was losing control of the plot, to his own detriment and survival. The time for subtlety had passed. Brutal efficiency was back in play.

The Bumper chose the spot with precision. He had eliminated the dental office as a kill spot because of the security teams that now surrounded the man. They looked to be professional, so if they weren't local police, they could be federal agents.

"Imagine that. American Federal Agents, the FBI, trying to stop The Bumper from completing his mission," he thought. *"After this, I will be famous."*

The Bumper had wanted to go twelve for twelve on the hit list from The Client. But with the authorities aware of his target, even he recognized that one scenario had simply been replaced with another. The "undetectable kill" thrill had been upgraded to a "heavily guarded target" challenge.

It might look different on the scorecard, but a kill was a kill. The Client, were they alive, would have understood.

Gone were the bee stings and gum wads. The Bumper was finished with bus tires and Great Lakes.

He had scoped out the backing neighbors for three days prior to Thanksgiving, and waited for which occupants would be traveling. His luck continued to hold.

Two houses emptied Wednesday night. He chose the house at the best angle.

The sightline was unimpeded, and his presence would go unnoticed.

He was banking on Nathan O'Neill making his appearance. Then it would be over. One moment, he was full of life, the next, a crime statistic.

And The Bumper would move on to December, then home two-and-a half-million dollars richer, with a reputation that would flood his bank account with more. Much more.

A misty grey spread slowly in the eastern sky, accompanied by its dawn winter wind. The killer eyed the house through his scope, centered on the rear corner window. All other movement was secondary. A glow from the back bedroom alerted The Bumper that the hour had come. Adrenaline flooded his veins in anticipation of the audacious kill. The killer tracked his prey, imagining the layout of the house until, finally, the victim entered center stage.

The killer eased back the bolt of the sniper's rifle and slowed his breathing. It could happen at any moment, though he knew preparations were needed before the victim would be in place. He tried to imagine it unfolding as he watched the frosted window. Then, the shadow passed across the glass. The Bumper squinted into the sight and locked in on that spot.

At the moment Nathan O'Neill's shadow passed the bathroom window a second time, the bullet shattered the thick glass and pierced his head, killing him before he hit the floor. The shower would run, pooling the blood from the exit wound as he lay, eyes open.

The Bumper quickly disassembled the rifle in the bedroom of the empty home, corralled the sack and slipped out the side door, waiting for sirens to split the morning silence. He knew from the angle of the shot that the police would descend upon this house within two minutes or fewer following the discovery. His rented Malibu sat on the road, pointing toward his getaway spot; an empty house owned by another family that had left for the Thanksgiving weekend, providing a perfect hiding spot in plain sight. He sped away from the sniper's nest and, a block later, wheeled into the empty driveway and up into the carport. Once the police began their dragnet, perhaps neighbors would remark about that car in the driveway that did not belong, but he would be gone by then.

The killer knew they would look for him, so the only goal now was evasion and survival.

Authorities would find the house with only the carpet indentations as proof of the nest, the abandoned car rented through fake ID with the murder weapon in the trunk, and a killer who had disappeared into thin air.

The Bumper felt he would be a legend. It was on to December, his ultimate act, then home for New Year's Day. If only the Client had lived to see his triumph.

When he walked around the corner from the drop-off house, he donned the Santa Claus hat and took up his place with the other volunteers at the Salvation Army kettle outside a neighborhood drugstore. No one asked him his name or wondered who he was.

Everyone smiled and gave change. It was the giving season, and The Bumper had much to be grateful for.

By ten o'clock, he'd be on a bus from the drugstore to the city center and out of town, never to see the lights of Harrisburg again.

Chapter Fifty-Four

Agent Downey silently stared at the boardroom table.

Agent Rhonda Perez paced the room, muttering, "We had him, we had him." While Agent Simms couldn't even open his laptop, Hannah shared their pain, but knew for them it was also a professional slight. They had been prepared and still beaten.

"Jacco, were you able to look into the four friends that Fitzpatrick's ex-wife sent you?" Hannah asked, breaking the mood.

Agent Simms exhaled and leaned forward, dragging open a file folder. "Yeah, I've got them here. You're welcome to see if anything is illuminating to you," he said, sliding the manila file to Hannah.

Frustration was running deep.

Hannah flipped it open and extracted the four sheets of paper, one per name. Each had standard information. Last known address, marital status, work experience, from which one could draw conclusions as to their relationship with the deceased Mel Fitzpatrick.

He lifted the page on Diane Jenkins. She was the only woman listed, though not a surprise that there weren't many. Sonya had said that women didn't last long. But maybe there was something different about Jenkins that was worth a more thorough investigation.

"Thanks, Jacco, this is great." Hannah said.

"Yeah, thanks Agent Simms." Downey said. "I think we're done for now. Nothing useful is going to come from us today," he said as he walked from the boardroom.

Agents Perez and Simms looked at each other in surprise and collected their files. They also beat a hasty retreat.

Hannah spread the four sheets across the boardroom table. He had only a slight advantage over the others in that when his disasters strike in poker, no one died. But you also had to collect the next hand and play on. As long as you had chips, you were alive.

Gerald Smith, Diane Jenkins, Paulo Rodriguez, Lonnie Banks.

Agent Simms had been diligent in searching their histories, though it had been impossible to find current information on them. Computer geniuses knew how to stay off the grid.

Gerald Smith got his start in Silicon Valley out of high school, having worked at six major corporations, three in one year. Head-hunters must have made a fortune, and it seemed a lot of young people jumped from bonus to bonus. Loyalty wasn't a prized commodity. After twenty-five years, he fell out of style around two-thousand-five, working in contract positions and a stint as a consultant. His on-line resume ended in twenty-twelve.

Diane Jenkins was an outlier. Agent Simms noted that there was quite a bit to know about the female programmer. She also had worked for the biggest names in the Valley in the late seventies, early eighties, so it was highly likely she would have known not only Mel Fitzpatrick, but the three other guys on the list as well. She disappeared from on-line searches in two-thousand-nine after being named as a plaintiff in a wrongful termination suit. The verdict hadn't been released, so there must have been a settlement. Hannah scanned the other three friends and found no mention of the lawsuit.

Paulo Rodriguez was a shining star in the Microsoft sphere, who got rich, then poor in the boom and bust. He was barely relevant by the year two thousand so Hannah couldn't see how he would have fit in with Fitzpatrick and the other three who worked for at least another ten years.

But a guy who had tasted wealth young, only to lose it when the tech bust blew your bubble was a strong motivating factor in The Client's creation.

Hannah slid Paulo Rodriguez's sheet off to the side.

Lonnie Banks, the fourth on the list, had a similar work path to Fitzpatrick. Clearly, they had been coworkers several times, perhaps good friends. That kind of familiarity would make a nefarious working arrangement not only possible, but understandable.

In a world of backstabbers, who do you trust?

Hannah stared at the names and wondered whether one of them was The Client, or were they missing the picture completely?

Paulo Rodriguez was the only one of the five who had been wealthy, so that could be the contributing factor. Did he have enough left over to pay an assassin? Lonnie Banks had the most intriguing name. It was the Big Banks that supplied the wealth, though Hannah had to admit it was a stretch. He had nothing else to go on.

All four had last known addresses from many years ago in northern California, as had Fitzpatrick, so The Client had to be one of these. It was unlikely Fitzy would have recently befriended someone his ex-wife hadn't met and pledged such trust that he would have embarked on such a daring scheme. It wouldn't have mattered how much money was involved.

Smith, Jenkins, Rodriguez, Banks…Fitzpatrick.

Five discarded genius-level computer pioneers with an ax to grind. All five had a motive, but who would take it to that next level? Who was angry enough and clever enough to create the scheme?

Smith, Jenkins, Rodriguez, Banks, Fitzpatrick.

Hannah's eyes danced over the names as he spoke them in his mind like a mantra, seeking a solution.

Then, a sliver of light cut through the haze. Hannah thought of the connection.

Who had the most experience in selecting a killer? A security expert. Who would be the more successful in the field, following The Bumper? A security expert.

Fitzpatrick had the motivation. He had the training. He had friends.

What he didn't have was imagination and money.

But they did. Rodriguez must have had some cash left after going bust, and Diane Jenkins had no doubt received a hush settlement. Did Lonnie Banks have cash? Maybe, but if not, depending upon how much they paid The Bumper, all they needed was a few hundred-thousand dollars to pay the piper and expense the travel. Maybe it was only one or two of them, not all four.

He knew for certain that one of them had been answering him on 'Hearts Elite.' But which?

Hannah paced around the table, settling in Agent Simms's chair. How would the brilliant junior agent view it?

Fitzpatrick had grown bitter over the years. Maybe he shows up to whatever get-togethers they have, and he throws out this revenge idea. His friends laughed, but did someone give it more than a passing thought? Did they call Mel later asking how workable it was?

Mel Fitzpatrick then disappears for six months before it all starts so he could work out the logistics. He had to have known how much it would cost, so who had the money?

It always came back to the money. Could Mel Fitzpatrick have had the cold brutality to execute the plan? Not according to his wife, but people change. If so, he would have needed someone he trusted to look after the cash. Maybe send payment to the assassin throughout the year to keep him motivated. Square up with the hotels and rental car companies.

Whoever had the money set up the scheme. Fitzpatrick was the foot soldier, screaming for revenge.

The Client had the money and created the game. That had to be the relationship.

Hannah spun to look out the window, picturing Agent Perez standing there, explaining the profilers' concerns. He heard echoes of *"Something flipped a switch in The Client. Something so profound that they would create a scheme so elaborate."*

"Who died that made you hate so much?" Hannah asked aloud. He looked at the whiteboard and pictured Sonya Fleming. *"There was a time in America where the family was a good thing for a man to have. In Silicon Valley, it was a crippling distraction."*

Hannah's mind buzzed with the elements and puzzles as clues bounced against theories, and theories wove into patterns, all meshing in a web of death.

"Something flipped a switch."

"Family was a crippling distraction."

Death.

The connection hit Hannah with a shock. He ran his revelation through the other elements, looking for a flaw. He thought of Hearts Elite, and how easily life changes in the blink of an eye, as fast as one hitting a switch.

A year-long murder spree, eleven victims instead of twelve, Mel Fitzpatrick tailing the killer, and a dating website for the rich.

Hannah argued the theory, tore it apart and put it back together until he was satisfied. It made too much sense.

He spun to the door and eased himself down the hall, ignoring the glances from agents who still wondered why he was a part of the investigation. Hannah caught Agent's Perez's eye, who was standing over Simms's desk while he studied his laptop. She tapped his shoulder, and they both followed Hannah into Agent Downey's office.

"By all means, don't knock," Downey said as the three of them slipped into the windowed corner suite. "What?"

Hannah nodded to Perez and Simms, then turned to his good friend, who had trusted him when no one else would.

"I've got it." Hannah said.

Chapter Fifty–Five

The Bumper landed just after three o'clock local time, grateful for the sudden burst of heat and sunshine. He feared using the airport after his picture had been made available, so he'd caught a Greyhound bus west until he reached St. Louis. From there, he could rent a hotel room near the airport and fly anywhere domestically, and no one would give him a second glance.

The killer had enough of the grey, flat middle of the United States, and was amazed at his first look at the desert. Even from the tarmac, it stretched out in all directions, with a brilliant rust color he'd only seen in films.

It was beautiful.

The unforgiving environment would be populated with predators of all kinds. Those that slithered, crawled, and soared. Those that traveled in packs, and those who attacked only at night. The desert was a bleak microcosm of the real world where only the smartest and most resilient could survive.

The Bumper finally felt at home.

Chapter Fifty-Six

Elaine Stafford read the chilling details of Nathan O'Neill's death on-line, searching out his profile on the site. There were a few photos, a couple with obvious signs of Photoshop, and one with an awful choice of hair color.

She completed the download of all his metadata, contacts, and chats, and filed it with the ten others from January through October.

Each victim had been given his own archival folder for safe-keeping. Then, she had frozen their accounts.

Stafford stared at the eleven icons on the screen, labeled by month as if they were centerfolds, amazed that these eleven men were dead because they had signed up on her website. That wasn't the only reason, of course, but it was a consistent, contributing factor.

'Hearts Elite' had tens of thousands of accounts, so losing these eleven wasn't even a consideration to the bottom line. No, it was the moral impact that had kept Stafford on edge.

As she dragged the eleven into a single packet for transfer, she pondered the future of her company.

She thought, as she reviewed her membership list, *"Maybe it's time I did something."*

Chapter Fifty-Seven

Agent Downey rocked in his office chair, giving Hannah's words serious consideration. He looked over at Agent Simms and Perez for confirmation. Perez was staring out the window while Simms was nodding, as if running it through his head.

"Fitzpatrick was the foot soldier, and The Client called the shots?" Downey asked.

Hannah stood by the door. "Yes. The Client, no doubt, had a major hand in hiring The Bumper, who had to be kept in the dark as long as possible. We know there is no way Fitzpatrick could have devised the scheme. He wanted to be part of the hunt and needed financial backing. The Client was someone who could choose the victims and run the operations with the money. They are two unique skills, and two important tasks. Fitzpatrick had to be out there making sure the job was being done, while the other partner ran the operation on-line, sending the information to the killer while communicating with Fitzpatrick."

Perez asked. "Is it one friend on the list, and, if so, which one? Or how about all of them?"

Hannah replied, "Just one. We believed the plan was twelve murders in twelve months, overseen by a vengeful computer security expert, spelling out a chilling phrase with corresponding initials. But why? The answer is very simple. Because it is the only way it would have worked."

"How did they use Heart's Elite without detection?" Downey asked.

"We have underestimated the brilliance of The Client's computer skills because we never considered the west coast, Silicon Valley connection. We were looking for new accounts and digital footprints. I'm sure hacking into the mainframe of data and profiles was child's play to them. That is why Stafford had no idea how it was happening. The Client was the proverbial ghost in the machine."

Agent Perez asked, "The thing that triggered The Client? You think you've figured out what happened?"

"I do," Hannah said, "and everything makes sense now. Why it started when it did, why single men were chosen, and why Mel Fitzpatrick was in the field. Everything is connected."

Simms sat back with an exhausted sigh, as Downey leaned in, intrigued.

"It had better be good, Pally, because it isn't obvious to me."

"I have Sonya Fleming to thank for the insight," Hannah said "Having a family killed your career. Being single was the freedom Their married friends all got divorced."

"The Client has a thing against marriage?" Downey asked, as Simms snapped his fingers.

"No," Simms said. "The young billionaires who took away their jobs prioritized being single. That is why the Client hunted single men. They represented the elite of Silicon Valley."

"Exactly," Hannah said, "and the young upstarts who took their jobs. But I'm convinced I know what kicked off the scheme eighteen months ago, and why Mel Fitzpatrick was crucial to the execution in the field. What could be so devastating that would trigger an aging, law-abiding computer programmer to unleash such a heinous plot?"

Three pairs of eyes bore into Hannah's. "Eleven single men, killed in eleven different cities, over eleven months, where it was impossible for The Client to be present. He would need Mel's help." He said.

Agent Simms broke from his trance, an idea flitting through his eyes.

"Someone went to their doctor and got a death sentence."

Chapter Fifty-Eight

The Bumper checked in for his final American hotel stay. He unpacked what few clothes he kept, opting to buy extra shirts and shorts. Gone are the black pants and grey sweaters. It's time for a new look.

He was immune to the jet lag that would have thrown off many people because he had travelled enough across Europe in his time, though he had lost track of days. Was it December second or third? Time was hardly a concern anymore. His target wasn't going anywhere and probably wasn't expecting him, either.

The Client had been kind, saving the easiest for last. But always lingering in the back of The Bumper's mind was that small voice reminding him that appearances can be deceiving. What may look like an easy kill could shroud the ultimate betrayal.

He moved about the large city, matching the pace of the pedestrians, blending in as best he could. There was a lot of red and orange in their clothing, and cotton was a common fabric. He darted into stores, looking for matching fashions, and added a couple of baseball caps with local university logos on them.

By the time he had returned to his hotel that night, The Bumper was ready to assume his final identity in this game of murder. He flipped open his laptop and scrambled the internet access. He read the memorized dossier again, just to familiarize himself with what he had seen today about the environment.

The Client must have used this as their home base.

It was almost as if he had been right here.

Chapter Fifty-Nine

Agent Perez broke the silence. "It makes sense. It answers the question 'Why now?'"

"That was always a stumbling block." Hannah admitted. "This was a well thought-out, long game approach. We just had to figure out what had kicked it off. And the profilers were right. There was a trigger."

"Which one of them is it, Robert?"

Hannah winced. "That I don't know yet, but hear me out."

"I'm all ears."

"The Client is too sick to be physically present at the murders, so that would be Mel's job. Fitzpatrick always had this crazy idea, but then one of them found out they have maybe a year to live, and after a few days of anger and regret, I'm sure that crazy plot floated through their mind. They reached out to Mel and put the plan together. They probably used all The Client's money because there was no one to leave it to, anyway."

"So, Fitzpatrick disappeared for a few months to plan and kicked it off in January. What if The Client died before it was over?" Perez asked.

Agent Simms said, "I think they worked that into the plan."

Hannah agreed. "The power of positive thinking. What better way to motivate a friend to stay active and use their genius in the face of a debilitating disease than to give them a reason to live? That, more than anything, explains the elaborate plot. Keep The Client busy and engaged. So, he created patterns and puzzles. To The Client, it was nothing but a game of revenge. Which is why December is the most important month, providing the ultimate twist. It is how we unmask The Client."

Agent Downey asked, "How do we do that, and why is the twelfth murder the most important?"

Hannah looked at Agent Simms. "I think Jacco knows. It is why the phrase was only eleven letters long."

Agent Simms said, "We need to find the one guy who links all these friends together. Either the one co-worker who screwed them over, or the one boss who had a hand in firing each of them. There is one guy who has been the face of this rage, their focus. I'll dig and see if I can find some candidates."

Downey said, "Oh, I bet you'll find a boatload of candidates. The question will be which one?"

Hannah said, "He'll be easy to pick out. His first name will start with a 'D' because of December and he will live in a city that makes sense to the phrase *KILL THE RICH*. He is the reason the phrase was eleven letters long. He is the reason the cities mattered. It has always been about him. We find him, we find The Bumper."

"*The ABC Murders*. He was the purpose of the entire spree." Downey concluded.

"Yes sir," Hannah said. "The motivation to keep The Client alive. To hang on long enough to see December's execution."

Downey turned to Agents Simms and Perez. "Can you get a list together tonight, Jacco?"

"You bet," Perez answered on his behalf. "I'll make sure he does. All hands on deck."

Hannah helped Curt and Laurel clear the table. He had been grateful for the invitation and appreciated the gesture.

The Downey house was awash with Christmas decorations, and an Elf on the Shelf spied on the three from a mischievous perch above the television. Stockings with the girls' names were hung on the stair bannisters, reminding Hannah to do some shopping. It would be the first time in a while he had cared enough to buy gifts, and he had a long list this year.

"Which one of the girls would like the drum set, and which would like the cat?" Hannah teased, looking under the tree.

"Don't even joke," Laurel said, pouring the mugs of coffee. "Uncle Robert doesn't need to play Santa this year. They will get spoiled enough. Bailey wants an iPad, for God's sake."

"I'm surprised the girls don't have one already." Hannah answered. "I assumed the hospitals hand them out in the maternity ward."

The three eased themselves into the living room and picked up the conversation without little ears overhearing. "So, California, huh?" Laurel said.

"It looks that way," Curt admitted. "I'll be back in a few days."

Laurel nodded with apprehension painted on her face. Hannah remembered his promise from months ago that danger would not find its way to their doorstep, but here was Curt called to be part of the final takedown of a killer he alone had initially detected. It was an honor to get the nod, and he knew his friend wasn't about to turn it down.

"On a scale of one to ten," she asked, clearly not for the first time. "How dangerous?"

Curt warmed to the regular question. "I'll be in more danger on the flight than on the ground. I'm in the reconnaissance vans, so I won't be anywhere near the action."

Laurel turned her hooded eyes and stared at Hannah over her steaming mug, with only a hint of humor in them. "I believe you promised me this wouldn't happen."

"Well, to be fair," Hannah reiterated, "I said that I wouldn't let anything dangerous happen to your family. But if Captain America wants to go to California, who am I to stop him? I'll tell you what. Why don't the three of us turn on our location notifications? That way, we'll all know where we are."

Curt shook his head with a nervous chuckle and thumbed through his phone.

With Laurel's concerns aired, they turned to the last details of the case. "You're sure you have the target?" She asked.

Hannah looked at Curt, who replied. "No, we aren't one hundred percent sure, but he is far and above the most likely."

He related the life story of Drew Bennett, who was a billionaire start-up success story. He had arrived on the scene with some money in his pocket, but with enough connections to be a success in whatever he wanted to do. He got in on the ground floor in the late nineteen-seventies, promoting computer technology to level the education field. If everyone had access to the same opportunity tools, then poverty could be eradicated. Bennett started several small companies, employing innovative technology at the time that would eventually morph into live digital streaming, and enhanced educational programs that could be accessed anywhere, anytime.

Each start-up company minnow was swallowed by a larger corporate fish until his initial crusade of eliminating the poverty gap ensured he would never be on the wrong side of it. Bennett's aim was incorporated into so many platforms that it was hard to see where his influence ended, or what his vision had become. But eliminating poverty was no longer a viable business model.

Like so many in Silicon Valley, Drew Bennett's idealism gave way to pragmatism. Higher ideals were stomped on the climb to greater profits.

"Each of the four people on Fitzpatrick's wife's list had crossed paths with Bennett at one time." Hannah continued. "All had worked for him, and three had been downsized from his companies when the takeovers started. In fact, Lonnie Banks had been let go twice."

"And the fourth?" Laurel asked.

"That's interesting. Diane Jenkins wrote a paper on Bennett's attempts to use the internet for good and praised his philanthropy in the face of corrupt practices that were emerging in the Valley. But when he and his companies turned their back on his original vision, she answered with a scathing rebuttal that got traction. That's what prompted her very public firing, and the eventual lawsuit. Agent Simms had to make a few calls today to nail it down. It had been gagged."

"Wow," Laurel said. "The last remaining decent people in Silicon Valley forced out, then turned vengeful. It is unbelievable."

"No," Hannah said. "As Sonya Fleming said, it's almost inevitable. Look around. The sentiment is everywhere."

They finished their coffees as Hannah stood to leave. "Thank you both very much for your hospitality tonight. I really appreciate the invitation, Laurel." He gave her a gentle hug and walked to the door.

"So how come you don't get to go?" She asked him, patting Curt's butt on the way past. "Who is going to look after my man?"

"Probably the one hundred other agents. Besides, I would only get in the way. It's not a big place."

She turned to Curt. "What's it called?"

"Drew Bennett has a huge spread just outside a small town in the Sierra-Nevada foothills. It's called Paradise."

Chapter Sixty

The Client lay silently in bed, thinking of death. At first, fearful following the diagnosis, the constant pain had altered their outlook.

Death would be a massive relief. And it would arrive soon.

A tear unexpectedly dropped from their eye when they thought of the morning when Mel had first made that preposterous boast. *"We could kill them all and get away with it. They made us invisible. It's their fault."*

It was a theme he would drag out time and time again until the group just stopped getting together. His obsession had spoiled what few friendships they had had.

Until the doctor pointed at x-rays and calendars.

Treatment would be expensive and could buy some time, but a full recovery was a pipe dream. So why spend that money on something that would do nothing but prop up pharmaceutical companies and *their* rich overlords? Couldn't the money be used for some worthwhile enterprise?

It had always been their vision when they started working in northern California that the better future would be found on-line. Education, the environment, and freedom. It could all be realized with equal opportunity offered at the dawn of the computer age. Wealth didn't matter, race didn't matter, orientation didn't matter. Nothing mattered but the human imagination, and the limitless possibilities they could fathom. What an amazing time to be alive and know that you had helped shape the brave new world.

It wouldn't matter if you were rich or poor.

So naïve. Of course, it mattered. It had always mattered.

The Client thought of the other hippies and hoped they had found their peace. Mel's death weighed heavily, although it had been his crazy idea in the first place, though perhaps they should have never made that phone call, offering the money.

"How would we do it? I can't kill anyone!"

Mel had reassured them. *"Leave that to me. We'll hire someone to do it for us. You just rest. There will be plenty to do soon."*

"How many should we kill? Five? Ten? A dozen?"

"Twelve sounds perfect. How about one a month?"

"Oh, I love that, Mel. But let's stop at eleven. I have an idea for the twelfth."

"Absolutely," Mel agreed. *"Start choosing the targets. And have some fun. I'll even let you pick how we do it."*

The Client felt a jolt of excitement. *What if each of these entitled bastards died a unique and puzzling death?*

Having cemented the motive behind each of the murders, how would one select the tailored means of death? It hadn't taken long for The Client to stumble upon the grotesque site called 'Hearts Elite'. Hacking into the database took some work, but owing to their expert training and unlimited time, The Client mirrored the commands and gained undetected access. Their first task was to troll profiles to see how easy it would be to pair up initials with their monthly murders, and glean as much information on each member's lavish, undeserved lifestyle to lure them to their death.

It couldn't have been easier.

The stroke of genius was landing on the taunting phrase. After selecting Jacob and Frank for January and February, the column of cities had started with K and I. Was there a suitable target whose first initial was *M*, who lived in a city that started with *L*?

Well, look at that. There was. Mason McKinley, a forty-year-old art dealer in Lansing, Michigan, who only accepted contact with women under twenty-one years of age.

Scum.

Alex Dunn from Louisville followed quickly, and the entire sequence, *KILL THE RICH*, dropped into place.

It was perfect. And completely untraceable.

All The Client had to do now was wait for death's frigid breath and the suffering would be over.

A glint of sun stung their eye off the corner of the laptop. They lay their hand on it, wishing that things could have been different. Could have been better.

The Client lifted the screen and thought about that Robert Hannah fellow. He seemed to be the only one who was even aware of what was happening, but could do nothing about it.

They brought up the 'Hearts Elite' account and found no new riddles. It was kind of sad. One last zinger would be satisfying. *"Go out on a high note"* and all that.

Their lips curled at the fun, brief message that ran through their mind. Despite the pain, the lively puzzler was still working inside.

"This is goodbye, and if it is all the same to you, let this bazaar year end."

After tapping send, The Client slid the laptop to the side of the bed, too tired to lift it onto the chair. Within seconds, they were asleep.

Hannah stared at the message. *"If it's all the same to you?"* He repeated. *"Let this bazaar year end?"*

He thought about texting Agent Simms, but it was Friday, December Twenty-second. Curt was expected back from California tomorrow with little to report on the hunt for The Bumper, and a terrified Drew Bennett had locked himself in at the FBI's insistence.

Everyone had poured their heart into the investigation, and here, The Client, was reaching out one last time. Hannah didn't want to spoil Simms and Perez's pre-Christmas weekend with a stupid little ditty. Especially since Bennett was locked down.

It must be an admission of defeat. No hard feelings. Just let it go.

Yet, he knew better than to take the message at face value. *"If it's all the same to you?"* He repeated. "Why would it be all the same to me?" His eye kept falling on the word bazaar. It seemed out of place.

Hannah spoke aloud to his own silent partner. "I wouldn't categorize this year as bazaar. It was tragic and horrific. No one would call it bazaar. Why would they? And why would that be *all the same to me?"*

Same. It had something to do with what was *the same*. Hannah grabbed the files to look for things that were the same, but struck out within minutes. There were far too many variables to find common links. But he was now certain it was a message.

"He's leaving one last clue. But for what? Is he pointing to Drew Bennett?"

Hannah wrote everything he could about Bennett.

Paradise, California, December…nothing remotely looked bazaar or the same.

He jumped at the mistake. But it wouldn't be a mistake. It would be intentional.

"That's not how you spell bazaar. It should be 'bizarre'".

Hannah went back to the initial message and read it slowly. *'If it's all the same to you, let this bazaar year end.'*

The first clue struck him when he realized why the misuse of 'bazaar' was necessary. The entire message sent him reeling when he solved it.

My God. Could it be true?

Hannah couldn't alert Curt because he wouldn't land in time and probably would try to talk him out of it. In fact, what if he was wrong? Instead, to be safe, he sent a group text. At least Curt would know then.

Hannah looked at the clock. Shit. Stacey!

As if on command, a gentle knock on the door announced his ex-wife's presence for a long-overdue Christmas drink and heart-to-heart talk. Hannah had offered it as her Christmas present, and she could not resist it. He had no illusions she would stay for the weekend and Christmas morning, but he knew that after what had happened this year, he was ready to try again.

He rushed to open the door to find Stacey holding a bottle of bubbly and an overnight bag.

She had wondered, too.

Hannah bit his lip. He hated doing this when inspiration struck. He would find out whether she was still the adventurous type.

"Oh, good, you're packed. I just got a message from The Client, and I know how it all ends. Will you come with me? Please?"

Stacey pulled a small pout of disappointment, but Hannah watched that unbridled, curious side brighten her eyes. "Where are we going?" She asked.

He answered. "Mesa, Arizona."

Chapter Sixty-One

Hannah and Stacey had settled in on the early morning flight. It departed Logan airport for Phoenix International at six-ten, scheduled to arrive in Arizona just after nine o'clock local time.

"I don't doubt your abilities with puzzles," Stacey said, "and I love the idea of a trip away for Christmas, but are you sure you're on the right track? I mean, you would hate yourself if you were wrong."

Hannah turned and smiled. "No, I'm right. The line 'if it's all the same to you' is an anagram, because The Client knows it's *not* the same to me. Not the *same* means an anagram of *same* which is Mesa. The misuse of bazaar contains the AZA that wouldn't have been in the proper use of bizarre."

"What does the AZA have to do with it?" Stacey asked.

"AZA is the airport designation for Phoenix." Hannah answered. He stared out the window at the growing light above the clouds, pondering the first steps upon landing. He'd need to get to his rental car and access Wi-Fi.

"You still make that face," Stacey said. "The one where you're so deep in thought that you forget you're even on a plane."

Hannah leaned over to his ex-wife and kissed her hair. "No, I'm here. The face may be the same, but my mind is right here. I just need to plan this out. We are running out of time."

"I just don't know how you think you can pull it off. We are looking for four people in a city of half a million, and we don't know where they are."

"I know," Hannah said. "But he gave me the clue. He wants me there. When we land, I'll send a message on the account. He will answer. For sure, it will be a puzzle, but it will lead me to The Client."

Stacey tilted her seat back on the full flight, just two days before Christmas, and said, "Well, it's a good thing I'm with you. Two heads are better than one, even if yours is genius level."

"No," Hannah declared. "I know how much you love getting into these scraps, but you're not getting anywhere near this. We'll find a pleasant hotel and hope it isn't full for the holiday, and you can relax."

"Robert, I won't be in any trouble just reading clues. Besides, if there is any real danger, then I won't let you out of my sight. You have no training for this kind of confrontation."

They both settled back, lost in their own thoughts, drifting in and out of sleep, with their fingers intertwined. As the plane descended into Phoenix, Hannah spied the expansive desert floor and remarked on the sand.

"It looks like the spot for a good treasure hunt."

The Client woke from a listless sleep. The pain would come in waves, and the daily medication could only dull the edge for so long. It was December twenty-third. The Bumper would complete his last task, and there would be peace. There was bittersweet satisfaction in knowing that their efforts and money had been worth it.

Breakfast arrived on the tray, and the inclined bed allowed a semblance of independence. The Client took their time, pondering the last days, wondering when it would end. Without Mel, who was to know when the killer would strike? There had been no correspondence concerning the late payment last month, so perhaps a scheduled payment for January first, along with a second deposit of the bonus, was the best way. When it was over, the bank account would be nearly depleted, but whatever little money remained would sit idle in a forgotten bank account forever. Or until the bank went under.

The Client pulled the laptop across the table and lifted the screen. As they logged on to the bank transfer, an icon caught their eye. When the laptop had last been closed, the window was still open, meaning they had not closed out of 'Hearts Elite.'

It seems Robert Hannah had sent a reply.

With the wire transfer forgotten, The Client checked Hannah's profile box and found, *"Mesa, Arizona, it is. See you tomorrow. Merry Christmas."*

The computer whiz, so close to death and in such pain, smiled for the first time since the death of their dear friend Mel Fitzpatrick. It had been so long since they'd had a visitor.

Stacey secured a hotel reservation while Hannah nailed down the rental car. Sensible sedans were all rented for the holidays, so they'd had to make do with a luxury SUV.

"We have an Escalade. I had my choice of white, white…or white."

"That's too bad," Stacey said. "I was hoping for off-white."

They inputted the hotel address into his phone GPS and drove east out of Phoenix into the desert along highway two-oh-two. They passed the exit signs to Tempe and continued until they reached highway Eighty-Seven, and the interchange to Mesa, which turned into North

Country Club Drive. The streets were busy with pedestrians, and the roads were congested with shoppers crossing off the last present from their list, or last-minute warriors just getting started.

The Desert Marriot was a four-floor hotel on the eastern outskirts of Mesa, strategically built just before the Boulder Mountains crushed the landscape. It offered free parking and breakfast. Hannah had been lucky when booking the room. Much like the rental car, there had been little selection. Non-smoking, one queen bed was all they had.

The front desk staff, wearing their Santa hats, welcomed them warmly and allowed an early check-in. Hannah and Stacey rushed to drop the overnight bags and log onto the Wi-Fi. He fired up his laptop while Stacey hit the vending and ice machines.

It was almost eleven-thirty when they had finally hit the 'Hearts Elite' website. The status wheel spun, searching for the link as Hannah prayed for a response. As it loaded, and he saw the telltale (one) in the chat box, his phone rang. He looked to see if Stacey had been locked out when he saw 'Curt.'

Hannah considered ignoring the call but knew that could easily come back to haunt him. He knew it would come to this, anyway.

"Hey," was all Hannah had to say before Curt laid into him.

"What the hell do you think you're doing in Arizona? Where are you?"

"I'm okay, and Stacey is with me. We're in a hotel. We're safe."

"Well, you stay in that hotel. I can have a couple of agents do whatever you think you are going to do. Are you crazy, Pally?"

"Look, Curt. I know it's a longshot, but The Client messaged me, and I think they want to meet. I don't think I'm in any danger. If we've been right about this, they aren't violent, and there is little they can do because they'll be dead before they see a courtroom."

"You don't know that, Pally. It is only a theory they may be dying. You are in way over your head here. This is one poker game when going all in gets you killed." Downey said.

"I'll be safe. I just sent the three of you the note because I wanted you to know where I was. If this blows back on you, do whatever covers your ass. I don't care. I want to do this. And I think The Client wants to play one last game. Hide and seek."

"How the hell did you convince Stacey to go with you?"

"Kind of a long story, but she's cool about it. She wants to help, too."

"Oh, my God. I'm going to alert the FBI in Phoenix to see if a couple of agents can monitor you two. If you're right, I don't want you walking in alone. Got that?"

"I do, Curt. And thank you."

Hannah hung up and turned to the laptop. He opened the chat window and read the reply.

"So much sand in the hourglass, but so little time. It's best to start at the beginning."

The beginning? Was The Client born here? Was the first clue a hospital?

If The Client was dying, then a hospital made a great deal of sense, but that could also be the ending. No, they only mentioned the beginning.

Stacey walked in with her arms full of soda bottles, small potato chip bags, and a full ice bucket. "Quick, I need your help," Hannah called. She dropped the goods on the dresser beside the TV and sidled up to him on the bed.

"The beginning? The beginning of Arizona?" She asked.

"Oh, I hadn't thought of that. Damn, I don't know."

Hannah had to think like The Client. The beginning was also the interest in computers.

"These friends were all computer whizzes. What about where they all started?"

"I thought they were in California?" Stacey asked.

"Yeah, but it can't be there. We're here." They sat quietly racking their brains when Stacey remarked, "They made the sand reference like you did. Do you think this is a buried treasure puzzle?"

"No, I'm hoping it will lead to their location," he answered.

Stacey nodded, then got up and walked to the door. "I'll be back in a few minutes. Keep going."

Hannah closed his eyes and prayed for inspiration. "Beginning of what?" He asked.

An idea snuck in. He searched the web until he found Mesa Community College. It offered several computer programming diplomas. Could that be it? Education?

Stacey returned with a folded booklet from a rack he'd seen in the lobby, full of maps and brochures. She dropped it beside Hannah. "It's a map of Mesa. We can circle the spots until we find somewhere that makes sense."

"Good idea." He picked up the map and unfolded it flat across the queen-size bed. Hannah hit the coordinates on the website for Mesa Community College and found its location on the map. He circled it in red.

"What's that?" She asked.

"It's the local community college that offers computer programs. It was how they all started. Young people working toward building education through computers." He tabbed back to 'Hearts Elite.' How should he answer?

Stacey leaned over and said, "Consider me enrolled. Where is my first class?"

"That's perfect," Hannah said, as Stacey grabbed the car keys. He looked up and asked where she was going.

"Robert, it's a treasure hunt. Grab the map. I'll drive."

Chapter Sixty-Two

The young woman brought in the lunch tray. The Client was sure they had never seen her before. "Yes," she replied when asked. "So many of the full-time staff have the holiday weekend off, so I'm just filling in for a couple of days. I'll be back when you're done, and Merry Christmas."

The Client abandoned and alone at the end, thought there was nothing worse than dying among strangers. They nibbled at the saltine cracker and sipped as much soup as they could manage.

The brightness of midday had prompted an orderly to close the blinds, casting a dull shadow across the floor. As it moved with the sun, so time was marching closer to claim them. It couldn't possibly be long now.

A note pinged from the laptop, piquing their curiosity. Perhaps Hannah was engaged in the puzzle. The Client was sure he would just run around asking people if they knew anyone who had been friends with Mel Fitzpatrick. He would be barking up the wrong cactus. No one here knew Mel Fitzpatrick, and no one knew them, either.

The Client had arrived in Mesa, Arizona, from Northern California to seek treatment for the fast-spreading cancer at the Mayo Pain Clinic. When the diagnosis had been made, and the end became certain, it was just easier to stay. Mel understood and was sympathetic. But it didn't take long before The Client and confidante of the plan realized their mistake.

When Mel had visited with the last details and execution of the plan that had begun in January, that was when the mistake was corrected. Full speed ahead.

The pained fingers lifted the laptop, and the patient clicked on the window.

"I'm enrolled. Where is my first course?"

The patient, despite the pain and weariness, was impressed. Even if he had the wrong spot, he was a dog with a bone. That counted for something.

The Client spread the on-line map across the screen and highlighted the Mesa Community College. They followed a line until they found their next destination.

'This could be a fun way to spend my last good day working on a puzzle map.'

They sent along the next riddle, and closed their eyes, hoping death let them be. They wanted to see how this one ended.

Stacey pulled into the empty student parking lot at Mesa Community College. Hannah got out and scanned the horizon but found no one. "Meeting here would have been too easy," he said.

"The Client wanted you to start here. Any reply yet?"

Hannah dropped back into the passenger seat and scanned his phone.

He read the new message aloud. *"What has wings, but does not fly? Was built to win and built to die?"*

Hannah read it aloud at various speeds as he thought of an answer.

"I thought you said this guy is dying? He sure seems on the ball to me," Stacey commented.

"He is a genius in his own way." Hannah agreed, trying out the phrase again. "What has wings but doesn't fly?"

"A large building, like a hospital? It has wings." Stacey said, sipping a soda.

"Of course, those kinds of wings." Hannah searched the map and found a half dozen hospital and health centers. "Which one is right? Does it matter?" He asked.

Stacey got up and peered over his shoulder. They were all spread too apart to make sense of the pattern. "Which one is closest to the College?"

Hannah looked down and stabbed at the paper. "This one," he said, reaching for a marker.

"Hang on." Stacey said. "That makes little sense with *built to win and built to die.*"

"People die in hospitals," Hannah offered. He was becoming annoyed that Stacey was doing a better job of keeping calm under pressure than he was. Hannah looked back at the map when his eye caught a strange symbol which denoted a tourist attraction.

Hannah read the corresponding name. "There, that's it!" He declared.

The Commemorative Air Force Airbase Museum housed military aircraft, as well as tour planes. *"What has wings but does not fly? Built to win and built to die?"* He repeated. "Decommissioned military aircraft." He circled the location on the map of Mesa. "How do I respond?"

"Use a rhyming couplet like they did." Stacey said, firing up the Escalade.

Hannah spun words in his head, searching for both a rhyme that answered the riddle, but one that also asked how many clues there would be.

He paused with his fingers on the keys before typing, "*Military aircraft ensured defeat, but I long for closure when we finally meet.*" He hit send and strapped himself in. They peeled off for the straight shot to the museum.

They arrived twenty-one minutes later, finding the lot empty just two days before Christmas. Hannah scanned his phone while Stacey walked through the lot.

There had been no reply.

Chapter Sixty-Three

The smartly dressed couple exited the Phoenix International airport and grabbed a shuttle to the rental car kiosk. They picked up a Mercedes convertible, peeled out of the parking lot, and headed east. There was little talk on the drive. It was all business.

The GPS setting alerted them to exit the highway and advance into downtown Mesa until it sent them east to the town limits in the shadows of the Boulder Mountains. From there, they spied the Desert Marriot and wheeled into an adjoining parking lot to wait.

Their job wasn't to confront or apprehend. Their job was to observe and report.

They sat in the late-morning desert sun and waited.

It took less than twenty minutes when the bright white Escalade with the unknown woman driving roared from the parking lot, heading west into downtown Mesa.

The Mercedes convertible purred into action and followed, keeping a safe distance behind without losing visual contact. The driver asked whether contact should be made, as the passenger texted an update. Upon the reply, she said, "No, just follow, but don't get made."

The driver laughed.

As if.

Chapter Sixty-Four

The weary patient puzzled over the reply before realizing the query. Hannah was growing impatient. One mustn't string him along forever.

The Client looked at the clock. It was three-thirty. All it would take is a couple of more clues. Not that they expected success for Hannah. Just a fun preoccupation for themselves.

They typed out the next clue and settled to listen to the ambient noises. Brushes of shoes in the hallway and the light tinkling of Christmas music from some distant room. It was still as a tomb. There was usually more activity, but with it being a weekend, and Christmas at that, these part-time caregivers were virtual strangers to each other and the residents. The thought of dying without loved ones brought a fresh wave of melancholy, as tears flooded their eyes. They knew very well what they had gotten into, the decisions they had made in their life, but it was sad to know it was almost over. Still, what a relief.

The patient thought of Drew Bennett and wondered what he was planning for Christmas. No doubt an extravagant meal with lots of presents, paid for by the work of the unappreciated, the expendable, the invisible.

The anger rose to vanquish the sorrow and claim its rightful place in their mind. Drew Bennett had caused all of this.

But it was time for the anger to end. It was time to put an end to it all.

"What does it say?" Stacey asked.

"Halfway there, my curious friend. Before my time, on them depend." Hannah read.

"Time? Why is it always about time?" She asked. "So, what would be before their time?"

Stacey pulled out of the lot and headed back to the downtown core. "Do you know?" Hannah asked.

"No, but whatever it is, it isn't around here. Sitting is a waste of time. Think it out and find it on the map. I'll just drive."

"Before my time, on them depend," He repeated. "What did we used to depend on that we don't anymore?"

"A lot of things," Stacey agreed, as the business section of Mesa appeared on the horizon.

Hannah said. "It has to mean that before the internet. *Before my time,* means before they helped to create home computers."

The Escalade got caught up in the late afternoon Christmas traffic and sat through a couple of stoplights before Hannah figured it out. "Look, a Kinko's!"

Stacey looked back, trying to change lanes to get moving, when she asked, "When did we depend on Kinko's?"

"No, that's what they mean. Before email, we depended on *the post office.*" He punched at his phone, then looked up at the intersection ahead. "You need to go left up here. Can you get over?"

She nudged the nose of the Escalade ahead of a Jeep whose driver exhibited a complete lack of Christmas spirit, and Stacey sped up to move into the left turning lane. She looked back when the Jeep honked in frustration after a black convertible Mercedes also cut them off.

"Okay, how far?" She asked.

"It looks like about two miles, but you'll need to turn again when we get closer. Stay in the left lane," he said.

"Are you going to reply now or wait until we get there? It's four-fifteen." Stacey said.

"I'm thinking, I'm thinking," Hannah said, giving in to the frustration. "Should I send back another riddle? There is only going to be one more clue after this one."

"Good thing too, because it will get dark by five o'clock."

The Escalade whipped left and followed traffic through green lights for two miles when Hannah directed her to turn left, then ease right around City Hall. The post office was just down the block.

It was a historic building with classical Arizona architecture. "It doesn't look like any post office I've seen back home," he commented.

"What's the reply, game boy?" Stacey asked.

"Okay, how about something with 'stamp of approval' in it? Like I'm complimenting their brilliance?" Hannah said.

Stacey nodded. "I like it. What other analogies work? Christmas package, mail, shipping, boxes…"

Hannah cut in. "Mail? Yes, perfect. You are a genius," he said, thumbing a furious reply.

Stacey checked her mirrors before pulling back out into traffic. "Naturally, too bad it has taken you this long to figure that out." Hannah settled back in his seat, but before he read his message, Stacey said. "I think we have company."

The Mercedes driver pulled into an open spot, with a clear view of the Escalade. As darkness swallowed the last of the day's light, the pair was grateful their quarry drove a large white SUV.

"Where do you suppose they are going?" He asked.

The passenger had texted an update. "I don't know, but there is a worry that all these stops could signal a problem. Either they are frantically lost, or being led into a trap."

"Perfect," the driver said.

Chapter Sixty-Five

The bedside table lamp provided barely enough light for the patient's eyesight. A reply notification prompted their uncomfortable shift in the hospital bed. The patient had to pull the laptop cord to gain access to the device. They were so weakened late in the day.

The Client had the last message ready to send, when Hannah's reply made them reconsider.

"He really is something, isn't he?" they breathed aloud, as a fresh dread set in. The implications of the message were that Hannah knew more than was deemed possible.

How could he have known about the group? Who would have told him?

The answer slid in from memories of the five computer visionaries, toasting the future, expecting their accolades, counting their future earnings.

But there weren't just five. There were six.

Clearly, with Mel's death, someone had talked to Sonya.

The investigators knew more than anyone had imagined.

The Client closed their eyes, rage boiling in their chest, cutting off oxygen. 'Settle, settle,' they thought. Now was not the time to die of a heart attack. What a terrible end to the game that would be. Utter uselessness.

Robert Hannah was thought to be just a curiosity, an on-line plaything. No, he was much worse.

The reply had a small digital picture of the post office, with the phrase, "*I have your three pieces of male. Where would you like it delivered?*"

This Robert Hannah knew the group had three men left after Mel's death, and the picture was more than an implied threat.

He was really here.

Hannah looked back over his shoulder. He could see headlights in the growing dusk, but not much more. "Are you sure?"

"The nice black car behind us cut off that Jeep way back, then followed us. Whoever is driving just pulled out of a parking spot. They stopped when we stopped. Robert, why are we being followed?" Stacey asked.

"Curt said he'd try to contact an FBI pair to help us out. Maybe it's them," he answered.

Stacey gave a throaty laugh. "Do you hear yourself? How did a pair of FBI agents in a city of half a million people find us, complete strangers, in a rented SUV in traffic?"

"I don't know, Stacey. It could be a coincidence."

"Robert, we are on the trail of a serial killer who you've been tracking for a year. Show a little more concern!"

"I'd rather get a reply on my phone. Just try to lose the tail." Hannah said.

"What? Like I'm a spy now?"

Hannah sighed. "Stacey, look, I'm sorry. I just need the last clue." He wheeled around. "Is it still back there?"

"I think so, but I'll make some turns and see what happens," she said.

As Stacey hit a fast right, Hannah's phone pinged. He slid it open to confirm the reply. He held the phone with one hand and his seat with the other as Stacey sped up and spun again. "When you think you've lost them, pull over. I need to read this."

Stacey made a quick left at a school crossing sign and pulled into the parking lot. Any other car pulling in would be highly suspicious.

"Four equal points can make a square, or, perhaps, some other measure. Create the sign to find me there, your long-awaited treasure."

Hannah read it aloud and looked at the map. "Where are we supposed to go?"

"We've only been to three places." Stacey said. "Unless you count the airport or the hotel."

Hannah shook his head. "The airport is too far away compared to the spots in Mesa."

"Where is the hotel on the map? Can you find it?" She asked.

"But the Client wouldn't know where we're staying." He straightened the map to find it.

"No, it's too far. It isn't an equal point…. *an equal point?*" Hannah repeated. He hit the overhead light and scrambled for his pen. He turned the map sideways so Stacey could see their route. "Look at our three stops. Here, here, and here. Three stops. They make a triangle. Now, if you wanted to make a square, you'd put in a point in the opposite direction just as far away. Like…here," he said, circling a small section of town. "It doesn't matter where we go. All we needed was four equal points. As long as we got the first three right, the fourth doesn't matter."

"Your guy wanted us to make a square? So, he's inside the square?" Stacey asked.

"No," Hannah said. "Not a square. *Create the sign to find me there, your long-awaited treasure.* We aren't supposed to make a square." He drew straight lines with his pen between the first pair of circles, then the other two.

"It makes an 'X'?" Stacey asked.

"X marks the spot. The location of every treasure hunt."

"Okay, but where is the X? It's an enormous area, Robert."

Hannah pulled up his phone and honed in on a one block radius in the southern area of Mesa.

There it was. Like a beacon.

"The 'X' we need is the spot where the two lines converge. It points to The Client." Hannah enlarged the map on his phone and pointed to the name.

The modern care hospital that lay beneath the converging lines on his map was a private facility that was part patient care, part hospice.

St. Xavier's.

Chapter Sixty-Six

St Xavier's Health Care Oasis was a two-story, three wing building at the end of an outlying cul-de-sac. The parking lot was constructed around the back of the building so as not to spoil the curb appeal for the prospective family members choosing a final hospice for their failing loved ones. The message was obvious. All deliveries around back.

Stacey whipped around the back corner, parking near an entrance door. She shut down the engine and turned to Hannah.

"I'm sure you have thought of this many times, but you could very well be walking into a trap. Are you sure this isn't the time to call Curt?" She asked.

"You're right, of course, but time is the one commodity we can't waste. The Client is inside and dying. Unless they have booby-trapped their room, the worst thing that could happen is that they will die before spilling it all out, which I know they want to do."

Stacey grabbed Hannah by the scruff of his shirt and pulled him to her. She kissed him hard, then shoved him against the passenger door. "Then go get them. I'll be right here, ready to go when you're done."

Hannah hopped out of the Escalade and hustled to the entrance door. It was five-forty-five and pitch dark. One pull on the entrance confirmed that visitor's hours were over. He pounded on the glass, trying to attract the attention of anyone nearby when a young attendant in scrubs walked over and pointed to her non-existent watch. "Closed to visitors," she mouthed. His frustration boiled over as he spread his arms. He didn't know what possessed him when he yelled, "But it's Christmas!"

The young lady softened her gaze and approached the door. Hannah pointed to his pale skin. "I've flown in today just to see my grandfather from back east. You are very busy, I know. I won't stay long."

The attendant bit her lip and looked around before pushing the crash bar. "I don't know all the procedures here, because I'm only working this weekend, but don't tell anyone I let you in."

"Thank you, and Merry Christmas."

"Merry Christmas to you, too. Do you know your grandfather's room?"

Hannah hadn't expected the question. "No, this is the first time I've been here since he moved out of the last place," he said, wondering if he sounded in any way credible. "I can just walk up a few corridors until I see his name."

"No, I can help. What is his last name?" She asked, moving behind the front desk. Hannah had been inside for less than thirty seconds, and his entire charade was in shambles. A young man in a white doctor's coat was working intently in the back office, so he kept his voice to a whisper. After a moment's pause, he said. "Banks, my grandfather's name is Leonard Banks. He goes by Lonnie."

The helpful service worker typed in a name and made a pensive look. "How long has he been here? I don't see his name."

Hannah stalled. "This is St. Xavier's, right? I was told he was here."

"Let me look again," she said, retyping. As she again showed confusion, an alert beeped and flashed above the workstation. "Oh, you'll have to excuse me. I'll be back soon."

As she trotted down the left wing of the facility, the doctor emerged from a side door with a tray of medicine. Hannah gave him a nervous smile and thought he might try another name with him, hoping to hit pay dirt. Then he remembered what the attendant had said, and what day it was. Everyone here was a part-time fill in. He doubted this doctor knew the identities of his patients.

Hannah slipped down the right hallway, moving his head from side to side to read the nameplates. He got to the end and peeled back, hoping the nurse hadn't returned to the front desk yet, giving him at least the chance to explore the other wing.

Hannah found the desk empty and hustled down the first few feet of the center corridor to avoid detection, when he spied the doctor strolling down the hallway before disappearing into an end room. He looked side to side at the nameplates, hoping against hope that The Client's name would be here before he had to encounter the doctor at the end, or the nurse at the front.

The hall grew gradually darker as he neared the last rooms, but one had the faint glow of a desk lamp. Hannah peeked in and saw the back of the doctor resting the medicine tray on a side table beside the sleeping patient. Hannah looked at the nameplate and found it blank. '*That's odd*,' he thought.

The doctor turned at the sound of Hannah's presence, unperturbed by his interruption. "Can I help you? You seem lost."

Hannah held his hands up apologetically. "No, I'm sorry. I was looking for a room. I didn't mean to bother you."

With a weak smile, the doctor returned to his tray. It held a medicine cup of pills, a plastic cup for water, and a syringe. The patient slept despite the glow of the light, and Hannah felt compassion for the sick and dying who held on for Christmas.

Having set the medicine aside, the doctor then brushed by Hannah without a word, and made his way back to the small office pharmacy. Hannah looked at the prone figure, then turned to leave when he spied a silver object beneath the medicine tray.

It was a laptop. His pulse raced as he pieced together the scene.

Single room.

No nameplate.

Laptop at the ready.

Hannah stared at the sleeping patient in the hospital bed, willing their eyes to open.

As they did, a smile etched itself among the wrinkles. "Hello, you must be Robert Hannah. I'm so glad to finally meet you. My name is Diane Jenkins."

Chapter Sixty-Seven

Hannah stepped to the bed, hovering over The Client. "It was you?"

Her eyes lacked the sparkle as she uttered, "Surprise!"

Hannah looked around the room and grabbed the only visitor's chair. He pulled it beside the bed, staring at the woman who had helped to devise the plan to kill eleven innocent victims. Hannah watched Jenkins try to turn her head to speak to him, so he pulled his chair farther down the bed.

"Why?" Hannah asked.

"Why?" She repeated. She gave a mirthless chuckle. "That's your opening question? *Why?* I should think that would be obvious by now. You know why."

"No, not really. Lots of people experience disappointment and betrayal without resorting to *this!*" He said.

The Client regarded Hannah with a serene look. "I'm intrigued. How much do you think you know? Tell me what you think I've done."

Hannah began. "Mel Fitzpatrick came up with a crazy scheme to kill off rich men as revenge for how you were all treated as computer visionaries in Silicon Valley. No one took him seriously until you got

361

sick. Then you contacted him to see how workable it was, offered him your remaining money, and set out to choose the victims and hire a killer. Then, you roamed the 'Hearts Elite' website, selecting men whose first initials matched the months of their deaths, and lived in cities that enabled you to spell out the phrase '*KILL THE RICH.*' How am I doing so far?"

Jenkins blinked as she took the narrative in. "Not bad, but a little off the mark. Mel had no imagination whatsoever. I created what you call 'the crazy scheme'. But please, continue. It's fascinating to me how you got as far as you did and find yourself in my room tonight."

Hannah pressed on. "Fitzy's job was to be on site and follow the killer to make sure the job was completed because you couldn't. He would report back to you and then, what? You'd send the next victim's dossier? Send some money?"

Jenkins nodded. "Not just 'some money.' A lot of money. One hundred-and-fifty-thousand dollars a kill. And if the killer completed the entire list undetected, a bonus of an additional seven-hundred-thousand dollars. That is two-and-a-half-million dollars for twelve month's work."

"Fitzpatrick had the resentment and training. He just needed the money."

"No, Robert," Jenkins said. "He needed a plan. If it was up to Mel, he'd have just gone in and tried to blow up a building for his revenge. No imagination whatsoever. He needed my help for a different approach."

Hannah watched her eyes flutter above the gray complexion. He didn't think she had much time. "How did it go from Mel lashing out at the world to this elaborate scheme?"

Jenkins nodded. "I had the money, but being bed-ridden, no way to spend it. If Mel wanted it, I insisted on an equal partnership. So, we agreed. My imagination, brains and cash. His eyes, ears, and legs."

"You hired The Bumper," Hannah stated.

"The Bumper? Well done, Robert. Of course I did. For all of his bluster, Mel Fitzpatrick was no killer. We both knew that. So, he made a few discrete inquiries," she breathed, "but I decided on Zach Betes, yes. A Bulgarian hitman who had never been to the United States was too perfect."

Hannah leaned in. "Where is The Bumper right now? Is he in Paradise, California?"

Jenkin's face showed genuine bewilderment. "I don't know where he is right now, but why would he be in Paradise, California?"

The doctor peeled off the white jacket and slipped back into the small pharmacy behind the front desk. The earlier attendant had returned, curious as to the missing visitor. He thought of relieving her of the annoyance but had bigger issues at the moment. The physician wanted to finish his tasks and get out in time for Christmas. He gave her a knowing smile and walked back to the far room. As he got closer, he was surprised to hear the patient was awake.

And talking to the lost, curious stranger.

Chapter Sixty-Eight

"Drew Bennett lives in Paradise, California. He is the December victim on your list!" Hannah said. "That's where The Bumper must be right now."

Jenkins looked puzzled. "Why would I want to kill Drew Bennett?"

It was his turn to be bewildered. "Well, you worked for him, and wrote a glowing paper on his accomplishments, but then turned when he sold out. Don't you blame him for all that happened to you? Isn't he the reason for the entire killing campaign?"

She closed her eyes and rested a moment before speaking. "Yes, he is. But I don't hate him. I was in love with him." She turned her head slightly to look directly at Hannah. "What I hate is how all that money changed him. He was a young idealist, like the rest of us. He had ideas that would revolutionize the world. I believed in him. I trusted him. I loved him."

Jenkins stopped and licked her parched lips. Hannah snatched the glass of water that accompanied the cup of pills and leaned over to help her drink. "Thank you, Robert. You are very kind." She leaned back, exhausted at the effort taken for a few sips. "Where was I?"

"The money corrupted Bennett?" He said.

"Yes. All those rich vipers. The parasites without ideas or morals with their bags of filthy money. They may have paid fair market value for Drew's companies, but they stole his soul, and I hate them for what they did to his vision."

"So you wrote the scathing article, and when you were fired, you sued him for unlawful termination?" Hannah asked.

"Yes, it was meant as a wake-up call, but he was too far gone. He paid me three million dollars to go away. After all we had meant to each other, he just paid me to get lost. I was devastated. Bennett never would have done that without the filthy rich getting their claws into him."

Hannah sat back in his chair, taking it in. "When you were diagnosed with cancer, you got in touch with Mel? Put those three million dollars to good use?"

A tear slid down her Jenkins' cheek, unwiped. It dropped onto her gown as she whispered, "No, Robert. This is the part you missed. I got in touch with Bennett. I wanted him to know I was dying with a terminal cancer that allowed me only eighteen more months." She turned to Hannah. "I still had my brain, and my skills. I could still do a lot of good in those eighteen months. The world could still be made a better place than I found it. Drew would understand, and he would know how. I wanted the old Drew to point me in that direction. Maybe it would wake him up from the coma that all that money caused. Start thinking of other people again."

Jenkins lay her head back, exhausted at her brief outburst. Hannah leaned closer and whispered. "And what did he reply?"

Tears flowed from both eyes as her fragile mask crumbled. Her mouth dragged lower in sorrow as the misery shook her body. It took almost a minute before a hint of composure returned. She replied, "He told me that since it was terminal, there was no sense wasting money on treatment, but he would cover my burial expenses."

Hannah cocked his head, as if he'd missed a step. "Sorry, he said what? Did you ask him to cover your treatment bills?"

Jenkins gained strength as she confirmed, "No, I did not. That is what all that cash did. I appealed to his inner goodness, and all he assumed was that I wanted money. Money, money, money. I don't need help with burial costs! I was talking about doing good while I was alive, and he was already thinking of the bills when I died! *Three million dollars!* I have three million dollars. I didn't need his blood money! But that answer confirmed to me that the real Drew Bennett, the one I loved and believed in, was no longer there."

She turned to gaze at Hannah. "I wouldn't have to kill him. To me, Drew Bennett is already dead."

Hannah stared at Jenkins, his stomach rolling. "If Bennett had given you what you asked for, a chance to make your final eighteen months count for something..."

She rolled her head back onto the pillow. "You'd be back in Boston right now, and eleven funerals would have been avoided."

A silence blanketed the room, smothering Hannah with the revelation. The trigger.

"That was the moment?" He asked, his voice shaking.

"The moment? Yes, I suppose it was. I forwarded Bennett's reply to Mel. That was when I reminded him of his crazy revenge scheme and said, 'I'm in.'" She winced as she sought comfort rolling onto her back. "And here we are."

Jenkins closed her eyes as Hannah eased himself from the chair and looked back out into the hallway. He wondered if the doctor was waiting to relieve her pain with the nightly injection until her visitor had left.

The hallway was empty. Hannah didn't have all he wanted, but withholding her medicine was tantamount to torture. If the doctor came back, he could easily slip out of the room.

Hannah stepped back in as Jenkins opened her eyes. "What do you think of me?"

He gave a blunt assessment. "I think you and Mel are murderers for what you did. I understand now why you did it. To prevent other young idealists from being ruined by the entitled rich, as you see it. But murder is murder."

Jenkins crinkled her mouth. "Is it?" she asked. "Tell me, if killing eleven entitled parasites saved the world from certain annihilation through their continued hoarding of opportunities and resources, wouldn't it be justified?"

"But that's not what happened here. They were just eleven men. How do you know they deserved to die? That their lives were going to ruin the world?" Hannah retorted.

Jenkins sealed her lips as if tasting something unpleasant, gaining vigor from the lively exchange. "Semantics," she said. "What about Nazis? How would you have felt if we had killed eleven skinhead Neo-Nazis? Would you have cried for them?"

Hannah answered quickly, "Now who's getting into semantics? It's a bullshit argument, and you know it. The law is clear. There is no room for what you believe."

Jenkins cracked a smile. "No, Robert. The law is what the rich say it is. But I'm going to give you a choice now. Let's see how virtuous you really are." She closed her eyes and swallowed hard before saying, "Or in a language you would understand. Let's put all our cards on the table," she said, turning her head to stare, "and go all-in."

The doctor had heard enough. He didn't know who this visitor was, but he knew why he was here. He always knew it would come to this.

The man denied the opportunity to inject the needle into the woman's arm rushed back to the pharmacy and grabbed his knapsack.

It was six o'clock on the night before Christmas Eve. City buses had all but stopped their routes, and certainly none were running out to St. Xavier's.

The man in the lab coat needed a ride.

Chapter Sixty-Nine

Hannah grew impatient. "Where is the killer? If he isn't in California, who is the last victim?"

"The last victim?" She wheezed. "So dramatic, Robert. Tsk-tsk."

"So, you set out to create a year long murder spree that only had eleven victims? Was that part of the puzzle?"

Jenkins turned to look at her laptop, and Hannah worried she was tuning him out. "Did you hear me? Why only eleven victims?"

She sighed and slowly turned her head. "Robert, there will be twelve deaths, but since it hasn't occurred to you, I'll make it easier. My name is…Diane."

Hannah's eyes widened at the simplicity of the ending. She said, "I would not consider myself a victim. It was my idea."

"D," Hannah said, looking at the floor. 'D' for Diane and 'December.'

"It's how the monthly pattern was hatched. I may look like the last victim, but I was really the first death agreed upon; the guarantee that my suffering would end if I hadn't died by December. Everything else was window dressing. I wanted to enjoy the thrill of the game until the very end."

"But why? Why not just end it?" He asked.

"Robert, Robert, Robert," she repeated with contempt. "I am in Arizona. Do you see the horrible mistake I made? *I am in Arizona.* The rich make the laws here too, and Arizona law says that I cannot legally assist in my death! So, while I lay here counting off the days, I could watch my three million dollars do some good.

Death is stalking me anyway, whether in California by my doing, or here by the Grim Reaper, unless I took matters into my own hands."

Hannah looked at the laptop, her instrument of death. He asked again, "Where is The Bumper?"

She answered in a whisper, "I honestly don't know where he is. Not now."

"Not now?" Hannah repeated.

Jenkins nodded her head. "So, this is where I give you a choice." She turned toward her laptop. "The Bumper will lose not only one hundred and fifty-thousand dollars if he doesn't kill me this month, but he also forfeits the seven hundred-thousand-dollar bonus. That is eight hundred and fifty thousand dollars, Robert." She turned and looked into his eyes. "And I will give it all to you if you will do one small thing. One tiny thing that will make no difference in your life at all. It will never be considered, and no one will know. Would you do that for me? For that much money? Can you swallow your virtue if no one knew, and you made almost one million dollars?"

Hannah paused, unsure of what to say. Jenkins interpreted the silence. "Yes, you are thinking about it. What almost one million dollars would do in the life of an elite, Harvard-educated, washed-up poker player? And what would you have to do? Virtually, nothing."

She turned again toward her laptop and tried to raise her hand, but it fell short. "All you'd have to do is move that syringe within reach of my fingers. That is all."

Hannah spun and jumped out of the room. The hall was dark and quiet.

"Robert," Jenkins called from her bed, "The Bumper was here and you let him get away. He just lost eight hundred and fifty-thousand dollars that I will give to you if you just slide the syringe over a couple feet and walk away. It's not like you injected the potassium cyanide. You merely thought you were doing a dying old woman a final favor. Two seconds of your time. Agree to do it, and I will have you open the laptop and send the banking link wherever you want. Do what The Bumper didn't do. Inject the poison. Move the syringe and it is all over. The case is solved, and you win the day. No one will know you had a hand in my death. You can tell them you left me alive."

"But The Bumper got away!" He argued.

"Aw, assassins are like the rich, Robert. Kill one, and five more pop up to take his place. Let him go. Take the money, have a better life. Maybe get back with your ex-wife."

'Stacey!' Hannah thought. He dove across the bed and grabbed the syringe from the medicine tray. He stared at Jenkins expectantly as her eyes begged him for the plunge. "Do it, leave, and the money is yours."

He leaned over again and yanked the laptop from beneath the tray, unplugging the power cord. Jenkins tried to sit herself up to type the cash transfer when Hannah's voice froze her.

"You'll get no help from me. And this laptop is heading to Quantico." Hannah turned to the small sink and pushed the plunger to empty the vial of its deadly contents. Jenkins wailed as the clear liquid circled the small drain. He shoved the needle into the plastic disposal box. "Stay alive. The cops are coming."

Jenkins' wails pierced the silence as Hannah raced down the hall, yelling to the attendant, "Where is that doctor that was back there earlier? Is he still here?"

She shook her head and pointed to the door. "No, he hurried out a few minutes ago."

Hannah crashed through the back entrance and scanned the darkened parking lot.

The White Escalade was gone.

Chapter Seventy

"I thought you died in Cleveland, but it seems I was mistaken. We finally meet face-to-face," the man with the gun said, waving his weapon at Stacey. "Just drive and do exactly what I tell you. Let us not play a game. You know who I am, and now, I finally know who *you* are," he said.

"I swear I have no idea what you are talking about. Just take the vehicle and let me go. I don't know anything about you." Stacey said.

"Do you think I am stupid?" The man asked, pushing the gun into her ribs as she drove. The Escalade pulled to the right with the jab, and Stacey yanked the wheel to straighten it out. "No, I don't think you are stupid," she said. "My ex-husband wanted to meet someone, but I don't know who."

"Yes, I know he did. I have known all along. You think I am so stupid because I am not from America," the man seethed. "*Oh, he is my ex-husband,*" the man mocked. "I am smarter than you, Client. You sit in the driver's seat of your expensive car and wait for news of my death, yes? You think you have won, but I will win."

Stacey had been terrified the second the man burst through the back entrance and raced to the SUV. He hoisted himself in, waving the gun and screamed for her to 'drive or die.' But his latest admission froze her. "Kill you? He wasn't here to kill anyone! Why would you think I am someone's client?"

The Bumper shouted in her face. *"I am not stupid. I know what the plan was all along*!" He quieted for a moment, then said, "Thank you for the money, which I will keep. But how dare you question my methods when you sit with your computer to keep your hands clean. Now I will do to this man what I did to The Witness you had following me, like I was a child! I will go back and finish the job properly. I now have what you Americans call 'the upper hand'."

Stacey's heart raced, trying to piece his rant together. "I swear you have me confused with someone else."

"No confusion," the man yelled. "I am clear, and you are The Lying, Coward Client. You lure me out to the middle of this nowhere to kill some old lady as a trap, huh? You think I am so stupid?" The man turned to Stacey and breathed in her ear, "Well, I show you who is stupid. Now, I am The Client, and you do what I say."

The man scanned the surrounding buildings, as if looking for cover. Stacey prayed it was not a secluded spot where he could ditch a witness.

"There," he pointed, centering the gun on her abdomen. "Turn into that mall and drive around to the back. Then we shall see who is in charge."

Stacey obeyed as tears filled her eyes. She knew without a doubt that she would die tonight in Mesa, Arizona.

She was only thirty-five-years-old.

"Curt, listen. The Bumper was here tonight. I saw him. He escaped with Stacey in our rented Escalade. I have the licence plate somewhere on my phone. You need to call the FBI and the locals to find them before anything happens."

"Robert, take it easy. I'll put out the APB immediately, but you need to think about whatever can help the authorities. Was The Bumper armed?"

"I don't know. He was disguised as a doctor."

"Okay, did you see his face? Was it Betes?" Downey asked.

"It didn't really register, but it could have been him. I just know that Jenkins identified him as The Bumper, and the Escalade with Stacey is gone!"

"All right, read me the license." Hannah spelled it out as best he could. Curt replied, "Robert, we will find her."

"You don't know that, Curt. You warned me and look what I've done. Please get her back."

"This is not the time to go there, Pally. Sit tight, and I'll call when…hang on."

Downey went silent as Hannah waited. "What, CD? What's happening?"

Downey whispered into the phone. "Robert, they found the Escalade…"

Chapter Seventy-One

Stacey pulled the Escalade along a loading dock spot behind a small supermarket. "Leave it running while you answer my questions." The armed man instructed her. She slid the SUV into park and waited for the bullet that would end her life. She hoped it would be quick.

"Where are all the computer files?" He asked. "I want everything."

"What files?"

"I lose such patience. You think Christmas will make me jolly, huh? It does not. I want files, I want transfers. I want all communication. Where is it?"

Stacey saw no way out of the vehicle alive. She vowed she would not let him see her cry. "I have no idea what you are talking about. If I knew anything, I would give it to you."

The man searched Stacey's eyes, as if looking for the truth. "I know why you hired me. Because you are weak. You are pathetic. You have others do your dirty work so you can be clean. You are worthless." He reached over and grabbed Stacey's chin, pulling it to his face. "You are a sad Client and I will kill you first, then go back for your friend."

With pain searing through her jaw, Stacey yelled, "You are making a mistake! I don't know anything."

The killer shoved Stacey's head against the driver's side window, his eyes brimming with rage. "I do not make mistakes," he spat, raising his Beretta. "I fix mistakes."

Stacey pressed her eyes closed, the thought racing through her mind that perhaps Robert would miss her. It all seemed so strange when the end arrived.

The bullet slammed through the glass before Stacey could register the pain.

She was grateful for that.

Chapter Seventy-Two

The Mercedes convertible followed the Escalade out of the St. Xavier Health Center from a trolling distance.

The couple watched the luxury SUV make a right-hand turn into a darkened strip mall and preceded around to the back of the building. The passenger turned to the driver, and with a glance, had him pull over. She slid from her seat, unstrapping her Glock. The black sedan rolled to the far side of the mall, effectively trapping the Escalade. Even though there were only the two of them, the SUV was surrounded, and the silent pair had the element of surprise. The Mercedes driver parked in a side spot, unholstered his weapon, and crept along the wall, looking for the spill of headlights.

The Escalade was still running, the occupants visible in the reflection of the headlights from a utility door in a nearby loading dock. From his vantage point, the Mercedes driver could see the armed killer in the passenger seat talking, though he was too far away to hear what was said. He approached the vehicle from the side, and knew that any shot he might heroically take would go through his window and exit the driver's side, possibly killing both occupants.

The shadow lunged when he saw the killer pressing the gun against the SUV's driver's temple. It was now or never.

Before he tightened the grip on his gun, a bullet shattered the glass, and all was quiet.

He raced to the Escalade with little regard for his own safety.

The female passenger from the Mercedes dropped into a shooting stance. The Escalade driver had her window cracked, and the sniper could hear snippets from the man. She heard "I do not make mistakes," and watched as an object, presumably a gun, was being pressed against the driver's temple.

The woman took a soft breath and held it as she fired through the windshield, directly at the man's forehead. The glass shattered, obscuring the result of the shot. She raced to the Escalade as her counterpart lunged forward from the side shadows. The woman grabbed the driver's door and dragged the female victim out of the SUV. She was in shock and covered in blood spray, and perhaps, brain matter. Her partner pulled open the passenger door and jumped back out of the direct line in reaction to any possible return fire.

He needn't have bothered. The man's face had been obliterated by the shot.

The Mercedes driver holstered his weapon and reported the result of the chase over his cell.

His partner, not yet aware of the damage she'd inflicted, comforted the driver, who began crying and shaking. "It's a natural response, ma'am," The Bumper's killer said. "Just breathe. That's good. I'm going to stay right here. Help is on its way."

The male agent raced over to the pair. "I've phoned it in. They will be here in a few minutes," he said. The woman looked up, nodding.

"You okay right now?" He asked. "You did what you had to do."

The female agent comforted the weeping Escalade driver before looking up.

"Thanks, Jacco. I think I'll be okay."

Chapter Seventy-Three

It was Sunday, December Thirty-first, and the small task force met unofficially at the boss's request. Captain Lockwood sat at the head of the boardroom table, as Agents Simms and Perez filled them in on the surveillance. "We weren't close enough to be of any help when The Bumper ran out of the building and jumped in the Escalade."

Lockwood replied, "He would have killed you and stolen your car. I know it would have been a tough call, but you were right to just follow."

"Sir, I don't know what possessed Hannah to go to Arizona. I wouldn't have allowed it had I known." Agent Downey said.

"I know, Curt," Lockwood said, "you said as much when you landed from California. That's why I sent Simms and Perez on the next flight out. You're too close to him. They reported to me."

"They've positively identified the victim as 'The Bumper?'" Agent Perez asked, dressed in more casual clothes than she was accustomed to in the office. She'd been suspended from duty pending the result of her first active shooter incident, but tailed along with Jacco for the debrief. Captain Lockwood welcomed her input.

"They have. Dental records would have been sketchy thanks to your precise aim, but the fingers were good. It was Betes all right." Lockwood said.

The Captain looked at his three agents. "Quite a year, guys. You all did amazing work."

Agent Downey replied, "Thank you sir, but it still doesn't feel like enough. What about Dennison and Farron? How long will they be in Arizona?

"They should be back right after the holiday later this week. Diane Jenkins reiterated much of what Hannah could remember of their talk before he tried running after The Bumper. Her confession pretty well clears it all up."

"What kind of charges will she face, sir?" Agent Simms asked.

"She will get them all. Eleven counts worth. Murder, conspiracy to commit the same. Wire fraud. But she'll be dead before the case hits a courtroom," The Captain said. "Anyway, we'll get the gang together and get a final debrief from Agents Dennison and Farron before we put it to bed. Quantico will help with the identification process and the legal steps. In the meantime, after New Year's Day tomorrow, we can go back to being New England FBI agents."

Lockwood dispersed the agents at four o'clock and bid them a happy new year.

Agent Downey stopped by Hannah's condo and gingerly knocked, as he had some eight months pervious. It felt like five years had passed. He stomped the snow from his shoes as he waited for Hannah to get to the door. He knew he might be in the bedroom, so Downey knocked again, with more urgency.

Downey heard the padding on the hardwood as the door swung open. "Come in." Hannah invited and moved aside. "Stacey's just lying down."

"Yeah, I guessed. How is she doing?" Curt asked.

"It's tough to tell. Physically, she's a champ. But emotionally, it has been a grueling week. She swings between the terror of facing her own mortality and the regret of wanting to go with me, and the relief she survived. I hate myself for asking her. I thought it would just be a game," Hannah answered.

"Yeah, I know. But how about you?" Downey followed up.

"I have a lot of guilt to deal with, but Stacey doesn't blame me. Not yet, anyway. She is going to think twice from now on about being an adrenaline junkie."

Downey sat on the couch, as he had back in April. "You know, I'm still mad you went to Arizona. But I also know that I got you into this, so whatever happened after I showed you the puzzle, it ultimately comes back to me. But I'm still mad."

"Yeah, well, I'm grateful I kept 'location finder' active on my phone. Otherwise, there was no way Simms and Perez would have found us in Arizona. I clearly hadn't thought about it all the way through. I expected 'The Bumper' to be in California. But the clues from Jenkins were goading me to come. It was too tempting to ignore." Hannah said. "By the way, did you thank the captain for sending Perez and Simms?"

Downey nodded. "I did. Perez is on-leave pending the investigation, which she will pass with flying colors. It was a good kill and a smart decision under pressure. She's an excellent agent. Could be the best one of us. I see her gaining a promotion to Quantico soon."

"Can Jacco go with her?" Hannah asked.

"Come on, Cupid. Life doesn't work that way. The FBI is not 'Hearts Elite.'"

"Speaking of the website, did you get the full package from Stafford?"

"I did," Downey said. "She drop-boxed the full profiles of the victims to aid in the investigation against Jenkins, who is fully cooperating anyway, though she clearly has little time left to live. But interestingly, Stafford is hanging it up. She told me she was resigning her position."

"Wow, that's a lot of money to walk away from. But she's bright. She'll catch on somewhere," Hannah said.

"Whatever. She wasn't very co-operative until we forced her to be. Apparently, the guilt set in that she could have done more to save lives. Stafford told me she resigned because she actually considered killing the entire site. Delete all the profiles. Reimburse all the paid members. Have a website fire-sale. That would have been epic."

Hannah laughed as a cough escaped the bedroom. He crept to the half-opened door and gently closed it. He turned back to Downey. "What do you and Laurel have planned for tonight? Stay up to midnight?" Hannah asked.

"No way. That hasn't happened since the girls were born. But if we do, how about a phone call to ring out these twelve months, and ring in a new year of goodness and possibilities," Downey said, nodding towards the door. "Yeah, okay," Hannah answered, "but I doubt Stacey will be awake."

Downey roused himself from the couch. "That's not what I meant. See you in the office on Wednesday, okay, Pally. The captain wants to see you."

"Of course, Agent Downey." Hannah leaned in and gave his best friend a rare, full hug. "Thank you for believing in me and not giving up. But mostly for looking after me. Without you, we'd be dead."

Downey smiled. "All in a day's work, Pally."

Chapter Seventy-Four

Hannah listened to the legal jargon being discussed by Agent Watson from Quantico concerning the transfer of evidence, which his friend Agent Downey comfortably reiterated.

The official record may never be complete with the recent death of Diane Jenkins, who passed away in the early morning hours of New Year's Day. The posted guards witnessed her last breath and had the coroner on hand to officiate the death.

It was as close to an execution watch as one could get without pulling the switch.

The other three friends, Paulo Rodrigues, Lonnie Banks and Gerald Smith, had all come forward when APBs had been posted, were all interrogated and found innocent of taking part in the scheme, though Rodrigues had his suspicions after reading about the bee stings in Ohio. He had a similar allergy and once told Jenkins to watch herself outdoors. He tried to reach out and wasn't getting any replies from her or Fitzpatrick about his misgivings.

"For just a few moments, I wondered if Fitzy was actually going through with it. But I had no idea."

Agent Watson wished the agents and Hannah a happy new year and made a point of letting the room know that Agent Perez would be reinstated within a couple of weeks and that a commendation would be forthcoming for the pair. Agent Simms sheepishly dropped his eyes. Hannah guessed he already knew it was coming.

As the meeting concluded, Hannah made a point of thanking all the agents individually, especially Agent Dennison, who had been so reluctant to work with him back in the spring. "Thank you for your patience. I've learned a lot, and I appreciate your professionalism. Thank you again." The agent returned the handshake and left the room.

Hannah figured Dennison wasn't a touchy-feely guy.

As he made the walk to the parking lot, he was hailed by Captain Lockwood, who waved him into his office.

"You wouldn't leave without saying goodbye, would you?" He asked.

"Well, it's like sneaking past the principal's office on the last day of school. The less said, the better," Hannah said, taking a seat in front of the large desk.

Lockwood answered, "Hmmm. I don't know. What are your plans? Back to the tables?"

"Maybe recreationally, sir. I'm working on reconciling with my ex-wife and straightening out a few other things in my life. New Year's resolutions, you know."

Lockwood chuckled. "Yeah, I haven't had a dessert yet this year, and it's only three days old. Making me crazy."

Hannah stood from his seat. "Thank you again, Captain, for your patience and professionalism. I really appreciate it."

Lockwood gave him a serious stare. "Hannah, when someone is in my office, they don't stand until I tell them to stand."

Hannah dropped again into his chair, his heart racing like he was back in his middle school principal's office. *Some things stay with you,* he thought.

"What I want to ask you was what you had planned...in your future?" Lockwood asked.

Hannah blinked. "Sir?"

Captain Lockwood peered over his reading glasses as he pulled a sheet from his desk. "This is a transfer request to Quantico regarding Agent Perez. I think you agree she is going places and will one day occupy an office such as mine, if not this *actual* office. I wanted your assessment on the transfer order."

Hannah looked around the office for the hidden camera. "Sir, Agent Perez has a keen intelligence that has been recognized and will be put to good use by brighter minds than mine. It is only a matter of time, and frankly, the sooner the better for the organization."

Lockwood nodded and grabbed a pen. "Done," he said, signing the paper with a flourish.

"Now," Lockwood said, removing the glasses, "what's to be done with Agent Jacco Simms?"

Hannah looked at the papers and saw no corresponding twin on Perez's transfer request. "Agent Simms will soon have his opportunity to shine as well. He has a strong, analytical mind that is very logic based. He is grounded in evidence, not theory, and will make a highly reliable investigator."

"My thoughts exactly," Lockwood said with a theatrical arm sweep, sliding back his chair. "Which leads me to my problem then, Mr. Hannah."

He waited for the captain to finish whatever he had up his sleeve so that he could go back to the condo where Stacey was packing for their trip to the South Carolina coast. Hannah had assured her he would be home by five o'clock, but it was already past four, and traffic would be heavy and slow because of the flurries that fell that morning. Resisting the battle of wills, Hannah relented. "What's that, sir?"

"I'm going to need to replace Agent Perez with a competent recruit capable of matching wits with Agent Simms. Now, I've gone through my files of applications, and I was wondering if you would help me pare down the list?"

Hannah exhaled, grateful for such a simple task. "Of course, sir, if you think I can help. Stacey, my ex-wife, and I are leaving for Hilton Head, South Carolina tonight and won't be back for a couple of weeks. Can I help you then?"

Lockwood gazed at him with a ruffled look. "Two weeks, huh? Fate of the free world and all, hinged on your return in fourteen days?"

Hannah snuck a peek at the door and contemplated making a run for it. "Yes sir. I suppose you could email me copies and I could read them while I'm away."

"Or you could just say 'yes,' Robert," Lockwood suggested.

"Yes, to what, sir?" Hannah asked.

Captain Lockwood pulled out a manila file folder from his desk drawer and slid it across. Hannah tentatively opened it and saw the words 'Federal Bureau of Investigation Application' across the top.

Much of the document had been filled out with respects to age, education, work experience, address, and social security number. A few blank spaces needed more personal information unavailable to the two signees that sponsored the application.

Captain Stuart Lockwood, and Agent Curtis Downey.

Hannah raised his head as Lockwood stared into his eyes, barely stifling a grin.

"Robert Hannah. What do you think about working for the FBI?"

Acknowledgements

First and foremost, I would like to thank Abby Macenka and the staff of Between The Lines Publishing for their dedication and unwavering support of the novel and author. You have been a joy to work with.

To Ken Salikof, the first editor to lay eyes on this novel. His assessment of "You may have a winner here" will forever hold a place in my heart. To editor Lea Vickery whose eyes and steady hand guided the manuscript into its final phase. Thank you for your efforts to bring the novel to the industry.

To all booksellers who have made space for "Kill Them All" on shelves, tables, and window displays. You are the true frontline heroes.

I would like to thank every librarian who has helped foster and nurture a love of reading. This novel could never have been possible without the seeds planted decades ago by countless librarians who have suggested new authors, ordered books, and set them aside. No truer friends exist in the world.

To authors everywhere who have sparked my imagination with your creativity and devotion to craft. Canadian thriller authors Linwood Barclay, Shari Lapena, and Rick Mofina have, in turn, offered insight, support and encouragement throughout my budding career. True inspiration is rare when the world gets so loud. Thank you for being a constant beacon.

To my radio friends, both on and off the air, coworkers, and listeners. You have all encouraged the creative process throughout my career that was necessary to complete my novel. Thank you for believing in me.

To you, my cherished reader. There are countless books published every year, and billions more on treasured shelves that you could have perused. It honors me that you have chosen to spend time and money on my story. Thank you.

Finally, to my beautiful, patient wife, Cathy. She has endured just one more paragraph, just one more page, just one more edit, and just one more read-through. Writing may be a lonely craft, but it is a team effort. She is the greatest teammate I could ever ask for.

Kill Them All has always been, from, its inception, a work of total fiction, though the cities, regions, and highways are completely real. Anything beyond that which approaches actual events or people is completely coincidental.

Finally, it is apparent that I have been guided by the spirit of the queen herself. To the memory of Dame Agatha Christie, I thank you across the void for the inspiration to follow in your gigantic footsteps. Though I am one of many, my gratitude is immense.

Mark Philbin is a retired radio broadcaster of thirty-five years. He is a sought-after speaker for a wide range of topics, including media, volunteerism, and writing. He currently lives in Belleville, Ontario, Canada, where he continues his writing and community initiatives.

www.ingramcontent.com/pod-product-compliance
Lightning Source LLC
Chambersburg PA
CBHW010557310726

48969CB00009B/2458